THE COMMANDMENT

The heat crawled slowly up his arms, as if he were submerging them in scalding water. He thought of the girl, of the wild chase, of the way the limb had caught her and dragged her down so that he could fall upon her with the knife. Who was she? A harlot and a whore, he thought, someone who had been brought to him for punishment, like the Negress. He knew that God's purposes were unfathomable, and that he could not guess what sidewise paths he would be asked to take on his mission. The girl had not been his intended victim, but she had been God's. She had been thrown deliberately into his path by a holy purpose that he could only partly understand. And now her face was being used to test him, swimming into his mind to deter him, to cause him to doubt his purpose.

He smiled. God was good, but He was also clever.

Books by Thomas H. Cook

BLOOD INNOCENTS
THE ORCHIDS
TABERNACLE

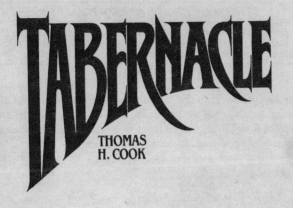

TABERNACLE

THOMAS H. COOK

PINNACLE BOOKS NEW YORK

TABERNACLE

Pinnacle Books edition, published by special arrangement with
Houghton Mifflin Company.

Houghton Mifflin edition published in 1983
Pinnacle edition/May 1985

ISBN: 0-523-42338-1
Can. ISBN: 0-523-43341-7

Printed in the United States of America

PINNACLE BOOKS, INC.
1430 Broadway
New York, New York 10018

9 8 7 6 5 4 3 2 1

To my mother and father
and
Lillian Ritter

The dove descending breaks the air
With flame of incandescent terror
Of which the tongues declare
The one discharge from sin and error.
The only hope, or else despair
    Lies in the choice of pyre or pyre—
    To be redeemed from fire by fire.
              T.S.Eliot, Four Quartets

TABERNACLE

PART
ONE

I

He inserted the key into the lock and opened it. The room was spare and uninviting, a place where people came for a few hours, then left forever.

He stepped inside. To the right he could see a scarred bureau with a dull, filmy mirror. A jagged crack ran diagonally across the glass, cutting its reflection of the opposite wall in half. Overhead, a square fixture of frosted glass diffused the light from the naked bulbs behind it. He could see the husks of small insects that had been trapped between the glass and the bulb, then burned alive.

He turned, closed the door, and locked it. He would open it only one more time, then his task would begin. Tilting his head upward, he sniffed the air. The fetid odors of the room made his stomach tighten. In his mind he could see the legions of tawdry women who must have stood before the cracked mirror splashing on their cheap perfume. He could imagine the artifacts of the place: paper cups half-filled with warm beer, ashtrays overflowing with stale cigarettes. Traces of these odors were still in the room, surrounding him, testing his dedication. He knew that part of the burden of his mission was to endure such debased places, with their unwholesome histories.

He walked to the center of the room and looked to the left. The door to the bathroom was open. He could see the toilet pushed up against the back wall, its base stained yellow, the seat chipped and pitted. The sink was on the left, rusty pipes protruding from the wall beneath it. He could not see the bath. He did not want to. Soon enough, he thought, and turned away.

The double bed stretched out toward the center of the room.

It was covered with a white bedspread that repeated washings had worn down. Looking at it, he could not imagine sleeping on such a thing, and for a moment he saw his own bed—the clean percale sheets, the thick down comforter. Soon he would be home, and he understood that for all the perils of his mission, it had mercies as well. And one of them was that each act took only a little time.

He took off his hat and dropped it on the bed. Then he slipped the surgical gloves from his coat pocket and pulled them onto his hands, wriggling his fingers, tugging the gloves tight against his finger tips. Part of the mission was that everything be done cleanly. Cleanliness was one of the commandments of the faith. Fastidiousness of body and purity of mind, these formed the twofold duty of man.

Glancing about him at the rusty air conditioner sagging from the window and the film of dust that covered everything, he understood once again the terrible dignity of his task. The world had always been besotted, rolling in its own physical and spiritual filth. But he had been born into the one faith that refused to be corrupted. And now this single refuge from the world's sordidness was being betrayed. The meaning of this betrayal suddenly filled him with an aching emptiness. Knowing that the enemy was everywhere, permeating everything, made his task seem all but impossible. And yet, he thought, it was part of the duty of men to resist despair. Although they had to see things clearly, even the harshest aspects of the world, they could not permit themselves to be defeated by their own lucidity.

Quickly, he stepped over to the phone beside the bed and picked up the receiver. He could hear the clicking of the switchboard in the motel office.

"Yes?"

"I wish to make a call."

"Sure. Give you an outside line."

"Thank you."

He heard a dial tone, then dialed the number.

"Hotel Utah. Good evening."

"I want to speak with William Casey."

"I'm sorry. I can't hear you."

He realized that he was whispering and raised his voice.

"William Casey, please."

"Just a minute, sir."

He waited, listening to distant voices, people moving about the hotel lobby. A beautiful place, he thought, the lobby of the Hotel Utah. He could see it in his mind. The ceiling of inlaid glass high above the plush red carpet. The magnificent crystal chandelier, great marble columns, and gilded balconies. He had once thought of the Utah as the perfect expression of the part of his faith that demanded elegance of manner and refinement of taste. Now it too had been subverted, and he hated the Hotel Utah as yet another place where material beauty masked corruption.

The receiver seemed to have grown very cold by the time he heard a voice on the other end.

"This is William Casey."

The voice was light, flippant; its casualness revolted him.

"Mr. Casey, I'm a visitor in Salt Lake," he said.

"What's that?"

He raised his voice again.

"I'm a visitor in Salt Lake."

He waited for Casey to speak, then went on.

"Did you hear me, Mr. Casey? I am a visitor in Salt Lake."

"Yes. I understand."

"Can we do business?"

"And why not?"

He felt his fingers tighten around the receiver.

"A Negress," he said.

"No problem. I can arrange it."

"Fine."

"Where?"

"Paradise Motel. Do you know where that is?"

There was a laugh on the other end, and he felt his hatred surge through the line. "I asked you if you know where it is."

"Sure, I know every place in Salt Lake. What time, pal?"

"Midnight. Room 17."

"It's almost midnight now, but I'll have her there."

He heard Casey slap the receiver into its cradle and hung up. He eased himself down on the bed and took a deep breath. It was the beginning. One day this moment would be exalted above all the other things he had ever done.

After a moment he stood up, walked into the bathroom, and took a washcloth from the rack above the bath. He moistened it in the sink, walked back out into the room, and began cleaning the bureau. He wiped the dust from its top and sides, then leaned over and carefully washed the mirror. In the glass his fake mustache seemed to darken his features. At first the fools would think he had used it as a disguise. In the end, they would know the truth. They would see that every aspect of this night had had a rational foundation. He smiled, then peeled the mustache from his upper lip and placed it in his pocket. Without the mustache, his face looked stern and handsome. Because of his looks, he had been horribly tempted in his life, but he had never gone astray, and he thought that this fidelity to his faith, this capacity to resist irresistible temptation, was perhaps the greatest reason for his being chosen to carry out the mission.

He glanced at his watch. He did not have much time. Walking quickly to the bed, he wiped the dust from the headboard, then bent down and straightened the cover. Its off-white color and coarse texture reminded him of the Great Salt Flats. His father had taken him deep into them once and had pointed up toward the great blue sky. "That is the eye of God," his father had said. "His eye surrounds the world and sees everything, sees *you.*" He had never forgotten the sudden thrill and dread of having God's presence made magnificently real: a great eye, watching *him.*

He walked to the back window, parted the venetian blinds, and carefully washed each blade. Outside it was very dark, but he knew that God's eye was not closed. He wiped the dust from the last of the blinds, then closed them.

Stepping into the bathroom, he carefully washed the small window, the sink, and then bent down and cleaned the base of the toilet. The room was a place of sacrifice, and must be made clean. More than anything, he had learned that God is not mocked. His instructions must be followed to the letter.

When he had finished with the bathroom, he walked back over to the bed and sat down. He did not feel tired, but he did not feel exhilarated either.

He peeled the gloves from his hands and put them in his coat pocket. Then he stood up, pulled off his coat, and hung it over the end of the bed. In a short time, he thought, it would be over and he would be home again, sitting quietly in his study, surrounded by his books. He knew he would complete his task, for part of the glory of God resided in the notion of completion, the sense of finality, of justice. Few men understood that all the days of their lives led to a single end. They scattered themselves in a thousand futile directions when there was only one direction worthy of life—the one that led through the pupil of God's eye and into that bliss of ultimate and everlasting union.

When the knock came, he felt his heart begin to pound within his chest. For a moment he could not move. He grasped the cover of the bed and squeezed.

The tapping came again. He rose and opened the door. The Negress stood before him, her face staring through the rusty screen. She had large eyes and full lips, but beyond this he could make out no details.

Then she smiled broadly, and her teeth gleamed in the slant of light that fell across her face.

"Evening, honey," she said.

He nodded.

"I am at the right place, ain't I?"

Unable to speak, he nodded again.

She squinted, and he thought he caught an edge of irritability in the grotesque stupidity of her face. "Well, you gone let Rayette in, or whut?"

She moved back and he opened the screen. She passed jauntily in front of him, and he caught the common odor of her perfume as she stepped to the center of the room and swung around to face him. "How you doin' tonight, honey?"

"Fine," he said.

"Good. That's good." She turned away from him to survey the room. He knew that she was used to such places, that she had rutted in these bleak rooms for years.

"Nice homey place," she said.

He dropped his hands into his trouser pockets and watched her.

She turned toward the mirror and looked at herself admiringly in the glass. She was tall and slender, with coarse, straight hair, and as she preened before the mirror he saw the absurdity of her pathetic vanity.

She placed her hands under her breasts and lifted them.

"You like?" she asked with a wink.

He did not speak. He felt his revulsion building, and because of that he knew his mission would be less difficult than he expected. In sending this ridiculous, posturing creature to him, God had made it easy.

Suddenly she moved toward him and he pulled away.

She stopped and looked at him oddly.

"What's the problem, honey?"

"Nothing."

She smiled indulgently. "Hey, look here, everybody's a little nervous. Ain't nothing to be worried 'bout."

Her eyes glanced up and down his body, but she did not move toward him. She was pretending to desire him, and this farcical play revolted him.

"Maybe you want Rayette to relax you?" she asked.

The lewd sultriness of her voice scraped across his ears like a blade.

She stepped forward slightly and lifted her hand.

"I'm a gentle woman," she said. "I bet you a gentle man, too."

He could feel his fists squeezing together rhythmically in his pockets.

She glanced at the movement of his hands and smiled.

"Maybe you jes' want to do everything yourself," she said.

He clenched his fists and did not release them.

"How'd you like to see Rayette all over?"

He stepped over to the bed, carefully avoiding her, and sat down.

She followed him with her eyes, shifting to the right to keep him in view.

"You a handsome man," she said.

He felt a smile tremble on his lips and struggled to keep it there.

"Let me get out of my coat, honey," she said. Slowly she dropped the coat from her shoulders, allowing it to collapse around her ankles.

Come here, he thought. Come here now. But he could not speak.

"You a salesman?" she asked.

"No."

She cocked her head to the left, flirtatiously.

"The strong, silent type, I bet," she said.

He felt his lips part, then close, then part again as he tried futilely to speak. He knew that he must not scare her away by acting too oddly.

"Are you from Salt Lake?" she asked.

"No," he said. His voice seemed high. He swallowed. "Are you?"

"Nah," she said, grinning warmly. "Can't you tell by my accent?"

She turned back toward the window and smoothed a wrinkle from her skirt, her hand drifting slowly over her hips while she watched him from the corner of her eye.

"Where are you from?" he asked feebly.

"Atlanta," she said. She reached behind her neck and tossed her hair. "Maybe I could give you a little massage, baby."

"No," he blurted loudly.

She stared at him suspiciously, and he was afraid she might flee from the room.

"I don't like massages," he added quickly.

She smiled easily, reassured. "Well, you know what they say, honey. I'm here to give you whatever you wants."

"Turn around," he said, but it did not seem that the words came from him. He knew then that God had taken control, and that for the rest of the time he would be merely the instrument of His immaculate will.

She walked to the bed and sat down with her back to him.

"You gon' give Rayette a massage, baby?"

"Yes," he said. The voice was soft, soothing, and he loved it.

"That's just fine, honey."

He started to move toward her, but the smell of her perfume seemed to push him away.

She stood up. "It's warm in here, baby. You know what I mean?"

He wondered if she were about to leave. For a moment he thought about reaching out for her, but she moved quickly and stood directly in front of him.

"You want me, baby?" she asked huskily. "You want Rayette real bad?"

He felt his eyes squeezing together and turned away slightly.

She slipped one finger beneath the strap over her right shoulder and slid it off.

"No need to be nervous, baby," she said.

He could feel her shadow settle on his body like a black shawl, but he did not move away.

She glided the other strap from her shoulder, and the dress fell to the floor. "Maybe you'd like to do the rest."

He shook his head quickly.

"Okay," she said lightly. She unloosed her bra and let it fall to the floor in front of her. Then she cupped her breasts in her hands and grinned.

Watching her, he could feel a terrible force building in his blood. Soon, he thought, soon.

She slipped out of her panties and stood naked before him. "I'm ready when you are, honey," she said softly.

He felt a voice rise within him. "Sit down."

She sat down on the bed beside him and giggled lightly. "I bet you a good loving man," she said, turning her back to him.

He pressed his hands against her back and moved them slowly upward.

"That feel real good, baby."

The touch of her skin felt like fire on his finger tips, and he knew that the spirit of God was burning in his hands.

"Oh, you got such a nice touch, baby," she purred, letting her head fall backward slightly.

He moved his hands up toward the back of her neck.

"Real nice, honey," she said. "You being real good to Rayette like that."

He circled her throat with his hands, turning his head away from her as he began to squeeze.

He could feel her body turn rigid as he squeezed, but he could no longer really feel his hands. His fingers were loops of knotted rope and something jerked at the end of them, pitching forward as the hands pulled back.

Then there was a sound, a low, muffled moan, and he could feel the rope of his fingers digging into something soft and warm. For a moment shadows flew about the room as if all the world were suddenly aglow in the holy light. Then the light went out as the room swam back into his mind, and he could see himself in the mirror, his hands clenched on the Negress's throat. Her fingers clawed weakly at his hands, then dropped away and fell into her lap, twitching in small, silent spasms against her thighs.

He knew then that it was over, that this part of his task was finished. Slowly, he released his grip on the woman's throat and felt something warm and moist caress his hands, soothing as the breath of God.

2

The weather Map in the Salt Lake *Tribune* told the story, and Tom Jackson could feel himself getting chilled just staring at it. An enormous cold front dipped south from Seattle, spread out to engulf most of Idaho, then swept down in a point toward Salt Lake, blanketing everything in snow. Tom turned the page. It was mid November, and the food stores were having a field day. Skaggs was selling turkey at forty-five cents a pound. Buy 'n' Save had cranberries at fifty-five cents a package. Lots of people were going to have their Thanksgiving dinners at home. He remembered his own holiday dinner the year before. He had taken Phyllis to the Plaza Restaurant and had sat there for almost three hours while she complained about Ballet West and the Utah Opera Company. Phyllis had expected excellence, he thought now, of everything but herself.

He folded the paper and dropped it on the floor beside his chair. For a moment he allowed his eyes to roam the room, shifting from the single painting of a mountain landscape to the large mirror, then down to the light blue sofa, which he had shoved against the wall, moving it from its former central location, his one act of redecoration. Phyllis had once suggested plants. He had said that he would get them if she would move in and water them. She had said no.

He looked at his watch. It was one-thirty in the afternoon. He had eaten a late Sunday breakfast, but it struck him now that there was nothing else for him to do but eat again. He stood up, grabbed his overcoat from the wooden peg by the door, and walked out of his apartment.

The luncheonette was just across the street. It was called The People's Choice, but not many people chose it, other than that transient population of cross-country truckers who didn't know any better. It was usually entirely deserted on Sundays, since all the Mormon Brotherhood were gathered around their family tables.

"Hi, Tom" Lucy said, as he took a seat at the counter. "Long time no see."

"How you doing?" Tom asked dully.

Lucy smiled. "Not bad for a poor lonely woman in need of a gentleman's companionship."

Tom let it pass, quietly refusing that gift she seemed always to be offering him.

"You must love this place, the way you keep coming back," Lucy said. "Hell, you only had breakfast a couple hours ago."

Tom grabbed the menu from the counter and casually looked it over. "Give me a hamburger and fries."

Lucy took the menu from Tom's hands. "You should be in church repenting a sinful life, Tom," she said lightly, "not in here indulging your appetite."

"Yeah, right."

"You and me, Tom, we're going to bust hell wide open someday."

"We'll know it when we get there," Tom said.

Lucy continued to stand before him, staring down, the menu cradled in her arms. "The way I figure it, you take the good times when they come your way and forget the rest."

Tom nodded. He remembered that Gentry had once told him just the opposite: "The way you get through it, Tom, you just bite down real hard on the pain."

Lucy turned and slapped a hamburger patty on the grill. The sizzling sound made Tom cringe.

"The Saints are always talking sacrifice," Lucy said. "Me, I'm finished with that. One life to live, that's the way it is."

Lucy did not turn from the grill, and watching her, it struck

Tom that the non-Mormons who lived in Salt Lake formed a kind of secret brotherhood of the damned. They floated in the bloodstream of the city like foreign objects, but they had nothing to hold them together except their shared isolation from the pervasive Mormon atmosphere.

"What'd you do last night?" Lucy asked, her back still to him.

"Watched TV. Slept. How about you?"

Lucy turned around and smiled. "I went to Rome for pizza," she said. "You know, Lear Jet. Just me and Paul Newman."

Tom took a copy of the *Deseret News* someone had left on the next stool and opened it. Another Mormon conference was coming up. Someone named Berryman was going to speak. Tom had never heard of him. He scanned the national and international news. Things did not look good in the Middle East. Things never looked good in the Middle East. Or anywhere else for that matter. He folded the paper and dropped it back on the stool.

"So where's that good-looking girl I see you with sometimes?" Lucy asked. "What's her name?"

"Phyllis."

"That's it. Haven't seen you dragging her around lately."

"She moved to Denver," Tom said. The thought of Phyllis darkened his mood. She had left in anything but a happy attitude, asserting that their "relationship had failed to deepen."

Lucy turned to face him. "Dropped her? Another heart broken by Tom Jackson?" she asked.

"She left because she wanted to." Tom felt a wave of bitterness pass over him. "She decided life would be better with a sensitive ski instructor."

Lucy smiled sympathetically. "I don't know what it is with people these days, Tom," she said. "If it's not one kind of bullshit, it's another."

Tom lifted his shoulders slowly, then let them drop. "Put some lettuce and tomato on that burger, will you?"

"Fifteen cents extra," Lucy said. "You got that kind of money on you?"

Tom tried to smile. "I brought my checkbook, but don't cash it before next week."

Lucy turned back to the grill and flipped the patty over.

"You know, since Phyllis is off with her ski instructor, maybe you ought to give me a whirl."

"Thanks, but no thanks."

"What's the matter, am I too intelligent for you?"

"Too fat."

Lucy turned around and glanced down at her body. "You won't get better than this for free, Tom," she said steadily.

"Probably not," Tom said.

Lucy laid the plate down in front of him. "Enjoy it."

Tom stared pleasurelessly at the food.

"What's the matter?" Lucy asked.

"Nothing. To tell the truth, I'm not really hungry."

"I don't know about you, Tom. But I think the trouble is, you need to get married."

"You should know," Tom said. "How many is it for you? Five? Ten? Twenty?"

Lucy leaned against the counter. "I'll tell you this—anything's better than being alone."

Tom shook his head. "No it's not, Lucy." He slowly lifted the burger to his mouth and took a small bite.

"So what happened between you and the ski bum?" Lucy asked seriously.

"She moved, like I said."

"Why?"

"Greener pastures."

"I'm asking you a serious question."

"There wasn't much between us when she was here," Tom said without emphasis. He took another bite from the burger.

"Why don't you open up a little, Tom?" Lucy asked.

Tom placed the burger firmly on the plate and stared at Lucy squarely. "I hear complaints all day, Lucy. I don't need to hear my own."

Lucy stepped back. She seemed to realize that this was as far as she would get. "You broke her heart, didn't you?" she said lightly. "You drove her to drink."

Tom popped a sliver of potato into his mouth and chewed it slowly. "I'm close to forty, and I look older than that. I don't drive anybody to anything, you know?"

"Sounds like a whine, Tom," Lucy said, smiling again.

"You drive me to it," Tom said. "Hey, give me a Coke and cut the crap."

Lucy stepped away to get the Coke and then returned. "So tell me, how's that nutty friend of yours, Epstein?"

"He's in the hopsital. I told you that yesterday."

Lucy leaned against the table. "How old's that goat, anyway?"

"Must be close to eighty," Tom said. "Maybe older.'

Lucy chuckled. "Tells crazy stories, don't he? You believe any of that shit?"

"Who knows," Tom said. He took a sip from the Coke. It was flat. He had grave doubts about the burger, too.

"What's the matter?" Lucy asked. "You gonna be sick or something?"

Tom lifted the top of the bun. "Hand me a slice of onion," he said. "I got a cold. They say a piece of raw onion is good for you."

Lucy handed Tom the onion and watched as he slid it onto the burger.

"You know what I think your problem is?" she asked.

"I give up."

"Mormonitis."

Tom looked up from the burger.

"Ever heard of it?" Lucy asked.

"Never."

"It's a special disease. You only get it in Salt Lake."

"And you're going to tell me all about it."

"It happens like this, Tom. One day you're going along, not feeling too good, but not feeling that bad. Then it hits you. Mormonitis. You just can't stand it anymore. You feel like a fly in a prayer book. The whole weight of Salt Lake just comes slamming down on you."

"Great," Tom said dully.

"Just like some fly in the Book of Mormon," Lucy said.

Tom nodded, finished the meal quickly, and walked out of the diner. Except for the range of dark gray, snowcapped mountains, the land was flat. Salt Lake was a city that sat like a huge mirage in the emptiness of the surrounding desert. It was inhumanly neat, Tom thought, as if each night God's tireless angels descended from Heaven and swept the streets and pol-

ished the tall glass buildings so that in the morning they shim-
mered under the huge, empty sky. Perhaps Lucy was right. Perhaps, after ten years, he had contracted Mormonitis. All he
knew was that he did not like Salt Lake very much and never
had. He did not like the wholesome cleanliness, the other-
worldly gleam. But there were oases of blight here and there, a
greasy diner or oil-stained gas station. And for a moment Tom
thought that he must be like them, curiously withdrawn from
the shining city, set apart and branded as unclean; a hard, af-
flicted island in a sea of perfect health.

Back in his apartment, Tom walked immediately to the refrigerator. There was very little in it, but that didn't matter. It
was all what Phyllis had called it, neurotic eating. He closed the
refrigerator door without taking anything out, started for the
living room, and felt relieved when the phone rang. It was police headquarters.

"Hey, Tom, you busy?"

Tom recognized Charlie Farrell's voice.

"No," he said. "What's up?"

"Some black whore got herself killed not too far from you.
The Paradise Motel. You live near there, right?"

"Yeah."

"That's what I thought," Charlie said. "The Chief says for
you to check it out."

"I'll be there," Tom said. He hung up the phone and for an
instant remembered that other time the phone had rung, on his
desk in the precinct house when he was still one of New York's
finest. It had been his partner, Gentry's, voice, low and full of a
terrible distress. "Tom," he had said. "Get over to the
Rodriguez apartment." He was breathing very hard. "Please,
hurry."

3

The flash from the police camera hit Tom squarely in the eyes as he walked into the motel room. Through the swirling sparks that clouded his vision, he could see his partner, Carl Redmon, standing on the other side of the room. Tall, erect, with close-cropped light brown hair, Redmon did not look at all ill at ease in the welter of activity—the flashing bulbs, hurried movement, and clipped conversation.

"How's it going, Carl?" Tom said as he elbowed his way toward him.

Carl smiled thinly. "Not the best way to spend the Sabbath, is it, Tom?" He waved a cloud of smoke from the air in front if him. "I never like it, smoking in a murder room. It seems disrespectful." He nodded toward the bed. "There's our work for today."

Tom turned and looked at the woman's body. It was fully clothed in a purple dress. Martinez took a final photograph, the flash washing across the body with a wave of hard, white light.

Tom looked back at Carl. "Who is she?"

"Somebody named Rayette Jones," Carl said. He raised his voice to be heard above the din. "Hey, Acheson, close her eyes, okay?"

Tom glanced back toward the body. "Strangled?"

"Very neat," Carl said. "With a strong pair of hands. Probably did it sometime around midnight."

Tom stepped away and walked slowly around the bed, his eyes carefully going over the body, the covers, anything that attracted his attention.

"Vice says she's a known prostitute," Carl said, "but no arrests in Salt Lake."

Tom's eyes continued to drift over the bed. "She couldn't have been in town very long if Vice hadn't nailed her."

"They rousted her about two months ago," Carl said, "but they couldn't really make a case."

"Just tossed her a little to work the fear in, right?"

Carl nodded. "That's the way they handled it. Too bad it didn't work. She might have gotten out of Salt Lake alive."

In a crevice between the bedsprings and the iron platform, Tom saw a brownish liquid. He pointed down toward the bed and looked at Redmon. "What's this?"

Redmon stepped over beside him and looked down. "Oh, that." He grimaced. "Lab guy figures it for vomit."

"The girl's?"

"Probably," Carl said. "Sometimes happens when you got a strangling."

"Then how come she didn't get any on her clothes?" Tom asked.

Carl's face tightened. "I don't know."

"Maybe she didn't have her clothes on when she died."

Carl seemed to think about it for a moment. Then he batted at the smoke again. "Let's step outside, Tom. This smoke is getting to me. I can't think in here."

Tom followed Carl out the door and they stood silently for a moment, staring out across the littered courtyard.

"Place looks like it's about to fall down," Carl said finally. "Look over there—no slate left on the roof, walls look like a mudbank." He looked at Tom. "Cheap place to die, Tom. Cheap way to die."

Tom looked back toward the room. The body still lay curled on the bed, but he could see the men from the coroner's office unfolding the large zippered bag that would transport Rayette Jones to the morgue.

"You'd think they'd learn after a while," Carl said.

Tom looked at him. "Who?"

"Prostitutes. You'd think they'd learn that they're all going to end up like this, dead in some fleabag."

Tom smiled slighly. "The thing is, they don't all end up this way, Carl. Some of them hook up with big shots and end up living the high life in Palm Springs.''

Carl stepped off the small asphalt walkway and looked out toward the range of mountains. "Remember that girl they found out on the Flats a couple years back? Throat cut?''

"I remember.''

"She was a prostitute, too, Tom,'' Carl said pointedly. "Look, I know you don't believe it, buy you reap what you sow, my friend.''

Tom didn't care to argue the point. "Did Rayette Jones have a pimp?''

"Sure did.'' Carl withdrew a small notepad from his coat pocket and flipped through it. "Here it is. The name is Pete Wilson. He's a small-time ex-con. Vice gave us the whole rundown on him. He's done a little time here and there, but nothing big.'' He closed the pad. "He's still in town as far as we know. Lives at that transient hotel on South Second.''

"The Richmont?''

"That's the one. Room 32.''

From inside the room Tom heard the slicing sound of the zipper as the bag closed around Rayette Jones's body.

"Who found her?'' Tom asked.

"The fellow who owns the place,'' Carl said. "I talked to him. He wasn't much help.'' He shook his head. "People who run places like this never are much help. They're like the people who come here. Everything finds its own level, you know?''

"Well, what did he say exactly? Tom asked.

"Said the guy was wearing a hat and overcoat. Didn't see a car, but the guy put down a license number. Probably a phony.''

Tom nodded. "Well, I guess we'd better start with Mr. Wilson.''

On the way to the hotel, Carl cracked the window on the driver's side just enough to send a steady stream of cold air across Tom's neck. "Charlie Michaels just got back from a visit to New York,'' he said. "It was his first trip. He said the pimps ride around Times Square in custom-made Cadillacs. Was it like that when you lived there?''

"More or less,'' Tom said dully.

Carl shook his head disapprovingly. "How can the authorities let something like that happen, Tom? I mean, that's a total breakdown of society. Total."

"Well, it's hard to clean something like that up," Tom said indifferently.

Carl shook his head. "You can eradicate that, those pimps, I mean, the way they flaunt it, flaunt us, the law, everything. You can eradicate that. It takes a lot of work, but it can be done."

Tom shifted slightly to the right, edging his shoulder against the door. Something in him envied the way Carl went at things with such certainty. Everything explained by that one ancient fall from grace in the garden, with everything gone rotten after that, except the one true faith and its promise of redemption.

"You bust them every time you see them," Carl went on. "You make the whole thing just one endless revolving door." He laughed. "I remember something my dad once said: 'You can't get rid of rats, but you can make sure they stay in the cellar.' "

Tom looked toward Carl and smiled. "You know what your trouble is, Carl, you have no taste for slime."

Carl sat up slightly. "And you think we ought to let things get like they are in New York, Tom?" He laughed. "Can you see it, Tom? All those pink Cadillacs parked front to back around Temple Square?"

Tom smiled. It was odd about Carl, he thought, the way at times he seemed so completely rigid, and at others he seemed to break through all that, becoming as he did so a warm, utterly approachable man.

"Even I wouldn't want that," Tom said.

"What? No taste for slime?"

After a moment the Richmont came into view, and as it did Carl stiffened once again.

"Look at that place," he said. "Falling down, just like the Paradise." He shook his head. "They should just take a bulldozer to South Second. Drive an expressway right through this section of Salt Lake. Get rid of it, once and for all."

Tom glanced at the ridge of storm clouds that was building to the north, then back toward the Richmont. It was a small building, five flights, with a brick facade that seemed older than it was, weathered, abandoned, the neon sign blinking palely, the windows covered with years of accumulated dust.

"Looks the part," Carl said.

Tom continued to watch the building. He could feel a growing dread, as if he were moving toward the final episode in the story of his life. He had felt that way before and survived. Because of that he dismissed the feeling, but he could never really get rid of it. Gentry had warned him that there might come a time when he simply couldn't bear to knock at one more closed door. Now he could hear his mind repeating the same sentence: I'm tired of this. Tired of it.

Carl guided the car up to the curb in front of the hotel. Then he leaned toward the windshield and glared up toward the third row of windows. "He's in Room 32. Most places, that'd be on the third floor." He smiled. "A place like this, though, it could be in the basement."

"Wherever," Tom said coolly. He could hear Gentry speaking again, this time a little differently: The way to get through it, Tom, is you just bite down hard on your fear.

Carl scratched his chin. "Well, Tom, let's hope our friend Wilson is not a bad person, you know?"

"Let's just hope he's in the room where he's supposed to be," Tom said. He got out of the car and waited for Carl to join him on the sidewalk. Through the glass doors he could see a few people lounging listlessly on sofas and chairs in the lobby. They were snoozing or staring inattentively at the television. It was in a hotel like this one, he remembered, that his father had died. It was a little brick building in the Bronx, and Tom could see the stained linoleum of the lobby, the littered stairs, the dull green walls. He had stood in his father's room for a long time, looking at the moth-eaten sheets, the empty whiskey bottles, the single black cockroach that watched him from its place on the wall near the ceiling.

"If Wilson killed her," Carl said as he stepped up next to Tom, "we won't find him here."

"Yeah," Tom said. Out of habit, he patted the shoulder holster beneath his arm.

Carl bounded up the few cement stairs, swung the door open, and followed Tom into the hotel lobby. A few of the people shifted uneasily, and Tom knew that most of them had long ago learned the look and walk and tone of a cop, even in plain-clothes.

The woman behind the desk eyed them carefully as they approached her. She had watery green eyes and a beehive of faded red hair.

Carl showed her his badge. "Does Pete Wilson live here?" he asked.

Under the fluorescent light, the woman's hair appeared almost orange. "I don't know if he's in," she said.

Carl smiled sarcastically. "We don't want you to ring him up, you know what I mean?"

The woman chewed her bottom lip mechanically. "I don't want no trouble," she said. "Last time you guys come in here, you just about tore this place apart."

"Did you see Wilson go out today?" Tom asked.

"I just come on at noon. I ain't seen him."

"Does he live alone?"

"Who he lives with ain't my business."

Carl placed his palm flat on the desk and leaned into it, glaring at her. "You have been asked an official question by a police officer."

The woman seemed to retreat a little. She glanced quickly at Tom. "What was the question? I forget things."

"Does Wilson live alone?" Carl blurted.

"He's got a couple females up there with him, I think," the woman said.

"He should," Carl said, "since he's a pimp."

The woman laughed. "That what he is? I figured him for one of them poly-type Mormons."

Carl's eyes narrowed. "Now let me tell you something. I'm not in a funny mood, so save the jokes. How many people are in that room with Wilson?"

The woman's eyes shifted from Carl to Tom. "I'm telling you the truth, I don't know who's up there. Maybe nobody. Maybe a damn army. I just come on at noon." She smiled slightly, and her heavy lipstick cracked at the corners of her mouth. To Tom, she seemed like one of those people who had simply been planted on the earth like dry weeds—mother, sister, daughter to no one. His father had had that look of having been sprung full-grown into existence and then living without anything you could call a life and dying without anything you could call a death, simply stopping in the middle of something that was nothing.

"We're not going to get anything out of her," Carl said to Tom. Then he looked at the woman. "Now, you must have heard this before, but I'll tell you again. We're going up to check out this Wilson pimp. You are not to warn him in any way, do you understand?"

The woman nodded half-heartedly. "Stairs are to the right."

Carl turned to Tom. "Okay, let's go."

Tom followed Carl as he moved up the stairs. He could feel his mouth turning dry, his hands clammy. In him mind he had always been able to picture the final moment: You kick down the door and there's a flash, then it's over; you never hear the sound it makes when it cuts you down.

Carl kicked a paper cup from his path. "This whole part of town is pure blight," he said. "It needs a bulldozer, maybe a wrecking ball, maybe just a big charge of dynamite."

By the time they reached the third floor, Tom could feel his fear in his throat. He had never been able to shake it off, and he suspected that if he had had a jot more of it, he would have been a coward.

"Well, that's nice," Carl said. "Wilson's room's right at the end of the hallway."

Tom glanced forward and saw the number on the door. "Just be careful, Carl."

Carl did not seem to hear him. He moved casually toward the door, as if he knew exactly what lay behind it, as if some invisible shield would rise to protect him from the force of hurling lead.

At Room 32, Carl took one side of the door and Tom the other.

"Ready?" Tom whispered.

"Sure."

Tom raised his hand, pausing at the door, and as always, something in his body seemed to speak: I do not want to die.

"Do it," Carl said.

Tom took a deep breath, then knocked at the door. "Police!" He could hear something scrambling behind the door. Instantly, he drew his pistol, stepped back, and kicked it open, slamming it against the interior wall. Carl bolted in with Tom behind him.

Wilson was at the bedroom window, tugging at it frantically. A naked woman stood beside him. She seemed frozen in place for a moment, then suddenly dove toward the bed, crawling into it and drawing the covers over her.

"Hold it right there," Carl shouted.

Wilson whirled around and flung his empty hands high into the air. "I got them up, man! Oh, God, don't shoot!"

"Don't move," Tom said. He could see the fading strength of Wilson's erection.

Carl laughed. "Sorry to have caught you at a bad time, Wilson."

Wilson remained rigidly in place, his arms stretched above his heads. "I didn't do nothing, man. I didn't do nothing."

Tom grabbed Wilson's clothes from the end of the bed and tossed them to him.

"Who's the girl?" Carl asked as Wilson began scrambling into his pants.

"She's my woman. JoAnn."

"That's cozy," Carl said, "but we hear you've got more than one woman."

Tom tossed the girl her clothes and she began putting them on under the covers. "What's your name?" he asked.

"JoAnn Blevins," she said. She was trembling wildly.

"Just relax," Tom said. "We want to ask some questions." He turned to Wilson. "You know a woman named Rayette Jones?"

Wilson zipped up his pants and pressed his back against the window.

"My friend asked you a question," Carl said stiffly.

Wilson nodded. "Yeah, I know her."

"We're not here to bust a lousy pimp, Wilson," Tom said.

Wilson looked mildly relieved, then confused. "What you want with me? Why you bustin' in here?"

"The police ask the questions in this town," Carl said. He chuckled. "Hey, you know what a pimp ought to do when he drives his Cadillac into Salt Lake?"

Wilson said nothing.

"He ought to keep driving it until he gets to L.A."

"We ain't been here long," Wilson said nervously. "We were just passing through."

"You've been passing through for more than two months," Carl said. "And you may be here a lot longer than you think."

"When was the last time you saw Rayette Jones?" Tom asked.

Wilson glanced apprehensively at Tom's pistol. Tom suddenly felt embarrassed. He had not even known that his pistol was still in his hand. He holstered it immediately.

"Answer, pimp," Carl demanded.

Wilson seemed to jump at the sound of Carl's voice. "Last night. That's the truth."

"When last night?" Tom asked.

"Around eleven, something like that."

"Did you set up a date for her?"

Wilson looked puzzled.

"Trick," Carl said. "Score. Hit. Whatever you pimps call it."

Wilson eased himself down from the windowsill. He grinned at Tom. "The dude for real, man?"

Carl stepped toward Wilson menacingly. "You want me to show you how *real* I am, man?"

Wilson stiffened.

"You're strictly L.A. garbage," Carl said. "We bury garbage in Salt Lake."

Wilson leaned back into the window, his eyes bulging. "Don't touch me, man."

Carl laughed. "Touch you? You're lucky I didn't blow your pimp head off."

"Take the girl out, Carl," Tom said calmly. "See if she knows anything."

Carl continued to glare hotly at Wilson. "We don't like your kind in Salt Lake."

"Take the girl out in the hall, Carl," Tom said firmly.

Carl stared at Wilson for a moment, then turned toward the girl. "Come with me, please," he said, his voice softening.

Tom waited until Carl and JoAnn had walked out of the room. He could hear Carl talking gently to her, the way he always talked to young women, even whores.

Wilson seemed to relax slightly. "Your friend got a temper, ain't he?" He offered Tom a toothy grin.

"Get that fucking smile off your face," Tom said.

The smile vanished.

"Rayette Jones is dead," Tom continued. "Your ass is in a sling."

Wilson's mouth dropped down. "Rayette? Dead?"

"Somebody strangled her. Early this morning. You said you saw her around eleven."

Wilson wiped his mouth with his fist. His lips were trembling. He was a small-time jerk, Tom thought. A real, hard-nosed pimp could look a cop dead in the eye and nothing ever trembled.

"Shit, man," Wilson said. "Oh, Jesus."

"You are prime meat for this, Wilson . . ."

"I didn't kill nobody," Wilson whined.

". . . and they still use a rope in Utah."

Wilson's eyes widened. "Christ, man, I didn't kill no Rayette Jones."

"Where were you early this morning?" Tom asked.

"Right here," Wilson said frantically. "You ask JoAnn if that ain't so."

"'Hell,'" Tom said. "A whore makes a great witness for her pimp."

"We was right here," Wilson cried desperately, "right here in this room."

"How do you run whores?" Tom asked.

Wilson hesitated, sweat building on his forehead. "You got to help me out," he said.

"No, I don't 'got to help you out.' "

"I didn't kill Rayette," Wilson whimpered. "I loved that girl."

Tom glanced at the bed, then back to Wilson. "I can see how much you loved her."

Wilson mopped his head with his hands. "Shit, man, I ain't no killer."

Tom stared evenly into Wilson's eyes. "You're running whores by phone, right?"

"Yeah," Wilson said weakly. "Yeah, that's right."

"When was her last trick?"

"I give her the place at around eleven. That's the last time I seen her. This morning, she ain't back. I was getting worried. I was 'bout to go see after her when you boys bust the door."

"The trick, did he call you?"

Wilson shook his head. "No."

Tom's eyes narrowed. "Don't bullshit me."

"I ain't, man. The mark didn't call me."

"Then how did he get to you?"

Wilson shifted nervously on his feet. "You can't do no street business in Salt Lake, man. You got to do it all by phone, you know?"

"Who called you, Wilson?" Tom asked. "Who set up that last trick?"

"Just a bellhop, man," Wilson said, "that's all. I give my number to some folks around town, you know. Bellhops and like that. They steer some action my way. They get a little piece of it."

"So one of your bellhops called you to set up the trick?"

Wilson nodded. "That's right."

"Which one?"

Wilson's shoulders seemed to slump. "Ah, please, man, I got to do business in this town."

"What business is that, Wilson?" Tom asked. "You're not doing any more business in this town. You might do time here, but no business. You're finished in Salt Lake. You understand?"

Wilson shook his head. "I can't tell you names, man."

Tom stepped over to Wilson, grabbed his shoulder, and squeezed hard. "You can and you will. Right now."

4

"It's strictly a phone business," Tom told Carl as they sat in the car outside the hotel.

"Which is why Vice didn't bust them yet," Carl said.

"That's right."

Carl grinned. "You see, that's the way a pimp ought to have to operate. Not drive down Temple Street in a pink Cadillac." He leaned back in the seat. "You know what I think, the guy came into town, a conventioneer, maybe, or a salesman. Anyway, he connected up with the whore. Then something went wrong. Maybe she didn't want to do exactly what he wanted. Maybe they had a dispute over the tab. Maybe the guy just wanted to cover his tracks."

"And so he killed her," Tom said.

"Simple as that, Tom."

"Maybe he even put the right name on the motel register, then," Tom said.

"The room was rented in the name of William B. Thornton," Carl said. "But that's probably a phoney. The license plate number was."

Tom looked out the side window and into the lobby of the Hotel Richmont. He wondered how many times his father had slumped down on some worn, spattered sofa in a dingy lobby, drunk and slowly losing consciousness. "How come he dressed her after he killed her, Carl?"

"We're not sure he did."

Tom turned around quickly. "How come he combed her hair?"

Carl squinted. "What?"

"Nobody just lays there and lets you strangle them to death, Carl," Tom said. "They fight like hell. They jerk around." He paused, watching Carl's face. "They even get their hair messed up."

Carl stared at Tom intently. "Go on."

"This woman's hair was neat as a pin," Tom said. "Not a hair out of place. She probably puked all over the place, but there was not a drop on her body. Just some stains on the bed and between the mattress and the frame. There were no stains on her dress. Which means, at least to me, that she was naked when she threw up. Which means he cleaned her, dressed her, and laid her on the bed—and combed her hair."

"So, you're saying we got a psycho on our hands," Carl said slowly.

"I don't think it's some conventioneer with a mean streak, Carl," Tom said. "You get anything from the girl?"

"Nothing much. Same old story. She's been with Wilson for several years. He met Rayette and a friend of hers named Peggy in Dallas. They moved on to L.A. together. Things got rough there—some kind of drug burn—and so they all came to Salt Lake."

"Maybe that's it," Tom said.

"What?"

"A drug burn rub-out. Maybe somebody from L.A. is trying to punish our friend Wilson."

Carl nodded. "Makes sense. Maybe this business with the hair and all is meant to mean something to him."

"They do their business by phone," Tom said. "The guy who made the last trick is somebody called William Casey. A bellhop at the Hotel Utah."

Carl's face seemed to pale. "Hotel Utah?"

"That's right."

"I don't believe it," Carl said. "That's the finest place in Salt Lake."

"Relax, Carl," Tom said. "It's just a bellhop with a phone number."

Carl's face hardened. "Let's bust him."

"We're working a *murder* case," Tom said. "Let Vice handle Casey."

"I don't like whores being run out of the Hotel Utah, Tom," Carl said sternly.

"Hotel Richmont. Hotel Utah. What's the difference?"

"Look there are parts of Salt Lake where the scum go, and there are parts where decent people go. The Utah has always been clean."

Tom could see that Carl was getting very agitated. "Look, why don't you go on home? I'll handle Casey."

Carl took a deep breath. "You make sure he gets my message," he said.

"I will."

"I mean it."

"Casey won't be stringing for a pimp anymore," Tom said. "You got my word."

Carl seemed to calm down slightly. "Okay, Tom, okay." He looked at Tom. "You know how I feel about things, don't you?"

Tom nodded silently.

Carl squeezed the steering wheel. "What's happening to this world? Garbage everywhere. Pimps and whores working out of the Hotel Utah. Where's it going to end, Tom? When are the decent people going to get together and straighten things out?"

Tom glanced at his watch. "You better drive me back to the Paradise Motel. I want to talk to Casey right away."

Carl hit the ignition and pulled the car into the street. "Listen, Tom," he said after a moment, "I know we don't have the same ideas about things, but we're still friends, right?"

"We get along," Tom said.

"Been partners for three years now," Carl said. There was a certain pride in his voice.

Tom glanced toward Carl, his eyes moving up from the thin black tie to the clean, well-scrubbed face. He looked like a marine on furlough.

"I mean, we're buddies, right?" Carl said.

It was a little boy's word, *buddies,* and Tom glanced away immediately, his eyes roaming the streets. He had had only one real friend in his life, a man much older than himself, a cop in New York named Gentry who had a round red face and snow-white hair and a faint trace of Irish brogue and who had once told him as they stood in the rain on the steps of Saint Patrick's that the secret to being a good Catholic was in knowing that it was all just so much bullshit but caring for it anyway.

Carl looked at Tom worriedly. "Which sort of brings me to my point."

Tom's eyes followed a tall, blond-haired woman as she skipped along the sidewalk. She was moving very quickly, her high heels popping along the cement walk. Automatically he glanced back to make sure no one was following her.

"Tom?" Carl said.

He turned back toward Redmon.

"As a friend, I just wanted to say something, Tom."

Tom watched him silently.

"Well, what with Phyllis gone and all, I was thinking, maybe you need someone in your life."

Tom did not disagree. But who?

"So, I thought maybe you'd like to come and have dinner with Jenny and me some night."

Tom could imagine the small, slightly chubby young woman they would have waiting for him. She would sit beside him at the table in Carl's tiny, crowded dining room, her hands squeezed together in her lap, her eyes faintly moist from the contact lenses she had not quite gotten used to.

"What do you think, Tom? Any time you say."

"Not any time soon, Carl." Tom turned back toward the window and watched the street life flow by.

"Still strung out over Phyllis, I guess," Carl said.

"I don't get that torn up about things," Tom said. They were moving toward the state capitol, and he could see the blue dome rising above the surrounding buildings like the tip of a huge bullet.

"You two made a terrific couple," Carl said. "You and Phyllis. I really thought you were going to take the vow on this one."

Tom watched a puff of gray cloud drift idly over the capitol dome. "People come and go," he said.

"That's not the way to look at it, Tom," Carl said firmly. He turned onto First Street, heading west.

The street life changed now. No more grimy streets or broken-down shops. From here the Hotel Richmont and the area around it could only be imagined as a foreign and strangely menacing world. Tom watched men in their dark suits strolling past jewelry shops and boutiques.

"You got to make an effort to keep things together, Tom," Carl said.

"I don't like to get stuck in things," Tom said. "Especially dead things." For a moment his mind returned to Rayette Jones. She seemed like just another dead thing, something he'd have to work over for a while, like a mortician, then bury.

The car glided past the Salt Palace Convention Center, and Tom watched the large crowd milling around in front, their bodies dwarfed by the great white rotunda. Signs advertised a solar power exhibition. "I'll be glad when it's summer again," he said.

Carl did not seem to hear him. "Man is not meant to be alone," he said.

Carl was always quoting something that sounded to Tom suspiciously like Scripture. "Some are," he said.

"You had a wife, you'd see the world in a better light, Tom."

Carl had a wife, Tom thought, and she had large breasts and a roving eye that Carl himself never seemed to notice.

"To tell you the truth, Tom," Carl said, "I don't know what I'd do without Jenny."

And he'd probably always feel that way, Tom thought, until he came home early one afternoon and found the milk truck parked outside and something gymnastic going on inside. That had happened to Gentry. It was the only thing he never talked about.

"You'll know what I mean someday," Carl said confidently.

Up ahead, Tom could see the battered sign of the Paradise Motel. "Just let me off at my car," he said.

Carl turned into the dusty parking lot and stopped. "I'm going to hold you to that dinner some night, Tom."

A quick wind sent a spray of sand into Tom's face as he stepped out of the car. "I'll check Casey out. Let you know what happened in the morning."

Carl's face seemed to harden. "You tell that joker there'll be no more running whores out of the Hotel Utah," he said fiercely.

"I'll tell him," Tom said as he closed the door. As Carl's car pulled away, he glanced back at Room 17 of the Paradise Motel. He could imagine Rayette's body in the chill, dark freezer in the morgue. Perhaps what his brother had once told him was true. His brother, the public school teacher with the little wire glasses and shiny pants. "Tom," he had said, fingering the bowl of his white meerschaum pipe, "you only fall in love with corpses."

5

Tom pulled up in front of the Hotel Utah and got out of the car. A knot of well-dressed businessmen huddled under the large awning, but for the most part the streets were deserted. On Sunday afternoons, Salt Lake took on a kind of asphalt emptiness, the gray sky yawning overhead, drawing the white light up into itself, turning the air an eerie blue.

Stepping up on the curb, Tom felt a slight cramp in his right thigh. He could no longer dismiss such small pains as the result of a sudden chill. It was age, gnawing at his bones and muscles like a mean, relentless little animal.

The lobby of the Hotel Utah was large and comfortably furnished, with large sofas and enormous red armchairs. Potted plants stood in clusters here and there, small oasis of vegetation that looked oddly out of place under the shimmering light of a gigantic crystal chandelier.

The desk clerk was tall and very thin. Even from a distance, Tom could pick up his quick, nervous manner, the hassled appearance of a person who looks busy even when he sleeps. He looked up as Tom drew nearer. Then he offered a small, wooden smile. "May I help you, sir?"

"I'm looking for William Casey," Tom said. "He's one of your bellhops."

"Right over there," the clerk said. He pointed to the right.

Tom turned and saw a man slumped near a pay telephone. He looked almost comical in his bellhop attire, an old man who was still playing in a high school band, still dressed up in a uniform that was at odds with his age and experience.

Tom walked across the lobby toward him, and when Casey caught him in his eye, he pushed himself up straight.

"You're William Casey?" Tom asked.

"That's right," Casey said. He watched Tom a little nervously, a debtor's eyes checking out a bill collector.

Tom could see a bit of gray hair peeping out from under the cap, giving Casey the appearance of a kindly grandfather. The eyes were light blue and watery. They made Casey look as if he had spent his life begging for forgiveness.

A well-dressed man stepped up and deposited a coin in the telephone.

"I need to talk to you about something," Tom said to Casey.

"Go ahead," Casey said. His voice had a manufactured hardness, like a phony steel.

"Privately."

"Okay." Casey led Tom to a small sofa several yards away and they both sat down.

"My name's Tom Jackson," Tom said.

Casey nodded quickly. "Let's make this short, okay? I don't want to miss any tips."

"I understand."

Suddenly Casey leaned forward, smiled, and said, "What can I do for you?"

Tom realized immediately that the old man was about to offer him a whore. "You know a pimp named Pete Wilson?" he asked bluntly.

Casey sat back and stared icily at Tom. "Who did you say you were?" he asked cautiously.

"Tom Jackson. Salt Lake Police."

Something seemed to darken behind Casey's eyes. "Police," he muttered softly.

"That's right. About Pete Wilson. You know him?"

Casey seemed to shrink inside his dark blue uniform. "Did you tell the desk clerk you were a cop?"

"No."

Casey looked relieved. "This is just between you and me, then, right?"

Tom said nothing.

"Listen, I want you to know something. I can't live on tips, you know what I mean?"

"Other people do," Tom said.

Casey's body suddenly went rigid, but he said nothing.

"What do you know about Wilson?"

"Not a thing when you come right down to it," Casey said. He glanced nervously about the room. "Did you bust him?"

"Not yet."

Casey looked suprised. "What's this about, then?"

"You know a woman named Rayette Jones?"

Casey's eyes squeezed together. He thought for a moment, then shook his head. "No, I don't think so," he said slowly.

"One of Wilson's whores."

"I never met any of them," Casey said quickly.

"Somebody killed her."

"Oh, shit," Casey groaned.

"She died last night. After her last trick. Around midnight. You set up that trick, Casey."

Casey's face paled. "Christ, look, I didn't have nothing to do with that."

"Wilson says you set up the last trick," Tom said evenly. "He says you called him up and made all the arrangements."

"That nigger bastard," Casey hissed.

"I thought he was a business partner."

Casey looked at Tom angrily. "Look, I got a sick wife to support. Would you like to live on a bellhop's take?"

"What was your deal with Wilson?"

"I don't have nothing to do with his whores. Like I said, I never met them."

"Answer my question."

Casey blinked quickly, then wiped his mouth with the back of his hand. "Once in a while, a guy asks me about a whore. It don't happen all the time. It ain't routine. But once in a while. Well, I got Wilson's number. I set things up. If everything works out, Wilson sends me a few bucks in the mail. Nothing much. Five, ten dollars. Something like that. Small stuff."

"And you set something up last night?" Tom asked.

Casey's eyes darted away from Tom's. "Yeah."

"Who was the john?"

Casey stared at Tom incredulously. "Jesus Christ, you think I know?"

"You didn't see him?"

"No."

"Then how did you set it up?"

"By phone," Casey said. He swallowed hard. "I got a bad heart, you know? I can't take much strain."

"Yeah, well, Rayette Jones's heart doesn't work at all anymore, you know? Now you're one step from being a pimp, Casey, and I got a woman in a rubber bag, and you set up her last trick. So excuse me, but fuck your goddamn heart."

Casey looked as if he had been struck. "I don't know who the man was. I swear to God, I just don't know." He paused, as if trying to decide what to say next. "This is Salt Lake. You can't run whores on the street. For Christ's sake, this ain't L.A., you know?"

"So you just got a telephone call?"

"That's right."

"And you didn't see the john."

Casey shook his head vigorously. "I didn't see him. It's just a voice on the phone."

"What did he say?"

Casey scratched the side of his face thoughtfully. "He said he wanted a girl. A black girl. A Negress, he said."

"He specified a black?"

"That's right."

"He used the word *Negress?*"

"Yeah, he did. He said, 'A Negress.' He wanted that in particular."

"What else did he say?"

"That's about it," Casey said. He looked at Tom closely. "Where you from? I mean, originally."

"New York."

Casey suddenly smiled. "New York, huh? I didn't think you were from Salt Lake."

"The voice on the phone," Tom asked. "Did you recognize it? Had he ever called before?"

Casey continued to watch Tom knowingly. "New York. I

knew it. You don't look like no Mormon type." He grinned.
"Too sloppy looking—no offense—and a mean mouth." He
place his hand lightly on Tom's shoulder. "I'm from the East,
too." He winked.

"We don't go along with this Mormon crap, do we?"

Instantly, Tom slapped Casey's hand from his shoulder.
"Let me tell you something, shithead," he said angrily. "If I
find out you've held anything back on me, I'll grind you down
to nothing, you understand?"

Casey's face froze. "I didn't mean no offense, mister," he
stammered.

"I think you better get out of the whore business," Tom
said. "I don't want to have your name popping up again. Understand?"

Casey bowed his head slightly. "You won't see my name
again," he murmured.

Tom waited a moment, then went on. "When did the call
come in?"

Casey looked up slowly, his face drawn, weary. "About ten-
thirty, maybe." He nodded toward the other side of the lobby.
"On that pay phone over there."

"Did you answer it?"

"No. Another guy. But the fellow—the john—he asked for
me."

"By name?"

"That's right."

"How did he get your name?"

Casey shook his head. "I don't know. Word gets around.
Maybe a friend told him. Somebody I'd set up before."

"What did he say exactly?"

Casey thought for a moment, then answered. "Well, like I
said, he wanted a black girl. He said he'd heard I could get him
one. I told him I thought I could, then he gave me the name and
room number of the Paradise Motel. He said the girl should be
there by midnight."

"That's all?"

Casey rubbed his eyes gently. "Yeah, that's all."

Tom stood up. "If you think of anything else, let me know."

Casey nodded but said nothing.

Driving away from the hotel, Tom thought of Casey, then of

New York. He remembered the grimy streets, the sooty air, the oily sludge in the gutters, the random, crazy noise, and he understood why he had left. And yet, after ten years in Salt Lake, New York still remained the closest thing he had to home. He had left it, but it had not left him, and Salt Lake seemed as foreign to him as ever, a place that was simply somewhere in between the place he had left behind and the place should have gone.

6

The sun had already set when Tom again pulled into the driveway of the Paradise Motel. He could see the manager standing behind the counter of the office. He looked up as Tom guided the car to the curb, the neon sign in the window bathing his face in a pinkish haze.

Tom got out of the car and walked into the office, a trio of bells jangling wildly as he opened the door.

The manager smiled. "I keep those bells so nobody'll surprise me, you know?"

Tom drew his badge from his coat pocket and showed it to the manager.

"Is there some new difficulty?" the man asked.

"I'm working on the homicide you had here this morning."

The manager nodded. "Yes, I presumed that. My name is Sims. Raymond Sims. What can I do for you?" He was a short, well-groomed man, rather formally dressed in a black suit and bow tie. He looked as if he should be managing a far less seedy establishment than the Paradise.

"I thought I'd take another look at the room," Tom said.

"Do as you like," Sims said. "I can assure you, no one has entered the room since you left." One eyebrow edged upward. "I don't recall talking to you today."

"You didn't," Tom said. "You talked to my partner, Carl Redmon."

"Athletic-looking fellow?"

"That's Carl."

"A football star going slightly to seed?"

"You could put it that way."

Sims smiled. "I have an eye for detail."

Tom laid his hand on the counter, palm up. "Could I have the key?"

"Of course." Sims turned around and took a set of keys from the wooden rack behind the counter. "This is it," he said, dropping the key into Tom's hand. "Feels odd now, the key. Cold. The mind does that, changes things."

Tom closed his fist around the key. "Was 17 the only room you had vacant last night?"

"Unfortunately, there were many others. We're not in the best location out here."

"Then why did you give him that room?"

"He asked for it."

"Specifically? By its number?"

"Yes."

Tom shoved the key into his pocket and walked out of the office. To his right he could see Room 17 at the far end of a long line of rooms. It was in a corner, facing the plaza, but the lights of the motel parking lot barely reached it, so that it sat in an area of deep shadows. Of all the rooms in the motel complex, Room 17 was the most difficult to see from the office. And the killer had asked for it specifically. To Tom, this meant that the murderer had planned his crime, and that the killing was not over a dispute about anything, as Carl thought. It was not the result of sudden rage, either.

Tom paused at the door, turned, and glanced about the surrounding area. Across the road, a bus came to a halt and two people emerged from it, then made their way to a small restaurant down the street. Tom remembered that Sims had claimed not to have seen a car, even though the killer had written a license number on the motel registry. He stepped to the side of the walkway and looked down at the dust on the driveway, as if somewhere amid all that littered ground the key lay undisturbed, but waiting to unlock the crime.

Tom turned, unlocked the door, and walked into the room. It was neat, orderly, drab. He closed the door behind him and moved toward the center of the room. In his mind, he tried to recreate what must have happened almost twenty-four hours before.

There had been a knock at the door. The killer had opened it, seen Rayette Jones, and perhaps offered her a smile. Then the screen door opened. Rayette walked in. The man closed the door and locked it. He turned around, offered Rayette a drink, or just told her he was glad to see her. At this point she was not afraid. There was no sign of a struggle in the room, which meant the killer had taken her by surprise, probably from behind. Tom tried to choreograph their movements from the time Rayette came through the door. She probably went into the center of the room and then turned around, looking here and there, checking the exits if she were smart, or maybe just glancing at the bed. At this point, maybe they began to talk a little. The man circled around Rayette, stalking her in his mind, but moving easily, casually. Maybe he went to the bed and sat down. Rayette was still standing. She took off her coat, or perhaps he had already taken it off and hung it on the chair where they found it the next morning. Now she was checking herself out in the mirror, while he either leaned in the corner, sat on the bed, or moved around appraising her legs and breasts. Then she took off more of her clothes. Perhaps she was on the bed at this time, feeling his hands explore her. After a while she was naked. Then his eyes changed. Maybe she saw it because he was on top of her looking down. Or maybe she didn't because he was behind her, his hands closing around her throat. Then she was dead and the room was silent.

Tom rubbed his eyes and stared at the bed. He believed that the murderer had probably killed Rayette there. In her agony, she had thrown up; he could still see the small brown stains that dotted a small area of the bed cover.

Tom walked to the head of the bed and drew back the cover. The sheets beneath were clean. This meant that the cover had not been pulled back: Rayette had not gotten into bed with anybody. The lab would be able to discover if she had had sex the night of her death. He drew the bedspread back over the pillows and straightened it neatly.

Tom turned and walked into the bathroom. The lab people had stripped it of towels and washcloths. The sink was stained with age and use, but otherwise it was clean. So was the bathtub. He leaned over it, parted the short blue curtains over the small window, and looked out. In the darkness he could only see the backs of several buildings in the distance. He pulled himself back up, glancing at the base of the window. A small residue of dust remained in the far right corner of the sill. The rest had been wiped clean, but a few chips of dry white paint dotted the window ledge near its center. Looking at the chips, Tom knew that they had to have fallen onto the ledge after the dust had been wiped away, or they would have been wiped away with it. He knew then that the killer had left the room through the bathroom window. He had slid out into the darkness and closed the window behind him. Some of the dried paint had fallen down onto the window ledge. He had not exited from the front because there was no need to. He did not have a car.

Quickly Tom walked out of the room and back to his own car. He took the flashlight from the glove compartment, circled around the office, and made his way to the rear of Room 17. Using the flashlight, he searched the ground immediately underneath the bathroom window and found two small impressions in the sand. They were not clear enough to identify as footprints, but Tom knew that that was what they were. The killer had dropped from the window, then circled around the motel. Then he either made his way to a car parked some distance away or took a bus.

Tom pocketed the flashlight, then walked back to the Paradise office. Sims looked up as the bells clangored over Tom's head.

"Did you find anything significant?"

"Were you here all of last night?" Tom asked.

"I was."

"My partner tells me you didn't see a car."

"You mean the car of the gentleman who rented Room 17?"

"Yes."

"No, I didn't."

"I noticed that when I drove into the lot, you looked up," Tom said.

"Certainly I looked up. I thought you were a customer."

"Wouldn't you normally do that?"

Sims nodded. "I suppose I would."

"If you didn't see the guy's car, what did you see?"

Sims shrugged. "Just him."

"At what point did you see him?"

Sims squinted. "What do you mean?"

"Did you see him before he came in the office? Before those bells rang?"

Sims thought about it. "Yes, I did."

"Where was he?"

"He came up from that direction," Sims said, pointing to the left toward the street.

"Did you see him cross the street?"

"No."

"You just saw him as he rounded that corner of the office, then?"

"That's when I caught sight of him," Sims said firmly. "He came around the corner that fronts the highway."

"And you're sure you never saw a car?"

"No car."

Tom glanced at the manager's large hands and wondered if perhaps no one had ever rented Room 17 at all and that the impressions beneath the bathroom window were Sims's.

"And you were here the whole night?" he asked again.

"Yes."

"You didn't leave the office for any reason."

"Well, the call of nature, maybe," Sims said lightly.

Tom did not smile. "How long have you lived in Salt Lake, Mr. Sims?"

"What's that got to do with anything?"

"We have to check everything out," Tom said.

"Including me, I suppose."

Tom nodded. "How long?"

"Ten years." Sims looked worriedly at Tom. "I didn't have anything to do with that girl's death."

Tom said nothing.

"You don't think I had anything to do with killing that girl, do you?" Sims asked.

Tom said nothing.

Sims smiled. "You have a way of looking at people. There's a note of intimidation. Do they teach you that at the academy?" He laughed easily. "The Strasburg Method for police."

Tom kept his eyes fixed on Sims. "If he'd had a car, you would have seen it, wouldn't you? That eye for detail you mentioned."

"He didn't have a car," Sims said. "Or at least he didn't park it around here."

"He came in here, didn't he?" Tom asked. "He had to register."

"He came in." Sims ran his finger delicately over his upper lip. Then he laughed. "That gesture, the finger at the lip. It's very good. I used it with scores of characters, especially aristocrats. It was perfect for the Scarlet Pimpernel." His face hardened. "You think I'm a joke, don't you? A failed actor. What could be more ridiculous?"

"What did he look like, the man who registered?"

"You really can't be diverted from your little inquiry, can you?"

"Not now."

"Careful, you may lose the human touch."

"What did he look like?"

"He was tall. He was dressed in an overcoat of some kind. It looked rather flimsy, worn at the cuff, the seams splitting a bit at the shoulder. It looked like a stage prop for some play about a man down on his luck."

"Could you see his face?"

Sims shook his haed. "Not very well. He had a floppy sort of hat, the kind the Okies wore in *The Grapes of Wrath*—the film, I mean."

"Could you make out anything about the face, anything at all?"

"He had a mustache. One of those big ones. Very thick."

"What color?"

"Black, perhaps very dark brown," Sims said. "The light in here is not the best for delineating subtle shades."

"Okay," Tom said. "When he came . . ."

"Look," Sims said, "if this is going to take much longer, maybe I should make us a pot of coffee."

"No, thanks."

"I have Brazillian. The very best. Like they say, it's good for what ails you."

"I just have a few more questions," Tom said.

Sims offered a thin smile. "Do I amuse you? One of those unfortunate creatures with neither home nor hearth. The male version of one of those heroines created by the late Tennessee Williams?"

"Just a few more questions," Tom repeated. "When he came in . . ."

"I imagine you work night hours too," Sims said.

"Sometimes," Tom said. He did not want to listen to any sob stories about the late shift.

"In this business, it's suicide," Sims went on. "You stand here from eight till dawn. Anybody can come through the door. You never know. That's the way it is. Maybe they want a room. Maybe they want something else. Maybe they'll take what they want and leave you alone. Maybe they won't. You just stand here. Waiting for them."

"You could say that about a lot of things," Tom said.

"Perhaps," Sims said. He smiled. "Ah, I'm just prattling on like an old woman, and you have all this urgent business to attend to. So, your question?"

Tom had almost forgotten it. "Well, about the man who rented the room. You said he asked for it specifically. Did he say why?"

Sims shook his head. "Not really. Nothing in detail, at least. He may have muttered something about wanting to get some sleep, not wanting to be disturbed. It's an old routine. Lots of people ask for the quiet rooms. You never know the reason."

"Did he say anything else to you while he was here?"

"No, nothing that I recall." Suddenly Sims seemed rather tired. "Anything else?"

"Just a few more things," Tom said. "The woman. Did you see her?"

"The prostitute?"

"How did you know she was a prostitute?"

"Because—to answer your first question—I saw her. That made it obvious. I'm not an unworldly man."

"Meaning what?"

"Meaning that when a black woman in a purple dress gets

out of a cab at a motel, and it's midnight, and the cab doesn't wait—I don't have to have a copy of *Nana* to figure out what's going on.''

''Had you ever seen her before?''

''No.''

''How about others? Other prostitutes.''

Sims smiled. ''Now it's my turn. Meaning what?''

Tom leaned across the counter and brought his face up close to Sims. ''I'm just going to ask you this question once,'' he said, ''and I'll let the answer be between you and me. But if I have to ask it again, it'll be in front of the district attorney.''

Sims's face hardened.

''You understand what I'm telling you?'' Tom asked.

Sims nodded vigorously.

''This Paradise Motel,'' Tom said slowly. ''Is this just a glorified whorehouse?''

Sims swallowed loudly but did not speak.

''Don't make me mention your name downtown, Sims.''

Sims's face seemed to pale. ''We have a little action here,'' he said. ''Nothing big.''

''Did you know Rayette Jones?''

''I swear I didn't know her,'' Sims said emphatically.

''How about her pimp, Pete Wilson?''

''I heard he worked around a little. I've heard the name. That's all.''

Tom turned away and looked out the front window. Another bus had pulled up across the street.

''What buses run up this line?'' he asked.

''A couple of different ones, I think.''

''That's all?''

''There's not much traffic out this way,'' Sims said. ''Beyond here it's just the desert all the way to Bonneville Flats.''

Tom turned from the window and stared at Sims. ''There aren't going to be any more whores working out of the Paradise Motel, are there?'' he said.

Sims shook his head slowly. ''Whatever you say.''

''Good.'' Tom turned and walked out of the office.

Outside, he could feel a late November chill in the air, an odd desert coldness. He turned his collar up against his neck and stared back at Room 17. Fernando Rodriguez's apartment had

had the same bleak and worn look, and Tom had never expected to see the inside of it until Gentry called that afternoon. A week before, Rodriguez had walked into the precinct house and said that he could recognize the man who had pushed Luis Fontana's body out of a speeding car, hurling it against the curb. And Gentry had sat down beside him, his eyes staring anxiously at Rodriguez, and had said, "Who?" Then Rodriguez had said the name, as casually as if it were his own brother: Angel Romero. And Gentry had looked at Tom as if all his dreams had just come true, because Romero was first-class scum and now they had a positive identification, and Gentry's lips had parted in a smile that grew slowly across his face until it seemed to light the room with joy.

Tom shook his shoulders against the chill and glanced up at the darkening sky. He could see a flock of pelicans sailing gracefully through the gathering darkness toward their crowded rooks on Guninson Island, and something in him envied them inexpressibly. It was Sunday night, and he was alone in a city of families, of small, knotted communities of fellowship and shared faith. And all of this seemed to him as impregnable as the stone walls of the Temple, and as remote from his own life as the spires that rose above it, pointing their dark, steady fingers toward the sky.

7

Epstein sat up in bed when Tom came into the room. He was bald, and the neon light over his bed worked on his pate like a fine furniture polish, turning it smooth and shiny. His eyes were small and round, and they darted about, forever following the bouncing ball across some lyric that was within him. He had a sparse mustache that looked as if it had been sketched across his upper lip by an artist who had never found the time to finish.

"Well, Tom," he said, "how are things in the cophouse?" He switched the television off and shifted his shoulders slightly. "Fucking game shows, they got them on at night now."

"How are you doing, Harry?" Tom pulled a chair up beside the bed and sat down.

Epstein scratched his forehead. "I hear you got a new stiff."

"Was that on TV already?"

Epstein put a forefinger to each temple and closed his eyes. "I see . . . I see . . . a black whore," he said.

"How'd you know that?"

Epstein grinned. "Well, they didn't say, 'Nigger whore found dead, X-rated film at eleven,' but I put it together. Paradise Hotel. A black. Murder. That don't add up to Marie Osmond collecting for Easter Seals." He scrutinized Tom closely. "Any leads?"

"Not much." Tom shrugged. "Not anything, really."

Epstein nodded. "Used to, when they found a black with a slit throat or a bullet in the head, used to, they wouldn't work a case like that. They'd take a picture of the dearly departed. You know, for the record, then they'd go back to the station, play a game of rummy."

"We don't work them like that anymore, Harry," Tom said.

"My ass. You think you don't," Epstein said. "But really you do. Nobody's going to be busting their buns for her."

Tom waved his hand. "I'd have brought the chessboard, but I didn't figure you'd be in the mood."

"I'm not," Epstein said. "I'm only in the mood for things I'm too old for."

Tom looked across the bed toward the window. He could see the lights of the Hotel Utah twinkling through the darkness. Once, while they stood across from the Plaza in New York, Gentry had nodded toward the hotel. "In the dining room, Tom," he had said, "they're drinking white wine with dishes you can't even pronounce."

"Speaking of things I'm too old for, you heard from Phyllis?"

"No."

"Pretty girl, Phyllis. Pretty, but stupid."

"You didn't say that when I was going with her."

"Who knows, you might have married her, and then for the rest of your life, you'd have known I thought your wife was a pinhead."

Tom smiled. "You're a wise man, Harry."

"I think before I speak, Tom," Epstein said. "That's the whole trick to being smart. And how's Lucy?"

"Fine."

"I'd marry her, " Epstein said lightly.

"Jesus, Harry," Tom said. "Give me a break."

"Fuck you," Epstein said. "I'd marry Lucy. In a minute. Hell, why not? How much longer have I got? Have a nice piece like that heating up the bed. Shit, I'd do it in a flash."

"You should ask her," Tom said jokingly.

Epstein shook his head. "It's you she's after, paisan." He looked up toward the television screen. "I must have watched that fucking box for twelve hours today."

"It's TV or a blank wall, Harry," Tom said.

Epstein laughed. "What's the difference?" he said, and the two men fell silent.

Epstein turned toward Tom. "I was doing a job in Miami. The nature of this job, well, the less said about that the better."

Tom nodded.

Epstein laughed again. "Anyway, I met this guy, hey, we'll call him Eddie. Anyway, we get to drinking one night out on the beach. Real nice. Waves coming in. Beautiful hotels there behind us. You ever been to Miami, Tom?"

"No," Tom said.

"Well, like I said, we was out on the beach, having a few drinks. Eddie gets a little in the wind, starts talking." His eyes rolled up toward his forehead. "This was maybe nineteen-fifty, something like that, and we're out there on the beach, and he says right out of the blue, he says, 'You know, Harry, this thing, television, it's going to make my job a lot easier.' " Epstein smiled broadly and took a sip of water from a plastic cup, then replaced it on the table beside the bed. "So I said, 'Oh yeah, what do you do?' I know he's shady, you know, but I don't know exactly how. Anyway, Eddie looks out at the ocean, just calm as you and me, and says, 'I hit people.' "

"Kills them," Tom said.

"That's right," Epstein said delightedly. "Bang, bang,

sayonara. So I said, 'Hey, that's something, I mean, but how is television gonna help you in that?' And he tells me he'd come down from New York to put a guy away, but the guy never comes out of his house so it turns out Eddie's got to go in after him, and shit, he finds the fucking guy in the living room staring at the television, and the fucking guy he don't hear Eddie, he don't see Eddie, he's just staring at the fucking tube, so Eddie, well, he does the hit, you know?'' Epstein laughed loudly. "So Eddie figures, dumb fuck that he is, well, this is the way it's going to be from now on. Go to the TV room put a soft-nosed twenty-two slug in their head, and take a vacation in the Virgins. Easy money. Never have to miss an episode of 'The Untouchables.' '' Epstein laughed again.

Epstein's stories almost always made Tom feel slightly dirty for having heard them. Still, there was something about the old man that drew Tom to him, as if they had both seen the world through the same murky glass.

Tom smiled. "Maybe I'll bring the chessboard next time," he said as he stood up. "Take care of yourself, Harry."

"Always do, copper," Epstein said with a wink. "But I'm surprised you're leaving so fast." He looked at Tom knowingly. "You got things on your mind, right?"

"A few."

"That whore," Epstein said. "Forget her."

Tom said nothing. He remembered a man he had once arrested for nearly beating his wife to death with a broken mop handle. On the way to the wagon, the man had turned to him and smiled. "Hey, come on," he had said. "Boys will be boys—right, pal?"

Epstein smiled. "On the news they made a lot out of the fact she was from out of town, you know."

Tom nodded and moved toward the door.

"That's the signal, friend," Epstein said. "Traveling scum, that's what they figure here in Salt Lake. They won't waste much tax money on some nigger nooky that's just passing through."

"Which is okay by you, right, Harry?" Tom said.

"You bet," Epstein said airily. "Look, if some pistol blows in here from Detroit and wastes me, what you think they'd do about it?" He smiled. "I can tell you. They look up my record and it all falls into place. Fucking old Jew with mob connections. Fuck him, shouldn't been living in a nice place like Salt Lake to begin with, right? Am I right?''

"It's not exactly like that, Harry."

"Close enough, Tom," Epstein said. "And to tell you the truth, I don't blame them. This is their town. They built it. You, me, that dead spade—shit, we're just something crawled out of the gutter."

Tom was standing at the door now. "I'll check in on you in in a couple days, Harry."

"Do that," Epstein said.

"Maybe I'll bring the chessboard."

"Whatever," Epstein said indifferently.

He closed the door, turned, and saw a tall, very lean man approach. A stethoscope hung from his neck.

"My name is Dr. Bennet," the man said. "I see you've just visited Mr. Epstein."

"That's right."

Bennet's face was stern. "Are you a friend of his?"

"You might say that."

"I see." Bennet glanced at the door to Epstein's room, then back at Tom. "His behavior has been inappropriate," he said crisply.

"That doesn't surprise me," Tom said.

"His language. His general attitude. Very disruptive."

Tom said nothing.

"Profanity. Vulgar stories. Very disruptive to the staff."

"Well, that's not really my business," Tom said.

"We don't tolerate that sort of thing in this hospital," Bennet said firmly.

"Well, why don't you just unhook the tubes and roll him out into the parking lot?" Tom said icily.

Bennet stiffened. "I had hoped that you might speak to him about his general deportment."

"Why don't you?"

Bennet's face reddened slightly. "I have. But to no effect."

"Well, he's sort of a hard case, doctor," Tom said. "So why don't you just get him well and get him out of here?"

Bennett thrust his hands into the pockets of his long white

coat. "Things would go more smoothly if Mr. Epstein behaved himself."

Tom could feel his irritation building. "Excuse me, doctor," he said. He edged away and walked down the hall, leaving Bennet standing rigidly in the middle of the corridor.

Outside the night had turned even colder than before, and as he pulled himself in behind the wheel of his car, Tom felt the chill penetrate his bones. He hit the ignition, pulled the car out of the parking lot, and headed toward downtown. Ahead he could see the office tower of the Zion's Cooperative Mercantile Center, the gigantic complex that the Church had built for the service of the faithful and that now loomed mightily over South Temple, reducing everything around it to a homey modesty. Here the Brotherhood came to buy those supplies they were commanded to keep on hand in case of emergency, a year's provision of everything. The architects had preserved the original facade of the ZCMI store, and it seemed to Tom that the Mormons had nothing if not a sense of history. Salt Lake City was their miracle, a safe haven in a hostile, forbidding world. And yet, in a way, Salt Lake was a city that seemed always to be poised, as if waiting for some greater miracle, the final one, which would boost the faithful into the house of God; a neat, clean, antiseptic temple where Dr. Bennett and his Brethren would dwell in an undisturbed harmony forever.

8

He looked at his watch. It was almost three-thirty. He had been waiting for over an hour. He edged around the cement pillar and glanced at the battered old Chevrolet parked ten yards away. It was caked with mud, its windshield spattered with flecks of dust and dried insects. A rotting hulk the owner did not care for. But that was not surprising, considering who the owner was.

He pulled himself back behind the column, turned, and leaned his back against it. He would wait forever if it were necessary. He bent his knees slightly to relax the strain in his legs. He could not let the tension wear him down. That had happened to others, and they had failed. Out of sheer physical weariness, they had renounced their duties.

He put his hand in his coat pocket and felt the grip of the .44 magnum. It was a heavy gun, one of awesome potential, and he had made it even more dreadful by using hollow-point shells. A little hole going in, small, red, not much larger than a dime. But then going out, the explosion.

He smiled. It was the perfect weapon. It had an absolute finality, a disintegrating force that struck with holy power. In its wake it left the afterimage of expended rage.

He pulled the pistol from his coat and quietly screwed on the silencer he had made for the barrel. Five twists of his fingers and the silencer was in place. He put the pistol back in his overcoat pocket and looked again at the door to this level of the garage. He would be coming from there, a short man with a bumbling, absentminded gait. From the position behind the pillar he could ease toward him, pull the pistol, and fire. With the silencer, the pistol would sound only a bit louder than a sudden expulsion of air. One shot, and the little man would be lifted out of his life with inhuman force.

He stepped back behind the pillar, the most wary of all predators. He did not like the crouching behind the column, the sense of criminal secrecy. He knew that they would call him a criminal, a mad killer, a fanatic. But the mission was all that mattered, and if it meant the slander of his memory, so be it. And if in order to carry out his task he had to slink about and crouch in shadows, he would do that too. One had to take the attitude of a warrior, the relentless, ruthless determination of a Ziska, who had led his army into battle blind and who had decreed that should he fall, a war drum be made on his flesh.

He pulled his hands from his pocket and rubbed them together vigorously. Most men, he thought, were made of two things, weakness and idiocy. He thought of the touch of the Negress's skin on his fingers. Many warriors would have failed at that moment, overcome by their own false morality. They would have succumbed to the weakness of the age, to its fawning sentimentality. And yet, he knew that he was himself not immune from such weakness. He could still feel her flesh on his fingers, and the sound of her breathing as it grew more shallow seemed to whistle through his mind.

He squeezed his eyes closed, trying to block out the light of the garage. But the Negress came back into his mind as if her image were engraved on the inside of his eyelids. He saw her face on the other side of the rusty screen door. Her mouth was moving but she made no sound. Her eyes were closed at first, then they opened suddenly and he saw his own face staring out from their pupils, two small white heads floating in tiny dark pools.

He shuddered and opened his eyes wide, flooding his mind with the gray light of the large, empty garage. For a moment he tried to lose himself in other memories. He thought of his son, then the green lawns of his estate. But still the face of the Negress washed back and forth into his mind, like something horrible carried on the surf. He turned toward the cement pillar and pressed his face against the rough texture of the blocks. He had to get her out of his mind or he would surely fail. He turned his face to the left and scraped his cheek along the pillar. He could tell that his eyes were filling with tears, and he batted them away, then rubbed his eyes with his gloved fists.

Plunging his hand into his pocket, he grabbed the handle of the pistol. It was firm, steady, absolutely resolute. He squeezed the handle with all his force, digging his palm into the carved grip until he could feel an edge of pain.

He took a deep breath and let it out slowly. He could tell that his eyes were drying now and that he was no longer sweating. The wildness of his pulse ebbed into a steady rhythm, and he felt himself gaining control of his body and mind once again.

He looked toward the garage door, and it was as if his eyes opened it, tugging at the metal handle with invisible wires.

The little man waddled out into the garage. He carried a battered brown briefcase and held the collar of his overcoat closed over his throat with his free hand. He was heading toward the car, his footsteps clacking loudly against the cement.

The grip of the pistol seemed to warm in his hand, radiating an otherworldly heat up his arm and throughout his body. He stepped from behind the column. His mouth opened. The voice was sweet.

"Mr. Fielding."

The old man turned toward the voice, his glasses misted over by the sudden warmth of the garage. He cocked his head to the right. "Who's that?" he asked.

"Mr. Fielding." He took a step toward him and pulled the pistol from his pocket.

Fielding dropped his briefcase to the ground and let go of the coat collar, then reached into his back pocket, drew out a handkerchief, and removed his glasses. "Just a moment," he said.

"Mr. Fielding." He took another step and lifted the pistol into the air.

The old man quickly wiped his glasses with the handkerchief. "Who is that talking?" he asked irritably.

"Mr. Fielding." The gun was in midair now, and it felt like a flaming sword. He could see the small, white head over the nub of the barrel.

Fielding quickly put the glasses on and squinted at the figure moving slowly toward him.

He pulled the trigger and the old man's head turned into a fine pink spray. His body flew backward and slammed against the front of the battered Chevrolet, then collapsed to the ground, a fount of blood gushing from the shattered skull.

He placed the magnum back in his overcoat pocket. The barrel was hot against the side of his leg, and its warmth seemed to flow into him with undreamed-of joy.

PART
TWO

9

"So we found this floater in the Beekman Reservoir," Baxter said with a smirk. "You seen a floater before, ain't you, Tom?"

"A few," Tom said. He had come into the office very early, but Baxter had already been there for some time, flipping through the morning paper as he puffed a huge black cigar.

Baxter grimaced. "This floater, Tom, it was real bad. Blowed up like a fucking beachball. A big, blue beachball."

The pathologist's report on Rayette Jones had been dropped on Tom's desk before he arrived. He did not look up from it.

"Now, the Beekman is up in the canyons," Baxter went on. "Swanky, you might say. Lot of movie people, that sort of thing."

Tom continued to scan the report. It did not tell him much he did not already know. Rayette Jones was a black female of a certain height and weight. She had died of strangulation.

Baxter stopped. "You ever been to L.A., Tom?"

Tom shook his head. In his mind he could see the pathologist's scalpel slice into Rayette Jones, then the rubber-gloved hands extracting, examining, and weighing Rayette's various organs.

"Used to get a lot of floaters in L.A.," Baxter said. "Disgusting things, look like they're about to bust right open."

"I've seen them," Tom said dully, Rayette Jones was no gourmet. She had eaten a tuna-fish sandwich and drunk a cup of coffee only a few minutes before her death. Tuna fish and coffee. A whore eating on the run.

"Anyway," Baxter continued, "this floater is just bobbing

up and down in the Beekman. There was a little breeze that day, caused the bobbing.'' He stopped again and glanced at the report. ''Anybody fuck that whore?''

''No,'' Tom said. ''There were no traces of semen anywhere.''

Baxter scratched his chin. ''Bad sign when they ain't been fucked, Tom. Means the guy that did it, means he's even crazier than you think.''

Tom continued to read the report. Rayette Jones had lost no blood from external lacerations. She had been strangled from behind with such force that her larynx had been crushed.

''She a hype?'' Baxter asked.

''No drugs beyond normal levels, it says.'' Small amounts of general grime and dried fingernail polish had been found beneath Rayette's fingernails, but no hair, particles of skin, or synthetic fibers.

''That just means her glands were working,'' Baxter said. ''How about dope?''

''No dope,'' Tom said.

Baxter nodded. ''Somebody came in, put her lights out. That's it.''

''And washed her up,'' Tom said. ''Soap residue all over her upper body and in her mouth.''

''That goes with the no fucking,'' Baxter said. ''Craziness. But anyway, about this floater.''

''Just a second, Ralph,'' Tom said. ''I want to check on something.'' He folded the report, put it in the top drawer of his desk, then picked up the phone and dialed the lab.

Jack Bemis answered.

''Jack? Tom Jackson. I was looking over the pathologist's report on Rayette Jones. The one we found strangled at the Paradise. Have you done the lab work on that yet?''

''Yeah,'' Bemis said, ''but I don't have much to give you.''

''Report mentions a blue fiber they found in her mouth. They send you that?''

''Yeah,'' Bemis said. ''It's from the washcloth we found in the bathroom of the motel. Guy must have used it to wash out her mouth. Fiber got caught.''

''Any prints at all? On her clothing? Anything?''

"Strictly clean," Bemis said. "No prints on the woman or in the motel room."

"Very professional," Tom said quietly.

"Guy knew what he was doing," Bemis said. "That all?"

"Yeah." Tom hung up. He looked at Baxter. "The floater," he said.

"Oh yeah," Baxter said. "Well, this floater, it looked even funnier than they usually do. Big goddamn thing. Long arms, too."

As he listened to Baxter, Tom's mind drifted back to Room 17. He tried to imagine what must have happened there after Rayette walked inside. Someone had been waiting for her. A man. He had to have been very strong, because he had crushed her throat like a matchbox, killing her very quickly.

"And there was not a hair on this thing, Tom," Baxter said loudly. "Not one goddamn hair on its whole body."

She had come into the room. Then she had undressed herself or allowed him to undress her. Then, at some later point, he had come up behind her, killed her, washed her body, dressed her, and laid her on the bed to be found the next morning.

"So I look at this thing," Baxter said. "Jesus, you should have seen it. So I look at this thing and I say to my partner, Tommy Davis was his name, and I say, 'Tommy, whatever this is, it ain't no normal human.' And Tommy, he looks at me like I've lost my mind or something and he says, 'So what do you think it is, Ralph, a fucking tugboat?' "

For a moment Tom considered his other recent cases. A young man had shot his girl friend and confessed within twenty-four hours. He remembered the boy's eyes, red-rimmed from crying.

"So I said to Tommy, 'I'll tell you one thing, shithead. I'll buy you the biggest octopus in Chinatown if this fucking thing is a normal human.' "

Then there was the other case. A man had killed his buddy in a brawl. No problem there. The evidence had all but stood up and saluted. There was a little muttering about temporary insanity and then some fast plea-bargaining.

Baxter lifted his face toward the ceiling and laughed. "So what do you think that big, disgusting floater was, Tom?"

Tom pulled the report of Rayette Jones from his desk drawer and began glancing through it once again. "I don't know."

"Turns out there's a guy works for a dogfood factory in the valley," Baxter said. "Well, one morning the guy who runs the place chews this kid out, then sends him on a pickup. The kid gets to fuming over the ass-chewing and dumps the pickup in the Beekman Reservoir. And the pickup was a fucking skinned gorilla from this research place up in the hills." Baxter slapped his knee and laughed loudly. "A goddamn gorilla!"

Tom forced himself to chuckle lightly.

"Ain't that something, Tom?" Baxter said. "Ain't that the craziest story you ever heard?"

"Yeah," Tom said.

"We don't get cases like that here in Salt Lake," Baxter said.

"Not very often," Tom said indifferently, his eyes still moving over the pages of the report.

"You must have had a few like that in New York, though," Baxter said coaxingly.

Tom had stories from New York, but none of them were funny.

"You got anything to top that?" Baxter asked.

"Afraid I don't, Ralph," Tom glanced up toward Baxter. "What are you working on?"

Baxter looked as if he had been gently reproached. "I got a few things." He stood up immediately and ambled over to his desk. For a few minutes he pretended to go over the memos and reports, then he gave up the act and picked up his newspaper, his feet stretched far out in front of him, a fisherman without a lake.

Slowly Tom's mind returned to Rayette Jones. This was not the usual sort of Salt Lake killing. But beyond that, nothing. He was still going over the case, routinely memorizing as many details as he could, when Carl walked into the room.

"How you doing, Tom?" he said, smiling.

Tom lifted the folder. "There's some strange stuff in in the report."

Carl grinned and sat down at his desk. "Always is. What she have, a seed in her hair that could only come from Siberia?"

"The guy washed her up after he killed her," Tom said. He

dropped the folder on his desk. "No sex of any kind. Just a straight kill."

"You look disappointed," Carl said lightly.

"It's oddball stuff, Carl. Which means the guy's pretty erratic, hard to trail."

Carl leaned forward, rubbing his hands together. "Truth is, that whore should never have landed in Salt Lake. There comes a time when you . . ."

"Reap what you sow."

"Just like I said yesterday," Carl said. He seemed satisfied with the opinion.

"So we should just forget it?"

Carl frowned. "Of course not. We'll work it, but it's a back-burner case."

"Well, there's not much on the front burner."

"That's right. And that's why Salt Lake is a good town." Carl shook his head. "You're still missing all that New York stuff, Tom. Even after ten years out here. You like them meaty. We get a clean murder, you can't stand it. We've solved two cases in the last month or so. They were perfectly good arrests. That kid who murdered his girl friend, and the other one, those two buddies. We nailed those two shut, and that's two stars in our crown."

Tom watched Carl silently. Epstein had been right, Rayette was just traveling scum. In a way, it had not been that different in New York. No one ever killed himself over some pusher who ended up in a landfill. Gentry had reduced it to a few words: Let the shit eat the shit.

"It's not that I don't care about that woman," Carl went on. "I want to make this clear. Maybe we got a difference of opinion on this, but I want you to know that I care about that woman. I'm sorry she's dead. You know why, Tom? Because she might have finally gotten it together and made a decent life. Now she'll never have the chance, and that's too bad. But in the end she brought it on herself. And I'll tell you something else. What happened to her could send a lot of Salt Lake whores heading out of town, and that's one for our side."

"Somebody else may still be in town," Tom said.

"You mean the killer?"

Tom nodded.

"I doubt it," Carl said, "but if he is, we'll get him. He's like Rayette, really. He's living the kind of life that will finally catch up to him."

Tom picked up the report, leaned forward across his desk, and handed it to Carl. "Here's what the lab has to say."

Carl took the report and began flipping through it. "I think it could be a drug-burn thing. We know they had some trouble in L.A. Or it could be a nut."

Tom stood up, stretched, and glanced at the clock. It was still early. "By the way, what are you doing in at this hour?" he asked.

Carl looked up from the report. "I went to the gym to get a little exercise." He patted his stomach and smiled. "I've been feeling a little soft in the midsection." He let his eyes drop toward Tom's stomach. "Maybe you could use a few situps yourself."

Tom shook his head. "I'm going outside for a while, get some air."

"Sure," Carl said. "I'll have this read by the time you get back. We'll go over it together."

Tom put on his overcoat and walked outside. The snow that had been predicted the day before was now falling slowly in large flakes. It gave Salt Lake a kind of postcard beauty, the white adorning the clean, clear air like Christmas ornaments. It was probably snowing in Denver, too, and Tom imagined Phyllis whistling down the slopes with her new man. Maybe she was a little stupid, as Epstein had said, but that wasn't the whole story. He had liked her laughter, her cutting humor, even that austere seriousness that sometimes came upon her suddenly and sat there like a black bird on her shoulder. Maybe that was really what he'd liked the best, that sense that there was something under all that West Coast optimism and flashy talk, something of New York and the gritty East, where even the snow turned gray and oily faster than it did here, as if it had grown suspicious of its own brief pleasantness and had quickly shaken it off.

He heard Carl call to him and turned toward the door.

"Did you finish the report?" he asked.

"No." Carl's face looked tense. "We got something else going."

10

Carl wheeled the car into the underground garage so that the force of the turn pressed Tom's shoulder hard into the passenger door.

"Jesus Christ!" Tom blurted.

Carl's fists tightened around the wheel. "What is it?"

"You're driving like a maniac."

Carl eased off the accelerator. "Really? I didn't realize it. I guess I'm still a little pumped up from the workout." He applied his foot to the brake. "I'll cool down."

Tom straightened himself. "Did they give you a name?"

"I don't think they had it yet."

Through the windshield Tom could see a group of uniformed policemen milling around a beat-up Chevrolet. "Over there," he said.

Carl guided the car to within a few feet of the line of men and stopped.

"Look at the way they huddle around, those uniformed guys," Tom said.

"They're just trying to learn about investigation," Carl said. "They don't want to be in blues forever." He looked at Tom. "Well, let's see how bad it is."

For a moment Tom hesitated.

"What's the matter?" Carl asked.

"I don't know," Tom said. "Just tired of seeing it, I guess."

Carl leaned toward him slightly. "Hey, Tom, we're the good guys, remember? Come on, let's go."

Tom got out of the car and met Carl on the other side. Together they walked toward the line of patrolmen who stood shielding the body from view. The men parted as Tom and Carl approached, and they saw a large canvas draped over the inert form that lay on the cement floor. Blood had spread out from under the canvas in a broad swath. It was drying now, turning almost orange.

A tall, uniformed patrolman stood directly in front of the body.

"What's your name?" Carl asked him.

"Matthews, sir."

"What do we know about this?"

"Victim shot one time through the head, sir," Matthews said crisply.

"Anything else?"

"Perpetrator positioned approximately directly in front of victim."

"That's it?" Carl asked.

"Victim is one Lester Robert Fielding. Victim was discovered early this morning—approximately six forty-five—by one Sherry Anne Maitlands. Victim was employed as reporter for one *Southwest Magazine.*"

Tom stepped to the side, bent forward, and removed the canvas. The head had been exploded by the shell, but he could see small tufts of white hair. Rust-colored bloodstains completely covered the old man's shirt and trousers. Tom straightened and pulled the covering back over the man's body..

"Victim was employed by one Charles David Robertson," Matthews went on. "Robertson last saw victim alive around three-thirty this morning."

"Where is Robertson?" Tom asked.

"Mr. Robertson is present, sir," Matthews said.

"Present?"

"On the premises, sir," Matthews added. He indicated a tall man who leaned against one of the cement pillars of the garage some distance away.

Tom turned back to Matthews. "Were you ever a Marine, by any chance?"

"Yes, sir," Matthews said loudly.

Tom glanced knowingly at Carl, then turned back to Matthews.

"Weapon?" he asked.

"I don't know, sir."

Tom took Carl's arm and led him a few yards away from the other policemen. "What is uniform division doing now, hiring right out of the zoo?"

"He's just a kid," Carl said dismissively.

"Let me tell you something about guys like that," Tom said. "You have to watch them every minute. They're bone breakers, and they should be on the other side."

"Well, you were a Marine, weren't you, Tom?" Carl asked.

Tom looked at Carl sourly. "Forget it. You want to talk to Robertson, or should I?"

"You take him. I'll check out the woman who found Fielding this morning."

"Okay." Tom turned and walked toward Robertson. As he came closer, he could see the pain etched in the man's face.

"My name's Tom Jackson," Tom said as he stopped in front of Robertson. "Homicide Division. I understand you were with Mr. Fielding last night."

Robertson stared over Tom's shoulder at the battered Chevrolet. "You know how long Les had that car?"

"No."

"Almost twenty years."

"Must have taken good care of it."

"He took good care of everything," Robertson said.

"How well did you know him?"

"Very well. All my life. We started *Southwest Magazine* together. I had the money. And you might say Les had the brains and the . . ."

"What?"

"Oh, I don't know. The heart, I guess."

"Was Fielding working last night?"

Robertson smiled sadly. "Yes."

"Did he do that often? Work on Sunday night?"

"You have to know him. He was an old bachelor, you see. No family or anything like that. No real home to speak of. Just an apartment. His work was all he had. Still, he'd only work after midnight Sunday. Monday morning, that is. He respected the Sabbath."

"And he was a reporter?"

"Yes, a reporter. Or I should say, a writer. The only real writer on the staff. Old School, you know what I mean?"

"Not really."

"He worked a story until he got everything that could be gotten from it," Robertson explained. "He never let anything slide."

"So it wasn't unusual for him to be in the office late at night?"

Robertson shook his head. "No."

"Even Sunday nights?"

"No," Robertson repeated. His eyes drifted back toward the car Fielding had died on. "He was up for the Pulitzer Prize in sixty-eight."

"Fielding?" Tom asked, surprised.

"That's right."

Tom glanced back toward the car. The green covering over the old man's body looked like a collapsed pup tent. He turned back to Robertson. "What kind of stories did he write?"

"The old kind," Robertson said gently. "Exposés. Hard hitting. Important. Not this gossipy trash you find around the supermarket."

"Was he writing something like that last night?"

An idea seemed to catch in Robertson's mind. "Yes, he was."

"What was it about?"

Robertson stroked his chin thoughtfully, then looked evenly at Tom. "No. There's no way he would have been killed over that story."

"You never know, Mr. Robertson," Tom said. "What was the story about?"

"It was about the Clayton Children's School."

"For juvenile delinquents?"

"That's the one."

"What about it?"

"Well, Les had found some things. You know, the usual stuff. Some financial mismanagement. Maybe some drug abuse. Neglect. That sort of thing. I haven't read the story, just talked to Les a couple times about it."

"Is it finished, the story?"

"No," Robertson said. "He'd just started the first draft last night."

"When he was murdered," Tom added.

"Yes," Robertson said quietly.

"I'd like to take a look at that story sometime," Tom said.

"Any time you say."

"I'll check into the Clayton School, too. But let me ask you this. Was he working on any other stories? Stories that might get somebody very scared or angry, anything like that?"

Robertson shook his head. "No. Les only worked one story at a time. That was the way he did things."

"This is important, Mr. Robertson," Tom said. "So think about it for a minute and be sure that he hadn't mentioned any other ideas he might have had, upcoming stories maybe, anything like that."

"I am sure," Robertson said firmly, as if protecting his old friend's reputation. "Les Fielding never worked more than one story at a time."

"How about enemies?" Tom asked.

Robertson looked surprised. "Les didn't have any enemies."

"Well, like they say, Mr. Robertson"—Tom glanced pointedly toward the crumpled body a few yards away—"he had one."

Robertson stiffened, but he said nothing.

"Now, reporters sometimes get into trouble, you know," Tom went on. "It doesn't happen often, but it happens. They step on the wrong toes and somebody tries to punish them. Do you know of anyone who might have felt that way about Mr. Fielding?"

Robertson shook his head vigorously. "Absolutely not."

"How about in his personal life?"

"I know this will be hard for you to understand," Robertson said, "but Les Fielding really didn't have much of a personal life."

"I don't mean just family," Tom said.

"Neither do I," Robertson said. "I mean a personal life of any kind."

At first Tom found this total absence of a private life difficult to believe. Then he realized that if Tom Jackson were found dead in an alley with blood pouring from his mouth, the same might be said of him. He could hear Carl saying it: Oh, poor Tom, poor devil, he had nothing, nobody, when you came right down to it.

Tom tried to get his mind back on track. "When did you see Fielding last?" he asked Robertson quickly.

"Last night, like I said."

"About what time?"

"Around three-thirty in the morning."

"You were here that late?"

"Yes," Robertson said. "I work hard too. That's one of the things Les and I had in common."

"Did you talk to him very much last night?"

"Not much. We discussed the Clayton School story a little. We discussed the magazine generally. That's all."

"Then you went home?"

"No," Robertson said. "Les did. He left the office around three-thirty."

"But you stayed?"

"Yes."

"Well, if you left after Fielding, why didn't you see his car still parked in the garage?"

"Because I don't park in the garage," Robertson said confidently. "I don't park at all, as a matter of fact. I take the bus."

"That late? Isn't that a little dangerous?"

"Not with policemen of your caliber guarding the city," Robertson said.

Tom let it pass. "So you didn't see Fielding after you left the office?"

"No."

"All right," Tom said. "That's all I have. I'll probably be talking to you again."

"I intend to offer a large reward for the murderer," Robertson added as Tom began to turn away.

"We'll find out who did this," Tom said, looking back at him.

Robertson was staring off toward the old car again. "He didn't have a personal life," he said quietly. "Nobody cared about Les but me."

Tom walked back to the car. Carl was still standing around, randomly checking the scene.

"Get anything from him?" he asked as Tom stepped up beside him.

"Nothing much. You?"

Carl looked confused. "Me? What?"

"You were supposed to check out the woman, the one who found Fielding this morning."

"I didn't do that yet," Carl said offhandedly. "I thought I'd look around the car first."

"The lab will do that, Carl," Tom said, masking his irritation. He turned around, casting his eyes here and there about the garage.

"I'll go talk to the woman now," Carl said quickly. "You want to come with me?"

Tom turned back toward Carl. "Fielding was working on a story about the Clayton Children's School."

"What kind of story?"

"An exposé."

"So?"

"Well, this is strictly a shot in the dark, but maybe somebody at the school decided to waste Fielding."

Carl stared at Tom unbelievingly.

"You know," Tom explained. "Somebody with his ass on the line."

"Killing a reporter? Not likely."

"It happened in Phoenix," Tom said.

"It did, but that was organized crime, not a reform school for underage car thieves. Still, I suppose we could check it out," Carl said unenthusiastically.

"No." Tom realized he didn't want Carl hanging around him anymore. "You go and interview the woman. I'll check the school."

"Fine with me," Carl said easily.

"Check on the Wilson pimp again, too," Tom said.

"Why?"

"I want to find out if this could have been a drug hit."

"That's what I think," Carl said.

Tom nodded, then turned to leave.

"You taking the car?" Carl asked quickly.

"I'm not going to walk all the way to the Clayton School."

"Yeah, but how am I going to check on Wilson and get back to the station?"

Tom shrugged. "Just wait for Baxter. He'll wander in after a while."

"I don't like working with him, Tom," Carl said. "I don't like being in the same car with him."

"You don't like the cigars?"

"I don't like Baxter," Carl said irritably. "We should have never hired him out of the L.A.P.D. Everybody's on the pad out there."

Tom turned back toward the squad car. "Relax, Carl. Everybody's on the take to something."

Carl seemed to stiffen. "Not me."

"Okay, Carl, Tom said wearily. "Everybody except you." He walked to the car. The dark air of the garage reminded him of another time in New York when he and Gentry had been waiting under the El, staking out a well-known gambling operation. They had been waiting for a murder suspect to show up, but two Vice cops showed up instead, ambling into the building, then out again, one of them laughing as he slid the bills into his wallet. Gentry had watched them with cold eyes. "Never go on the pad, Tom," he had said, almost to himself. "Then you won't have to feel your stomach turn over at midnight when somebody comes knocking at your door."

11

Under the glow of the lamplight on his desk, his hands seemed to shine with the radiance of their purpose. He had brought a sword into the world. He had become a warrior for the faith, and he knew that a price must be paid. He formed his hands into fists. They would say he was insane, a fanatic against whom all the fortitude of the faith was powerless. He smiled. Insane, indeed. Was he insane because he practiced his faith to the fullest, because he was not seduced by the laxity of the times, because he adhered with invincible devotion to the commandment: "Be ye, therefore, perfect."

He stood up, walked to the window of his study, and parted the dark curtains. Outside he could see his son walking beside the covered pool. More than anything, he regretted that the boy would have to bear the burden of his commitment. For a time, he had actually thought of killing his son the day before his final act. But that would be vile and unholy, and it would undoubtedly brand him as a madman forever. Only religious lunatics hurled their children from buildings or burned them in their beds. He knew that he had to separate himself from such fanatics, and he had already begun to compose the statement that would accomplish this. It would be his testament; it would be written clearly and precisely, shunning the wildly rhetorical; a work as lucid as his mind. In the writing, he would avoid all the chaotic, tumbling fire of religious frenzy. Instead he would present a quiet, reasoned argument. It would state simply that one had either to accept the faith wholly, or wholly reject it; the faith did not alter with the times. God spoke but once. His words were not subject to revision. God did not modify, extemporize, or hesitate. These things only men did, and did them to their everlasting damnation.

He released the curtain and let it fall back over the window, darkening the room. He turned and looked about. No one could mistake this room, with its dark-hued floor-to-ceiling bookshelves, large mahogany desk, and delicately woven Oriental rug, for a madman's cell. It was, instead, a scholar's redoubt, as orderly and restrained as a scholar's mind, and he knew that when the photographers came here with their harsh lights, when the reporters scurried about glancing at his books and notes, when the police stumbled around, tipping the vases from their pedestals, all of them would know—as surely as he himself knew—that it was not a madman who dwelt here. There were no crude images of a bleeding Christ, no Bibles nailed to moldering walls, no tools of flagellation. Only the world of books and ideas, the intellectual legacy of Attica and Christendom neatly arranged on shelf after imposing shelf.

He sat down behind his desk, leaned back in his chair, and allowed his eyes to fall upon a worn volume of Hobbes's *Leviathan*. Of all the secular voices to which he had given heed, Hobbes had spoken most clearly of man's nature, a nature wholly depraved, driven by greed alone. He thought of the paintings of Hieronymus Bosch, the hellish, anarchic landscapes of rape and pillage. This was the world as Hobbes knew it, the universal nightmare made flesh by man's demented soul. How different it was, he thought, from the immaculate modeling of classical sculpture, from the polished surfaces of the Dutch masters, from the idyllic romanticism of Rousseau. They showed a world of sheer delusion, a mere fantasy. But in the real world, man slithered about in his own slime. Into that world there had come but one miracle: out of the swollen excesses of the Roman world and clothed in the bitter robes of Jewish sectarianism, God-made-man had come to bring a sword of righteousness.

He looked at his hands again, and a chill passed over his body. In his mind he saw the fingers close around the Negress's throat. Then his right hand jerked, and he realized that he had felt again the jar of the pistol as it fired before the old man's face.

He stood up again, trembling, surprised at the tension his memories had imposed upon him. The tension was part of his weakness. He knew then that the legacy of guilt remained a powerful force within him. He could contend with the limited intelligences of those who regarded him as a deranged killer. It was the perversion in his own mind he dreaded. For to some extent his own mind remained cast in the simpering moral code of his time, and he hated this weakness. He had to guard against it, harden his will, so that the mission might be accomplished despite his misgivings.

He walked out of the office, closing the heavy door behind him, and strode across the neat, carpeted foyer, pausing to glance at the curved staircase to the second floor. There was, he thought, an angelic quality to the construction of the stairs, a sense of something effortlessly lifting itself toward heaven. It was deceptive in its simplicity, immensely beautiful, and wholly false in its illusion of ease. For one could not mount the heights without tremendous force of will.

He grasped the polished newel post at the foot of the stairs and massaged it gently with his fingers. Everything should be as perfectly made as polished wood, as hard and flawless and resistant to injury. Surely chief among man's sins, he thought, was his incapacity to take the harder route toward salvation and hold firmly to that path, moving willfully toward the destination God intended.

Releasing the post, he strolled down the long hallway and outside. His son stood idly under one of the great trees that shaded the back lawn—a beautiful boy, tall, lean, with sparkling eyes. One day, he thought, the boy would come to understand his father's mission. The women of the house would weep and wail, but the boy would hold firm. He smiled, raised his hand, and called to his son. When the boy reached him, he placed his hand on his cheek and held it there for a moment, watching the beautiful face as it looked up toward him. "I must take you on a hunt soon," he said. "I must teach you how to kill cleanly.

12

The Clayton Children's School sat right in the middle of a prosperous Salt Lake suburb. It was surrounded by a high iron fence, and beyond the bars Tom could see a well-tended lawn.

Tom got out of the car and walked through the gate, then up the stairs and into the building. A guard in a dark blue uniform met him just inside the door.

"May I help you, sir?"

Tom could see the slight bulge of a pistol under the man's coat. He flashed his shield, and the guard seemed to snap to attention.

"Who's in charge of this place?" Tom asked.

"That would be Mr. Danforth."

"What does he do?"

"He's the director." The guard pointed to the left down a long hallway. "His office is down there. Last door on your right."

"Thanks," Tom said. He went down the hall and turned into the director's office. A woman sat behind a metal desk. She was so small her typewriter seemed to dwarf her.

"Is Mr. Danforth in?" Tom asked.

The woman looked up. There was a smudge on her right cheek. "I can't get this in," she said, lifting a tangled type-writer ribbon.

"I need to see Mr. Danforth." Tom did not intend to get hooked into unraveling yards of black ribbon.

The woman lowered her hands to the desk. "Do you have an appointment?"

"No."

"Well, he has to go to a meeting in five minutes."

"I'm with the police," Tom said. "Homicide Division."

The woman looked at him as if she hadn't quite caught it. "The police?"

"I'd like to see Mr. Danforth now," Tom said.

"Just a minute," the woman said quickly. She stood up, walked into an office next to hers, then reappeared. "Mr. Danforth will see you now."

"Thanks," Tom said.

Danforth sat behind a large wooden desk that looked as if it had just been polished. It looked strangely uncluttered, as if he used it only for display.

"My secretary didn't catch your name," Danforth said as Tom entered the room. He stood up but did not offer his hand.

"Tom Jackson."

"Have a seat," Danforth said. He was very tall, with slightly bowed shoulders. His hair was white, but he had the face of a robust middle-aged man.

Tom took a seat in front of the desk.

"Now, what can I do for you?" Danforth smiled pleasantly. "We don't get too many visits from the police. At least not from the homocide squad."

"I'm investigating a murder," Tom said flatly.

Danforth did not look moved.

"Do you know a man named Lester Fielding?"

Danforth's face seemed to turn sour. "I know him." There was an edge in his voice.

"How well?"

"We weren't friends," Danforth said dryly. He sat back in his seat, and a little American flag in his lapel winked as it caught the light from the desk lamp to his right.

"Somebody shot Fielding last night."

Danforth watched Tom calmly. "Killed him, I suppose?"

"Yes."

Danforth nodded but said nothing.

"You say you and Fielding weren't friends, right?"

Danforth smiled. "No need for the cat-and-mouse stuff, Mr. Jackson. You must already know that Fielding was working on a story about the school. He was a reporter for *Southwest Magazine.*"

"Yes," Tom said.

Danforth did not seem the least perturbed. He kept his eyes steadily on Tom's. "The story, as you must also know, was not going to be very flattering. Mr. Fielding does not have a reputation for revealing the best in people of institutions."

"Did you talk to him?" Tom asked.

"Of course, but it was more in the nature of a jousting match than a conversation."

"You didn't get along with him?"

Danforth rubbed his palms together softly. "You would have to have known Fielding to know how impossible that was."

"How did it go? The interview, I mean."

Danforth smiled. "How did it go? It was a disaster. Fielding had been gathering his little facts, such as they were. When he thought he had enough, he came storming into my office to do battle with the evil director."

"What did Fielding have on the school?" Tom asked. "What was he going to write about?"

Danforth's voice softened. "Look, this is a large institution. It is not a heavenly creation. There are problems here, as in any other human endeavor."

Tom kept his eyes fixed on Danforth's face. "What problems?"

Danforth shrugged. "Some of the staff sometimes mistreat

the residents. We do our best to weed such people out. We try not to hire them in the first place. But, as I said, we aren't perfect. The truth of the matter is that an ambitious reporter could go into any school for delinquents in the country and find some abuse, some mismanagement, some petty crime. Then he could blow these things into a big story.''

"Well, the way I hear it," Tom said, "Fielding had a pretty long list. Drug abuse. Physical abuse. Neglect.''

Danforth put up his hand. "No need to go on. I know what Fielding had. I know how it will look when the story is presented. I know how I will look when the TV reporters swarm around asking me questions. The Clayton School will look like hell, and I will resemble Satan.''

"Well, what about these things, these charges?" Tom asked.

Danforth smiled contentedly. "All of them are true, I imagine. All of the things Fielding told me probably happened. If you're trying to get me to deny everything, you won't. I'm not a liar. I do the best I can. I make mistakes. So does every other member of the staff. So do the people who keep the books and records and make the meals and do the wash. Fielding found human frailty, Mr. Jackson, not crime. And I suspect he could find such frailty anywhere he looked.'' He grinned almost impishly. "Even in the Homicide Division of our own Salt Lake police.''

Suddenly, Tom found himself rather liking Mr. Danforth. There was a strong resilience in him, a sense of his own battered worth.

"I don't like people who play Martin Luther," Danforth said, "who nail their ninety-five theses on someone's door.''

"Then what Fielding was going to write didn't bother you?"

Danforth bent forward and began to fill the bowl of a dark briar pipe with tobacco. "Not very much. Why should it? I would not ultimately be vulnerable to a man like Fielding.''

"Why not?"

Danforth put his pipe into his mouth and lit it. "Because I know who I am, what I am. So do other people who have considerably more power in Salt Lake than that, well, scribbler. Besides, his so-called 'findings' were utterly trivial.''

"He didn't have anything serious to write about, is that what you're saying?" Tom asked.

"Small matters," Danforth said. He puffed serenely on his pipe. "By today's standards, they were minor infractions. Peccadilloes in a corrupt age."

"But he had some facts, didn't he?"

Danforth leaned back in his chair. "A few whining children told exaggerated stories. A bruise became somthing terrible. Also, the books are badly kept. Evidently some money—a small amount—is unaccounted for. Well, we can't afford to hire Price Waterhouse. You know who does our books? A retired investment counselor with bad eyes. He does it for free, and the money we save goes to buy supplies for the school. Supplies we need, Mr. Jackson, a good deal more than we ever needed Fielding's snooping."

"What about drugs?"

Danforth casually fanned a cloud of smoke from his face. "From time to time we administer Thorazine. Some people are dangerous to themselves and others. We don't use this or any other drug routinely. Some institutions do."

"You paint a pretty nice picture, Mr. Danforth." Tom kept an edge of suspicion in his voice.

"I'm closer to the truth than Fielding was," Danforth said. "You may be sure of that."

Tom smiled, but he held a coldness in his eyes. "How come the guard at the door has a gun?"

Danforth's eyes rolled toward the ceiling. "Ah, yes, the gun. Fielding made a lot of that." He chuckled. "It's perfectly explainable, Mr. Jackson. The kids have parents. Once in a while a parent attempts to seize a child illegally. We can usually handle it. But two months ago a man came for his son. He brought a shotgun with him. After that, we armed the guard. It's strictly for security, and the bullets are kept in the guard's pocket, not in the pistol."

"Did you tell Fielding all this when you talked to him?" Tom asked.

"Of course."

"What did he say?"

"Nothing."

"Then as far as you knew, he was going to write the story anyway?"

"I expected that he would," Danforth said. "Fielding was a decent man, but he had what you might call a philosophical flaw."

"Which was?"

"He believed in perfection. And he was wounded by imperfection."

"Could someone else have been worried about that article?" Danforth shook his head. "I doubt it."

"Someone on the board, someone like that?"

"No. By the way, have you read it?"

"No," Tom said. "But I intend to."

Danforth placed the pipe in an ashtray. "Too bad about Fielding." He looked pointedly at Tom. "To speak plainly, I'm not surprised he's dead."

"Really?"

"No. He looked like someone who might even have welcomed it a bit, welcomed death."

"Why?"

"Just a sadness. It was in his eyes. One often sees it in old men."

"Not all of them."

"No, not all. But people in a certain kind of work. People who've seen the worst the world offers."

"People like Fielding," Tom said.

"Yes." Danforth lifted his eyes from the pipe. "And people like you."

They talked a while longer, Danforth adroitly countering any suspicions Tom might offer. He seemed very confident of his own integrity, but Tom noticed a nervousness in his hands, a tendency to relight his pipe before it went out, the gestures of someone who might or might not have something to hide.

"You don't really think I could have had anything to do with Fielding's death, do you?" Danforth asked finally.

"The investigation has just begun," Tom said.

"But it's so absurd. I've lived in this community all my life."

"Which only means you know the streets."

Danforth stood up immediately. "Is that all for now?" he asked crisply.

Tom nodded. He knew that the interrogation was over, whether he wanted it to be or not. He had known other people like Danforth, people who kept their calm. Circumstances never seemed to matter. They just had the calm—wore it like a badge, or like a shield. Sometimes it meant they were innocent. Sometimes it meant they were guilty. It was impossible to tell.

Later, sitting in his car, staring at the imposing structure of the Clayton Children's School, Tom tried to decide what he thought of Danforth. There was something in the man's manner that he liked, the sense of being in control, unassailable. But there was also something he didn't like, Danforth's arrogance and imperturbability, his sense that he could rise above anything, because the great blue wave was nothing other than himself and all the rest mere scattered sand. Romero had had that, too, that mood of contempt. He had sat in a chair in a squad room, smirking at everything around him—his slick black hair gleaming under the lights, the pencil-thin mustache resting on his lip like the edge of a razor, the small, black eyes never darting from your own, never looking away while he sat facing you, and lied and lied and lied. Gentry brought him in not long after Rodriguez told them what he had seen, and Romero had sat at Tom's desk, his legs crossed casually over one another, the cream-colored suit almost glinting in the light that poured through the precinct windows. They had tried to break him, but couldn't, and finally Gentry had stepped forward and slapped his face with his open hand, the sound echoing against the dirty walls of the squad room, echoing back again and again, until it seemed like music played to soothe the soul.

13

Carl was sitting at his tan metal desk in the detective bullpen when Tom entered the room.

"Did you talk to Wilson?" Tom asked.

Carl turned the newspaper he had been reading so that Tom could see the front-page headline: SOUTHWEST MAGAZINE REPORTER MURDERED. "Great for tourist trade."

Tom nodded. "What about Wilson?"

"I talked to him. Nothing. He says the people in L.A. were mean enough to rough him up a little, but that's all."

"You believe him?"

Carl turned back to the paper and flipped through it to the sports page. "Why not?" he said casually.

"I'm thinking maybe that dumb-ass wouldn't know a heavy mark if he saw one."

Carl's eyes drifted up and down the sports columns. "If he thought they'd kill Jones, would he still be hanging around Salt Lake?"

"I guess not."

"That stupid, he ain't." Carl folded the paper and placed it on the top of his desk. "Jones is a psycho thing. Hundred to one, the guy that did it is long gone."

In his mind Tom could see him going, a man on a bus or sitting first class in a plane, ordering his drink, polite to the stewardess, and on his mind that image of his hands closing around a throat.

"A murder like this makes me nervous," he said.

"Sure it does," Carl said. "Very sad thing. But out of our control. Hundred to one on that." He sat up slightly. "Now,

80

Fielding, that's another story. There's plenty on that we can work. What did you find out at the school?"

"Nothing much." Tom could feel his unease growing, that tension Gentry said would someday go away, but never did.

"Well, something'll break on that one," Carl said confidently.

"Yeah, right," Tom said hurriedly. "Listen, I'm going to check something out."

"Want me to go with you?" Carl asked.

Tom shook his head. "Nah, it's just an idea."

"Oh yeah? What?"

"I want to see what's on the street."

"A snitch?"

"Yeah."

"You're not going to crack these killings with a snitch," Carl said assuredly.

"Maybe not, but I want to give it a try."

"Why bother?" Carl asked.

Suddenly Tom's anxiety hardened into irritation. "We got two murders, Carl," he blurted. "What are you doing sitting around reading the fucking sports page?"

Carl stared at Tom, stunned. "What?"

"You heard me."

Carl stood up. "What's the matter with you?"

"Nothing," Tom snapped. He turned to leave.

Carl grabbed his arm. "Is it Phyllis?"

Tom whirled around. "Fuck Phyllis. You've been harping on that shit for a month."

"Take it easy, Tom." Carl looked wounded.

"Look, Carl," Tom said, quieting himself, "my private life is my business. But just for the record, it has nothing to do with the way I feel right now."

Carl said nothing.

"You understand?" Tom asked. "We've had two murders in two days. That is, by definition, a Salt Lake crime wave. Now that makes me jumpy, Carl."

"Okay," Carl said finally, releasing Tom's arm. "I didn't do anything to upset you, did I, Tom?"

Tom took a deep breath. "Look, I'm going to check some

things on the street. You do whatever you want." Then he turned quickly and walked away.

Tom found Eddie Donovan where he had expected, sitting in a diner not far from the Hotel Richmont. Eddie was staring languidly into an empty cup of coffee while his fingers drummed on a stained paper napkin.

"Hello, Eddie," Tom said as he pulled himself into the booth and sat opposite him.

Eddie did not look up from the cup. He was dressed in a soiled flannel shirt with a torn pocket. His hair was combed straight back and plastered down across his skull like a black bathing cap.

"Eddie?"

Eddie looked up and a thin smile crossed his lips. "Well, now, it's Tom Jackson. Good old Tom from the good old neighborhood. You come to talk about the good old days?"

Tom had known Eddie in New York, where they had both run into hard times. Tom had gone into the Marines; Eddie had hitch-hiked west, found nothing but a wife who quickly left him, and after that, just nothing.

"Grand to see you, Tom," Eddie said, slurring his words slightly. "Just grand."

Eddie was a pig for drugs, but he heard more than most street people, and he remembered everything.

"Listen, Eddie," Tom said. "I—"

"You know, Tom," Eddie interrupted, "I been thinking maybe I should go to college."

Tom drummed his fingers on the table.

"You don't believe me?"

Tom said nothing.

"You have no faith in human nature, Tom."

"How old are you, Eddie?" Tom asked.

"Thirty-seven," Eddie said, his head drooping forward slightly. "You trying to tell me something?"

Tom looked out the window and watched a workman begin to tear up the street with a hydraulic drill.

Eddie jerked his head back up and opened his eyes very wide. "I have lived the life of a drifter," he announced.

Tom turned to him. "Save it for a priest, Eddie."

Eddie's body slumped a bit to the left. "I'm a high school graduate, Tom, did you know that?"

"I knew."

"Could have gone to college on a boxing scholarship."

Tom lit a cigarette and offered it to Eddie.

"No, thanks."

Tom crushed the cigarette into the ashtray. "So what's new on the street, Eddie?"

Eddie giggled and pressed his fingers to his mouth. "You caught me at a bad time, Tom," he said. Then he laughed.

"What are you on, Eddie?"

Eddie's eyes drifted toward the ceiling. "Could have gone to college on a boxing scholarship."

"Tales from Palookaville," Tom said.

Eddie scratched half-heartedly at the black stubble on his cheek. "I have lived the life of a drifter."

Tom could tell that Eddie was going into a drug haze. "Listen," he said quickly, "I got a dead whore I want to talk to you about."

Suddenly Eddie sat up rigidly. "Am I crying?" he asked. "Am I doing that?"

"No."

Eddie shrugged. "Just as well." He balled the napkin in his fist. "You like baseball, son?"

"Cut the bullshit, Eddie."

Eddie blinked rapidly and shook his head violently. Tom could tell the rush was coming on him. "This whore's named Rayette Jones," he said. "She lived over at the Richmont."

"Whore," Eddie repeated, his eyes half-closed.

"That's right."

"Stupid fucker," Eddie hissed.

"What do you know about it?"

Eddie craned his neck. "Where's the bathroom? How far to the bathroom?"

"If you used all your strength you could make it," Tom said.

"Jesus," Eddie muttered. "Jesus Christ."

Tom reached across the table and shook Eddie's shoulders, "I want you to concentrate," he said loudly. "I want to ask you a few questions."

Eddie's eyes closed very slowly.

Tom shook him vigorously.

The eyes opened, hazed in yellow.

"This whore," Tom said. "Somebody killed her. At the Paradise Motel. You know anything about it?"

Eddie swatted at something invisible in front of his face. "Did you hear from Samantha lately?" he asked.

"I never met your wife, Eddie," Tom said wearily. "I'm not in touch with her. You know that."

"She don't write to you?"

"I never met her, Eddie."

Eddie's head flopped from side to side. "She don't write me, neither."

Tom leaned forward and slapped Eddie's face gently. "Tell me about the whore, Eddie."

"Samantha a whore now?"

"Rayette Jones."

"She got strangled," Eddie said.

"What else?"

"Nothing else."

"No talk on the street?"

Eddie smiled maniacally. "Silence. That's all."

"Are you sure?"

Eddie's head lolled forward, and Tom suddenly remembered the way he had hit the long balls on Ninety-sixth Street: Eddie the Stick, they had called him.

Tom shook Eddie gently. "Eddie?" The head did not move. Tom pressed his palm against the forehead and pushed it backward. "Eddie?" The eyes were closed. Tom let go and Eddie's head drooped forward.

Tom stood up and walked back to his car. Through the windshield he could see Eddie's head jerk backward slightly, then slam forward onto the table, sending the empty cup crashing to the floor.

Tom turned the ignition and pulled the car into the street. It was a bright, cloudless day, and far in the distance he saw pelicans. They were the most beautiful things in Salt Lake, and he loved to watch them in their unhindered flight, their black-fringed wings stretched out against the deep blue panoply of the sky. For a moment he wondered what it would be like to be like them, to have a place to go, a place that felt like home. He imagined his place as a remote cabin tucked away in some rocky, inaccessible hinterland, In his mind, at times, he could hear the streams, sometimes he couldn't, but always he could smell the scent of pines.

14

He saw the pelicans wheel to the right under the dazzling sky, and for a moment their beauty seemed to hold him in place, then lift him up toward the eye of their Creator.

"Look, son," he said.

The boy raised his head and a slight breeze caught a lock of hair, lifting it slightly from his forehead.

"Where are they going?" the boy asked.

"To be with their own, kind," he said. "That is nature's way of protecting each creature."

The boy nodded, still watching the great white birds as they banked back to the right again.

He pulled an arrow from the quiver that hung from his shoulder and held the nock between his thumb and finger, the head pointing toward the ground.

"Never touch the feathers," he said. "If they are bent in any way, then the arrow's flight will not be true."

The boy looked at the arrow as it dangled from his father's hand. "It's a very long arrow."

"It's a hunting arrow," he said, watching the boy closely. "It is not meant to be used by amateurs."

"Yes, father."

"And you must use the precise name for everything," he went on. "Only fools are unfamiliar with technical language. This unfamiliarity betrays them as amateurs."

The boy nodded.

He touched the end of the feather very carefully. "This part

of the arrow is called the fletching. You must not call it feathers.''

The boy shook his head. "No, I shouldn't.''

He drew the arrow onto the bow. "This is a weapon, not a
toy. It was designed by man to do only one thing, kill.''

The boy stared hypnotically at the bow. "Yes, father.''

He stepped to the left, edging away from the boy, and pulled
the nock of the arrow into place along the bowstring.

"It is an ancient and perfect weapon," he said. "Silent,
swift, and deadly.''

The boy's eyes widened, but he said nothing.

When the arrow was in place, he drew it back quickly and
with terrific force, so that the hilt of the arrow touched the hand
grip of the bow.

"Watch now," he said. Then he let go of the arrow and it
shot away at an incredible speed, then slammed into the large,
straw target in the distance.

The boy clapped his hands. "Bull's eye!" he shouted.

He looked at the target approvingly. The arrow had sunk almost to the hilt into the round, black circle at the center of the
target.

"That's great," the boy said jubilantly.

He drew another arrow from the quiver and placed it on his
bow.

"When you become proficient with the bow," he said,
"then stationary targets will pose no problem for your ability.
You will have achieved a certain technical skill." He looked at
the boy closely. "But skill is not enough," he added. "You
must be able to exercise a certain amount of will.''

They boy looked at him, puzzled.

He turned slightly to the left and raised his hand into the air.
"See that?''

The boy looked in the direction his father indicated and saw a
small gray squirrel hopping about in the distance. He nodded.

He drew the bow up toward him and steadied it, his eyes still
on his son.

"If you had the skill," he asked, "could you kill it?''

The boy continued to watch the squirrel as it rose up on its
hind legs and peered about, its nose sniffing at the air.

"Could you kill it?" he repeated.

"Yes," the boy said in a low voice.

He smiled and drew back the bowstring. He could see the squirrel's body over the tip of the arrow.

"Are you sure?"

"I'm sure," the boy said.

He released the string and watched the arrow explode away from him.

The squirrel seemed to hear the whirring of the arrow. It turned its head slightly as the shaft plunged through it and drove into the earth, impaling it where it stood, so that it remained standing, its body held up by the arrow.

He watched as the squirrel struggled to free itself, its feet scraping at the ground, its head craning wildly left and right until finally it slumped forward, the tiny, furry chin resting on the arrow shaft.

"That is what it is like to kill," he said.

The boy turned to him, blinking quickly, his mouth open slightly.

He watched the boy's face, his love sweeping out toward him.

"It's is not an easy thing to do, is it?" he asked.

The boy shook his head.

"The squirrel died for two reasons," he said. "First, because it is inferior." He glanced at the small, gray body that hung limply from the arrow.

"What's the second reason?" the boy asked.

He turned to his son, smiled, and gently stroked his cheek. "Because it was put here for our delight," he said, "and we have dominion over it and may use it as we will."

The boy nodded.

He dropped his hand from the boy's cheek and rested it upon his small, round shoulder. "I am not cruel," he said, "you must understand that."

The boy nodded again.

He drew his hand from the boy's shoulder. "There may come a time when people will say terrible things about me," he said.

The boy looked at him oddly. "Why?"

He took a deep breath and let his eyes drift back toward the squirrel. Blood was dripping from it onto the earth.

"Because I have done my duty," he said, "and they have not."

15

Bemis dropped a sliver of metal into a small glass tray. "We'll get, let me see, five or ten of these, maybe a few more fragments, but it doesn't add up to much."

The sliver had come from a piece of Lester Fielding's shattered skull, but resting in the clean glass tray under the silvery fluorescent light gave it a wholly innocent look. The harmless appearance of a weapon after it had been used struck Tom as one of the chief oddities of his profession.

"What are we dealing with here?" he asked.

"A regular cannon," Bemis said. He picked the sliver up with a pair of tweezers and examined it carefully.

"Magnum?" Tom asked.

"Of course." Bemis had the square-jawed look of an aging football player. "Forty-four. Hollow point." He looked at Tom. "Head wound the only one?"

"Yeah."

"Bemis's eyes shifted back to the sliver. "Only need one, of course. You saw it?"

Tom nodded.

"Probably looked like a watermelon after it had been thrown off the Empire State Building."

"That's about right, Jack."

"Nasty thing, hollow point." Bemis dropped the sliver back into the glass tray and looked at Tom. "Can't help you much on this."

"You can get hollow points easily," Tom said, almost to himself.

"Yeah. Easy to make, too. Take a knife, saw through the copper jacket. Same effect. Very nasty."

"Makes a very loud noise, a magnum."

"Loud enough."

Tom stared at the sliver. "He was an old guy, Jack. Christ, why would anybody want to kill him?"

"Way I hear it, you got motive problems with that whore, too."

"Yeah."

Bemis smiled faintly. "How long you been a cop, Tom?"

"Close to twenty years."

Bemis nodded. "Maybe I'm wrong, but the way I see it, things have gotten a lot stranger the past few years."

"How's that, Jack?"

"Well, used to be, if you had a killing, it wasn't that hard to come up with the reason behind it. Usually it made a certain amount of sense. A nagging wife gets shot. Or there's money involved. Stuff like that. Follow the blood or the money and you'd get your man."

"And now?"

Bemis shook his head despairingly. "Now, it could be anything. Like the kids used to say: far out. It could be far out, the reasons can be, I mean."

"Maybe so," Tom said.

"Mark my words, Tom, the more weird the world gets, the tougher it'll be for a cop."

Carl was questioning a thin boy with thick blond hair when Tom walked into the bullpen.

"Now when did you get to the garage?" Carl asked.

"I work midnight to eight in the morning," the boy said.

Tom pulled up a chair next to Carl's desk. "Who's this?" he asked, nodding toward the boy.

"Name's Mark Collins," Carl said. "He's the garage attendant where Fielding was killed."

The boy smiled politely, as if he had just been introduced.

"They're taking my statement," the boy said proudly.

"Yeah," Carl said. "We've already gone over everything with him verbally. I'm just taking it down for the record."

"What'd you get from him?" Tom asked.

"Z-e-r-o," Carl said.

The boy looked hurt to hear that all his information added up to nothing.

"Mind if I ask a few questions?" Tom asked.

"Go ahead," Carl said.

Tom turned to the boy. "I heard you say you worked the midnight-to-eight shift, is that right?"

"That's it. Been doing it for two years."

"Must be pretty dull after it gets late."

"I listen to the radio," the boy said, rolling up one sleeve of his shirt.

"Where do you listen to it?"

"In the office."

"On the ground floor?"

"Right there at the entrace. Yeah, that's the ground floor."

"Fielding was killed on the second floor," Tom said. "You didn't hear anything?"

"Not a sound," the boy said. He turned to Carl, his eyes widening slightly. "I was awake, too," he said quickly. "I don't sleep on the job."

"Mr. Fielding was killed with a very loud weapon," Tom said.

The boy sat up in his seat. "Couldn't have been. I would have heard it."

"Maybe you get hungry and wander down to the coffee shop once in a while," Tom said.

"I never do that," the boy said.

"So you were there in the office for the full eight hours."

"I sure was," the boy said assuredly.

"But you didn't hear anything?"

"That garage is usually pretty quiet if no cars are coming in and out," the boy said.

"Was there any traffic in the garage between three and four in the morning?" Tom asked.

"No."

"You're sure?"

"I checked my tickets. Nobody came in or out after two."

Tom looked at Carl. "Robertson, the man who owns *Southwest Magazine*, told me he saw Fielding around three-thirty.

That's when Fielding left the office. He was probably killed just a few minutes after that."

"Okay," Carl said, "but where does that leave us?"

"The killer must have used a silencer. And he didn't drive into the garage himself." Tom turned back to the boy. "How would you get up to the second floor if you didn't have a car?"

"There's a staircase."

"Can you see it from the office?"

The boy thought about it for a moment. "Not really. It's sort of behind me."

"Would you have heard anybody if they tried to go up the stairs?"

"I think I would."

Tom smiled calmly. "Think, now. Did you hear anybody?"

The boy's face crinkled slightly. "You know, I think I did hear that door open," he said slowly, "but it was earlier then four."

"How much earlier?"

"An hour, maybe. Maybe less."

Tom leaned forward in his chair. "Did you see anything?"

The boy shook his head. "No."

"Did any cars come down the ramp after you heard someone take the stairs?"

"No, I don't think so."

"Are you sure?"

"No, no one came down," the boy said finally. "I didn't have any checkouts after two o'clock."

"If there's so little activity after midnight," Carl said, "why do they keep a guy working there?"

The boy shrugged. "I don't know. Security, I guess. Some of the tenants in the building want to know that if they work late, somebody'll be around, you know, sort of looking after things."

Tom looked at Carl. "Did you talk to Sherry Anne Maitlands?"

"Yeah."

"Anything?"

"She just found him," Carl said. "She'd come in early that morning to catch up on some work. She was the first one in the garage. From what she says, it was real bad, you know? She was pretty upset about it.''

Tom nodded. ''Who's handling the canvass?''

''Baxter,'' Carl said. ''You might want to get a rundown from him.''

''Okay.''

Tom turned and walked over to Baxter's desk.

''How you doing, Tom?'' Baxter asked as Tom sat down opposite him.

''You check the neighborhood around the garage?'' Tom asked.

''Sure did.''

''What'd you get?''

''Just what you see, Tom, older and fatter.''

''How about the coffee shop across from the garage?''

Baxter chuckled. ''They got a waitress in there looks like Dumbo the Dancing Elephant.''

''Is that place open all night?''

''Closes midnight,'' Baxter said. ''You know, when the lab crew turned Fielding over, he had a shine to the seat of his pants, Tom.''

''What?''

''A shine. Right in the ass of his pants. I thought those magazine writers made money.''

''Is that coffee shop the only one open on the block?''

''It ain't open after midnight, and it stays open later than anything else. So that's it. No witnesses.''

''Surely there was somebody around,'' Tom said.

''In Salt Lake? At midnight? If anybody's on the downtown streets 'round three or four in the morning, it's only for—like we used to say in L.A.—a criminal purpose.''

''How about the offices in the building?''

''Nothing,'' Baxter said. He took a sip from a can of soda. ''Who put a fire under you, Tom?''

''I just want to touch all the bases.''

''You have touched them, buddy.'' Baxter glanced toward the small window to the right. ''Getting dark, Tom. Relax. Go on home. I'll keep the lawless element quiet until you return.''

Tom stood up. ''Let me know if you hear anything.''

"You'll be the very first," Baxter said without looking up from the can.

"I want to do this one right," Tom said emphatically.

Baxter slowly turned his face toward Tom and squeezed his eyes together. "Let me tell you something, Tom. I was blowing the heat off a thirty-eight special before you were born." He stood up more quickly than Tom thought possible and stood facing him, eye to eye. "And I can still chase a mark till the collar's on, understand?"

"I understand, Ralph," Tom said quietly.

Baxter let a smile ease onto his face. "Good," he said and sat back down.

Tom walked back to his desk, glancing back only once, very quickly, to see Baxter hunched over his soda once again—an old hound, grown mean with age, but one who could still run the length of the trail.

Tom was still thinking about Baxter when he pulled up in front of his apartment. He did not want to end up like that, but he did not know how to avoid it either. There came a time, it seemed, when you could be nothing else but what you already were, and even if you could think of options, you no longer had what it took to take them.

Inside his apartment, Tom switched on the light and stared around. It looked like a display window for the Salvation Army thrift store, and Tom could not keep from smiling—sadly, but smiling nonetheless. He sat down in his chair and turned on the television. He wanted to wash his mind, but the ridiculous stories and loud commercials irritated him, so he turned the set off and sat in the darkness, nervously eyeing his room, already impatient for the dawn.

When he couldn't take the sitting anymore, he walked out into the empty square of the apartment complex. For a moment he stood motionless, watching the sky, his hands tucked deep into his trouser pockets. The moon slid behind a cloud, darkening the air around him, then peeped out again. It amazed him that people had actually walked on the moon, and he resented the violation, the ugly footprints that were probably still there, a stigma of invasion, human scars. He shook his head and walked to the empty swimming pool. With the water drained

for the winter season, the pool looked like a plain cement rec-
tangle dug out of the sand and gravel surrounding it. Ugly in its
uselessness and abandonment, it seemed to make everything
around it a little uglier too.

He turned away and strode across the drive. For a moment he
started to turn back, then moved on until he stood beside the
road. He watched the late-evening traffic whisk by him, right
and left. He felt the impulse to stick out his thumb and hitch-
hike somewhere. Anywhere. Instead, he pulled a cigarette from
the pack in his shirt pocket and lit it. Glancing up the highway
to the left, he saw the small orange glow of his cigarette reflected in an oncoming car. Briefly he saw himself reflected in
the glass as the car drove past, and it struck him that he must
look threatening to the people inside, a lone rogue standing in
the darkness beside the road, idly smoking a cigarette. How
could they know that it was just Tom Jackson from the neighborhood and not someone else altogether? Someone deranged
and lethal eyeing them through a mask of cigarette smoke.

He turned away quickly and headed back toward his apartment. As before, he switched on the television, watched it for a
short time, then switched it off. He smoked another cigarette,
picked up the newspaper, read a story about a new development
in transplant surgery, then folded the paper and dropped it to
the floor beside his chair.

He stood up, sat down, stood up again, walked to the refrigerator for something to eat, realized that he was not hungry, and
returned to his chair, easing himself into it with a heavy, point-
less groan. For a moment he thought of Gentry, of the way the
old man had stood under the streetlight, waving good-bye to
him the night he left New York for Salt Lake. ''You're going to
live alone all your life, Tom,'' Gentry had warned him, ''and
all your life you're going to hate it.''

He leaned back in the chair and tried to relax. He thought of
landscapes, of small animals in their underground burrows, and
cloudless skies, but he could not pluck peace from anything.
The landscapes were suddenly overrun with locusts. The furry
animals sensed something watching them in the darkness of
their burrows. The skies filled with circling vultures. Everywhere and in everything, he sensed a third force that leered
from behind the clouds and from time to time struck out with a

mindless, burning fury. "You want to make everything new, Tom," Gentry had once said. "but the trouble is, everything is already very old."

16

He walked out onto the second-floor balcony of his home, grasped the wrought-iron railing, and gazed up toward the moon. So far, it had been possible for him to strike during the night, but he knew that soon he would have to engage the light. It would be the second stage of his challenge, the second test of his determination. He would slip from beneath the shield of night and strike in full light of day. And although this would certainly increase his danger, it would also shed the creeping, disreputable nature of nocturnal acts. For it seemed to him that the darkness that had protected him so far had also cast a shade of iniquity across his deeds. He had hated the blackness beyond the motel window and the shadows of the garage. Acts done in darkness had the flavor of acts about which one was ashamed. But soon he would work beneath the sun, shedding forever that cloak of evening which he despised.

He turned and walked back into his bedroom. He could hear his wife padding up the stairs with her tray of milk and cookies. Each night she sat beside him in bed, munching mindlessly at her snacks, her eyes pinned stupidly to the television. She was a caricature of housewifery, the frumpy, empty-headed housemate of popular cartoons. In her snickering foolishness she had neglected the rightful rearing of their daughter, and so the girl had grown up without any sense of the actual duties of womanhood. She would not be given the same chance with his son. By his acts he would teach the boy the meaning of dedication.

The bedroom door opened and he turned to watch his wife stagger into the room, the tray swaying precariously in her hands. Quickly he turned away and stared out into the darkness. He felt the mattress sag as she drew herself into the bed and heard her grunt softly as she plopped herself down and dropped the tray onto her lap.

He stood up instantly and marched out of the room, closing the door behind him. For a few seconds he stood alone in the hallway. Saint Paul had remained a bachelor all his life, he thought, and had recommended marriage only for the purpose of soothing the rage of thwarted sexuality. It had been years since he had felt the slightest desire for his wife, but he recognized that it was desire that had moved him toward her in the first place. It was part of the idiocy of youth to mistake for love that which was merely appetite, and he hoped that his son would know more than he, himself, had known.

He drew his lips into a sneer and walked down the stairs to his office. Here, alone, he felt at peace, his books his only friends. Yet even here something gnawed at him. For a moment he could not guess what it was, then he realized that he still had the odor of his wife lingering in his nostrils. He strode into the adjoining lavatory and vigorously washed his face, rubbing the washcloth against his skin until his face reddened and grew raw.

He folded the washcloth and hung it neatly on the stainless steel rack. Then he dried his face, stroking his cheeks softly, soothing the inflamed skin.

He walked out of the lavatory and back into his study. The large globe on the other side of the room caught his eye and he watched it steadily. In its spherical perfection, the globe seemed to convey the dream of God to make all things perfect in their form and content. The universe was made of symmetries and in their brilliant completedness they were, as Blake had called them, truly fearful.

He smiled to himself. There was somthing fearful in perfection and he thought that perhaps God never so fully realized Himself as in his wrath. Wrath was itself beautiful, and its beauty resided in the purity of its intent. Even at their best, all other emotions were crude, corrupted alloys. Wrath was an element, a thing that could not be broken down into weaker parts.

PART
THREE

17

Carl taped a large pasteboard turkey to the front of his desk, then turned to Tom.

"How's it look?"

Tom glanced up from a pile of papers on his desk. "How's it supposed to look?"

"It's supposed to add the holiday spirit, I guess. You doing anything special for Thanksgiving?"

Tom shook his head. "No." He looked at the turkey again. It looked very odd, a brightly colored holiday bird hanging stiffly from the edge of a homicide detective's metal desk. Then he thought of Rayette's purple dress, of her dark, swollen lips, and the black, spike-heeled shoes strapped neatly to her feet.

"You don't like it, right?" Carl asked.

Tom blinked quickly. "What?"

"The turkey. You don't like it."

"It looks a little out of place," Tom said.

Carl frowned. "I don't have any holiday spirit, Tom," he said mournfully.

"Neither do I." Tom let his eyes drift back toward his desk. "It comes with the job."

"Did you ever go to the Macy's Thanksgiving Parade?" Carl asked. "When you lived in New York, I mean."

Tom stared at the black and white police photo of Lester Fielding's body. "No, I didn't."

"Really? Never?"

"Never." Tom picked up the police photo of Rayette Jones. She lay on her back in the bed, her hands folded neatly over her belly, her eyes open, staring at the ceiling.

Carl craned his neck to see. "What you got there?"

"Just the pictures."

"Of what?"

"Jones and Fielding."

Carl shivered slightly. "How can you look at those things, Tom?"

Tom continued to stare at the photograph of Rayette Jones. "I can't figure why he would lay her out like that ."

"Because he's nuts," Carl said. "As in crazy. One of those guys that likes dead people."

Tom looked up. "But he didn't do anything to her. Sexually, I mean."

"Maybe killing her was enough. It is for some men," Carl said. "You got pictures of Fielding, too?"

"Yeah."

Carl leaned back in his chair. "Now I figure that for a mob hit."

That was the first Tom had heard of that. "Mob hit?"

"That's right."

"Why?"

"The look of it. Very clean."

"We don't have much mob action in Salt Lake, Carl."

"Yeah, but we also don't know what Fielding might have been looking into." Carl leaned over his desk and looked at the turkey. "Do you think this looks silly? The turkey, I mean."

"Fielding was evidently only working one story," Tom said, "and that was about the Clayton School. Why would the mob care about that?"

Carl sat back in his chair. "Who knows? Maybe they were just now getting around to nailing him for something he did before." He tapped his index finger against his temple. "In the mob they don't forget, you know?"

Tom tried to keep from smiling. The only thing Carl knew about the mob was what he saw on television or at the movies. "I don't think there's a mob connection with Fielding," he said.

Carl did not argue the point. "I got a court date this morning. That convenience store thing about six months ago. You got anything on the stove?"

"I'll be checking out a few things," Tom said. "Which reminds me. When you talked to that guy, the motel manager, he told you he saw a cab, right?''

"Cab?"

"The one that brought Rayette Jones to the Paradise," Tom said.

"Oh, yeah, sure. It was a cab."

"Did he mention the company?"

"Blue Dot, that's what he said."

"When's your court date?"

"Ten-thirty."

"That'll kill the day for you," Tom said. He stood up. "I'm going to run a few things down." He picked up the pictures of Jones and Fielding, folded them, and put them in the breast pocket of his coat.

"Taking those with you?" Carl asked, puzzled.

"Yeah."

"We got regular shots of them," Carl said. "You don't have to take those ugly things."

"It's something an old detective back in New York used to do," Tom said. "He always kept the police shots of the victimes in his breast pocket. He said they reminded him of what had been done to them, and kept them close to his heart." And he saw Gentry's face, and felt cold.

Driving over to the offices of the Blue Dot Cab, Tom kept trying to pump up his energy. He had seen enough murder now to be dulled by it, the critical edge worn off from overuse. Once, not long before he left New York, he had asked Gentry how, at his age and after what he had seen, he kept up his relentlessness, his almost inhuman zeal. He remembered that Gentry had smiled slightly. "Well," he had said, "just remember that the next case may be the thousandth murder for you, but for the victim, it was the very first."

Tom pulled over to the curb in front of the Blue Dot Cab Company and walked inside. For the most part, it was a garage, but he could see a line of glass-enclosed offices to his right. He picked one and walked in.

"My name is Tom Jackson," he said to the man behind a battered wooden desk. "Salt Lake police."

The man looked up. "What can I do for you?"

"You may have read about a murder last Saturday at the Paradise Motel," Tom said.

The man shook his head.

"Well, anyway," Tom said, "we understand the murdered woman was brought to the motel in a Blue Dot cab."

"I see."

"I'd like to find out who drove her there."

"What time would he have dropped her off?" the man asked.

"Close to midnight."

"I'll check it for you," the man said. He stood up and left the room.

Tom's eyes idly scanned the room. It was a typically second-rate office except that it was neater than most, the papers placed in boxes or stacked on shelves. Behind the desk, staring down from the wall, was a large portrait of Brigham Young. That was typical of Salt Lake. Young's picture hung in restaurants and clothing stores, groceries and coffee shops—the Salt Lake version of the cult personality. At first, Tom had found it interesting, but as the years passed, it had grown to annoy him as one more thing about Salt Lake he didn't like, and it struck him that he had never known he was a man without faith until he moved to a place where faith was everything.

"The driver was Jerry Phillips," the man said as he entered the room.

Tom turned toward him. "Where would I find Mr. Phillips?"

"Well, he's on duty now, so I can't be sure, but he usually keeps close to the ZCMI Center when he's not on call."

"Where in the Center?"

"Across from the Deseret Book Store. You know where that is?"

"Yeah," Tom said.

"I'll radio him and tell him you'll be waiting for him," the man said.

"Thanks." Tom walked back to his car and headed toward the ZCMI Center. It only took a few minutes to get there.

Deseret Books had large display windows and faced a small pedestrian mall. One window was filled with stacks of the Book of Mormon, another with various Mormon cookbooks and travel guides, and still another with posters advertising Brigham Young University.

Tom turned back toward the street and leaned against the window. Across the way he could see the great stone facade of the Hotel Utah. It was topped with a beehive finial, which Phyllis had once told him, in her travelogue fashion, was meant to symbolize efficient industry.

"Sir?"

Tom turned and saw a small woman with neat gray hair. He pointed to himself. "Me?"

"Yes," the woman said sheepishly. "Please don't think I'm rude, but could you not lean on the window here? We're trying to give maximum exposure to this display."

Tom edged away from the window. "Better?"

"Much better." The woman smiled brightly. "Thank you very much." She turned briskly and walked back into the store.

Tom walked to the curb and glanced left and right, his eye searching for any Blue Dot cab that might come into his view. After a moment, he saw one and waved it over to him.

"Are you Jerry Phillips?" he asked the driver.

"Yes," the driver said. "You must be the police officer. They radioed that you wanted to see me."

"I just have a few questions."

"No trouble." The man got out of the cab. He was short and stocky, with large, strong arms.

"I suppose they told you what I wanted to see you about," Tom said.

"About the murdered woman," Phillips said. "The one at the Paradise." His face grew intense. "That's a seedy place, the Paradise, but I guess you know that."

"Yeah."

Phillips folded his arms together and leaned against the cab. "Well, how can I help you?"

"You let her off at around midnight, right?" Tom asked.

"Yeah."

"And she was alone?"

"That's right."

"Say, Jerry, how you doing?" someone called in the distance.

Phillips lifted his hand and smiled. "Hey, Frank." He

turned back to Tom. "Sorry, friend of mine. We go to the same ward."

"Did the woman say anything while she was in the cab?" Tom asked.

"No. Real quiet. I sort of like to talk to people while I drive, but her, I knew what she was."

"What did you know?"

"That she was . . . a prostitute."

"How did you know that?"

"The look. It's easy to tell. She was from out of town."

"Atlanta," Tom said.

"That's right, I guess. Southern accent."

"Did she mention any names while she was with you?"

Phillips shook his head. "No. She didn't say a thing. Minute I knew the type she was, I guess I sort of clammed up, too. I don't go in for that, prostitution." He glanced upward and smiled. "Beautiful when the sun shines on it," he said.

"What?"

"The tower."

Tom turned around. The huge, glass-paneled face of the ZCMI tower broke the sunlight into a thousand brilliant shards.

"Like the burning bush," Phillips said.

"Where did you pick the woman up?" Tom asked.

"At another dive. The Richmont."

"And she just gave you the address she wanted to go to?"

"That's all." Phillips leaned toward Tom. "Between you and me, I'm not picking any more of them up."

"More of whom?"

"People down there at the Richmont," Phillips said disgustedly. "Nothing but prostitutes like that woman, and drunks and dope addicts."

"Did you notice what room the woman went to?"

"She just headed back toward the right corner of the place," Phillips said. "Normally, with a woman customer, I mean, I would have waited to see she got in all right. But not this one. She knew where she was going. She could take care of herself, too, I'll bet. They carry knives, I hear."

"How about cars? Did you see any parked at the Paradise?"

Phillips shook his head. "Place looked like a ghost town." He shrugged. "Mostly, it always does."

"Did you see anybody around the motel?"

"No, I didn't," Phillips said. "Just the woman, that's all."

"Can you think of anything at all that might help me?" Tom asked.

"I really can't," Phillips said. "I wish I could. I really do. I like to think that I am as much a friend of the police as they are friends to me."

Tom smiled thinly.

"I'm serious," Phillips said. "You guys do a great job, and I'd help you if I could." He smiled brightly. "I mean, I'd have to, wouldn't I, with *him* looking over my shoulder?"

"Who?"

"Him." Phillips turned and pointed to the tallest spire of the Mormon Temple and the burnished gold statue that rested on it. "The Angel Moroni."

Tom nodded. "I guess that's all I have for you."

"Really sorry I couldn't be of more help," Phillips said.

"Just let me know if anything comes to mind."

"Sure will," Phillips said brightly. "You can depend on it." He turned and got back in his cab.

Tom walked back to his car and pulled himself in behind the wheel. For a moment he thought of the people like Phillips, who wanted to give too much to the police too quickly. Then he thought of the others like Romero, who never gave anything to anybody, who only took until there was nothing left to take and then wanted more. He remembered the way Romero's face had turned bright red after Gentry slapped him, but he knew at that very moment when Gentry hit him that they had lost, that Romero would not break and that the only hope was that Rodriguez would hold firm, that Romero would not be able to get to him with money or with fear. But then, a few days later, the phone had rung on his desk, and it was Gentry telling him that something terrible had happened in the Rodriguez apartment, and the shakiness in Gentry's voice, the remote, barely controlled desperation had told him all he needed to know about the little man who saw Luis Fontana's body hit the curb and who had sat smiling and given Gentry his address, the apartment where he lived, or once had.

18

Baxter met Tom in the hallway leading to the squad room.

"You got a honey-colored one waiting for you, Tom," he said with a grin. "Real cute. Looks like she might have escaped the whole shebang without contracting a social disease."

"What are you talking about?"

"The still-surviving half of that pimp's financial resources. Says her name's JoAnn Blevins."

"Rayette's friend," Tom said.

"Bosom buddy, you might say," Baxter added. "And that little button nose didn't come from no pickaninny grandpa."

"Where is she?"

"Sitting right at your own little desk, Tom. Right there in our homey little squad room." Baxter smiled. "Sic 'em, King." Then he lumbered down the hall.

JoAnn nodded faintly as Tom came through the door. She was dressed in a plain checked blouse and black skirt that gave her the appearance of a college coed.

"I come to see you," she said.

Tom pulled out his desk chair and sat down. "What's on your mind, Miss Blevins?"

JoAnn ran a finger down the length of her face. "I don't want any more trouble here in Salt Lake. So I come to tell you. Pete's skipped town. He left last night. He told me to keep my mouth shut about it, but I know better." She grinned sardonically. "He thinks I'm just a little fool, but I know the law, and I'm not taking the rap for him."

"You did the right thing," Tom said. "Where'd he go?"

"Back south, where he come from," JoAnn said. "Atlanta.

106

He asked me to go with him, but I'm too smart for that. I'm through with him."

"Do you know where he went in Atlanta?"

JoAnn smirked. "Yeah, I know. Back to his mama. That's the way he is."

"Do you know her name?"

"No. He just always called her Mama."

"We can find him." Tom leaned forward slightly. "Do we need to?"

"What do you mean?"

"Did he have anything to do with Rayette's murder?"

JoAnn laughed slightly. "Him? God, no. He wouldn't have the guts for something like that."

"What kind of trouble did he get into in L.A.?"

"Stupid bastard," JoAnn said. "He was pushing baking soda for cocaine. Pushing it to these little wet-nosed rich kids up in the hills. They didn't know the difference till they stuck it up their nose."

"But what was the trouble?"

"Well, the real pushers got tired of him burning people. It was giving the business a bad name around there."

"And they did what?"

"Told him to go somewhere else with that game."

"That's all?"

"That's it. Nothing really mean going on."

Tom nodded, keeping his eyes on her. "The night Rayette was killed, Wilson said he spent that night with you."

"He did," JoAnn said. "You should know that from the way you found us the next morning."

"How well did you know Rayette?"

"Pretty well," JoAnn said. "She was one of those Southern blacks, dumb as hell, but sort of sweet, you know?"

"When did you meet her?"

"Just a few months ago." JoAnn leaned forward and smoothed a wrinkle from her skirt. "I'd come to L.A. from Syracuse, that's my home town. I'd come to L.A. to try to get some modeling." She looked at Tom and smiled. "My mama, back in Syracuse, she used to be dressing me up, you know, and she'd run her hand down my side and she'd say, 'That's your gold mine, honey. That's what's gone get you out of all this.' She'd rub her hand there and she'd say, 'That's your gold mine, baby.'"

"But you didn't get any modeling," Tom said matter-of-factly.

"You think I'm pretty, don't you?"

Tom said nothing.

JoAnn smiled. "You know I am." She tossed her head back slightly. "You thought I'd come in here dressed up like some street hustler, right? Flashy colors and all that tacky, low-life stuff. That was Rayette's thing, not mine."

"I didn't think you'd come in at all," Tom said.

"He left me flat, you know? Left me completely broke. Took all the money back to his mama."

"Sorry to hear it."

JoAnn dropped her eyes toward her lap, then let them rise slowly toward Tom. "Anything you could do for me?"

"Afraid not."

JoAnn continued to stare at Tom languidly. "You seemed like a nice fellow that time, you know, busting down the door, but sort of in a nice way."

Tom said nothing.

JoAnn drew a white handkerchief from her purse and began twining it slowly through her fingers. "I'm broke. Flat broke."

"I'm not exactly rich myself," Tom said.

"You know, you could come over to my place, I might—"

"I wouldn't go any further than that if I were you."

JoAnn smiled. "What, you made of steel, that it? Superman, maybe?"

"There's nothing I can do for you, Miss Blevins," Tom said flatly.

JoAnn watched Tom knowingly. "Everybody needs a treat, right? You're no different."

"Rayette's last trick," Tom said. "You know anything about that?"

JoAnn laughed. "Rayette? Shit, I know Rayette's not what's on your mind."

Tom let his face harden. "It could have been you, you know. Instead of her. The odds were fifty-fifty."

JoAnn's lips parted slightly.

"You may not wear the tacky clothes, but it's the same tacky life, and you could have ended up spread out on that bed just like Rayette."

JoAnn's body seemed to slump back into the chair.

"Have you seen the pictures of her?" Tom asked.

JoAnn shook her head.

Tom stared at her icily. "You want to?"

JoAnn said nothing.

"That guy's still out there on the streets," Tom said. "Maybe next time he'll connect with you."

JoAnn lifted a finger to her mouth and began to chew nervously on the nail.

"Had Rayette mentioned anything strange going on with another john?" Tom asked.

"No," JoAnn said.

"Anything weird or freaky?"

"She never said anything."

"What about repeaters? Regular johns? Did she have any of those?"

"No," JoAnn said weakly.

"Did anybody call up and ask for her by name?"

JoAnn shook her head. "Not that she ever said."

"Anybody ever get a little rough with her?"

"Rayette didn't go in for that."

"Sometimes that doesn't matter," Tom said. "Did she ever come back bruised, rope burns, anything like that?"

"No," JoAnn said. "We never had any trouble."

"Can you think of anything that might help me, Miss Blevins?" Tom asked.

"She just went out alive and she came back dead," JoAnn said. Her voice had begun to tremble. "She wasn't a bad girl, just sort of dumb." She began massaging the arm of the chair with her palm. "I want to get out of here, out of Salt Lake. I got to. I don't have to stay, do I?"

"I don't think so," Tom said.

JoAnn stood up quickly. "Pete did this to her. He filled her up with all kinds of big ideas about going to Hollywood. He didn't do it, but he caused it."

Tom drew himself up from the chair.

"He just fucked her and threw her away," JoAnn said bitterly. "Me too." She turned abruptly on her heels and strode toward the door, bumping into Baxter as she went through it.

"Must have made a hit with the little missus," Baxter said.

Tom sat down at his desk as Baxter moved toward him. "That bitch give you anything you didn't already know?"

"Not much," Tom said.

"Figures." Baxter leaned over to glance at Tom's face. "You got that look again."

"What look?"

"That end-of-the-line look you get when nothing's breaking on a case."

"Nothing's breaking, that's true."

"Surely you didn't expect to get anything from that hooker, even if she did come in all by herself."

"The pimp, Wilson, he's cut out."

Baxter put a fist on his hip. "Well, that does it, Tom, breaks my faith in human nature."

"I could put a warrant out on him," Tom said. "But I don't know what good it would do."

"Probably none." Baxter slapped Tom lightly on the back. "I'll tell you how you're going to break this case, Tom. One day some rookie patrolmen are going to pull a guy over on a busted taillight. They're going to ask the little fucker if he knows his goddamn taillight's busted, and he's going to say, 'Yeah, it is, and you remember that nigger whore somebody killed two years ago, I did that.'"

"You may be right," Tom said.

"You bet, buddy. Take it from an old pro."

19

Tom found Robertson in his office at *Southwest Magazine*. He was standing at his window, absently watching the traffic on the street below.

"Mr. Robertson?"

Robertson turned from the window. "Yes?"

"You remember me? Tom Jackson."

"Of course," Robertson said. "Come on in. As you can see, the door is open."

Tom walked into the office. It was more disheveled than he had expected—manuscripts piled on the floor, or stuffed into any available space along bookshelves or under chairs.

"Have a seat," Robertson said.

Tom sat down. "That piece Fielding was writing on the Clayton School . . ."

"I suppose you read about the reward," Robertson said. He was still standing, and the light from the window threw his shadow across Tom's face.

"No, I didn't," Tom said.

"Today's paper. Full-page ad."

Tom nodded.

"You don't think it'll do any good?"

"You usually get a lot of phony leads from something like that," Tom said.

"People who want the money," Robertson said.

"People who can imagine things if the price is right."

Robertson sat down at his desk. "I was just thinking of Les when you came in, just remembering what he was like when he was young. It's hard to imagine *Southwest* going on without him."

"The last time I talked to you," Tom said, "you mentioned a piece he was doing on the Clayton Children's School."

"That's right," Robertson said. "Les had already written a first draft."

"I'd like to read it."

"I see." Robertson looked worried.

"You still have it, don't you?"

"Yes, I still have it," Robertson said, his voice measured. "There's nothing in it that would really do serious harm to anybody."

"Where is it?" Tom asked.

"Right where Les left it, on top of his desk. In his office. Next door on the left."

Tom stood up. "Thanks."

Robertson watched him cautiously.

"Is there something you want to tell me?" Tom asked.

Robertson shook his head. "Read the article first," he said slowly, "then we'll talk."

Tom walked into Fielding's office, sat down at his desk, and began reading the piece on the Clayton Children's School. It was unlike anything Tom had ever read, punctuated with strange references to odd names he had never heard, and it ended with what appeared to be a verse of Scripture: "And ye will not suffer your children that they go hungry, or naked . . . But ye will teach them to walk in the way of truth and soberness . . ." For the most part of it was all spitting rage, but very little else, and it seemed to Tom that Danforth was right: Fielding had come looking for something evil and then had insisted upon finding it, evidence or not.

When he had finished, Tom took the draft back into Robertson's office. "He didn't have much of anything on the Clayton School, did he?"

Robertson shook his head. "No."

Tom thumbed through the manuscript until he found what he was looking for. "What is an Amulonite?"

"You're not a Mormon?" Robertson asked.

"No."

"The Amulonites were a tribe mentioned in the Book of Mormon. They refused conversion."

"Why did he call Danforth that?"

"You must understand something, Mr. Jackson," Robertson said. "In the past few years, Les had become somewhat more religiously inclined."

"So that word, it was just used as . . . what?"

"An accusation, perhaps," Robertson said. "Admittedly, an unfair one."

Tom lifted the papers slightly. "Would you have published this?"

"No," Robertson said without hesitation. "First of all, we would have been liable, legally liable for the things in the article. As you know now, there was very little evidence of anything really bad going on at the school."

"Yes."

"But second, that piece is not really journalism," Robertson added. "When you get right down to it, it's just a jeremiad."

"Jeremiad?"

"A lamentation, a tale of woe, something like that. Very religious in its tone."

"But *Southwest* is not a religious magazine, is it?"

"No," Robertson said. "And that's one of the reasons we would not have published Les's article." He cleared his throat softly. "It should be obvious, Mr. Jackson, that Les Fielding was slipping a bit. He was old, and he was tired. We had not published anything by him for months."

"But you kept him on the payroll."

"Yes," Robertson said. "What would you have done, fired him?"

"That's usually what happens."

"Not at this magazine," Robertson said proudly.

"You said Fielding wasn't working on anything else, is that right?"

"One story at a time, that's the way Les worked."

"You're sure?"

"Absolutely."

Suddenly something Carl had said struck Tom as important, the idea that someone could have gone after Fielding not because of his writing, but because of something he had already written: revenge. "Do you think anybody could have killed Fielding for something you'd already published?"

"I doubt it."

"Did Fielding ever mention a threat of any kind?"

"No."

"Did he gamble? Have any debts?"

Robertson smiled sadly. "If you'd known Les, you'd know how mistaken such ideas are."

"Did he ever mention any personal problems to you?"

"No."

"Would you have been the person he mentioned them to? Did he have any close friends? Closer than you, I mean."

"I think, honestly think, that I was his one and only friend in the world." Robertson glanced down at his desk, then back up toward Tom. "Some people say that if you're homeless on earth, you'll be homeless in Heaven. Do you believe that's true, Mr. Jackson?"

"I wouldn't know. Do you keep back issues of the magazine?"

"Of course we do."

"Could I see them?"

"Yes, but why?"

"To see if there might be anything in them that might have caused someone to kill Lester Fielding."

"You do grasp for straws, don't you, Mr. Jackson?"

"When they're all I have," Tom said. He hoped that in looking through the back issues of *Southwest Magazine* he would finally find something rising from the page, like a curl of smoke.

20

He heard the sound of the door opening and quickly closed the desk drawer. Looking up, he could see his wife peeping cautiously from behind the edge of the door.

"Are you all right?" she asked.

"You're supposed to knock," he said.

"Sorry, darling." She took two halting steps toward him, then stopped and stood watching him.

"Close the door behind you," he said.

She closed the door softly, then turned back toward him.

"What is it?" he asked.

"I didn't mean to disturb you."

"What is it?"

She nervously stroked the broad collar of her light blue housecoat. "I thought we might talk about Margaret."

The sight of his wife made him cringe. He could picture her body aging under the robe, the flaccid belly drooping limply forward, the legs lined with raised blue veins, the wrinkled, spotty skin. He had not touched her for years.

"Do you want to talk about Margaret?" his wife asked weakly.

"What about her?"

"About the marriage."

"That's none of my concern."

"Well, she is your daughter, darling."

The girlishness in his wife's voice seemed to come at him from the past, a high, light tone without resonance. He could not imagine what he had ever seen in her.

"I told you to make all the arrangements yourself."

She nodded. "Well, I just wanted to tell you that we've sort of selected the date. A June wedding. Is that all right with you?"

"Fine," he said crisply. He would be long dead by then. Good. One of the unsought blessings of his mission.

"Would you prefer any particular day in June?" she asked.

"No."

"We were thinking of the fifteenth."

"Fine."

"I'll tell her you approve."

"Tell her anything you like."

She took a small, almost frightened step toward him and lifted one of her hands. "Please, darling, try to be good about this."

He watched her watery green eyes and wondered what she could possibly know of goodness or evil. It was one of the blessings of stupidity, he thought, to hold words in such low esteem. Be good about this, she had said. What could she possibly know about the nature of goodness, or the sacrifices necessary for its triumph?

"Margaret wanted me to ask *you* if the fifteenth would be all right."

"Why?"

"She wanted your approval."

Approval, he thought contemptuously. She had not asked for his approval when, some years ago, she had marched off to the hinterlands of ecstasy, changing idiotically into her saffron robes. During that time she had seemed the perfect expression of the modern temperament, a fool who believed that she could find the complex mysteries of God within a guru's murky eyes.

"Tell her she has it," he said coldly.

His wife smiled meekly. "She really does want you to be active in the wedding, you know."

"That is impossible."

The smile on her face disappeared. "Can't you please make peace with her?" she said. "Can't you just forgive and forget?"

That was his wife's mind, he thought. A flutter of homilies, thoughts stripped of all richness, honed down to the shallowness of a wall sampler.

"Can't you please," she said, "just please be nice to her?"

The sweetness in her voice sickened him as few things ever had. It was the sweetness of the pathetic, the fawning, the indolent of mind. In his youth he had been seduced by it, had mistaken ignorance for innocence and inanity for guilelessness.

"Darling?" she asked again. "Can you?"

He stared at her icily and said nothing.

"Just for the wedding," she pleaded. "Just for one day."

"When that day comes," he said, "you'll know."

She looked at him strangely, her hand drawing back to her side. "It's so important to Margaret," she said.

Her eyes, he thought, were like the eyes of sheep in the slaughterhouse, vacant and uncomprehending until the very instant the hammer hits.

"Handle the wedding as you please," he said flatly.

Her eyes closed wearily, but the mournful look did not leave her face. In the early days, he remembered, she had used this pose of martyrdom to good effect, but he had long since rejected it as no more than a crude parody of emotional suffering. Great souls suffer, he thought; small ones merely ache.

He stood up. "Is that all?"

She stiffened at his tone of dismissal, and for a moment he thought he saw a glint of steel in her character. Then, almost instantly, her shoulders slumped forward and she turned from him, dragging herself from the room, her padded house shoes flopping against the polished wooden floor.

"Close the door," he said.

She did and was gone.

He was alone now. He sat down and leaned back in his chair, allowing the warmth of his isolation to encircle him. He could sense the terror in such utter aloneness, but he could sense its jubilation too. There were times when it was dizzying, as if he were able to look down upon the whole besotted world from the great height of his solitude. To be immaculate, he thought, was in some sense to be alone, and one only gained a true awareness of one's own powers by discarding all earthly connections save the most intimate and exalted—those between the devotee and his faith, the father and his son, the predator and his prey.

He glanced at the telephone on his desk. Once he had thought of it only as a faceless tool. But now he knew that greatness of purpose could transform even the most pedestrian object, and as he watched it, the plain black phone—featureless and ordinary—suddenly took on the radiance of its mission, shining with terrible light. Soon he would pick it up. For it was now one more weapon within the invincible arsenal of God.

21

"We keep all the back issues of the magazine in this room," Robertson said as he opened the door. He stepped inside and allowed Tom to pass in front of him.

The room was small and cramped, the walls lined with gray metal shelves. A small desk rested in the middle of the room.

"This desk is a sort of museum piece," Robertson said. "It was here from the beginning." He stepped over to it and ran his fingers along its surface. "Did you ever see the movie *Citizen Kane?*"

Tom nodded.

"We were like that. Or felt we were." Robertson looked at Tom. "I was Kane, the guy with the money and the big ideas. And Les, he was the honest man, the one played by Joseph Cotten in the movie." He shook his head sorrowfully. "To see him deteriorate as he did, it was terrible."

"What happened, exactly?"

Robertson leaned against the desk. "Les was always a very devout man," he said.

"That piece on the Clayton School," Tom said, "that was more than devout."

Robertson looked at him curiously. "Was it?"

"Didn't you think so?"

"That piece wasn't acceptable journalism," Robertson said. "That's as far as I would go in judging it."

"Does the Church have anything to do with the Clayton School?" Tom asked.

"I don't think so."

"Is that why Fielding went after it?"

Robertson straightened himself immediately. "Absolutely not," he said fiercely. "You're like so many of the . . . the . . . outsiders. You think we're all a bunch of fanatics."

"No, I don't."

"Lester Fielding wrote about injustice. He wrote about inhumanity and corruption. He wrote about it wherever he saw it, and he didn't single out any group for praise or blame." Robertson's eyes fell back toward the desk. "At least not for most of his life." He looked up at Tom. "In a way, it's good Les went when he did. It was a favor to him. From God, I think. I believe it was a kind of euthanasia." He turned and walked out of the room, closing the door behind him.

For the next few hours Jackson worked steadily, reading one article after another, slowly realizing that Robertson was right—Fielding had not singled anybody out for special attention or condemnation. He was a champion of underdogs: of an old woman against the electric company, of a private land-owner against a consortium of developers, of a young college student against an unscrupulous automobile company. And as he read, it seemed to Tom that Fielding himself had become a kind of ultimate underdog, almost always losing the battles he chose to fight. Only during the last months of his life had Fielding's work taken on a different color, moving more and more into polemic, relying more and more heavily on religious symbolism and sheer moral rage. Perhaps Robertson had been right about this, too, Tom thought—perhaps Fielding had died before he had time to diminish what he had already done.

The door to the small room opened, and Tom saw Robertson standing in the hallway.

"Find anything yet?" he asked.

Tom shook his head.

"How far have you gotten?"

"I just finished his last piece."

Robertson smiled and opened the door wider. "Not bad. You must be a pretty quick reader."

"I did some scanning," Tom admitted. He stood up and stretched. He could feel a slow, throbbing pain behind his eyes.

"Like to have a drink before you go?" Robertson asked.

Tom was surprised by the invitation. "Coffee, if you have it."

"Sure."

Tom followed Robertson into his office and watched as he poured the coffee into a large styrofoam cup.

"I don't drink it myself," Robertson said, handing the coffee to Tom. "But I keep it in my office for other people. Sorry I don't have any cream."

Tom took a sip from the cup. "It's all right." He took another sip.

"So you didn't come up with anything?"

"Nothing much."

"I didn't think you would."

Tom glanced at a large painting that hung behind Robertson's desk. It showed an old man, naked from the waist, who appeared to be undergoing some sort of royal judgment, kings and princes staring down at him angrily.

"Who is that?" he asked. "Saint Paul?"

Robertson chuckled. "No, no. I'm afraid not. That is Abinadi. From the Book of Mormon. He was a prophet who denounced evildoers. He was sent to prison.'' Robertson looked up at the painting. "Abinadi was sort of our inspiration at *Southwest*. For me at least, and for Les.''

"Oh.''

"You're not from Salt Lake, are you, Mr. Jackson?''

"No.''

"Back east?''

"New York City.''

"Ah,'' Robertson said, as if it had all come clear in his mind. "How did you end up way out here?''

"Just drifted, you might say.''

"You don't look like the sort who drifts.''

"I got tired of New York,'' Tom said, and added nothing.

"Yearning for the open spaces of the great Southwest?''

"Just tired of New York.''

Robertson stared attentively into Tom's face for a moment, then leaned forward, placing his elbows on top of the desk. "I've found something that might interest you.''

"What?''

"I'm sorry I didn't think of it sooner, but I don't think that matters.''

Tom placed the cup on the small wooden table beside his chair. "What is it?''

"As you can imagine, *Southwest Magazine* has gotten a few crazy letters in the past,'' Robertson began. "Not every one always agreed with the positions we took. Particularly the positions Les took.''

"Yes.''

"As a joke, when we first got started, Les and I had a box. We called it the Crazy Box. And these crazy letters, from crackpots calling us Communists or agents of the Antichrist, things like that, these letters, we decided to save them. That's what the Crazy Box was. The place where we kept them.''

"We would normally go through all Fielding's letters,'' Tom said. "That would be the next step.''

"You wouldn't have found these, because he didn't keep them in his normal correspondence. That's precisely what the Crazy Box was for. Such letters. To get rid of them without really getting rid of them, if you know what I mean.''

Tom nodded. "Go on."

"This Crazy Box," Robertson said, "it was just something young people do. I haven't put anything in there in years, and I didn't think Les had either."

"I see."

"But then I remembered seeing him do just that, put something in the box."

"Letters," Tom said.

"A stack of letters, actually," Robertson said. "He put them in about a week before he died. As I said, I saw him do it. I thought nothing of it at the time."

"Where are they?"

"Here." Robertson opened a drawer and dropped them on the top of his desk. "While you were in the other room, I read them."

"Who are they from?"

"His wife," Robertson said.

Tom raised his head slightly. "I thought you said he had no family."

Robertson sat back in his chair. "He hasn't. At least for the last forty years."

"But he was married a long time ago?"

"That's right. When he was a very young man. Her name Barbara Tompkins, and she was quite a beauty. A coed at Brigham Young. She was nineteen when they married. Les was was a year older."

"When did they divorce?"

"Well," Robertson said, "they never really did. Unlike other people, Saints do not divorce at the drop of a hat."

"How long did they live together?"

"Only a few years. Then they separated. Permanently. Time passed, as they say, and Les became completely absorbed in his work. I think he had more or less forgotten that he even had a wife."

"Until he got the letters," Tom said.

"Yes."

"She had never written to him before?"

"Only at the beginning of the separation, as I recall. And they were awful letters. They accused Les of everything imaginable. Being a red, being a homosexual. Terrible stuff."

Tom nodded toward the letters. "What about these?"

"Pretty much the same," Robertson said. "They're the letters of an insane person. Barbara was institutionalized for many years."

"When did she get out?"

"A year or so ago, evidently. And there's one other thing. Her father was a very wealthy man, and he only died a few months ago. According to the papers, Barbara inherited everything. A great deal of money. And since she was not in an institution and there were no other heirs to challenge her father's will, it can be assumed that she actually received the money."

"And bought some stamps," Tom said.

"Maybe more," Robertson said, "but it's just a thought."

"What?"

"She might have been just crazy enough to have done it," Robertson said darkly.

"Killed Fielding?"

Robertson nodded. "Of course, I don't think she would do it herself."

"You think she hired someone?"

"It's only speculation."

"Professional killers usually don't work for distraught wives," Tom said, "or crazy people of any kind."

"It's only a thought."

And, it seemed to Tom, one worth pursuing. "Where does she live now?"

"Right here in Salt Lake."

"You have an address?"

Robertson bent forward and pushed the letters across the desk. "She was kind enough to include a return address."

Tom put the bundle of letters into his coat pocket. "Did Fielding ever mention her at all?"

"No," Robertson said. "But I don't think he would have felt the need. Barbara was just something in his past, very distant past. She was too sick to be hated. Besides, Les was not a hateful man."

Tom stood up. "Thanks."

Robertson got to his feet. "I hope that's your answer," he said. "Those letters, I mean."

"So do I," Tom said.

"Don't judge her too harshly," Robertson added. "Les

would have wanted that." He smiled faintly. "We are taught to be watchful, but to leave our vengeance to the Lord."

22

Donald Olsen waved to his secretary, Betty Carpenter, as he walked by her desk and into his office.

"Long lunch," Betty said, following behind him.

"Very," Olsen said. "Lots to do, with the conference coming up." He sat down behind his desk. "Any calls?"

"Luckily, just one."

"Who?"

"He didn't give his name. He just said he needed to see you."

"About what?"

"He didn't say that either. Just that he'd call back around three."

Olsen glanced at his watch. "Fine, that should be any minute now."

Betty Carpenter left the office, and Olsen began routinely going through the mail that was routed to him in his capacity as a Church spokesman in the Public Communications Department. It was the usual: requests for information of various kinds, complaints about Church positions, inquiries on how one might join the Saints. He was relieved, leaned back in his chair, and considered the host of plans to be completed before the conference.

After a moment the buzzer on his phone sounded. Olsen straightened himself and pressed the button on his intercom. "Yes?"

"It's the man who called earlier."

"Put him through." Olsen heard the click as Betty connected

the two lines. "Hello," he said. "This is Donald Olsen. What can I do for you?"

The voice on the other end was so soft Olsen had trouble hearing it. "I'm sorry, what was that?"

The voice seemed to harden. "I need to see you, Mr. Olsen."

"May I ask who this is?" Olsen asked gently.

"Please, I'd rather not give my name at this time. I trust you can understand that?"

"I suppose," Olsen said.

The caller hesitated for a moment, then continued. "For a long time I have been interested in the Church. I have read deeply in its history and philosophy."

A convert, Olsen thought, and he was surprised at how quickly the joy rose in him at the prospect of bringing a new member into the Church. "That's very good to hear," he said.

"I know the teachings well."

The voice trailed off into silence.

"Please go on," Olsen said after a moment.

"Each person has many options," the man said, "both in secular and religious life." Then there was another silence, sudden and abrupt.

"Yes?"

"Many options," the voice began again, "but only one true way."

"Absolutely," Olsen said.

"Though it may not be easy."

"Not easy, no."

Again the silence. Olsen could hear the measured breathing through the line. "Not easy," he repeated. Then he waited. Nothing. "But sometimes," he added, "the more difficult the journey, the greater the reward." He listened for a reply. Nothing. But there was something intense, even in the silence. "Please go on," he said.

"We are made from one creation." The voice was deep again now, strong, a bit louder than before.

"One creation, yes," Olsen said quickly.

"God's creation."

"Yes, absolutely."

"But we are not all equal in God's eyes."

"But we are all equally available to God's love," Olsen said.

Silence.

"Don't you think so?" Olsen asked.

Still no answer.

"Sir?"

"The Saints are like no other people," the voice said. "Theirs is a unique faith."

"We think so, yes."

"Think?" Abrupt, almost an accusation.

"I mean that we believe ourselves to be possessed of a unique understanding of God's will," Olsen said hurriedly. The sound of his own words gave him a renewed sense of the grandeur of his faith.

"Absolutely unique," the voice said resolutely.

"Yes, absolutely," Olsen said.

"Pure."

"As close as man can come to perceiving the will of God." Olsen pressed his ear to the phone and waited.

"Flawed man," the voice said.

Olsen felt a terrible sadness in the other man. "Unfortunately flawed, yes."

"Fallen."

"Fallen by our own hand," Olsen added, "but not without the prospect of redemption."

"I am seeking redemption," the voice said. Then, a faint hiss.

"That is the first step in gaining it," Olsen said.

"But painful," the voice added.

Olsen could feel the pain, like a hard edge pressing into his body. He had heard it now, he thought, the voice of spiritual agony. "Our pain makes us special in God's eyes," he said.

"Yes," the voice said, and then a heaving breath.

"Sometimes those who come late to the Community of Saints add the most to its spiritual life," Olsen said.

"A pleasing thought."

Olsen thought he caught a sudden edge of sarcasm. "You disagree?" he asked.

Silence.

"I mean to say," Olsen went on, "that people who join the

Saints, though they come from other faiths, such people sometimes have a special commitment to the Church.''

"Commitment?''

Olson thought he heard a piercing sharpness underneath the
word, a barely detectable mockery.

"Really it's very simple,'' he said. "By commitment I just
mean that if you—''

"I have commitment.''

"I'm sure you do.''

There was a pause, and Olsen thought he could hear labored
breathing on the other end. "Are you all right?''

"Only a few can possibly know what real commitment to
God means.''

"Very true,'' Olsen said quickly, trying to renew his hold on
the caller's attention.

"Nothing less than total dedication is worthy.''

"Yes,'' Olsen said. "Quite right. And, of course—''

"Full of trials and tribulations.''

"In the commitment, yes.''

"Terrible tests of the will of the Saints.''

The voice seemed to Olsen to be deeply interior, as if it were
coming directly from the soul. He felt powerfully attracted to
it. "Faith always has a price,'' he said.

"Indeed,'' the voice said glumly, and Olsen recognized that
he was not dealing with some simple-minded enthusiast, but
with a man sufficiently educated to recognize a homily when he
heard one.

"I feel . . . feel that I am failing you,'' Olsen said slowly.

Silence.

"I mean to say, you are obviously an educated man,'' he
went on after a moment, "and I sense—correct me if I am
wrong in this, please—but I sense that you are a man who has
experienced some . . . suffering?''

There was no sound on the other end.

Olsen waited a bit longer.

Nothing.

"Tell me,'' Olsen said. "Have you recently experienced
some deep personal tragedy?''

Olsen thought he heard a muffled groan, but he could not be
sure.

"I wish I could make myself more clear," he said.

Silence.

"Please," Olsen said, "I can feel your need, but I feel inadequate in some way."

"I understand," the caller said immediately, but there was no gentleness in the voice.

"I'm glad you do," Olsen said, even though he could not be sure of the exact nature of the "understanding" the caller claimed; there seemed to be an edge of superiority in it, of pride. He waited for the caller to say something else, but there was only the silence again, and the breathing. "I'm still not sure what you want from me," Olsen said finally.

"Perhaps we could meet," the man said.

"That would be fine," Olsen said. "I would like to meet you very much." He waited. The breathing seemed to grow more shallow, coming in short, almost gasping bursts. "Very much," Olsen repeated.

"Yes."

"I'm free almost anytime,"-Olsen said.

"Fine."

"We could make an appointment for you," Olsen added. "You could come to my office."

"No."

The refusal was flat, absolute, and Olsen did not try to counter it. "Then, when would you like to meet?" he asked.

"Today."

Again the voice was very firm, and Olsen sensed that the meeting would take place either today or never. "That's sort of short notice," he said cautiously.

Silence.

"But," Olsen added quickly, "I think I could arrange it."

"Fine."

"Where would you like to meet?" Olsen asked.

"Do you know Markham Road?"

"You mean out near the mountains?"

"Yes."

"I know where it is," Olsen said. "Do you live out that way?"

"Take it three miles after you turn onto it from Cleveland," the caller said. "You will see a small trail at exactly that point.

On your right. Follow it three hundred yards, and you will see a cabin.''

"Cabin?" Olsen said. "I didn't know there were any cabins up that way."

"If you're uncertain, don't come," the caller said.

"No, no. Not at all," Olsen said quickly. He did not intend to miss so interesting a conversion. "I'll be there, of course."

"Five sharp."

"That will be fine." Olsen was about to thank the man for calling him, but the click on the other side cut him off.

23

A large, bald man with a wide mustache opened the door at Barbara Fielding's house.

"I'm looking for Mrs. Fielding," Tom said.

The man eyed him carefully, his hands squeezing a towel draped around his neck. "What for?"

Tom pulled out his badge. "Police business."

The man did not seemed impressed. "I was just about to go out on a little errand."

Tom watched the man's large arm muscles flex as he continued rhythmically squeezing the towel.

"Like I said, what you want with Barbara?"

"Her husband was murdered," Tom said.

The man laughed lightly. "No shit. Poor old Les. I read it in the paper."

"Where is Mrs. Fielding?"

"Save yourself some time, chump," the man said. "Barbara hasn't seen that fuck in years."

"That so?" Tom said. "I hear she was writing letters to him."

The man suddenly tensed. "Letters? What kind of letters?"

"That's my business," Tom said. "By the way, who are you?"

The man's eyes narrowed. "I live here, pal. You got any objection?"

Tom tried to force down the fear that was rising in him. The man was big, very big. And he had the mean look of a person who had broken a few bones in the past.

The man seemed to sense Tom's uneasiness. He smiled. "So why don't you just trot on back to the cophouse, tell them you couldn't find anybody at home." The smile vanished. "Okay?"

Tom cleared his throat. "Why don't you just trot on inside and get Mrs. Fielding?"

"Maybe I'm not in the mood," the man said.

"What's your name?"

"Santa Claus," the man said with a grin.

Tom summoned up his most lethal stare. "Name, fuckhead."

The man did not seem at all intimidated, but he gave the name anyway. "Harris. Ted Harris."

"Go get Mrs. Fielding."

"Maybe she don't want to see you."

"Let her tell me that."

"Look," Harris said, "she's in no shape to be bothered by a cop right now."

Tom felt his body tighten. He had broken some ice with the tough-guy pose. He decided to keep it up. "Tough shit," he said.

A low moan came from inside the house.

"What's that?" Tom asked.

"My bitch's in heat," Harris said mockingly.

"What's going on there?"

Harris's face suddenly grew taut. "Nothing."

"I want to see Mrs. Fielding," Tom said firmly.

Harris seemed to root himself in place. "Like I said, she's sick."

Tom moved toward the door, and Harris stepped forward, blocking him.

"Get out of my way." Tom could feel dread building in him,

the sense of being only so much easily spilled blood and broken bone.

"You got no right to come in here," Harris said darkly.

There was another moan, and Tom guessed that it came from a closed door he could see just over Harris's shoulder. He took a step toward the door.

Harris stepped forward and raised his hand. "You got a warrant, chump?"

Tom said nothing.

Harris smiled. "I didn't think so." His voice hardened. "Go get one, shithead, then you can see whoever you want to."

Tom stared at Harris for a moment, gauging him, calculating his strength. He could feel his heart thumping wildly. He stepped back. "Okay," he said.

Harris's smile broadened. "Good boy," he said. "By the book."

Tom turned slowly, watching Harris's hand glide back down to his side, then he wheeled around and plunged his fist into Harris's stomach.

Harris groaned and doubled over, one arm stretched out, his fingers grabbing for the floor.

Tom clenched his hands together, lifted them high into the air, and brought them down with terrifc force on the back of Harris's head. The head seemed to bounce back from the blow, then crash to the floor as Harris's body slid out of the doorway, his face scraping across the cement floor of the porch.

Tom bent down and cuffed Harris's hands behind his back. "Don't you even think about getting up," he said.

A third low moan came from the room, and Tom hurried over to the door. He knocked lightly. "Mrs. Fielding?"

Another moan, this one somewhat higher than the others.

Tom opened the door slowly. "Mrs. Fielding?"

Across the room he could see a thin, very pale woman lying on her back on a mattress. The mattress rested on the floor amid a pile of soiled sheets.

Tom walked over to the mattress and bent down. "Are you Barbara Fielding?"

The woman's watery eyes moved toward him. "Les," she breathed, "help me."

Tom could smell the woman's body, and it was clear that she

had not been bathed for days. From the level of her emaciation, it appeared that she had not been fed very regularly either.

"Listen," Tom said. "I'm with the police. I'm going to get you to a hospital."

"Les," the woman whispered weakly. "Water."

Tom stood up quickly and searched the house for a telephone. He found it in the kitchen, called for an ambulance, then returned to the room, knelt down beside Mrs. Fielding, and gave her a drink of water.

"Les," she muttered. One of her hands lifted slightly, the fingers brushing Tom's face.

"We'll take care of you," Tom said.

Mrs. Fielding stared at the ceiling, her eyes dull and filmy.

Tom bent down and put his lips next to her ear. "Don't worry," he said. "You're going to be all right now."

Mrs. Fielding's eyes closed slowly. Tom tucked his hand under the sheets, found her wrist, and felt her pulse. It was slow, but steady. "I've got an ambulance coming," he said softly.

Mrs. Fielding's eyes opened, moving over to the right, and staring at a painting of Jesus in the Garden that looked as if it had been cut out of some magazine and taped to the wall under the windowsill.

Tom placed his hand gently on Mrs. Fielding's forehead. "You'll be okay," he said. "Just don't let go."

Then he walked out to the porch and pulled Harris over on his back, then up to a sitting position.

Harris's breathing was still coming in short spurts. His eyes drifted over toward Tom. "Not a bad punch, fuckhead."

"Want another one?"

Harris did not seem in the least agitated. "I fell for that stupid trick."

"I'm going to shitcan you," Tom said coldly.

Harris shrugged. "Go ahead. I've seen the slammer before. It's nothing new to me."

"How long has Mrs. Fielding been like that?"

"She's good as dead," Harris said indifferently.

"If she dies," Tom said, "so are you."

"Bullshit," Harris said. "You don't have anything on me. So why don't you just shut up."

There had been a time, Tom remembered from New York,

when punk talk like that got you an instant tour of the emergency room. He placed his hand on Harris's throat and squeezed. "You were starving her to death," he said.

Harris laughed. "Bullshit."

"Why were you doing it?"

Harris sneered. "I wasn't doing anything, asshole. You found a sick old fart, that's all. Say what you want, I wasn't trying to kill nobody. You can't prove a thing. I been a yardbird long enough to know that."

"Where'd you meet her?"

"She hired me."

"For what?"

"Take care of her, what do you think?" Harris shifted slightly, edging his throat from Tom's grasp.

"You were doing a real good job," Tom said.

"You slammed me for no good reason, asshole," Harris shouted. "That's assault."

Tom pulled Harris violently toward him. "Lester Fielding was getting threatening letters not long before he died. You know anything about that?"

Harris shifted his eyes away from Tom. "I was just born yesterday."

"Those letters came from Mrs. Fielding," Tom said. "Does she look like she's able to write anything?"

"Ask her."

"You wrote them, Harris."

"Prove it."

Tom grabbed Harris by the jaw and jerked his face forward. "That won't be hard to do, and you know it."

Harris eyed Tom carefully. "What can you do for me?"

"Nothing."

"Then why should I tell you anything?"

"Because you're a murder suspect right now, Harris," Tom said.

"Fielding?" Harris said. "I didn't kill that bastard."

"Why were you writing those letters."

"Look," Harris said, "I been down for the count a couple times. Small stuff. Selling bod. Some con games. But that's all. I don't fall for murder."

"You don't decide what you fall for," Tom said icily.

Harris swallowed hard and blinked his eyes. "Okay, I was pulling something on the old lady, but I'm not in this for murder."

"What were you doing with Mrs. Fielding?"

"Look at her," Harris said. "Christ, she's got all that cash and no way to spend it. I mean, let's face it, either way it goes, that old broad ain't got many good fucks left. I mean, the mind's gone, man, and the bod ain't that far behind."

"Let's get to the good part, Harris," Tom said.

"All right," Harris said. "The old lady has nobody. No relatives. Nothing. And she's got a lot of money. She dies and you know who gets it?"

"Fielding."

"Bingo."

"He's her only living relative, fucking husband she ain't seen in years," Harris said. "But since there's no will—and she ain't got one, too loony if you ask me—well, she dies, he gets it all just because they're still legally married."

"What does that have to do with the letters?" Tom asked.

"I wanted to stir him up a little," Harris said calmly, making it all sound perfectly reasonable. "You know, I figured that if I could really get on his ass, maybe he'd go ahead and divorce the old lady, either that or so piss her off in some way that she'd divorce him."

"And then make a will," Tom said.

"That's right."

"With you as beneficiary."

Harris smiled. "That would have been the easy part."

"You're scum, Harris," Tom said.

Harris actually looked offended. "Yeah? Well, let me ask you this. Who's been wiping her ass for the past year? Me or her darling, faithful husband?"

Tom stood up. "You're going down again, Harris."

Harris turned his head toward the street, drew a deep breath, held it for a moment, then exhaled slowly. "Don't worry," he said casually, "I'll land on my feet." His eyes shifted back to Tom. "I always do."

The ambulance pulled up in front of the house, and Tom signaled the attendants to follow him. He led them into Mrs. Fielding's room and watched as she was bundled up on a

stretcher. Her eyes were closed, and her breathing had become
more strained. On the way out to the front door, Tom took her
hand. "Hold on now," he said gently. "Just hold on." Then
he let her hand slip from his and watched as the men rushed her
to the ambulance and lifted her in. Years ago he had watched
them do the same thing to Rodriguez and his daughter, Tina.
He had stood on the street, his arms dangling helplessly at his
sides, and watched the two stretchers hoisted into the ambulance, blood draining from them as they were tilted upward.
Rodriguez had been shot in the back of the head. Tina, only
nine years old, had been shot in the face, her body slumped into
the corner of the kitchen where she had tried to hide. Gentry
had stood beside him, his face pale and trembling under the
streetlight, and Tom had turned to him. "Romero did this," he
had said. And Gentry had nodded slowly, his eyes staring at the
ambulance as it pulled away.

24

As he took the trail toward the mountains, the intoxicating
sweetness of the air seemed to lift him upward. In the distance,
he could see the great dark face of the Wasatch Mountains, the
snowcaps towering high above the valley. Everything he did
now would someday be written of in the history of his faith, and
that, it seemed to him, made all the places he went and all the
objects he used in some way sacred, tools in the fulfillment of
his purpose. He smiled faintly and circled his fingers around the
long hunting knife in his overcoat pocket.

   The trail led upward in a winding path through the rocks and
brush. Over his shoulder he could see the highway stretching
back toward Salt Lake, or in the other direction toward the
Great Salt Flats. He paused for a moment, breathing heavily,
for he had already walked a long way. He leaned against a large

rock and looked down at the stony earth. He marveled that any people could have taken such inhospitable, rocky soil and turned it into a land of riches. That they had survived against so cruel a physical environment was miracle enough, but that they had grown wealthy beyond their own imagining, this seemed no less than a clear sign that they had once been, in those early days, a chosen people, exactly as they claimed.

He glanced down at the pocket of his overcoat and drew out the knife. It had a polished wooden grip, partly obscured by tape he had rolled around it. He had to be sure that the blade would not slip from his hand, and the tape gave the grip added traction. He pulled the knife from his pocket entirely and plunged the blade deep into the crusty ground. Flesh, he knew, would not feel like this. It would be soft and pliable, and the blood would come in a great gush, like water released from dry earth. The ground around the blade seemed to sizzle as he withdrew the knife and returned it to his pocket.

He looked up. It was late in the afternoon now, and the blue haze that surrounded Salt Lake gave the city an almost mystical appearance, as if it had already been lifted into Heaven by the hand of God. But that was only an illusion, he thought, his lips curling downward bitterly—only an illusion, for the truth lay somewhere else entirely. Not in an exalted appearance, but in a debased reality. Salt Lake had degenerated, had allowed itself to be mongrelized by a thousand alien forms. It was no longer the City of the Saints, but rather, a place where sainthood was befouled, where Saint and Gentile rolled together in a stifling atmosphere of moral rot. All of that had been to some extent endurable. But they had finally reached into the pit and come up with an ultimate betrayal, one that was clothed in the shining light of revelation, but which, in fact, was nothing more than a monstrous, satanic abomination.

His hand clenched the handle of the knife, and the heat of the blade radiated upward into his forearm. He would strike with the flaming sword that had guarded Eden. Now the heat was like a torch raked across his arm, singeing his hair, boiling the moisture on his lips.

He straightened himself once again and began walking up the gentle slope that rose toward the base of the mountain. The crunch of his boots on the pebbly soil reminded him of his days in Korea, the endless hours of marching through snow toward an enemy they could never seem to find. There were times when he thought his betrayals had begun there, when he was just a boy, blindly following orders, going where he was told to go, stopping where he was told to stop, watching as his friends fell at his side, steam rising from their warm blood as it spilled onto the snow. Now he was being asked to do it again, to follow because he was commanded to follow by men who were inferior to himself in every way one man could be inferior to another. They claimed the insights of revelation, but their eyes never lifted toward Heaven. What they wanted, in their treachery, was the approval of other men. And in their mindless expediency they had denied everything, had declared the first revelations false, had turned their backs on history and tradition and the moral order, which was inseparable from the natural one.

He sat down, his breath coming in short gasps. But he knew his weariness did not come from physical exertion. It arose from the burden of his memory, a burden that, at times, seemed almost too much for him, a history of failure, treason, lost chances, and deceptions, of weakness and moral incompetence. And although he thought it had begun in Korea, he knew it had not ended there. He had come home and found a renewed stability in the incorruptible body of his faith. And so he had labored for that faith in one way or another all his life. He knew that it was the bedrock of his existence, the ground upon which his spirit stood; when it had begun to tremble, to totter and grow insubstantial, it was as if the world had been torn from beneath him, and he knew that he must act to stop them and all their manifold corruptions and deceits. If he did not, no one would, and the People of the Book would perish forever.

He looked up toward the mountains and resumed his climb. He moved urgently, digging his feet forcefully into the ground, shouldering his way through the slightly thickening brush. He knew the spot would be waiting for him, that it had been prepared for just this moment, just this act, and that in the history to come, it would be a shrine, a place where pilgrims would come to remember what some men could do when guided by the light.

He found it easily, for he had prayed here from time to time in an attempt to clarify the exact nature of his mission. Sitting down on a smooth stone that rose up from the small clearing, he remembered his early confusion, the many voices that had seemed to come at him from all sides, commanding him to this thing or that. Finally, in an agony of doubt, he had called upon God to make the way clear once and for all, and it was as if he had been sliced by a sword of light. And then, at that moment, as he stood shuddering before his Master, he knew with perfect understanding the task for which he had been chosen.

For a time he waited, his eyes watching the clouds pass overhead, or searching through the surrounding woods. Then he heard someone moving toward him. He looked to the right and saw Olsen thrashing his way through the bushes. He smiled. Olsen was a man perfectly made for the spoiled repose of the City of the Saints. A modern man with no respect for the hazards of the natural world, who could move only with the greatest difficulty through unpaved streets or unbroken fields.

He stepped back and watched Olsen elbowing his way through the low-slung limbs. His eyes seemed to burn away the leaves separating him from his target. He thrust his hand into his pocket and grasped the knife.

Then, ridiculously, Olsen tottered and fell to the ground, sprawling out into the dust. He jumped up immediately, brushing the dust from his suit. Then he moved forward again, staggering into the small circular clearing.

For a moment he watched Olsen turn around and about in the clearing, his large eyes blinking in the mottled sunlight, a look of mute, bovine confusion on his face. Then very quickly he stepped out into the clearing and watched as Olsen turned toward him, an amiable, idiotic smile growing like a thin red vine on his face.

He stepped forward, almost rushing, and Olsen seemed to step back, watching him curiously.

"You know," Olsen said, extending his hand, "you look like—"

Instantly he pulled the knife and charged forward, thrusting the blade deep into Olsen's chest.

Olsen groaned loudly and tried to push away, but he held him close to his own body and thrust the knife in again.

Olsen's head dropped backward, his eyes staring disbelievingly into his face, a trickle of blood oozing from one corner of his mouth, his lips fluttering wordlessly.

He held Olsen up by one shoulder, pulled the knife out, then plunged it in again. Olsen's head lolled to the left, his eyes growing lifeless. Then he did it again, sinking the knife in to the hilt. Olsen's face paled and dropped forward.

He let go and Olsen's body slumped to the ground, his knees drawing up under him like a sleeping child.

He stepped back, drew a handkerchief from his back pocket, and began wiping the knife. The blade seemed to glow with a white-hot flame.

He put the knife back in his pocket. The front of his overcoat was soaked in blood, but the blood looked beautiful, a coat of crimson armor for a soldier of the faith.

He drew back another step and looked at Olsen's body with the deepest repulsion. The ground was soaking up his blood, he thought, as Hell was soaking up his soul.

He turned to head back down the mountain, and then suddenly he heard it: a sound, very slight, no more than the quick snapping of a twig. Instantly he whirled around and saw a glint of sun as it fell upon a long strand of blond hair. He dropped to his knees, his eyes searching through the tangle of brush. He could see it: a pair of pale, thin legs running away from him.

He leaped up, pulled the knife, and bolted forward in pursuit. Ahead, he could see the girl running wildly toward the downhill slope, her white arms flailing at the limbs. For a moment he thought of calling to her, but the foolishness of such an idea was obvious. He knew what she had seen. And that she must be stopped.

He was running now with all his strength, slapping at the limbs as they rushed toward him, raking the leaves from his eyes. He could tell that he was gaining on her, drawing closer to her with each step, her body growing larger and larger in his view. He lowered his head, driving himself forward, and after a moment he heard the low, breathless whimpering as the girl raced toward the clearing at the base of the slope.

He seemed to be flying toward her now, driven by a powerful wind, lifted up on great white sails, soaring through the leaves and branches, which seemed to shatter and dissolve as he approached them. He could hear the girl's feet as they tore across the ground, crumbling the earth beneath them, and he plunged forward toward that sound, tearing his mind from every other thought.

He saw her stagger briefly, regain her footing, then plow onward, still tottering, growing more and more exhausted as she fled him. The sight of her as she began to tire seemed to make his own flight more powerful, and he felt that he was moving beyond the earth, driving through the clouds, an insubstantial spirit moving with terrific force toward its destination.

A limb caught her in the face and knocked her backward. She stopped for a moment, stunned, then slowly began to lumber forward, her body lurching left and right, her feet sliding wearily against the earth.

He drove through the thinning brush toward her, his eyes burning into the blond hair, his hands reaching out toward her shoulder. Suddenly she turned around as she ran, caught sight of his face, and started to scream. He lunged toward her, knocking her to the ground, then fell on top of her, crushing his face against hers. He could feel her breath on his lips. He reached for the knife.

Her eyes opened, then her lips. "My God—"

He clapped his hand over her mouth, then plunged the knife between her ribs. He could feel her body buckle upward, and he pressed the knife in more deeply.

Her eyes dulled in an instant, but he did not remove the knife until he felt the last beat of her heart as it pulsed through the blade.

25

"Where the fuck's the wagon?" Harris said. He was still slumped on the floor, his hands cuffed behing his back.

Tom sat at the edge of the porch, watching the street. "You in a rush, Harris?"

"Why don't you take these goddamn cuffs off," Harris said. "What's the matter, I won't bite you."

"You look good with them on."

Harris laughed. "That right? Think they become me, huh?"

Tom continued to watch the street.

"What's your name, anyway?" Harris said.

"Jackson."

"Well, Jackson, I'll say this for you, you've got a good punch."

Tom glanced at his watch and wondered why it was taking so long for the patrol car to show up. He had called for it right after the ambulance left with Mrs. Fielding.

"You look sort of fidgety, Jackson," Harris said.

"I got work to do."

"Captain America," Harris scoffed.

Tom turned toward him. "Shut up."

Harris smiled. "You ought to have a better sense of humor, Jackson."

Tom turned back toward the street. Except for an occasional passing car, it was very quiet.

"How about a cigarette?" Harris said.

Tom said nothing.

"Hey, Jackson. Come on, cigarette?"

Tom turned and nodded toward the cuffs. "How you going to smoke it?"

"I'll manage."

Tom pulled a pack from his coat pocket.

"Jesus," Harris said, "that all you got, that low-tar crap?"

"You want one or not?"

"I'll have to settle for it."

Tom drew a cigarette out of the pack, placed it in Harris's mouth, and lit it.

"Ah, thanks," Harris said after the first puff. He was holding it between his teeth and blowing the smoke out both corners of his mouth.

Tom inched back against one of the wooden pillars of the porch. The late-afternoon cold was just beginning to chill the air. He looked back at Harris, still naked from the waist up except for the towel around his neck.

"You need a blanket over you?" Tom asked.

"Nah." Harris took three more deep puffs on the cigarette, then blew the stub onto the lawn. "That was a nice break. I needed a smoke."

Tom looked at him. "Where were you yesterday at around four in the morning, Harris?"

Harris laughed. "You mean when the old man got iced?"

Tom nodded.

"Playing cards with some buddies," Harris said. "They'll back me up."

"I'm sure they will."

"And they won't have to lie, either." Harris looked at Tom seriously. "I really didn't kill that old man. I never even met the bastard."

Tom heard a car round the corner to the right. He looked to see if it was a patrol wagon. It wasn't.

"How'd you come by the letters?" Harris said. "Going through old Lester's dirty underwear?"

Tom said nothing. The car moved slowly down the street and passed the house. There was a little girl with light brown hair in the back seat. She seemed to watch him for a moment, then laugh.

"She loved the old fart, you know," Harris said.

"Who?"

"Mrs. Fielding. She had a real thing for Lester. Even though they'd been separated for years. Talked about him a lot."

Tom withdrew the letters from his coat pocket.

"Well, I'll be damned," Harris said. "The written word."

"It's against the law to write a threatening letter," Tom said.

"I know that," Harris said. "That's why you won't find a single threat anywhere in that shit."

"You forged Mrs. Fielding's signature."

"Suppose I told you that she asked me to."

"Did she?"

Harris smiled. "Like they say, that's for the courts to determine. Right, Jackson?"

Tom opened the first letter and read it. It was filled with crude, even hysterical accusations, but not a single threat.

"Didn't I tell you?" Harris said. "I'm no fucking fool."

Tom folded the letter, placed it with the others, and returned the stack to his pocket.

"I'm what they called state-raised, Jackson," Harris said. "Did you know that?"

Tom said nothing.

"Orphanage to juvenile detention to slammer."

"Better stop now," Tom said. "I cry easily."

Harris turned away and looked through the open front door toward Mrs. Fielding's room. "Filthy old bitch." He looked at Tom. "I'm glad it's over."

"Her too, I imagine."

"She was born richer than we'll ever be, Jackson."

"Did her a lot of good, didn't it."

"The old man was into copper," Harris said. "Made his fortune that way. Part of it, at least."

"Who are you talking about?"

"Her old man. Mrs. Fielding's father."

Tom nodded.

Harris shivered slightly but did not ask for a blanket. "You ever been out to the Oquirrh Mountains, Jackson?"

"No."

"Kennecott runs the copper mines out there. You should see the way they mine it." Harris's eyes grew almost mystical. "Beautiful. Like a whirlpool. Rings of copper." He looked at Tom. "You know how much money just one of those mines must be worth?"

Tom did not answer.

"Just one," Harris said dreamily. "Just one fucking little mine." He said nothing for a moment, lost in his visions, then he turned back toward Mrs. Fielding's room. "She was my big chance, Jackson." He turned to Tom. "I met her, found out all about the money, then this thing with the lost husband. So I figured, this it it, Teddy-boy, your pot of gold at last."

"Ever think about a job?" Tom asked facetiously.

Harris smiled. "Digging copper for Kennecott, something like that?"

"Maybe."

Harris leaned back slightly, resting his head on the door jamb. "You think you've got it all figured out, don't you? You figure that if you play by the rules, do everything by the book, then somehow it'll all work out for you." He shook his head slightly. "That's bullshit, Jackson."

Tom pulled out a cigarette and lit it.

"You're drowning in the same scum I am, Jackson," Harris said, "but you don't know it."

Tom blew a shaft of white smoke into the air.

"She had some money, you know," Harris said quietly. "Here in the house, I mean." He stared at Jackson closely. "Enough to make a new start. Interested?"

"Where is it?"

Harris hesitated.

Tom turned away. "Patrol car'll be here soon."

"Under the refrigerator."

Tom did not look at him. "How much?"

"Close to thirty thousand by now, I'd say."

Tom nodded, and to his amazement, for a moment, just the briefest moment, he considered it. Then he knew, instantly knew, what must have happened in New York. "I'll tell the uniform patrol to pick it up," he said.

The eagerness in Harris's eyes dissolved. "You're a fool, Jackson."

"Maybe I am," Tom said.

A few minutes later the patrol car pulled up. Tom stood up and met the two patrolmen in the yard.

"Took you long enough," he said irritably.

"Yeah," one of the patrolmen started to explain, "there's been this—"

"Mrs. Fielding," Tom interrupted. "The woman who owns the house. She's already gone to the hospital." He pointed to Harris. "Take him downtown now. I'll file charges later."

One of the patrolmen nodded quickly. "You're Redmon's partner, right?"

"Yeah."

"He's been looking all over for you. They've found two bodies out in the woods off Markham Road. You're supposed to get out there right away."

26

The highway stretching out toward the mountains was lined with police cars, their lights flashing rhythmically in the deepening haze. As he pulled over to the side of the road, Tom could see small knots of men standing in various places along the trail that led up toward the base of the mountain. He got out of the car and began climbing the trail. He met Baxter about halfway up the slope.

"Interesting week, isn't it, Tom?"

"What have we got, exactly?"

Baxter dropped his cigar onto the ground and crushed it with the toe of his shoe. "Exactly one man, exactly one woman," he said.

"Bodies still here?"

"Yeah."

Tom looked up toward the stand of trees at the base of the tall, jagged cliffs.

"Very messy, Tom," Baxter said. "Very, very untidy."

"Hollow points again?"

Baxter shook his head. "Not even bullets," he said. "And don't I wish it was."

"What, then?"

"Slice job. Broad-blade knife, looks like. I ain't seen nothing like this since I left L.A."

"Did they find the knife?"

"Wouldn't you know? That thoughtless killer took it with him." Baxter pulled a handkerchief from his back pocket and mopped his forehead. "Long climb up there, makes you sweat." He shoved the handkerchief back in his pocket. "You look a little worn yourself, Tom."

"It's been a long day."

"No shit," Baxter said. "And it's going to get longer."

"I imagine so."

"Your friend Redmon, he's been calling all over for you."

"I heard."

Baxter smiled. "Can't piss without you there to flush it, can he, Tom?"

"Is he up in the hills?"

"Sure is," Baxter said. "And hopping around like a Chinaman in a whorehouse."

Tom nodded.

"They tell you who we got up there?" Baxter asked.

"Just a man and a woman."

"Not just a regular man, though," Baxter said. "Donald Olsen."

Tom's face registered nothing.

"You don't know who that is, do you, Tom?"

"No."

"I didn't either," Baxter said, "but the Saints sure did. Evidently he's big shit with the Church."

"What about the other one, the girl?"

Baxter shrugged. "Just some coed from Brigham Young."

"Were they together?"

Baxter winked. "Well, they sure weren't too far apart. Wonder what Mrs. Olsen's going to think about that."

Tom said nothing.

"The Saints are real upset about this one, Tom. And your buddy Redmon—shit, man, he's practically pulling his hair out."

"Okay, thanks." Tom pushed by Baxter and sprinted up the slope, elbowing his way through the brush until he could see Carl standing among a group of men in a small clearing. As he made his way through the trees, he could see the chief of detectives leaning against a large stone, talking to the chief of police.

Tom was out of breath by the time he made it to where Carl was standing. "Sorry you had trouble finding me," he said.

Carl turned around. His face was taut, strained.

"This is a terrible thing, Tom," he said desperately.

"Yeah."

Carl pointed to a large green tarpaulin. "That's Donald Olsen under there. Stabbed in the heart." He shook his head mournfully. "I don't understand how something like this can happen. Donald Olsen was a fine man."

"Baxter said there was a woman, too."

Carl's face suddenly turned angry. "Baxter, he's enjoying this, Tom. He's enjoying it a lot. He likes to see the great brought low. That's the way he is."

"Who was she?"

Carl shrugged his shoulders. "We just know she was a student at Brigham Young. She had a student ID on her. Name's Jennifer Dale Warren." He kept his eyes trained on the intent conversation between the police chief, Sam Marshall, and the chief of detectives, Charlie Philby. "They're going to go crazy over this one," he muttered. He looked intently at Tom. "We've got to find the guy who did this. We've got to do it fast."

"What do you know about Olsen?"

Carl's eyes drifted toward the covered body. "I know that he was a decent man."

"Besides all that."

Carl looked at Tom with suspicion. "What do you mean?"

Tom was about to answer when the police chief and the chief of detectives walked over to them.

Philby nodded. "Hello, Brother Redmon," he said. He turned and touched the brim of his hat. "Tom."

"Terrible thing, sir," Carl said mournfully.

"Yes, it is." Philby glanced at Marshall, then back to Tom and Redmon. "We've got a strange situation on our hands up here." He looked intently at Redmon. "Delicate, you might say." His eyes drifted over toward Tom. "I'm sure that both of you know what I mean."

"Absolutely," Carl said quickly.

"The thing is," Marshall said, "we just don't know exactly what was going on up here. We have to keep that in mind, the fact that we have no clear idea. So, as far as we know, two people were killed, and that's all we know."

"Yes, Chief," Carl said.

"And what we don't want," Marshall went on, "is any . . .

well . . . any speculation, you might say." He looked for some sign of recognition in their eyes. "To be frank with you, fellows, I'm talking about the girl."

"That's right," Philby said. "Now, Brother Redmon, I'm sure you know who Donald Olsen was." He looked at Tom. "You probably do too, Tom."

"I do now."

"Yes, right," Philby said. "Anyway, we've got this thing under control at the moment. We've kept the press pretty much out of here, and that's the way it's got to stay. No leaks. No off-the-record remarks. And absolutely no speculation about what these two people were doing up here. We have two murders—that's tragic, very tragic—but that's all we have, just the murders."

"What was Donald Olsen doing way out here?" Tom asked bluntly.

Philby's face tightened. "We don't know, Tom. That's the point I'm trying to make. And what we don't know, we don't talk about. Is that clear?"

Tom nodded.

"Now, I'm sure Brother Redmon will cooperate in this matter," Marshall said. "And I know you will too, Tom."

Tom said nothing.

"One thing, chief," Carl said. "We do have a little problem."

"What is that, Brother Redmon?"

"Another police officer. Baxter."

"What about Baxter?" Philby asked quickly.

"He's sort of what you might call a troublemaker," Carl said.

Marshall and Philby glanced at each other apprehensively.

"What do you mean, troublemaker?" Philby asked.

"He has a big mouth," Carl said.

"Has he been up here?" Marshall asked.

"Yes, sir," Carl said. "I didn't see him, but Tom did."

Philby's eyes shot over to Tom. "What did he say to you?"

"Nothing much," Tom said.

"What?" Marshall asked firmly.

"He made some . . . insinuations."

"Like what?" Philby asked.

"Like maybe there was something going on between Olsen and the girl."

"Good grief," Marshall hissed.

Philby closed his eyes slowly.

"I want you to understand something, Tom," Marshall said. "We have absolutely no evidence of any such thing. Do you understand that?"

"Yes."

"Donald Olsen was an upstanding member of this community," Philby said emphatically. "He was a high Church official with a spotless record of service. He was a fine, stable family man. And we have absolutely no indication that he had any connection with this poor girl."

"It looks to us, Tom, like somebody went berserk up here," Marshall said calmly. "Killed the first two people he saw. There's no reason to think anything else."

Carl squared his shoulders manfully and looked at Philby. "You want me to talk to Baxter?"

"No," Philby said. "I'll handle Baxter. Everyone is being told the same things you are," he said, addressing both Tom and Carl. "They're being told to keep their mouths shut until all the evidence is in." Then he seemed to single out Tom with his eyes. "Do you have any problem with this, Tom?"

"I guess not."

"Good," Philby said, relieved.

"We'll do our duty," Carl said.

Philby nodded, then turned to Marshall. "Do you have anything else you want to say?"

"Just one thing," Marshall said. "I want you . . . everybody . . . to keep in mind that we are only doing one thing—trying to make sure an honorable man is not needlessly slandered in death. Now doesn't that seem reasonable?"

"Absolutely," Carl said immediately.

"And you, Tom? Does that seem reasonable?"

"Sure."

"Fine, then," Marshall said. "Do your best, and let's nail this psycho fast."

They turned and walked slowly past Tom and Carl, moving into the clearing once again, then stopping to talk softly to each other.

"Those are two good men," Carl said admiringly.

"Where's the girl?" Tom asked.

"Over there." Carl pointed to the left. "Come on, I'll show you."

Tom followed Carl through the brush, allowing him to clear the way as they walked.

"They were right, you know, Tom," Carl said. "I mean about Brother Olsen, about not letting rumors get around."

Tom stopped. "Let me ask you something, Carl. What if Olsen *was* out here to meet that girl?"

Carl turned toward Tom and stared at him seriously. "I don't think anyone would have to know that."

"Of course they'd have to know."

Carl looked at Tom, puzzled. "Why? Why would they?"

"Because they *would*. It would all come out. In court, if no-where else."

Carl shook his head. "We're looking for a murderer; that's all we're looking for."

"Carl, don't you see that—"

Carl put up his hand. "A murderer. That's it. Whose side are you on, Tom? Baxter's? Are you like him?"

"No, but—"

"Then there's no problem." Carl turned abruptly and continued to make his way through the limbs.

Several policemen were milling around the woman's body, or fanning out in all directions, stomping through the bushes looking for any stray piece of cloth or hair that might lead them to the killer.

The body was covered with a tarpaulin. One white hand extended beyond the cover, the fingers curled.

"You want to see her?" Carl asked.

"Yes."

Carl bent down and drew back the tarpaulin. The girl looked to be in her early twenties. She lay on her back, one arm at her side, the other flung out over her head. Her eyes were wide open, staring. A pool of blood swept out from her left side, soaking the pebbly ground with a dark stain.

"Okay," Tom said, turning away. "Cover her up."

"Fully clothed, Tom," Carl said, as if clearing up something that might have otherwise cast some suspicion on Donald Olsen.

Tom nodded.

"A hiker, maybe," Carl said.

"No backpack," Tom said. "No binoculars or camera or canteen or anything like that."

Carl draped the covering back over the girl's body. "So what?"

"Well, there's nothing to indicate what the hell she was doing out here, like hiking."

"As opposed to what?" Carl said.

"As opposed to meeting Donald Olsen," Tom said. "It doesn't matter to me, but these bodies were pretty close together, and this is not Times Square."

"So?"

"So, in the end, you have to wonder what these two were doing up here."

"Nothing at all, Tom."

"You can't just blank it out."

"Maybe she was taking a walk from the university," Carl said.

"That's miles from here."

"She could have taken a bus," Carl said. "They come up here all the time from Brigham Young."

"Maybe," Tom said. He thought about the whole thing for a moment. "Look, Carl," he said, "we're going against each other in this thing, and it's just going to get worse."

"You got a solution?"

"Yeah, I do."

"And?"

"I'm working two murders already," Tom said. "I've got all I can handle. So suppose you just take over this case yourself."

Carl shook his head. "Can't you see that all I'm trying to do is protect a man's reputation?"

"I know," Tom said, "and that's why I think I'll just leave it to you."

"Okay," Carl said reluctantly, "if that's what you want to do."

"It is."

"Where are you going now?" Carl asked, following him.

"I'm through for today."

"Okay," Carl said. "I'll walk you to your car."

They walked in silence all the way down the hill and across the field to Tom's car.

"Well, be seeing you around, I guess," Carl said.

Up ahead Tom could see Philby and Marshall talking to a very tall man in a neat three-piece black suit. "Who's that talking to Philby and Marshall?" he asked.

Carl turned to look. "Goodness, Tom, you must live in a shell."

"What do you mean?"

"How can you live in Salt Lake and not know who that is?"

"The face looks familiar."

"It should," Carl said. "That's Mordecai McBride. He's one of the twelve Apostles of the Mormon Church."

27

"I see you didn't bring the chessboard," Epstein said as Tom came into the room. He lifted his shoulders slightly. "I could have used a chess game."

"Sorry."

"Didn't bring me no cigars, either," Epstein said lightly. "Or whiskey."

"Not in your condition."

Epstein waved his hand. "I'll worry about my condition, Tom, and you worry about yours." He straightened himself slightly in the bed. "When you was a cop in New York, Tom, did you ever work the Lower East Side?"

Tom shook his head. "Mostly midtown," he said, "and, for a while, the Village." The Village—but it seemed that he had only worked it that one afternoon over ten years ago.

"That's where I got my start," Epstein said. "The Lower East Side. Numbers mostly, nothing big."

For a moment Harris's sneering face swam into Tom's mind, then dissolved almost instantly into the bleak marquee of the St. Mark's Theater and the two men he had seen standing there.

"Tom? You listening?"

Tom blinked quickly. "What? Sure. Numbers."

"Yeah, right." Epstein laughed. "Christ, Tom, running numbers in those days, it was fucking great. Found money. Easy."

"Yeah."

"Used to carry the fucking stuff around in a little paper bag," Epstein went on. "Can you believe?" He laughed again. "And sometimes I didn't even carry a piece with me. Christ, Tom, it was just that goddamn safe."

"Long time ago," Tom said.

"Yeah. Do it today, you better carry an H-bomb in a side holster."

"It was that way when I left," Tom said.

Epstein scratched his cheek. "You know, Tom, you never did tell me why you packed up and left the city."

"Change of heart."

"About what?"

Tom could still see the two men in his mind. He remembered that a mist had gathered on the window, and he wiped it off so that he could see more clearly. "Just a change of heart," he said, "about the city."

"About New York?"

"Yeah."

Epstein nodded slowly.

"Go on with the story," Tom said.

"To tell the truth, Tom, you don't look that interested."

"Sure I am, Harry." Tom struggled to bring a small, limp smile to his lips.

"Okay," Epstein said. "One day I was walking along Delancey Street. Christ, it's a sunny day and the street vendors are swarming all over, and I look out, like from the left corner of my eye, and I see this guy I knew once, Joey something-or-other, and he comes up and he says . . ."

Tom continued to listen, but his mind seemed drawn away

from the room, from Epstein's voice, from the light that poured down over his body from the lamp above his bed.

". . . both start heading south, like we was brokers running for a killing around Wall Street, something like that, and . . ."

And he was moving through the blue haze that had surrounded the porch at Mrs. Fielding's house, and he could see Harris slumped in the door, the towel hanging from his neck.

". . . by then we were running so hard because this patrol car had started around the corner, sort of cruising around, checking us out, you know, so we . . ."

Then the great, gray mountains were before him and he was moving up the slope, watching Baxter come toward him, the sweat dripping from his face, staining his lapels.

". . . and so Joey finally says, 'Shit, Harry, we ain't never going to shake those fucks,' and we can see the goddamn patrol car not more than a block or so behind us . . ."

And then he was standing rigidly, listening to the drone of Philby and Marshall discussing Olsen and the girl.

". . . drop to our knees and Joey says, 'Here,' and hands me one of the sandwiches from his bag and takes the other one and says, 'Stuff the bills in the sandwiches and let's start eating,' and that's what we did, and I'll be goddamned but . . ."

And then he was standing over the girl and her eyes were wide open and staring back.

". . . so that by the time the fucking cops passed us, we looked like we was just a couple of assholes nibbling sandwiches on our fucking lunch break . . ."

Staring back.

Epstein laughed. "Fooled those fuckheads!"

Tom laughed, but he did not know at what. He had only caught snatches of the story.

"Ain't that a killer, Tom!" Epstein cried.

"Yeah," Tom said, and he could feel his mind moving back toward New York again, toward the Village, toward the two men standing beneath the dark marquee, and his face seemed to be pressing toward the window again as his hand wiped the mist from the glass.

PART
FOUR

28

When Tom got to the squad room the next morning, it was clear that the word had come down on the Olsen murder. Detectives were scrambling back and forth, looking hunted themselves, as if everything was on the line for the Olsen case—jobs, careers, everything.

"Regular three-ring circus, ain't it, Tom?" Baxter said as he passed by.

Watching the other detectives scurrying about, Tom decided that he had done the right thing in taking himself off the case: there was too much craziness in it, too many passions that would remain incomprehensible to him. It was Mormon business now, he thought, and he was well out of it.

"Listen, Tom," Carl said as he rushed up to him. "You got any time to do something for me?"

"Like what?"

"Like run a few things down on the Olsen case."

Tom shook his head. "No, thanks."

"It wouldn't take you more than an hour. The rest of us are up to our necks."

"No," Tom said firmly, his voice barely audible over the roar of activity. "I don't want anything to do with this case."

"Forget I asked," Carl said crisply. He wheeled around, strode to his desk, and snapped up the telephone.

Tom walked to his desk and sat down. All around him, detectives were moving about with more purposefulness than he had ever seen. Usually it was a simple matter: someone killed someone else, then the machinery began chugging, and it continued to lurch and sputter until either someone got nailed or the machine ground everything into a fine, insubstantial powder, leaving nothing to go on, nowhere to go. It seemed to Tom that his own cases had just about reached that point. He could feel the photographs of Rayette Jones and Lester Fielding in his pocket, but he had no idea what to do about them. Kiss them. That's what Gentry had told him once, with a full, hard wink. Kiss them right on the goddamn mouth, then take a deep breath and start all over again.

Tom stood up, the tension in his legs acting like a wound spring, snapping him to his feet. He walked out of the building and headed down the street toward the Desert Inn.

Tom saw Baxter sitting alone at one of the tables, his fingers toying with the brown blinds.

"Come to join me, Tom?" Baxter said when he caught Jackson in his eye.

Tom walked over to the table, pulled out a chair, and sat down. "Things are really hopping out there."

"Yeah, and it's just going to get worse." Baxter smiled. "I remember a time in L.A. We had this priest-killer running loose. He'd hit Father Mickey in one parish and Father Paddy in another. Christ, a real screwball." He looked toward the coffee machine, then back to Tom. "You a Catholic, Tom?"

"Sort of."

"Me, too," Baxter said, "but I ain't seen a Mass card in years."

"You were saying?"

Baxter laughed. "Oh, yeah, the priest-killer. Anyway, the Catholic boys really got hot under the collar on that one. Jesus, running around, busting everything in town, putting the arm on their snitches, muttering novenas every time they got a little lead." His face grew serious. "And they burned their covers bad, Tom. Even the narc boys got into it."

Tom nodded.

"They're going up to the mountains again this afternoon," Baxter said.

"For what?"

"Another search." He took a sip of hot chocolate.

"Maybe they'll find something."

Baxter shrugged. "Maybe they will. Me? I ain't going on no treasure hunt up there." He straightened himself in his chair.

"I got back trouble. Goes out easy. Running up and down hills—shit, I can't do that no more." He smiled. "You know me, Tom. The joke of the department. Old fart, sits in the lounge, waiting to retire."

For a moment Tom remembered Gentry again, an old man with a simple dream of a little house in Florida where he could sit out in the back yard and watch the gulls sweep across the sea.

"How long you got, Ralph?"

"One more year in this shithole, Tom." Baxter took a hesitant, dodging sip of the steaming hot chocolate.

"Then what?"

"Then who knows," Baxter said. He glanced toward the counter. "Want an ice cream, Tom?"

"No, thanks."

Baxter seemed to think about getting one for himself. "Yeah, you're right," he said finally. "Too much sugar in that stuff. Fucks up the kidneys." He glanced at the cup of hot chocolate. "They get this goddamn stuff so hot, takes an hour for it to cool down, you know?" He took another sip, then looked at Tom. "So, Tom, got your hiking boots ready?"

"For what?"

"Go up to the woods with the rest of those assholes."

Tom shook his head. "I'm not working that case."

"Really?"

"I got enough to do with Jones and Fielding."

Baxter looked puzzled. "Who's Jones?"

"Black prostitute down at the Paradise."

Baxter laughed. "You're not going to get in the Detective's Hall of Fame working that slime pit."

"It's all I got," Tom said dully.

"The headlines are with the Olsen case, my friend," Baxter said, the old pro filling in the new guy on how things really worked. Then he thought about it for a moment. "I don't know, Tom. Maybe you're right staying off that fucking case." He smiled impishly. "What you lose in newsprint, you'll gain in shoe leather."

"Maybe."

"Fielding," Baxter said thoughtfully. "I'll tell you, Tom,

that was a professional hit. He fucked somebody over, and they got him for it.''

"It looks that way," Tom said, "but something bothers me about it."

Baxter's eyes slid over toward Tom. "Yeah? What?"

"You should know, being from L.A."

Baxter looked interested. "Know what?"

"Well, you must have run across a few pro hits in your time, Ralph."

Baxter smiled, the worldly man. "I've seen a few snuffed canaries. Some territorial problems." He arched his eyebrows. "Four guys one time on the south side. Used a mean air-cooled, semiautomatic weapon on those fucks."

"In a single hit, though," Tom said, "you must know what those guys usually use."

"Twenty-twos," Baxter said immediately.

"That's right."

"Muzzle velocity one thousand feet per second. Short range, that'll do the job."

"And they want a short range."

"Sure do, from behind." Baxter placed his hand on the lower part of his skull, just behind his head. "Little hole there, bullet goes right to the fucking brain."

"That's right," Tom said. "So with a professional hit, we're not talking field scopes."

"Close range," Baxter said. "Always right on the button."

"Little powder burn on the shirt collar, maybe?"

"Sometimes." Baxter looked at Tom closely. "What are you getting at, Tom?"

"We know a pro hit when we see one, Ralph. We've both worked the big-time cophouses."

Baxter nodded attentively.

"Twenty-twos, like you said," Tom went on. "Little pistol, easy to hide in the palm of your hand. And you don't need a silencer long as a ballbat to keep things quiet."

"True," Baxter said, "but what's that got to do with Fielding?"

"Well, you must have read the report on that case."

Baxter waved his hand. "I don't read nothing I ain't told to read."

"Well, compared to a twenty-two, Fielding was hit with a field howitzer."

"What?"

"Forty-four magnum."

"Jesus."

"And right downstairs, the garage attendant didn't hear a thing. That means he must have had a suppressor on that thing almost as big as the magnum."

"Had to be," Baxter said. "A magnum—Christ, you can die from the sound of that fucking thing."

"He was hit from quite a distance, too," Tom said, "and from the front. That's target-shooting style, Ralph."

Baxter laughed. "Fuck, I've seen a few hotshit hit men couldn't hit a Volkswagen they didn't stick the barrel up the grill."

"Yeah."

"So you don't think it was a pro," Baxter said.

"I got my doubts. Maybe it's an amateur, thinks he's a pro."

"Could be," Baxter said. "Stranger things have crawled up my pants, you know?"

"The pros get close, Ralph," Tom said. "The amateurs, they stay back."

"Yeah. Or maybe you just got a guy likes to do things his own way."

"You don't get a button by being unconventional," Tom said.

"Yeah," Baxter said. "Whatever this Fielding snuff may be, it ain't *alla Siciliana.*"

Tom nodded.

"So who's the button man, Tom?"

"I don't know."

"And what's the beef?"

"I don't know that either."

"So you're nowhere."

Tom shrugged. "I'm running around on this one, but I'm not bumping into anything." He stood up and began to walk away.

Baxter took his arm and stopped him. "Hey, listen, Tom. You know I'm not doing much around here anymore. Like I said, old fart waiting to retire. So look—if you need a little help, let me know, okay?"

Tom smiled. "Sure. I'll let you know."

"Like you said, Tom, we're from the big-time cophouses."

"Yeah."

Baxter frowned. "And stay out of the hills, Tom. It don't pay."

Tom pulled his arm gently from Baxter's grasp. "I'll be talking to you."

"You do that." Baxter turned back toward the table.

Back in the squad room, almost everybody was gearing up for another search of the hills where Olsen and the girl were found. They looked like a bunch of cowhands getting ready for a cattle drive.

Tom sat down at his desk. Carl stood a few feet away, strapping on a canteen.

"If there's anything up there," he said, "we're going to find it."

"They should let the uniform guys handle this," Tom said.

"They'll be up there. In droves. But you know how it is with them. They don't know evidence when they see it."

"You get too many people up there stomping around, you'll bury more than you'll find."

Carl smiled coolly. "Well, you're not on this case, right, Tom?"

Tom nodded and turned away, waiting for the rest of the detectives to leave. They would be swarming over the mountain like vultures, he thought. Vultures. For a moment he remembered a story Gentry had once told him about a time in Africa when a bunch of GIs had come across some of their dead comrades. The dead had been stretched out on the desert floor for some time, and the whole area was covered with vultures. For a moment, Gentry had said, the soldiers stood silent, stunned by the horror. Then they acted, mounting their guns on tripods, the coiled cartridge belts hanging limply beneath the feed plates. Then, when all was ready, they fired. "You should have seen it, Tom," Gentry said. "Those birds just exploded, like grenades going off in their bellies." Then some impenetrably distant look came into Gentry's eyes, and he walked away, leaving Tom's mind caught in the picture of birds blown from the sky, of new death plunging toward the old, of dead soldiers buried beneath mounds of glistening black feathers.

Tom rubbed his eyes, stood up, and walked to the window. Through the clear glass he could see the edge of the Wasatch Mountains rising like a huge gray slab from the desert plain. In a little while, he thought, they would be there, scurrying about the brush, poking into crevices, turning over stones, a desperate Mormon army bent upon revelation and revenge.

29

The girl was watching him again, her face frozen, two thin shafts of piercing white light shooting toward him from the pupils of her eyes. He clapped his hands over his face and drew in a long, deep breath. The image dissolved, formed again, dissolved. He pressed his palms into the sockets of his eyes and twisted them slowly. A heavy black cloth floated over the girl's face, cutting off the shafts of light. Then the face vanished.

"O Father," he said in a whisper, "give me strength."

He removed his hands but did not open his eyes. He was afraid of what he might see. Another vision to taunt and accuse him, another version of the girl's face, this time with the purple lips parted in a scream.

He wheeled around in his chair and opened his eyes. A small breeze was stirring the trees outside his window, and he watched the few remaining leaves turn up slightly, then drop back down as the wind passed through them.

There was a knock at the door. He turned toward it. "Come in."

The door opened and he could see his daughter standing in the doorway. She looked at him strangely. "Are you all right?" she asked.

The concern in her eyes sickened him. He said nothing.

"Father?"

"I am fine." He could feel his hands clenching together under his desk.

"You've been in here all night," she said. "I was worried about you."

"I am fine," he repeated.

She did not move. "Are you going to have breakfast with us?"

"No. I am not."

"But you haven't eaten anything," she said.

He watched her with contempt. The musky smell of her body revolted him.

"You must be hungry," she said.

"I have work to do," he said coldly.

Her lips drew together scornfully. "I'm just trying to be nice," she said petulantly. She tossed her hair. "You don't have to be so touchy."

"Get out of here," he said.

She drew back slightly. "Please don't speak to me like that."

He stood up. "Get out of here," he said loudly.

"I want us to be friends again." She tossed her hair girlishly, as if trying to attract him.

"You have your life," he said. "Live it."

She placed one hand on her hip. "Why can't you forgive me?"

"It is not up to me to forgive you."

"All right, I did a terrible thing," she said. "I left home without your approval. But I'm back now, and I want us to be friends."

He said nothing. For an instant he was the face of the girl in the woods superimposed upon his daughter's face.

"All that I want is for you to begin to forgive me," she said, her eyes glistening. "Is that too much to ask?"

"Yes," he said. "It is too much."

She lowered her head, muttering something he could not understand.

"You may go now," he repeated.

She turned slowly toward the door, her head still bowed. It was a gesture of submission he despised.

"Never come in here again," he said.

She nodded gently and left the room, closing the door behind her.

He turned toward the window, watching the wind move in the trees, their branches stark and empty. That was what his life could have been, he thought—bleak and bare, his arms stretched upward toward a limitless sky, stretched upward futilely, ignorantly, rising like twisted prayers to which the ear of God was deaf, to which His eye was blind.

He spun around to his desk and felt a sudden heat sweep over his hands. Olsen had died clinging to him, his breath licking at his face. He had died like a pig hoisted up in the slaughter-house, squealing wildly as his blood drained into the pebbly soil. No. That was not true. He had to remember it clearly. Olsen had not squealed, only groaned. He had not struggled, but had given in immediately to his death, given in as if he knew he deserved to die, knew *why* he was dying. Perhaps, in some way, God had told him.

The heat crawled slowly up his arms, as if he were submerging them in scalding water. He thought of the girl, of the wild chase, of the way the limb had caught her and dragged her down so that he could fall upon her with the knife. Who was she? A harlot and a whore, he thought, someone who had been brought to him for punishment, like the Negress. He knew that God's purposes were unfathomable, and that he could not guess what sidewise paths he would be asked to take on his mission. The girl had not been his intended victim, but she had been God's. She had been thrown deliberately into his path by a holy purpose that he could only partly understand. And now her face was being used to test him, swimming into his mind to deter him, to cause him to doubt his purpose.

He smiled. God was good, but He was also clever.

30

Tom sat at his desk for a long time after the others had left. For a while he thought about questioning Harris again, but it was hard for him to come up with any real reason for it, and he hated busy-work. Then there was Mrs. Fielding, but it took only one call to the hospital to determine that her condition had worsened markedly and that she could not be questioned for some time, if ever.

Finally Tom stood up, walked outside, and wandered more or less aimlessly, his mind still occupied by the Jones and Fielding murders. He tried to imagine the kind of man who would kill a naked woman, then clean her up, dress her neatly, and lay her out on the bed of a cheap motel. Perhaps Carl had been right: a drifting psycho, a rogue male who wandered from place to place, killing according to some private ritual. Bundy had done that—a killer who never stayed very long in one place but simply roamed, buying gas with credit cards and then picking up somebody, anybody, as long as it was a woman. Within a few minutes of meeting him, they were dead, and he was on the road again, his hair lifting in the breeze from the side window as he hummed along with the radio.

Then there was Fielding. The more he thought about it, the less Tom could see that murder as a professional hit. There were too many false notes. And then, to top it all, there was the massive overkill of the magnum, as if the killer had wanted not only to murder Fielding, but to obliterate him, disintegrating his head in one terrible explosion. And hollow points. Completely unnecessary. There again, the overkill. The annihilating

166

power that, it seemed to Tom, expressed an almost other-worldly fury.

A few minutes later Tom found himself on Temple Street. He turned, walked down the sidewalk, and took a seat on some steps near the Temple itself. Overhead, the spires stretched up toward the sky.

For a moment Tom hugged his knees and tried to think his way through everything. But it seemed that walls closed off every direction. No prints. No weapons. No witnesses. No motives. It was as if these two people had been struck down by the air itself, victims of some sudden, invisible malice.

Tom released his knees and stretched his legs out, scraping his heels across the concrete walk. A tall, well-dressed woman strolled by, glancing at him oddly. He wondered if he appeared to be a derelict, sitting on the steps the way he was, his worn suit looking as if it had not been pressed for weeks, which it hadn't. He drew his feet back up and straightened himself. It would, after all, be embarrassing for some gung-ho rookie patrolman to step up to him and ask to see some identification. He stared about at the line of squat buildings surrounding Temple Square, buildings Salt Lake boosters still insisted on calling "tall."

After a while a black limousine pulled up to the curb only a few yards away, and Tom followed it with his eyes. Almost immediately Mordecai McBride stepped out and stretched his long body in the sun. Then another man emerged from the car, and the two stood talking for a few minutes, the shorter man gesturing wildly until McBride placed his large palm on the man's shoulder and lifted a single finger of the other hand to his lips. The short man immediately stopped talking, then, a few seconds later, returned to the car. McBride stood and watched as the limousine pulled slowly away.

McBride turned casually toward the Temple, raked his long fingers through his sleek, white hair, and waited, staring at the dark spires as if he were receiving a radio signal from Heaven. Tom leaned forward, watching, and it seemed to him that McBride was the very prototype of the tall, lean Westerner. He could imagine him stretched out on a large leather sofa, his boots dangling over one arm, his head resting on the other, his eyes closed, contented, utterly unafraid, the man of the West, at home in large spaces. Easterners tended to crouch, to sleep in the fetal position, to keep their eyes forever glancing over their slightly hunched shoulders. But McBride seemed wholly at peace with his environment of great range land and bottomless blue lakes.

McBride turned and began walking toward the steps. Then his eyes caught Tom's huddled body a few paces from him, and for just an instant his pace seemed to falter, to lose its hard, sure beat. Then he regained it and moved boldly toward the steps until he was standing over Tom like a great black obelisk.

"You're Tom Jackson, I believe." McBride's voice was very deep and seemed to come from some place lower than his throat.

Tom looked up. "That's right."

"I thought so," McBride said. He added nothing. His eyes remained fixed on Tom's upturned face.

Tom got to his feet. "Do I know you?" he asked—unnecessarily, but he thought to good effect. For it seemed to Tom that McBride was not the sort of man who liked to think he needed to be introduced.

"Mordecai McBride," he said.

Tom said nothing and let McBride guess for himself what that meant.

"You were over at the mountain," McBride said slowly. "With the police."

"The Olsen case."

"Yes."

"I'm not working that case," Tom said.

McBride's hand unconsciously moved up to straighten his dark blue tie. "So I've been told."

"Told?"

"I've been kept informed about it."

McBride was so tall, Tom had to tilt his head upward to see his face. "Well, Carl Redmon is on the Olsen case."

"I know that too," McBride said. "Of course, he's not the only one."

"No," Tom said. "Just about the whole department."

"And that bothers you?" McBride asked. One white eyebrow slid upward.

Tom said nothing.

"Actually, I had intended to have a little talk with you today," McBride said, "but I had arrangements to make having to do with the general conference. So, meeting you here like this is . . . what, serendipity?"

"You were planning to talk to me?"

"Yes."

"Why?"

"Do you not know who I am, Tom?"

"I saw you at the mountains," Tom said, and went no further.

"Yes, well, I'm given to understand that you are not a member of our Church."

"That's right."

McBride allowed a smile to crease his lips. "You've made that clear on a number of occasions, I understand."

"What about it?"

"Nothing at all, Tom," McBride said. "Except that that is the main reason I felt it necessary to talk to you."

"If this is about Olsen, there's nothing to talk about," Tom said. "Like I said, I'm off that case."

McBride dropped one of his great hands on Tom's shoulder. "Yes, I know. And if you don't mind my saying so, that's part of the . . . well . . . the problem."

"Is there a problem?"

"Yes, there is," McBride said. "And I think you know exactly what it is."

"I don't know anything, Mr. McBride."

"Call me Mordecai."

Tom knew he could not do that. The man was too imposing, too gigantic, too fully in charge of his surroundings. He had a way of turning everyone around him into a menial.

"What do you want to talk to me about?" Tom asked.

"I understand that you asked to be taken off the Olsen case," McBride said.

"That's right."

"Of your own volition, that is."

"I asked to be taken off myself, if that's what you mean."

"I wanted to make sure of that," McBride said. "I wanted to be sure that no one had given the slightest hint of any, shall we say, pressure for you to take yourself off the case."

"No one did," Tom assured him.

McBride smiled again. "Now, that brings me to my second question, Tom. Why?"

"Why what?"

"Why did you ask to be taken off the Olsen case?"

Tom shrugged. "I've got my hands full, Mr. McBride. I'm already working two other cases."

"Two? Murders?"

"Yes."

McBride looked as if something had slipped past him. "I heard of the Lester Fielding murder," he said, "but two?"

"That's right."

"What was the other one?"

"A black prostitute at the Paradise Motel."

"Ah," McBride said, as if that explained the fact that he had heard nothing about it.

"That's a lot of work, two murders," Tom said.

McBride smiled knowingly. "Yes, I'm sure it is, Tom. But overwork, that is not the real reason you asked to be taken off the Olsen case, is it?"

Tom shifted slightly. He was being interrogated by a pro, and he didn't like it. "Not entirely," he said.

McBride shook his shoulders. "It's a bit chilly, don't you think? Perhaps we can go inside somewhere."

"I need to get back to headquarters," Tom said.

"No, no, please, Tom," McBride said amiably. "Do me a favor. I don't really want to be seen at police headquarters. I'd much rather talk to you some place more . . . comfortable. Now. And don't worry about your superiors. I'll speak with them."

"I'm not worried about my superiors."

"Good," McBride said easily. He smiled. "Would you like to join me for lunch in the dining room of the Hotel Utah?"

"No, thanks," Tom said.

"Anywhere you like, then."

"There's a coffee shop down the street. We could go there."

"Fine," McBride said. "Let's do."

They walked slowly down the block, cut to the left, and found the coffee shop only a few blocks from the Temple. Tom ordered a coffee and listened to McBride's small talk until it came.

"That's why I love Salt Lake," McBride was saying, ending a particularly long and loving portrait of his native city. "Because I think it is about as close as one can get to Heaven."

Tom took a sip from the coffee and stared unenthusiastically into McBride's face.

McBride caught Tom's indifference quickly. "You're not much of a booster for our city, are you, Tom?"

"Not much."

McBride leaned forward and watched Tom intently. "All right, let's drop the amenities. I want to know why you dropped out of the Olsen case."

"I thought Carl could handle it better," Tom said.

"What do you mean, better?"

"He'd know what to do."

"About what?"

"About the girl," Tom said bluntly.

McBride sat back slowly. "You mean about Donald Olsen, am I right?"

"Him, too."

"And you think Carl would handle it—as you say—better because he is one of us?"

"One of *you*," Tom said.

McBride's eyes narrowed. "I think I know what you're getting at. Would you tell me if I am correct?"

"Yes."

"A coverup," he said. Then he smiled. "A sort of Mormongate."

"Maybe."

"Do you honestly think we are that corrupt?" McBride asked, a sense of wounded honor in his tone.

"No."

"You're implying it."

"Look," Tom said, "I know how a murder investigation works. You can't just exclude an entire area of investigation and expect to do the job. You've got to check out everything."

"And you think we won't?"

"There was a girl up there with Donald Olsen. Maybe they

knew each other. Maybe they didn't. But in any normal investigation, that's the first thing you'd need to find out.''

''Agreed. So?''

''They're not looking in that direction,'' Tom said.

''I see.''

''They don't want for there to be any relationship between the girl and Olsen.''

''Maybe there wasn't one,'' McBride said.

''Maybe there wasn't,'' Tom said. ''But from my experience I've learned that if you don't want to find something, you won't, whether it's there or not.''

McBride glanced about the room, then leaned forward again. ''Does the word *discretion* mean anything to you, Tom?''

''Yes, it does.''

''Is it wrong for us to want simply to be discreet in this matter?''

Tom shook his head. ''No, in itself, that's not wrong.''

''Then what's bothering you?''

''Nothing,'' Tom said coolly.

''I don't think that's true, Tom.''

''All right, McBride,'' Tom said. ''There is something that bothers me.''

''What?''

''What if that had just been some nobody who was sliced to ribbons up there in the mountains?''

''Ah, I see,'' McBride said. ''You think we are being hypocritical in our concern for Olsen.''

''Yes, I do,'' Tom said. ''Don't you think you are?''

''No, I don't,'' McBride said. ''Shall I tell you why?''

''Yeah, tell me.''

''All right, I will,'' McBride said calmly. ''A man is just a man, Tom. Every man is just a man. But the Church, its integrity, that is something much larger and and more important than any particular human being. If a man meets a young girl in the woods and they both end up dead, that's one thing. It is a tragic thing, admittedly. But if, on the other hand, that man is closely associated with the Church, well, that's an entirely different matter, Tom. And it is a different matter not because one man's life is more important than another's, more valuable than another's, but simply because one man dressed in ordinary clothes, while the other was wrapped in the garments of the Church.'' McBride stopped, his eyes peering deeply into Tom's. ''Now, as I see it, that is not hypocrisy at all. For you see, Tom, if we're concerned about Olsen, it's not because of who he was personally, although we certainly care about him as a human being. Still, the greater concern—for Olsen is, after all, dead—is for the Church and the place he had in it, and the fact—which cannot be ignored by us—that Olsen, as a person, represented the Mormon Church. Believe me, Tom, the Church has not gotten to where it is in this country by being indifferent to such matters.''

Tom smiled. ''You sound like a Catholic, McBride.''

''I sound like a man of faith, Tom,'' McBride said. ''That is what the Church, any church, is all about.''

''Well, I'm just a cop,'' Tom said, ''and when I see somebody murdered, I want to find out who did it. That's what being a cop is all about.''

''I understand,'' McBride said. ''And believe me, we want to find out who killed Donald Olsen, too. But let me add this, and I hope it's something a secular person like yourself can understand. If, without any real evidence, you go sniffing about, trying to dig up something between this girl and Olsen, and find nothing, do you think no harm will have been done? Do you think the insinuation—no matter how groundless—will simply disappear?'' McBride shook his head. ''It won't, Tom. Once you let something like that out, it lingers forever.''

''Sometimes that can't be helped,'' Tom said. ''And another thing. Those two bodies were close together. That's an insinuation that won't go away either. But the point is, I'm not on the case, so they can handle it any way you want.''

''That's not the point at all, Tom,'' McBride said. ''At least not the only one. Think about this. Suppose somebody found out that you've asked to be taken off the Olsen case. How does that look?''

''That's not my problem.''

''No, but it's our problem, the Church's problem. It looks like an honest cop took himself off a case rather than become involved in a coverup.'' McBride looked at Tom intently. ''There is no coverup, Tom. I give you my word on that, do you understand?''

"What do you want me to do, then?" Tom asked.

"I want you to stay on the case."

"The whole damn department's working on it."

"One more investigator can't hurt." McBride smiled. "Who knows, maybe you'll be the one to break it."

"And what about the girl?"

"Maybe you should work that area yourself, Tom," McBride said. "I think you understand what I mean by discretion now."

Tom nodded. "Tell me this. How did you know I was off the case."

"Word gets around," McBride said. "You have to understand something about the Saints. We were greatly persecuted. Our leaders were killed. We were driven from place to place until we found Salt Lake. A people with that sort of past is very careful about its future. Very self-protective of what they have, because it took them so long to get it. Maybe sometimes we overreact. But just remember where all that comes from. We're not a bitter people, Tom, just one that has been tempered by long distress."

Tom thought of the wealth of the Church, of those vast stock and real estate holdings it never divulged, of the banks and hotels and industries. He smiled. "It's been quite some time since the Church felt much distress."

McBride looked at Tom almost sadly. "That's a narrow way of looking at it, Tom."

"Is it?"

"Yes, it is. And it makes me wonder if perhaps I've been wasting my time talking to you."

"I guess we'll both have to find that out, McBride."

"We are used to waiting," McBride said. "We teach the present, but also the past and the future. There is a wholeness to our vision, a completeness. We are used to waiting. And we will know when it is finished."

"I don't know anything about that," Tom said. "I'm just a cop."

"Then be one," McBride said.

Tom looked closely at McBride's face. He had seen such visages before. They were usually carved in stone.

"Just a cop," he repeated.

"And I am just your brother," McBride said. Then he stood up and walked away.

31

The man's face seemed to sag the moment his eye caught Tom's police identification. "Is this really necessary?" he asked wearily.

"I'm afraid so."

"I've already talked to someone from the police."

"Yes," Tom said gently, "but you never know when something else might come up."

The man nodded mordantly, his eyelids drooping somewhat. "All right." He stepped back and opened the door.

"I'll try to make this brief," Tom said as he stepped inside the house.

"Please do." The man waved his arm, indicating a large, carpeted living room. "We can talk in there."

Tom walked into the room and sat down. "I know this is hard," he said.

"But it can't be helped," the man added, finishing Tom's sentence.

"No, it can't. Just to be sure, you're Jennifer Warren's father?"

"Yes." Mr. Warren shook his head. "I wake up in the morning, and I can't believe Jennifer's dead. My wife has just fallen apart. She lays in bed all day. Hardly ever speaks." He sat down in a large wing chair and folded his arms over his chest. "I'm sorry, I don't want to get you off track. What is it that you need to know?"

"Just a few basic things."

"Go ahead," Mr. Warren said. "I'll be as helpful as I can."

"I don't suppose you know of anyone who might have had a motive for what happened."

"No."

"Did your daughter go up to the mountains often, Mr. Warren?"

"She enjoyed the mountains," Mr. Warren said. "She was interested in nature. She was a very spiritual person, Mr. Jackson."

"What does that mean, exactly?"

"She was religious, first of all," Mr. Warren said.

"More than average?"

"I think so."

"In what way?"

"Well, for one thing, she was majoring in theology at Brigham Young."

"I see."

"She was an A student all the way," Mr. Warren added. "Straight A's."

"And so maybe she thought of the mountains in some sort of . . . what do you mean? . . . religious way?"

"Oh, no," Mr. Warren said. "She was not a pantheist. It's just that I think she sometimes thought of natural beauty as, well, as a kind of religious experience."

"So she would go up in the mountains? Why?"

"Well, I'm reduced to a cliché, I'm afraid. To commune with nature."

Tom nodded and glanced around the room. Jennifer Warren had lived well. It was a nice, large house with everything in place and no dust on the piano or water rings on the end tables.

"Did she live at home?" Tom asked.

"No. At the university. A dormitory."

"Which one?"

"Budge Hall."

"Did she have any special friends at the university?"

"Her best friend was another girl, very nice, named Mary Tilman."

Tom took out his notebook and wrote down the name.

"Does she live at the same dormitory?"

"Yes. She was Jennifer's roommate."

Tom looked up from his notebook. "Did she have a boy friend?"

"Mary?"

"Jennifer."

"No," Mr. Warren said flatly.

"Are you sure?"

Mr. Warren's face seemed to tighten. "Jennifer was a very serious student. She did not have time for boys."

"I see."

"Jennifer was a very good girl," Mr. Warren added emphatically.

"I'm sure she was," Tom said. And he knew what that meant. That Jennifer was a good Mormon girl from a good Mormon home, and that her death in the Wasatch Mountains had nothing to do with the way she had lived her life. Who, after all, would take a blade to such a person, except some psycho who'd blown in from L.A.?

Mr. Warren watched Tom suspiciously. "Jennifer was a very serious person—academically, I mean. She really didn't have time to develop much of a social life."

Tom nodded. "How about Donald Olsen?"

"What about him?"

"Did she know him?"

Mr. Warren leaned forward slightly. "What are you talking about?"

"Your daughter was religious, right?"

"Yes."

"And Mr. Olsen was a prominent Church official."

"So?"

"She might have had some contact with him," Tom said.

Mr. Warren sat back. "She probably knew who Mr. Olsen was, but I doubt that she could be said to have known him in any real sense."

"You don't think she could possibly have known him personally?"

Mr. Warren shook his head. "I don't see how. Jennifer lived at the university and at home. She knew very few people outside that circle."

"Were you close to your daughter, Mr. Warren?" Tom asked.

"Very," Mr. Warren said. His voice seemed to break very slightly.

"So if she had had a problem of any kind, you would have known it?"

"Yes."

"She would have spoken to you about it?"

"Absolutely." Mr. Warren looked down at his hands, his voice softening. "I loved my daughter very much. I mourn her very much." He looked up at Tom. "I can't think of any reason why anyone would have done this to her."

For a moment Tom's mind flashed to the body of Tina Rodriguez as it lay slumped to the side of a spattered wall, trails of blood running down her legs. He could not think of any reason for that, either, or at least none that made any final sense.

"I suppose you gave the other detectives a list of your daughter's acquaintances," Tom said.

"Yes, I did."

"Have any of them contacted you?"

"Of course," Mr. Warren said. "Many. Beautiful telephone calls. Lots of people loved Jennifer."

Tom nodded.

"We received a beautiful letter from one of her teachers," Mr. Warren added. "It must have been hand-delivered to our mailbox."

"A teacher?"

"Yes."

Tom placed his pencil on the notebook. "Which one?"

"A Professor Martin. At Brigham Young."

"You still have that letter?"

"Of course."

"May I see it?"

Mr. Warren looked puzzled. "It was just a very beautiful letter. There's nothing of importance in it, except of course to us."

"I'd like to see it anyway," Tom said.

"All right," Mr. Warren said. "It's upstairs. In Jennifer's room. I'll go get it."

Tom sat quietly in the living room while Mr. Warren made his way up the stairs, holding tightly to the banister like a man who had suddenly grown very old and weak. While he waited,

Tom's eyes roamed the room. It was broad and spacious, the walls painted light blue, pictures of sedate Western vistas hanging here and there like windows to the natural world. He thought of his own apartment, of the clutter, the randomness, the mess, and it seemed to him that these people were more rooted than he had ever been. For a moment he saw himself as they must see him—as a person floating rudderlessly in the world, tossed this way and that, whirling like a piece of sludge in a swampy culvert.

"Here it is," Mr. Warren said as he eased himself down from the last step. He held a small envelope. "It's a very beautiful letter," he added as he handed it to Tom.

"Okay if I keep it for a while?" Tom asked.

"Just please return it to me when you're through," Mr. Warren said. "It's very precious to us. It helps us remember what a wonderful person Jennifer was."

Tom placed the letter in his breast pocket, along with the photographs of Rayette Jones and Lester Fielding. "I won't keep it long."

Mr. Warren sat down. He looked troubled. "You're digging through her life, aren't you?"

"We have to do a little bit of that," Tom said.

"My daughter's life was beyond reproach," Mr. Warren said firmly.

"I'm sure it was."

"So what is it you're looking for?"

"Her killer," Tom said.

Mr. Warren lifted his head slightly. "The man who killed my daughter, he killed Donald Olsen too, didn't he?"

"Yes, he did."

Mr. Warren shook his head. "Terrible. Terrible what the world has become." He looked at Tom very intently. "Do you enjoy it?"

"What?"

"Digging around in other people's lives."

"No," Tom said, "I don't." He watched Mr. Warren for a moment. "And I don't make the world what it is. I just clean up after it."

Mr. Warren seemed to study Tom's face. "The other detectives, they didn't ask about Jennifer's life the way you did, about boy friends, things like that."

Tom said nothing.

"I told them my daughter was beyond reproach, and they believed me."

Tom stood up. "Thanks for your help, Mr. Warren."

Mr. Warren followed Tom to the door and opened it. "The others, they accepted what I said. They didn't question it."

"Maybe they have more faith," Tom said. Then he stepped out of the house, and the bright light of midday seemed to close around him like a hand.

32

The young man sat across from him, his face strained, worried. He could barely endure the petty concerns that had brought him here at midday, back to this cramped office he despised. He yearned to return to the spacious one in his home, to draw the great curtains together and sit in the darkness behind his huge mahogany desk.

"I'm sorry to trouble you," the young man said.

He nodded. "What did you want to see me about?"

The young man drew his finger across his upper lip, wiping away the tiny beads of sweat that had formed there. "I know I'm not performing very well, sir."

"No, you're not," he said, his eyes fixed on the young man's face, watching his nervousness, this dark night of his little soul.

"I'm just having a hard time, I guess," the young man sputtered.

Looking at the young man's clean white face, his watery light blue eyes, it was hard for him to contain his seething contempt. What could such a person know of hard times? He had been reared at the breast of ease and simple-mindedness, and in this he was like all the rest of his weak and insubstantial generation. They had been born into a land brought to them by endless struggle and suffering. They were the inheritors of an estate of which they were entirely unworthy.

"Part of the trouble is that I fell in love," the young man said.

He closed his eyes. He knew what was coming. A tale of romantic woe, of *Sturm und Drang* and the excesses of the heart. There had been a time when such puerility would have amazed him. Now it was commonplace.

"I know I shouldn't have let myself be carried away," the young man said, "but I couldn't help it."

He opened his eyes and stared lethally at the young man. "You could have used your will," he said.

The young man looked at him, puzzled.

"Will. Human will. Have you ever heard of it?"

The young man seemed to draw back into his chair.

"Have you?" he demanded, glaring at the young man.

The young man lowered his head penitently. "Yes, sir."

"Well, why couldn't you have used it?"

"I'm sorry, sir," the young man said softly.

He found the young man's submissiveness repulsive. He was like the rest of them—spineless, merely one more member of a people who had become wasted through excess, through comfort, through their own mindless cowardice.

The young man looked up at him helplessly. "I'm so sorry, sir. I feel so disappointed in myself."

He glanced away with a sudden jerk of his head. He could not bear the sight of his simpering expression or the sound of his thin, whining voice.

"I want to do better," the young man said.

"Indeed," he said coldly.

"I really do, sir," the young man said.

"But you need help, is that it?" he asked.

The young man nodded. "Yes, sir."

"What kind of help?"

"If you could just give me a little more time on the—"

"No," he said.

"But, I know that if—"

"No," he repeated loudly.

The young man stared down at his hands and said nothing.

He could feel his rage building again. He wanted to take the young man's throat in his hands and crush it. The weak deserved nothing, he thought, but they had inherited the earth.

"Is there anything else?" he asked crisply.

The young man shook his head.

"Then you may go."

The young man rose slowly from his chair.

"Close the door on the way out," he said.

The young man turned, walked to the door, and then turned back toward him. "Sir," he said meekly, "if I could just—"

"You have done what you have done," he said quickly. He folded his hands on his desk. "You are responsible for yourself. Now please leave my office."

The young man stepped out into the hallway and closed the door gently behind him.

He turned toward the window and looked out. It was a bright, beautiful day that God had made, that God had seen fit to give him for the penultimate phase of his mission.

33

Tom sat down on a bench and waited. He had called Mary Tilman not long after leaving Jennifer Warren's house, and she had agreed to meet him between classes at Brigham Young. Her voice had been clipped, hurried, but thorough. Administration Building. Bench to the left of the building. That was where Tom sat now, his eyes drifting across the spacious campus. Students moved about all around him. They had young, fresh faces and they were neatly dressed. No long hair. No beards. Times had changed. Or perhaps, at Brigham Young, they had stood still, leaving the university unrumpled by the crazy sixties, the flags and marches, and the lots and lots of overtime that Tom remembered—the long hours of standing in place, eyeing the crowds, hoping nobody would throw a rock or fire a cap pistol and bring the whole goddamn thing to some terrible conclusion.

After a moment he took Martin's letter out and read it. It was a terse three sentences:

Dear Mr. and Mrs. Warren:

As one of Jennifer's professors, I would like to convey my deep sadness at her death. She was an extraordinarily gifted young woman, a credit to Brigham Young, and an immense joy to all who knew her. I commend her memory to your keeping and assure you that she will be greatly missed, and is greatly mourned, by the university in general, and by her classmates and teachers in particular.

With deepest sympathy,
Timothy Martin

Tom folded the letter and placed it in his pocket. It was no more, no less, than what he had expected. It almost sounded official, which, in a way, seemed the oddest thing about it.

"You must be Mr. Jackson."

Tom looked up and saw a tall, thin girl with long, straight black hair. "That's right. And you're Mary Tilman?"

The girl did not move. She stood hugging her books to her breast. "Yes."

Tom scooted over on the bench. "Want to sit down?"

"Okay." Mary sat down. "Terrible about Jennifer."

"Yes, it is."

"Such a surprise. You never expect anything like that to happen to someone you know."

"I guess not," Tom said. "How well did you know Jennifer?"

"Pretty well, I guess," Mary said. "We were roommates. And close friends, too, in a way."

"Why, 'in a way'?"

"Well, Jennifer didn't have many friends. She was sort of

shy. That always struck me as sort of unusual. In a pretty girl, I mean. And Jennifer was very pretty."

"Yes, she was."

"Pretty girls are usually very lively," Mary said.

"But Jennifer wasn't . . . lively?"

"Not really. She was really into her studies. School was really important to her."

"Yeah, that's what I've been told."

"Oh, yes, very important." Mary said excitedly. "Have you talked to anyone else? About Jennifer, I mean."

"No," Tom said. "I was hoping you might lead me to other people."

Mary shrugged. "She really didn't know that many other people, at least on campus."

"No boy friends?"

For a moment Mary seemed to hesitate. "No, I don't think so."

"Very unusual for a pretty girl."

"Yeah, I guess."

"When did you see her last?" Tom asked.

Mary thought for a moment. "The day she died. I saw her in the morning at the dorm. I mean, we woke up together, you know. Then I saw her in the afternoon."

"The afternoon of her death?"

"Yes."

"Where did you see her?"

"She was getting on a bus. She waved to me."

"Was anybody with her?"

"No."

"Did you ask her where she was going?"

Mary shook her head. "No, I didn't."

A few yards away two young men had begun tossing a Frisbee. Tom watched them for a moment, then turned back to Mary. "That bus, which one was it?"

"It had a number, I think," Mary said immediately. "There aren't that many that run out here."

"Where does it go?"

"All over, I guess," Mary said. "I don't know exactly."

"Does it run all the way back to the mountains?"

"You mean where Jennifer died?"

"Yeah."

"I think so. She used to go out there sometimes, and she didn't have a car. So I guess she took the bus."

"What was she doing out there, Miss Tilman?"

Mary shook her head. "I don't know."

"Her father says she liked, or had an interest in, nature. Is that true?"

"Oh yes," Mary said. "She was really into hiking and that sort of thing."

"Did she have hiking gear?"

"Yes."

"Did she have it on when she left? When you saw her get on the bus?"

For a moment Mary seemed to grow puzzled. "No," she said slowly. "She didn't."

"Did she usually take it with her when she went to the mountains?"

Mary nodded. "Yes, she did." She squinted. "That's funny, I wonder why she didn't take it. I hadn't thought of it before. But she definitely didn't take it. I mean, I know that for sure, because it's all still in our room at the dorm. In the closet."

"Had she ever done that before?"

"I don't think so," Mary said.

"Are you sure she was going to the mountains? Maybe she was going somewhere else."

"No," Mary said. "She was going to the mountains."

"How do you know?"

"Because she told me," Mary said. "She waved to me and I went over to her. The bus was just pulling up. She said she was going to the mountains and that she'd be back later in the evening. I said fine. And then she got on the bus. That was the last time I saw her."

"And that's all you know?" Tom said.

Mary glanced away quickly. "Yes."

"That's absolutely everything you know?" Tom said evenly.

Mary looked at him but said nothing.

"What is it, Miss Tilman?"

Mary tightened her arms around the books. "I don't want to get Jennifer into trouble."

"I don't think you can."

"I mean . . . her reputation."

"She's dead, and the man who killed her is still out there," Tom said.

"I know," Mary said, "but still, her father . . . what she was . . . I don't want to get her into trouble."

Tom leaned forward slightly and brought his eyes down on Mary with a deadly earnestness. "This is a murder investigation," he said in his most authoritative voice. "Concealing any sort of evidence is not only a big mistake, Miss Tilman, it's a crime."

Mary's eyes blinked.

"Do you understand what I'm saying?" Tom asked.

"Yes," Mary said nervously.

"All right, then. What is this about Jennifer Warren's reputation?"

Mary cleared her throat. She did not seem to know where to begin.

"Miss Tilman?"

"Jennifer was having some kind of relationship," Mary began.

"Relationship?"

"With a man," Mary added. "I don't know exactly what kind of relationship it was."

"I thought she didn't have any boy friends," Tom said.

"He's, well, not exactly a boy." Mary shook her head. "Jennifer would just die if she knew I was telling anybody this."

"Go on."

"It was with an older man," Mary said. "Much older." She stopped and glanced out toward the Administration Building. "A married man."

Tom pulled out his notebook. "What's his name?"

"Oh, God," Mary said, her eyes on the notebook.

"Name?"

"He's a professor here. One of Jennifer's teachers."

"Name."

"Professor Martin. Timothy Martin."

Tom could feel Martin's letter in his pocket. "How long had this relationship been going on?" he asked.

"Almost a year," Mary said. "And please, like I said, I don't know exactly what kind of relationship it was. I don't want you to jump to conclusions."

"How did you find out about it?"

"Jennifer told me."

"Why?"

"I think she needed to tell somebody," Mary said. "Like to confess or something."

"What did she tell you, exactly?"

"She was crying when she told me," Mary said. "We were talking one night, and she just broke down and came out with it."

"What did she say?"

"She told me that she'd had a course with him, Professor Martin, and that they had been meeting ever since, and that he was a married man. She felt terribly guilty about that."

"When did it start, the relationship?"

"Almost a year ago."

"Was she going to end it?"

"She said she wanted to, but that she just didn't know what to do."

"When did she tell you this?"

"About a month ago," Mary said.

"And she was thinking about ending it?"

"Yes, but she didn't know if she could or not." Mary looked at Tom plaintively. "She loved him. She really did."

"Do you know this man, this Professor Martin?"

"No, I don't. I mean, I know who he is, but I don't really know him as a person."

"He still teaches here?"

"Yes."

"What department?"

"Theology."

Tom nodded, then placed the notebook back in his pocket.

"Please don't tell anybody about this," Mary said.

Tom said nothing.

"I guess you'll have to talk to Professor Martin, won't you?" Mary asked.

"Yes."

"Please don't tell him I told you."

"I won't."

"I really think that whatever it was between them—well, that it was innocent. I'm sure he didn't have anything to do with Jennifer—I mean, with her death."

"Had she told him that she was thinking about breaking off with him?" Tom asked.

Mary shook her head. "I don't know."

"Do you know where they used to meet?"

"No."

"Did she say anything about the kind of person he was, that he was very upset, or had a temper, or anything like that?"

"She only mentioned him that one time," Mary said. "Just that once when she cried."

Tom glanced toward the open green of the campus. The boys with the Frisbees had disappeared, and the afternoon chill was moving in.

34

Tom walked to the nearest telephone he could find, dialed university information, and got the number of Professor Martin's office. Then he dialed the number and a man picked up the phone almost immediately.

"Hello?"

"Professor Martin?"

"Yes."

"My name is Tom Jackson. I'm with the Salt Lake police."

"Police?"

"Yes. I'm looking into the murder of Jennifer Warren."

There was silence for a moment on the other end.

"I understand you knew Miss Warren," Tom said.

"Yes, I did."

"I'd like to talk to you about her."

There was another short silence. "Well, I didn't know her very well. She was a student of mine. I wrote a letter of condolence to the family."

"Well, I've heard something a little different from that, to tell you the truth," Tom said as gently as he could.

"I see."

"I don't think we should go into this over the telephone," Tom said.

"No, of course not."

"I'm here on campus," Tom added. "I could come over to your office."

"No," the man said quickly. "I'd rather you not do that, if you don't mind."

"Where, then?"

"I was just leaving for the city," the man said. "Are you going back to Salt Lake?"

"Yes."

"Perhaps we could meet there."

"At police headquarters?"

"Oh, no," the man said fearfully. "Not there. We could meet in the dining room of the Hotel Utah. Would that be all right with you?"

"Yes. In a half hour?"

"I'm leaving now."

The dining room of the Hotel Utah was an elaborate affair. It was located on the roof, and the dark spires of the Temple could be seen easily through the large windows.

The maître d' looked at Tom apprehensively, glancing down toward the scruffy shoes, then up at the fading, weathered sport coat. "May I help you?"

"Did a Professor Martin arrive yet?" Tom asked.

"I'm afraid not."

"When he does, tell him where I am," Tom said. "The name is Jackson."

"Certainly, sir. And where would you like to sit?"

"Anywhere."

The maître d' nodded and led Tom all the way across the dining room, seating him beside one of the broad windows.

"Thanks," Tom said. "You can bring me a cup of coffee."

"Certainly," said the maître d'. "Someone will be right with you."

The coffee came almost immediately, brought by a young man in a short brown coat with a gold vest and a large bow tie, who looked as if he had just been roundly scolded.

"Would you like to see a menu?" he asked.

"No, thank you," Tom said.

The waiter looked surprised. He moved away quickly.

Tom took out Professor Martin's letter and reread it. It was very much as Jennifer's father had described. Beautiful. There was a clearly visible sense of loss in the writing, but no suggestion that the relationship between Martin and Jennifer had ever gone beyond that of a teacher and a gifted, personable student.

"Mr. Jackson?"

Tom looked up. The letter was still in his hands.

"I'm Timothy Martin." He noticed the letter. "Where did you get that?"

"From Jennifer's father." Tom folded the letter and put it in his pocket. "Sit down, Mr. Martin."

Martin sat down, the gray hair around his temples turning silver in a shaft of light. He was handsome in a very masculine sort of way, with a firmly set jaw and dark blue eyes. It was easy to see how a young girl could be attracted to him.

"I can't tell you what Jennifer's death has done to the university," he said.

"What?" Tom asked bluntly.

Martin looked taken aback by the question. "Well, I mean that one of our students—that such a thing could happen."

"How well did you know Jennifer Warren?"

"She was a student of mine, a very good student."

"We've already been through this," Tom said coolly. Something crawled into Martin's eyes—sadness, maybe, but there was anxiety, too. He did not speak.

"I'd like to make this meeting as short as possible," Tom said.

"So would I, believe me."

"Then just answer the questions," Tom said. "It'll be easier that way."

"Fine."

Tom noticed the waiter approaching again and waved him away. "I don't imagine you're in the mood for a late lunch," he said.

"No, of course not." Martin folded his hands together on the table and leaned forward. "I'm going to be totally honest with you, Mr. Jackson, and I hope you will be the same with me."

"I have no reason not to."

"Fine. Ask your questions."

"I know this much," Tom said. "Jennifer Warren was more than just a student."

"You learned that from Jennifer's roommate," Martin said.

Tom did not indicate if that was true or false.

"I know you did, Mr. Jackson," Martin went on. "Because Jennifer told me that she had spoken to Mary about us. And I also know that Mary was the only person on earth who knew."

"Who told me what doesn't matter," Tom said flatly.

"Just so there are no secrets between us."

"Okay," Tom said. "No secrets. At least not on my side."

"There won't be any on mine either," Martin said. "Believe me, Mr. Jackson, I intend to be perfectly frank with you. But you must understand something, too. When I am finished, you will have my reputation—and Jennifer's—in your hands."

"They'll be safe there," Tom said.

"I hope so."

"When did you meet Jennifer?"

"Not quite a year ago."

"What happened?"

"Nothing. At least not for a very long time." Martin sat up. "I know what you think of me at this moment. That I'm some kind of crass individual who preys on young girls while teaching God's place on earth. You are wrong."

"What I think doesn't matter."

"Yes, it does," Martin said. "It matters to me. And I'll tell you this. I am a sinner. I don't deny that. And if all of this finally comes out, I won't deny it then, either. I haven't taught the necessity of individual responsibility all my life for nothing."

Tom nodded.

"And at least in this matter, I am not a hypocrite."

"What was the nature of your relationship to Jennifer Warren, exactly?" Tom asked.

"I fell in love with her," Martin said without hesitation. "I have been married for twenty years, and I love my wife, but I also fell in love with Jennifer. And to tell you the truth, I feel a certain amount of gratification that she also, I believe, fell in love with me."

"I really can't beat around the bush on this," Tom said. "This relationship, this love, was it physical?"

Martin sat back. The fear was gone from his face, but the sadness remained. "Why do you have to know that?" he asked softly.

"Part of my job."

"Then your job is not a very good one." Martin watched Tom uneasily. "You think if you know that about us, what we did together, the physical thing, you think if you know that, you'll know everything. But you won't."

Tom waited.

"All right," Martin said finally. "It was, as you say, physical—on one occasion. It wasn't very successful. We were too aware of what we were doing. It was rather sad, if you want to know the truth. Not at all what you probably think."

"I don't need the details, Mr. Martin," Tom said. "I just need to know what this thing between you and Jennifer was."

"I'm trying to tell you," Martin said. "It was love." He shook his head. "It was wrong, but it was love." He lowered his head for a moment, then looked up. "That one time. The physical time. When it was over, we both cried."

"Was she going to end it, the relationship?"

"We both were."

"But you hadn't already?"

"No," Martin said. "We were going to meet one more time, just to say those things we both thought should be said before it all came to an end."

"Do you have any idea what she was doing in those mountains?" Tom asked.

Martin looked surprised. "Well, of course I do. She had come there to meet me."

"The day she was killed?"

"Yes," Martin said. "We had arranged to meet at this little clearing where we used to go to talk. There was a large stone there, and we would sit on it and look out over the valley."

"So you were up there too?" Tom asked immediately.

"No, I got delayed. Sudden department problem. A student who had to speak to me. I got to the mountains very late, and that's when I saw all the police cars."

"So you didn't go up to the clearing?"

"No, I didn't." Martin's lower lip trembled slightly. "I saw the cars, the flashing lights, and I got this terrible foreboding."

"And what did you do?"

"I turned around and left," Martin said. "I feel very ashamed of that."

"Did you think something had happened to Jennifer?"

"I didn't know. But I knew she was up there, and I knew she would wait until I came. The cars, the police cars—seeing them, I knew that something must have happened, and I sensed, really deep down, that it had happened to Jennifer." He lifted his hands. "I mean, who else would have been up there but her?"

"Donald Olsen was," Tom said.

"Yes, I know that now."

"Did she know him?"

"I don't think so."

"She never mentioned him?"

"No."

"You don't think she could possibly have had any kind of . . . relationship with him?"

Martin smiled sadly. "If you had known Jennifer, you'd know how absurd such an idea is." For a moment he seemed to retreat within himself, his eyes fading slightly as if small lights were turning off behind them.

"I didn't mean to accuse you of anything," Tom said after a moment.

"You don't have to. I've already done that myself."

Tom watched him a moment. There seemed something faintly admirable about a man so careful of his goodness that he could not enjoy a woman, even a pretty woman, even one he loved and who loved him back.

35

He walked to the closet and pulled out the small carpetbag. He could feel the weight of the .44 in it. He placed the bag on his desk, opened it, and drew out the pistol. He turned it over in his hand, his fingers gliding over the walnut stock, then up around the side plate, and finally pinching delicately at the tip of the hammer.

He glanced at the clock on his desk and realized he was slightly behind schedule. He quickly dropped his hand back into the bag, fished around under the coat and hat, and found the small box of cartridges. He placed the pistol on the table, opened the box, and spilled out the cartridges. Their copper cases glinted in the light from the desk lamp. He smiled, picked up one of the cartridges, and ran his finger over the dark, flat nose. Then he picked up the pistol, threw open the loading gate, and inserted the first cartridge. He could see the dark primer at the base of the case where the hammer would hit when he pulled the trigger. The hammer would slam down on that tiny point and then the pistol would explode, the bullet plunging from the barrel at incredible speed, a miracle of efficient, deadly force.

He finished loading the pistol and returned it to the bag, pushing it securely under the coat and hat. Then he picked up the bag and walked out of the office.

Down the hallway he could see the rest of the staff working dutifully at their petty jobs. They were preoccupied with the minuscule details of administration, and their incessant business struck him as entirely contemptible.

"Well, how are you today?" someone said cheerfully as he passed by in the hallway.

He did not reply. The bag was heavy in his hand, and it was as if he were being led by it, guided toward his mission by its hard, certain grasp.

He walked down the stairs and out into the open air. Others bundled themselves up in coats and scarves. He had no need of such things. His purpose gave him all the warmth he needed or would ever need. The brightness of the day itself was a sign of God's approval.

He walked steadily through the crowds that wandered about the walkway or huddled together on the lawn. They were all full of their own emptiness, drowning in their own nonentity.

Suddenly someone called to him from behind. He turned and saw a short, chubby young woman staring at him from behind an enormous pair of thick-rimmed glasses.

"I want to talk to you about Bill," she said.

He looked at her quizzically.

"Bill," she explained. "He came to see you this morning about his work.

So this was the overweight, pathetic object of the young man's affection.

"What is it?" he asked.

"He really does want to do better," she said.

"Then maybe he will," he said coolly.

"He needs a chance," she said. "I don't mean to be pushy or anything, but I just want you to know that he needs a little help."

The weight of the bag seemed to tug at his hand, pulling him away from her.

"He must help himself," he said hurriedly.

"But it's all my fault," she said in a high, plaintive voice.

"Then you take responsibility for it."

"But I don't think it's fair for one mistake to—"

"What you think is fair or unfair means very little to me."

"But if you could just help him a little," she whined, "give him a little extra time, I'm sure he could do everything he needs to."

He could feel the bag pulling him with rough, sudden jerks,

as if it were alive, an angry, impatient animal tugging at its leash.

"Please," the girl begged.

"No."

She looked at him oddly, slanting her head to the right. "Is there something wrong?" she asked. "Are you all right?"

"Get away from me," he hissed.

She drew back and continued to stare at him, her eyes widening fearfully.

He tried to regain control of himself. "I'm not going to discuss this any further," he blurted.

She nodded quickly. "All right, " she said. "Fine." She took a step backward and away from him, as if shrinking away from something dreadful.

He could feel a scream forming in his throat and tried to keep it down.

"I didn't mean to disturb you," the girl said. She took another step backward, moving away from him cautiously.

He felt a terrible wrath sweep over him and tried to keep his body from trembling.

The girl raised one hand toward him, palm out, a gesture of self-defense.

"It's fine," she said. "Really. I'm sorry to have bothered you."

He turned quickly and walked away. He could hear his shoes slapping against the sidewalk, clear and hard as steel on steel. He glanced at his watch and stepped up his pace until he seemed to take flight for a moment, then fall to earth again, then rise above the cement walkway, then land again, hard, almost bouncing, but still moving forward, his hair pushed back across his forehead as his head raced against the stale and motionless air.

36

"How's it going, Carl?" Tom asked as he walked into the squad room.

Redmon was standing at his desk, brushing dust from his pants. "We combed those hills top to bottom, Tom. There's nothing up there."

"The department has to look busy," Tom said offhandedly. "That's what a search like that is all about."

Carl did not like to hear the department criticized. "Well, you never know when you might find something," he said. He finished brushing himself off and sat down behind his desk. "What about you? What have you been up to?"

"I talked to Jennifer Warren's father," Tom said.

Carl looked surprised. "You did? I thought you weren't going to work the Olsen case."

"I changed my mind."

"Well, I talked to the girl's father," Carl said. "If you'd told me you were going over there, I'd have saved you a trip."

"Yeah."

"We're sort of working at cross purposes if we don't stay in touch, Tom."

"Well, it's always a good idea to do a follow-up interrogation," Tom said.

"So? Did you find out anything?"

Tom shook his head. "Not really."

"I didn't think you would," Carl said. "How's his wife, still real upset?"

"So Mr. Warren said."

"Terrible thing, Tom, about that girl," Carl said. "And she was a fine young woman, too."

"Yes, she was."

"Hey, Jackson, get in here!"

Tom turned and saw Chief Philby standing in the doorway of his office, one fist on his hip—a bad sign.

Tom looked at Carl. "What's this about?"

"Beats me."

"Hurry up!" Philby shouted, retreating back into his office.

Tom followed Philby into the office and remained standing as Philby slid in behind his desk.

"I hear you paid a little visit to Jennifer Warren's father," Philby said.

"That's right."

"I had already sent Redmon over there," Philby said irritably. "What's the matter, Tom, you feel you got to double-check what your partner does?"

"No."

"Then why did you go over there?"

"People sometimes remember more the second time around."

Philby did not look satisfied. "What did you say to Mr. Warren, Tom?"

"What do you mean?"

"What do I mean?" Philby asked rhetorically. His voice was thin, angry. "What I mean is this, I just got a call from Mr. Warren that would melt the phone." He folded his arms over his chest. "Now suppose you just tell what happened between you and him."

"I didn't think anything happened between us," Tom said.

"Well, he tells it a little bit different."

"What did he say?"

"He said that you made certain remarks, Tom, like about his daughter, like maybe she wasn't the nice little girl he always thought she was."

"I never said anything like that."

"So he made it all up? That what you're telling me?"

"I asked Mr. Warren if he knew whether or not Jennifer had a boy friend." Tom looked at Philby sternly. "You know, it's an old story. Somethimes the boy friend kills the girl friend."

"And what did he say?"

"That she didn't."

"So what did you do, Tom, laugh in his face?"

"I took it for the truth."

"He got a different feeling about that."

"That's his problem."

Philby leaned forward toward his desk. "No, no, Tom, you get a victim's father upset, that's your problem."

"He upset himself," Tom said. "I can't help what I have to do."

"Did you mention Donald Olsen?"

"Of course I did."

"Why?"

"They died in a remote area only a few hundred feet apart, Charlie." Tom could not keep a thin tone of sarcasm from his voice.

"What did you say about Olsen?"

"I asked if Jennifer knew him."

"Why would she?"

"That's what I wanted to find out. If she knew him, how she knew him, and why."

"And did you find out anything?"

"About what?"

"The girl and Olsen."

"No."

"Did you insinuate that there was something going on between them?"

"No."

"He thought you did."

"I can't help what he thought, Charlie."

Philby shook his head wearily. "You're a fish out of water, Tom. This is Salt Lake, not some New York slum. You can't just walk into a citizen's house and start laying a lot of crap around about his dead daughter."

"I asked routine questions," Tom said.

"This is *not* a routine case," Philby said hotly, "and I want you to get that through your head. A routine murder is somebody blows away the wife or two guys take it to the wire over an extra ace of spades." He picked up a pencil and began tapping it rapidly on the top of his desk. "Now get this, Tom. Jennifer Warren was a white, upper-middle-class college girl with good grades and a spotless reputation. She was a native of Salt Lake with a daddy who loved her and a mother who can't get out of bed she's so broken up about what happened to her little girl. Now do you understand what I'm saying to you, Tom?''

"Yeah."

"There's such a thing as delicacy, Tom," Philby went on. "And you come in with mud on your shoes, start talking about the only daughter like maybe she's not so nice. Don't you understand how that sounds?"

"I didn't tell him his daughter was blowing guys at the bus station, Charlie," Tom said hotly.

Philby's fists clenched together. "Well, maybe it sounded just that way to Mr. Warren. You're not dealing with New York slime anymore, Tom."

"You made that point, Charlie."

"Yeah, and I'll make it again, Tom." Philby said. "And I'll keep making it until you get it through your head that we do things differently in Salt Lake."

Tom nodded impatiently, his eyes casting about the room.

"Okay," Philby said. "Something else. What was the letter you took from Mr. Warren?"

"Just a letter," Tom said. "I read it. It was just a nice letter, like Warren said."

"So he told you the truth about the letter, right, Tom?"

"Yes, he did."

"And so maybe, just maybe, he told the truth about his daughter."

Tom said nothing.

"Maybe she was exactly the kind of girl he thinks she was, right, Tom?"

Tom dropped his hands into his pockets.

"Did you find anything that indicated otherwise?" Philby asked accusingly.

Tom stalled.

"Well, Mr. Big Shot Tough Detective, did you?"

"No," Tom said.

A look of immense satisfaction swept into Philby's face. "I could have told you that from the beginning," he said.

Tom leaned against the door jamb.

"I hope this has taught you a lesson, Tom," Philby said, his voice softening.

"Yeah," Tom said.

"Good," Philby said. "You can go now."

Tom stepped out of Philby's office and walked back to his desk.

Redmon swiveled his chair around to face him. "What was that all about?"

"The girl's father," Tom said. "He called up and said I made some remarks about his daughter, some insinuations."

"Did you?"

"No!"

Carl looked at Tom doubtfully.

"I didn't," Tom said emphatically.

"Okay, Tom," Carl said, but the look remained on his face. "So are you back off the Olsen case again?"

"No." Tom sat down at his desk. "No, I'm not."

"Let me fill you in. I talked to Olsen's secretary, and it's pretty clear that Olsen was set up."

"How do you know?"

"Somebody called him and talked to him for a while. No name, of course. Anyway, the person asked Olsen to meet him in the mountains."

"For what?"

"Nobody knows. Olsen just talked to the guy, and then he told the secretary he was going out to meet him later in the afternoon. He said he was going to the mountains and that he wouldn't be back in the office until the next morning. Right now, that's all we have."

"He didn't mention anything about what the guy said?" Tom asked.

"Not a word."

"Did he look worried, anything like that?"

"Not according to the secretary."

"So that's all you have?"

"That's it for now," Carl said. "I'm going over to talk to his wife." He started to get up.

"There's something you need to know, Carl," Tom said. "But keep it between you and me."

Carl eased himself back down in his chair. "What?"

"I found out what Jennifer Warren was doing in the mountains," Tom said. "And it had nothing to do with Olsen. So it seems to me we're probably dealing with a witness killing here. If Olsen was set up, then Jennifer must have seen it, and that's the reason she was killed."

Carl nodded. "So there was nothing between the girl and Olsen?"

"Nothing at all."

Carl looked relieved. "I didn't think so." For a moment he looked as though he might ask another question, about what Tom had found out about Jennifer Warren. Then his lips tightened.

"I'm going to go check out Mrs. Olsen now," he said. "You want to come along?"

Tom shook his head. "No. I'll talk to the secretary again, maybe look over Olsen's correspondence."

"Good idea." Carl stood up and walked out of the squad room.

For a few moments Tom sat at his desk, his hands rhythmically squeezing the arms of his chair. He was still irritated by his encounter with Philby. He felt like a small boy who had been taken out behind the barn and given a good thrashing. But, in a way, he suspected that Philby was right—he never had really gotten New York out of his system. He thought of Romero again, the little dark slits he had for eyes, the slick black hair pulled tightly across the top of his skull, the sweet smell of his cologne. With Romero you knew what you were up against, and it had felt good, very good, to be up against such men.

He shook his head. Maybe he was working Salt Lake like a shitcan New York neighborhood where everybody shot up, skinned their neighbors, and worked the streets like their own private crap game. New York was the life he had left. Salt Lake was the one he had come to. There was a difference between them, all right, but not one in which he took much comfort.

Shifting in the seat, he felt a sudden pain in his back. Getting chewed out by Philby had tensed every bone in his body. But maybe Philby had been right. Maybe he had handled the case all wrong. Besides, he knew that he was not the best cop in the world. He remembered one time back in New York when he had completely misread everything. From the very beginning, he had fingered the wrong guy, and then spent weeks going up blind alleys trying to nail him. Then Gentry had collared the right one, and he had felt like the victim of a first-class con, one he had pulled on himself. That had put him in a black mood for days, and he remembered spending hours at his desk, gnawing at it, blaming himself because there was no one else to blame. Then one afternoon Gentry had sidled up to his desk, winked, and made the sign of the cross in the hot, stifling air of the precinct house. "Te absolvo, Tom," Gentry had said with a grin. Then they had both begun to laugh, the laughter of the one stirring the laughter of the other until they laughed so loudly and for so long that the little withered junkie in the holding cell began to giggle along with them, his lean, pale hands shaking at his mouth.

37

Betty Carpenter looked up from her desk as Tom entered Olsen's office. She seemed to know immediately that he was from the police. "Can I help you?" she asked.

Tom flashed his identification. "I'm working on the murder of Mr. Olsen."

Betty nodded.

"You were his secretary?"

"Yes."

"I understand Mr. Olsen received a call from someone telling him to meet him in the mountains."

"Yes, he did," Betty's eyes were red-rimmed, and her voice seemed to tremble. "I haven't touched anything in the office. They told me not to. Everything is just the way he left it."

"You took the call?" Tom said. "I mean, from the person who wanted Mr. Olsen to meet him."

"Yes, I did," Betty said.

"What time did it come in?"

"The first one came in at about two."

"There was more than one?"

"Yes." Betty dabbed a small handkerchief at her nose. "Mr. Olsen was out of the office when the first call came. The man who called said he would call again at three."

"And he did?"

"Yes."

"Did you take that call too?"

"Yes."

"What did he say?"

"Only that he wanted to talk to Mr. Olsen."

"It was a man's voice?"

"Yes, definitely."

"Could you describe it? Low? High? Did the man sound nervous? Anything at all."

Betty tilted her head, thinking. "Well, he didn't really sound nervous. But the voice was very low and sort of whispering."

"Did he sound like he was out of breath?"

"No."

"Asthmatic?"

"No, not like that," Betty said. "Just that he was sort of whispering, like he couldn't get his voice out of his mouth. It's hard to describe."

"Did he have any sort of speech impediment? Did he lisp?"

"No," Betty said, "but you know he only said a few words to me."

"What did Mr. Olsen say to you before he left?"

"Just that the man had asked him to meet him in the mountains."

"He didn't tell you anything else about what the man had said?"

"No, that's all."

"Had the man called before, do you think? I mean before the day Mr. Olsen died."

"I don't think so," Betty said.

"Had he had any unusual calls of any kind?"

"He didn't mention any."

"Had anyone unusual been by his office?"

"No."

"You're here all the time?"

"Yes."

Tom nodded. "Had Mr. Olsen mentioned any particular problem he might have been having?"

Betty looked at Tom oddly.

"Any personal problems," Tom explained.

"I don't think he had any," Betty said.

"What about the mail, do you see it?"

"Yes, I screen Mr. Olsen's mail."

"Any crank letters?"

"There are always a few of those."

"Threatening?"

"Oh, no, nothing like that," Betty said. "We don't get letters like that very often."

"But you do get some?"

"Of course."

"Had you gotten any recently?"

Betty shook her head. "No."

"Where do you keep that sort of letter?" Tom asked.

"We file such things with all the other correspondence. We treat it just like any other letter."

"Do you have all of Mr. Olsen's correspondence for the last month or two?"

"Yes."

"Could I see it?"

Betty hesitated for a moment. "I don't want to do anything that might be wrong," she said.

"Well, I'm a policeman," Tom said. "I don't think you'd be doing anything wrong to show me Mr. Olsen's correspondence."

That seemed to satisfy her.

"Of course not," she said. "I don't think anybody would object. Least of all Mr. Olsen."

Betty led Tom into Mr. Olsen's office. "You can sit down at his desk if you want," she said.

"I'll just take this chair over here," Tom said.

"Fine." Betty walked to a file cabinet across the room and pulled two large folders from it.

"This is for the last two months," she said as she walked back to Tom and handed him the folders.

"Thank you."

"I'll be in the outer office if you need me."

Tom nodded. "This won't take long."

Betty smiled. "Take as long as you like. No one uses this office now." Then she left, closing the door behind her.

Tom opened the folder and began reading through the correspondence. Most of it was very businesslike and had to do with the internal workings of the Public Communications Department of the Mormon Church. Other letters contained requests for information about the Church. Letters from students working on dissertations on the history of Mormonism, or from reporters inquiring about the financial holdings of the Church. Carbon copies of Olsen's replies were stapled to each letter, and in every case, Olsen had responded with the utmost courtesy and civility, helping where he could, fending off inquiries where he could not. The man who emerged from this correspondence was a cool professional who seemed to know exactly what he could and could not do in regard to giving out information about the Church. But there were also a few crank letters. One suggested that the Mormon Church was an agent of international communism, another that it was responsible for the water shortage in the West. There were also a few protests against various positions the Church had taken. One letter urged the Church to use its influence to bring legalized gambling to Utah, another requested the Church to end its ban on the consumption of alcoholic beverages, and still another advocated the return to polygamy.

Tom closed the folder for the first month, rubbed his eyes with his fist, then opened the folder containing Olsen's most recent correspondence. It was much the same, and Tom leafed through it almost casually, his eyes glancing up and down the pages, skipping whole paragraphs, getting only the basic sense of the letter, then going on to the next. Again, it was business correspondence, requests for information, mild protests, and an occasional harmless crank.

Then suddenly, as he neared the end of the folder, one letter caught his attention.

Dear Mr. Olsen:

    I write as one who has admired your work for some

time. During the long ordeal of the Harrison affair, your writings were an inspiration. Calmly, and with consummate reason, you argued the position of the faith in regard to this matter. The high level of your commitment, and the clarity of your prose, served to explain our position with great skill to that benighted world which chooses to see us wrongly. It is with the deepest disappointment, then, that I have observed the change that has overtaken you, a change so deep as to constitute betrayal.

> With deep and abiding sadness,
> Wm. B. Thornton

For a moment Tom could only stare at the letter, his eyes riveted to the signature. *William B. Thornton.* Then he stood up and walked into the outer office.

Betty was sitting at the desk. "Finished?" she asked.

"I think so," Tom said. "Do you know anyone by the name of William B. Thornton?"

"No, I don't think so," Betty said.

Tom showed her the letter and waited while she read it.

When she had finished, she looked up. "It's a rather common letter," she said.

"You don't recognize the name?"

She shook her head. "No."

"Have you received any other letters from him?"

"Not that I know of."

"Did Mr. Olsen ever mention knowing such a person?"

"No," Betty said. "Who is he?"

"I don't know," Tom said.

Betty looked at him curiously. "I'm a little confused."

"Listen." Tom said quickly. "Could you go over Mr. Olsen's correspondence as far back as you can and see if this name crops up again?"

"Is it that important?"

"Yes, it is."

"Then I'd be happy to."

"I'd be interested in knowing about anything you find," Tom said.

"I'll let you know immediately," Betty said.

Tom glanced at the notebook. "Would you mind if I took this letter?"

Again, Betty seemed undecided.

"It's official police business," Tom assured her.

"All right, then," Betty said, "if you take full responsibility for returning it."

"I do."

Betty looked down at the newspaper on her desk, then back up at Tom. "Are you working on other cases? I mean the one about Lester Fielding?"

"Yes."

"There's a full-page ad in the paper today," Betty said. "A ten-thousand-dollar reward."

Tom smiled faintly. "I work on salary."

38

The ride into Salt Lake was a long one, and he tried to busy himself with thoughts of what he would do if anyone tried to stop him. He tried to calculate exactly how long it would take him to reach into the bag, search under the coat and hat, draw the pistol from its hiding place, and fire. He ran through the procedure in his mind, clocking each step. He decided it would take him approximately five seconds.

He looked out the window, watching the desert speed by the bus window. This was the land he loved and had come to save, long beautiful stretches of flat ground that rose only gently toward great snowcapped peaks. He took in a deep breath and let it out slowly, concentrating, readying his body for the rigors ahead.

He turned back from the window and closed his eyes. The hum of the engine as he sat at the back of the bus soothed him, and he could feel a wonderful calm descending upon him, as if the fingers of God were at work massaging his back and neck, gently rolling over his forehead, cheeks, and eyes.

After a moment he opened his eyes and stared down the aisle at the other few people who had gotten on the bus. The backs of their heads were perfect targets, little round protuberances that fit the sights of his pistol with extraordinary neatness. He relished his secret power, his knowledge that within a matter of seconds he could turn the interior of the bus into a slaughterhouse if such were his wish. Madmen did such things, killed with monstrous impartiality, their very arbitrariness a perfect symbol of their lunacy. Whatever else they might say of him, he thought, they would never be able to slander him as a random, wanton killer. There would be no blood spattered against bus windows, no bodies sprawled chaotically across the seats or stretched out in the aisle. The secret of power, he thought, resided in correctly choosing when to use it, and against whom.

He leaned back slightly, stretching his long legs under the seat in front of him. Up ahead he could see the bus driver's face reflected in his rearview mirror. He had picked his seat carefully, as he always did. From the angle he chose, the driver could see very little, the back of the seat in front of him shielding almost his entire body from view. He smiled, pleased at his own resourcefulness. Madmen were not resourceful. They plunged ahead, heedless of the consequences, both to themselves and others. Men of mission were different from that. They dealt in plans of immense complexity, acts of extraordinary subtlety, and as a result received rewards of incalculable beauty.

He allowed his head to loll gently left and right with the movement of the bus. There was a beauty in this giving up of self to forces larger than the world, to forces that were themselves the world's Creator. Part of the mission was to understand fully one's place in this larger scheme of creation. Small minds could not do this, and even if they could, they lacked the will to act on their understanding. He closed his eyes again, and it seemed he was floating on a great cushion of shining air. The rumble of the bus became the low, steady hum of a great cathedral organ, and he tried to lose himself in the majesty of its sound. He imagined that he had already completed his mission and been taken up to the altar of God, a gleaming example of man's possibilities. He reveled in the idea of his ascension and glorification, and for a moment he wondered if this might not be the sin of pride. He shook his head gently, his eyes still closed. No, not the sin of pride, but only the recognition that there were vast gradations in the achievements of men on this earth and that these differences would ultimately be realized and rewarded. That was nothing more than a sense of justice that was truly divine.

He opened his eyes. He could see Salt Lake in the distance, the ZCMI tower rising above the smaller buildings of the city like a white obelisk. The blue of late afternoon was beginning to cover the city like a thin Arabian veil, and this lovely, gentle blueness suggested the eternal nature of God's protection. Salt Lake was still His capital on earth, still the city raised by His noble, chosen people. All that this people had done to betray Him, all the evil that they had done, all of this had still not finally separated them from God. Even in their fallen state they retained the favor of their Creator, and as he watched the city come within view, he felt the power, the naked, consummate power of His abiding love.

39

Tom had only casually followed the long, tortuous confrontation between Barbara Harrison and the Mormon Church which Thornton had mentioned in his letter to Donald Olsen. It had raged for months, filling the Salt Lake newspapers with column after column of charges and countercharges. For a time it had become the hottest issue in the city, and hearing it spoken of continually in the squad room and on the streets had only served to distance Tom further from his surroundings, to reinforce his alienation. Finally the controversy had ended with Mrs. Harrison's excommunication, and then the city seemed to relax again, sinking into its own unruffled calm.

Mrs. Harrison's picture had been in the paper many times, but when she opened the door, Tom hardly recognized her. She no longer had the pert, slightly impish look that had made her appear at times to be engaged in a great prank, rather than what was for her a profound moral battle.

"Who are you?" she asked immediately through a crack in the door.

Tom pulled his identification from his pocket and showed it to her. "I'm sorry to bother you," he said, "but it's important."

Mrs. Harrison watched him suspiciously, her light blue eyes flashing in the slant of sun that crossed her face. "I don't like to let strangers into my house," she said softly.

"You can call downtown to verify who I am," Tom said. "I'll wait here on the porch until you're satisfied."

"All right," Mrs. Harrison said quickly. She closed the door, and Tom could hear her jangling chains and throwing dead bolts behind it. He turned toward the street, glancing left and right. It was a nice, tidy neighborhood, one of those places that stays so quiet you wonder if anything left around is still alive. In New York the streets had been filled with wild, chaotic, and unceasing noise, and part of what Tom had liked at first about Salt Lake was the quiet. Now this same silence made him nervous, and sometimes he lay in his bed hoping for something to rattle unexplainably outside his window.

After a moment he heard the chains and bolts again. Then the door opened, and he could see Mrs. Harrison plainly. She was smaller than he had imagined, a little woman bound tightly together, as if by invisible ropes.

"I checked on you," she said.

"And?"

"I guess it's okay for you to come in."

She stepped back and opened the door all the way.

Tom walked into the foyer. The house was very dark, the shades drawn down over the windows like the eyelids of the dead. The air inside was a smokeless gray.

"I don't have any real idea what this is about," Mrs. Harrison said. She did not close the door or move away from it. Instead, she stood rigidly in place, her hand holding tightly to the door as if it were a weapon.

"I just have a few questions," Tom said. "I won't stay here long."

"All right." Mrs. Harrison nodded toward the living room off to the right. "You can have a seat in there."

Tom walked into the living room and sat down. Mrs. Harrison continued standing at the door, watching him.

Tom pulled his notebook from his coat pocket. "I'll write down a few answers, if you don't mind," he said.

Mrs. Harrison seemed somehow reassured by the open notepad. She closed the door, walked into the living room, and sat down on a small sofa opposite Tom.

"You're sort of a famous person here in Salt Lake," Tom said, trying to relax her by bringing a bit of lightness to his voice.

Mrs. Harrison stared at him pleasurelessly.

Tom drew the small smile from his lips. He knew that he had to relax her, or the whole interrogation would be one long sparring match.

"I'm not a Mormon," he said.

A tiny light seemed to come on behind Mrs. Harrison's eyes. "You're not?"

Tom shook his head. "And if it matters to you, Mrs. Harrison," he said, "during that whole big deal with the Church—I mean, for what it's worth, I was more or less on your side."

Mrs. Harrison did not seem moved.

"Well, it wouldn't have mattered to you anyway, would it," she said, "since you have no interest in the Church?"

"I guess not," Tom said.

Mrs. Harrison closed her eyes slowly, and it looked to Tom as though all the passion of the previous battle had been scooped out of her, like the insides of an animal, and she was left now without anything, a flap of skin drying on the desert floor.

When Mrs. Harrison opened her eyes again, they seemed to have aged beneath the lids, to have grown more weary. She took a long, deep breath and folded her hands in her lap.

"What is it you want with me?" she asked. "On the telephone just now, they said something about a murder."

Tom drew a pencil from his pocket and held it poised over the open notebook. "Did they say which one?" Tom asked.

"Well, no, but I can only assume this has to do with Donald Olsen."

"Why do you assume that, Mrs. Harrison?"

"Well, I suppose Mr. Olsen could be thought of as an enemy of mine."

"Was he?"

"I barely knew him."

"Well, it's not—"

"But what I knew, I respected," Mrs. Harrison interrupted. "He was a good man. He was on my side about many things. He was socially responsible. He had opposed the MX missile, and he supported the admission of blacks into the Church."

How did he stand on your own problem?" Tom asked.

"Problem?"

"With the Church."

"He supported my excommunication," Mrs. Harrison said, "but I never held that against him." She stared evenly at Tom. "I need hardly add that I had nothing to do with his death."

"I wasn't thinking of you as a suspect."

Mrs. Harrison said nothing. She curled one of her hands into the fist of the other and continued to stare determinedly into Tom's eyes.

"Did you think I was thinking of you as a suspect?" Tom asked.

"Mr. Olsen wrote approvingly of my excommunication," Mrs. Harrison said. "Some people might think that a motive. Certain minds move in that sort of direction."

"Mine doesn't," Tom said. "And besides, Mr. Olsen was killed very brutally. Frankly, you don't look strong enough for that."

"Really? And could I have hired someone to do it for me?"

"I don't think so."

"Why not?"

"Experience," Tom said, and left it at that.

"Lester Fielding was killed too," Mrs. Harrison said matter-of-factly, "and he was on the other side of the question."

"Yes, he was."

"You knew that?"

"I read the piece he did about you," Tom said. "Very favorable."

"That was quite some time ago."

"I only read it a couple days ago. I'm also working on his case."

"Well, at least I don't suppose I'm a suspect in that one," Mrs. Harrison said.

"No, you're not," Tom said. "I'm not even here about Fielding."

"Olsen, then?'

"Yes."

"What about him?"

"I've been going through his correspondence." Tom pulled the letter from his coat pocket. "I found this."

Mrs. Harrison looked at the letter but said nothing.

"It's about you." Tom lifted the letter toward her. "Read it."

Mrs. Harrison took the letter and read it carefully. "This is very mild, as far as it concerns me," she said.

"Yes, I guess it is."

"Nothing like some of the letters I received during that other time." A small, bitter smile rose on her lips. "Crude letters. Hateful. Threatening. Obscene." For a moment she seemed to retreat into herself. "Very painful. I could show you letters that would—"

"Would what?"

"It doesn't matter," Mrs. Harrison said stiffly.

"What did you do with those letters?" Tom asked.

"I turned them over to the police."

"Who did you give them to?"

"A fat man, very unkempt," Mrs. Harrison said. "I don't remember his name."

"Baxter?"

"Yes, that's it. He never got back in touch with me."

"Did he give them back?"

Mrs. Harrison shook her head. "No. He still has them, I suppose. They are not the sort of things I care about having returned to me."

Tom nodded. "Did you notice the signature on that letter?" he asked.

Mrs. Harrison looked down at the letter. "William B. Thornton."

"Have you ever heard that name before?"

"No."

"You're sure?"

"I know of no such person," Mrs. Harrison said firmly.

"Did you get any letters from anyone by that name?"

"I might have," Mrs. Harrison said. "I didn't memorize the names."

"It's very important."

"You'll have to look at the letters yourself," Mrs. Harrison said.

"I will," Tom said, "but I'd like for you to try to think if you have ever heard that name."

"I've tried, and I can tell that that name, Thornton, means nothing whatever to me."

"Do you live alone, Mrs. Harrison?" Tom asked.

Mrs. Harrison looked at Tom curiously. "Why do you want to know?"

"Well, the man who killed Olsen, we don't know what he might do."

"Come after me?"

"It's just a thought. It doesn't hurt to be careful."

"Well, for your information," Mrs. Harrison said, "my husband divorced me not long after my excommunication. He also gained custody of my children. So, I suppose you could say that I live alone."

There was a certain hardness about her, a resolution, that Tom admired. "I'm sorry," he said.

Mrs. Harrison arched one eyebrow. "About what? My sacrifice?"

"I don't know about sacrifice, but I'm sorry you have to live alone."

Mrs. Harrison's face softened somewhat. "People get the wrong idea about me," she said. "When the trouble was going on, and for some time after that, people would come with their hearts bleeding for me. They'd come filled with a ridiculous admiration. They expected some sort of flaming feminist." She smiled. "And what did they get for all their effort and support? A little Mormon wife and mother who no longer has her husband or her children. You may be sure that such people went away disappointed.''

"I'm sorry about that, too.''

"Fielding,'' Mrs. Harrison said. "Now he was different.''

"In what way?''

Mrs. Harrison shook her head slightly. "You wouldn't understand.''

"Why not?''

"Because you're not one of us. But let me tell you about Lester Fielding anyway. Maybe he changed a little later. His writing certainly did. But let me tell you about Mr. Fielding before that happened. Early on he wrote that favorable article about me, the one you read. Then all the trouble kept increasing, and in the end I was excommunicated. Well, the day after that, Lester Fielding came by my house, and he put my hand in his and he said, 'Mrs. Harrison, because of you, I will always know what conscience is.' '' Tears welled up in her eyes. "Now that was a man to be remembered.''

"Yes,'' Tom said.

"The other people,'' Mrs. Harrison went on, "the people like you, from the outside, they just disappeared. They were secularists. They never cared about the faith. And when the trouble was over, they vanished. They went on to the next cause.'' She turned and glanced at one of the shaded windows. "But my people, the ones of my faith, my brothers and sisters in the Church, they cared more about me, before and after the trouble, than any of those others.'' She lowered her eyes to her hands. "They are right outside my window. And in a sense, they want nothing more to do with me.'' She looked up at Tom. "But I can tell you this. They still pray for me. They still do that. They feel the trouble in my soul. Who else does? Do any of those people who flew in to sing my praises? No.''

Tom closed his notebook. He had written nothing. "Thank you for your time,'' he said. "I hope everything works out for you.''

"It already has,'' Mrs. Harrison said. "We're all part of a plan, a great plan. We're all part of it. You. Me. Everyone.''

"Maybe so,'' Tom said. .

"You'll see.'' Tom got up, walked to the door, then opened it and went out to his car. As he pulled away, he saw Mrs. Harrison standing in the open doorway, watching him. One part of the plan, he thought, keeping a very close eye on another.

40

Tom found Baxter standing at a urinal in the station men's room. "I just had a talk with Barbara Harrison," he said.

"I'm pissing, Tom. You mind?"

Tom stepped back slightly and waited.

Baxter shook his penis, pushed it back into his pants, then turned toward Tom. "Now, what were you saying?"

"I said I had a talk with Barbara Harrison a few minutes ago."

Baxter zipped up his fly. "So?"

"It was about those letters."

Baxter moved over to the sink, turned on the water, and began washing his hands. "You say Harrison, huh?"

"Yeah."

"Why you working that case, Tom?" Baxter splashed water up to the elbows of both arms.

"It has to do with the Olsen thing."

Baxter glanced up, leveling his eyes on Tom. "I heard you took yourself off that one."

"I'm back on it."

"Philby make you?"

"No."

Baxter nodded and turned back toward the sink. "So what's our friend Harrison got to do with our friend Olsen?"

"Maybe nothing," Tom said. "That's why I wanted to ask you about the letters."

Baxter turned off the water, pulled two paper towels from the rack above the sink, and began drying his hands.

"Mrs. Harrison said there were some very mean threats in the letters," Tom said.

"There were," Baxter said casually. "What would you expect? She made a spectacle of herself."

"You still have the letters?"

"Yeah." Baxter dropped the towels into a basket under the sink. "Tell you the truth, Tom, that was a shitty thing to work. I may not be the best cop in the fucking world, but I'm Homicide, and I don't like pulling double duty. Shit, a rookie could have handled those letters, but Philby pulled my chain, and I had to hustle over to old lady Harrison's." He grinned mischievously. "I'm beginning to think Philby don't like me, you know?"

"Did you check them out, the threats?"

Baxter's lips curled down. "Well, it ain't like there's much to check out. Where you been all your life, Tom? People don't put their addresses on that kind of crap."

"Where are they?"

"The letters?"

"Yeah."

"My desk."

"I'd like to see them."

"Be my guest," Baxter said indifferently. "Bottom drawer. Left-hand side. I'll be in the lounge if you need me."

Tom walked out of the men's room and down the hallway to Baxter's desk. He sat down in Baxter's chair, pulled out the left bottom drawer, and withdrew a stack of letters. They were all sizes and colors. Some were written in a neat hand, some in a scrawl. Some were typed, some carefully printed. But they all had one thing in common—a raging desire to wound Barbara Harrison by turning language into a weapon of attack. They slashed at her with the crudest vulgarities and insults. And reading them, Tom could not imagine the pain of receiving such things in the morning mail, along with the routine bills and advertisements, and knowing that there were people in the world who felt this way about you, and that these same people could probably walk into their local sporting-goods store and buy a Walther P-38 and a neat little box of nine-millimeter slugs.

After reading the last letter, Tom replaced the stack and started to get up.

"Find anything?" Baxter asked, as he walked up to the desk.

"Not much."

"Goofballs. I've seen this kind of crap a million times. You gotta be a real dim bulb to write that kind of shit."

Tom nodded.

"Real fuckheads, you ask me," Baxter went on. "They read something in the newspaper and, bingo, fire off some loonytune letter to somebody they don't even know."

"What kind of work did you do on the letters, Ralph?"

"I read them," Baxter said, "then I went to the toilet."

"You didn't check anything out?"

"What could I do? All I had to go on was postmarks. None of them were from Salt Lake. The South. The East. Places like that." He looked at Tom curiously. "What's your angle on this?"

"I was looking through Olsen's correspondence," Tom said, "and I found a letter to him about Barbara Harrison."

"Threatening letter?"

"Not exactly."

Baxter smiled. "So what's the point?"

"The letter, the one to Olsen, it was signed William B. Thornton."

Baxter stared at Tom expressionlessly.

"That name means nothing to you, Ralph?"

Baxter scratched his chin. "Maybe my poor old mind is weaseling out on me, Tom."

"You remember that Jones killing? The one at the Paradise?"

"Sure."

"Well, the guy who checked into Room 17, where Jones was killed, he signed the motel register William B. Thornton."

Tom could hear Baxter's breath suck in.

"Now that looks like a connection to me," Tom added.

Baxter nodded. "Maybe."

"The address in the motel register was a phony," Tom went on, "and there was no address at all on the letter to Olsen."

Baxter smiled knowingly. "You got a problem, Tom."

"What do you mean?"

"You got a connection, a murder connection, between a dirty little whore and a big shot in the Mormon Church."

"Yeah."

"And that's not all, either. What about that girl got wasted the same time as our friend Olsen?"

"She didn't even know Olsen," Tom said.

"Yeah?" Baxter said unbelievingly. "How do you know?"

"I did a little work."

"Maybe you didn't do enough."

"Well, what makes you think there was something between Olsen and the girl?"

"Birds and the bees, Tom," Baxter said. "And another thing, we've all been told to keep our fucking mouths shut about anything cropping up about Olsen and the girl."

"I know."

"Now why do you think they're doing that, Tom?"

"To protect both of them," Tom said.

Baxter grinned. "Or maybe they already know something we don't know, and are trying to make sure we never know it."

"I don't think so."

Baxter's smile widened. "You're a trusting soul, Tom."

A trusting soul, Tom thought, and his eyes were up against the car window again, and the two men were staring at each other beneath the marquee of the St. Mark's Theater, their faces slowly coming clear.

41

The bus was almost empty by the time it pulled onto Highland Drive. Up ahead he could see the corner of Highland Drive and Murphy's Lane. It was time to act, and he could feel energy building in his muscles. He opened the bag, took out the coat, and slipped it on, his eyes watching the face of the bus driver in the mirror. Then he pulled out the hat and placed it on his head, drawing the brim low over his forehead, shielding his eyes.

There would come a time when it would no longer matter who recognized him, but until that moment it was necessary for him to conceal himself. He took the mustache from the bag and pressed it in place. Now, he thought. The time is at hand.

He stood up, walked to the side entrance, and waited for the bus to pull over to the curb at the corner of Murphy's Lane and Highland Drive. When the door opened, he hopped out onto the sidewalk and began walking up Murphy's Lane. He could see the house only a hundred yards up the street, and the sight filled him with a strange joy.

He looked around. The streets were deserted, and that pleased him immeasurably. It seemed that they had been swept clean for his coming. Then he heard a sound behind him, a child's voice. He turned quickly and saw a newsboy pedaling in his direction. He laughed to himself, amused at his own nervousness.

The boy passed quickly, and he moved on up the street at a steady pace. The weight of the .44 now seemed very slight, as if it were moving without his help, as if it had a momentum of its own.

The house was getting nearer now, moving toward him with each stride. Finally he was there. He stopped and turned toward the house. It seemed to pulse and grow red as he stared at it.

He walked to the door and knocked lightly. He waited for a moment, then knocked again. Then he pulled the bag toward him, pushed one hand into it, and took hold of the pistol.

The door opened.

The man standing in the doorway looked at him curiously for a moment, then a smile broke across his face. "Well, now, what are you made up for?" he asked with a laugh.

"How do I look?"

"I never figured you for a costume party," the man said. He swung open the door. "Come on in. What are you doing out this way?"

He stepped inside and waited for the man to close the door.

"Annie would love to see you." The man shook his head, chuckling.

He felt his hand grip the pistol, his finger edge over onto the trigger. "Close the door," he said.

The man closed the door and stepped in front of him, shaking his head. "Annie would get such a kick out of this," he said, "but she's not here."

"I know," he said. He pulled the hammer and heard the click as it fell into place, a small, muffled beat.

"Come into the kitchen," the man said cheerfully. "I'll fix you a lemonade." He looked at him affectionately. "Missed seeing you at the library lately."

"Yes," he said.

The man's eyes moved up and down his body. "You got to tell me what you're doing in that getup," he said, moving toward the kitchen. "Come in here, we'll have a little refreshment."

He drew out the pistol and let the bag fall to the floor beside his feet.

"Ben," he said.

The man turned. "Good grief, what a blunderbuss! Where'd you get that thing?"

"From Heaven," he said, and fired.

The man's body flew backward and slammed into the rear wall of the living room, then collapsed to the floor.

The recoil of the pistol was still rushing up and down his arm when he heard a whimper to his right. He turned and saw the two boys standing frozen down the hallway. For a moment he felt a terrible confusion. He knew that the children had been scheduled for day camp and that Ben's wife, Annie, was supposed to be with them. But there they were in the hall, staring at him, and for the briefest instant he did not know what to do. Then the pistol jerked forward and he saw the barrel press down toward them. He fired, and the taller boy plunged backward, lifted into midair, one of his shoes flying toward the ceiling. The other boy turned, but it was as if he were struck in time, his movements slow, unreal, a grinding, lethargic dance. And the barrel came down again while he could still feel the jarring in his arm, and he fired again as the boy turned to run, and the explosion hit him in the neck and seemed to tear up toward the back of his head like a red scarf suddenly jerked up from behind his collar, and the small body tumbled forward and slid down across the carpet.

Then there was only a silence that seemed to last forever while he stood in place, staring down the hallway at the sprawled, contorted bodies, and he looked down at the pistol and it seemed to shake itself from his hand and fall away from him very slowly, like a stone falling into the valley of the night.

42

"How are you doing, Harry?" Tom said, walking into Epstein's room.

Epstein closed his eyes slowly, then opened them, a gesture of resignation.

"They took that fucking tube out of my dick," Epstein said. "That's an improvement, I guess."

Tom pulled a chair up near Epstein's bed and sat down. "Need anything?"

"You got maybe a couple of shots from the Fountain of Youth?" Epstein said. "You know, I was just remembering New York." He smiled. "I met Meyer Lansky, the gangster, once, Tom, did you know that?"

"No."

"I was strictly small-time," Epstein said, "and Lansky was king of the hill, but I met him. I was running booze, bringing in a full truck. It was this garage in lower Manhattan. That's where I met him. Lansky. He happened to be hanging around the garage when me and Petie pulled the truck in."

"Is that right?"

"Oh, yeah," Epstein said. "Well, me and Petie pulled in. Petie's a spade. Big nose, bigger than mine. He wasn't so fucking black, you'd figure him for one of my own."

"Lansky," Tom said.

"Yeah, Lansky. He watched the truck pull in. Dressed real nice, Lansky. Nice overcoat. Had his hand stuck way down in the pockets. Probably got two thirty-eights down there."

"And?"

"Well, Lansky gives us a real close look-over. He don't say nothing. Just keeps those two little eyes on us. He liked to stare people down, I think. Liked to scare the shit out of them. Way he got his kicks. He was a short little fucker. Maybe he was mean from that, who knows."

"And he was staring at you. You and Petie."

"Staring a hole right through us," Epstein said. "So we start to open up the back of the truck, and Lansky steps around to keep an eye on what's going on. Makes me nervous, that scumbag. But I just keep at what I'm doing, and Petie, he does the same thing." He glanced at a small yellow plastic cup on the table beside his bed. "Pour me some water, will you, Tom?"

Tom stood up, poured the water, and handed it to Epstein.

Epstein gulped down a couple of swallows, then turned his head away. "Okay, that's enough. I don't want to drown myself."

Tom placed the cup back on the table.

"Anyway," Epstein went on, "Lansky, he keeps staring at us. Finally he comes over to me. He says, 'Hey, what's your name, shithead?' I tell him. He says, 'Tell the shine to go play with himself.' " Epstein laughed. "Petie hears this, he thinks maybe he's going down for the count. He starts sort of shaking, so I calm him down. I tell him Mr. Lansky would like him to disappear for a little while. I point to the other side of the garage. 'Over there,' I tell him. Well, Petie, he don't care to argue, you know? He goes right where I tell him and that's where he fucking stays."

Tom nodded.

"So then Lansky turns to me," Epstein continued. "He says, 'So, schmuck, you a Jew?' I say that's right. He says, 'You know this neighborhood?' I say yeah, I know it a little. He says, 'You know who I am?' I nod my head. Who's he supposed to fucking be? The king of Siam?" He laughed. "Then you know what the mean-faced bastard says, Tom?"

Tom shook his head.

"He looks me right in the eye, Lansky does, and he says, 'I want a salt bagel.' " Epstein's eyes widened. "Jesus Christ! Fucking Meyer Lansky wants a goddamn salt bagel. What am I supposed to do, Tom? I mean, I ain't got one on me. Shit, I ain't even got no heat to speak of.''

"So what'd you do?" Tom asked.

"I just looked at the fuck," Epstein said. "Christ's sake, it's after midnight. Maybe two in the morning. Where the hell can I get a goddamn bagel that time of day?" He stopped and took a deep breath. "So I tell Lansky there's a little mom-and-pop bakery down the street. Maybe two blocks. But I tell him the truth, it ain't open." He stopped again, pausing for effect. "And what do you think Lansky says? He winks, and he says, 'Don't worry, fuckhead, I'll open it.' ''

Epstein laughed loudly. "Fucking guy, he can do what he wants whenever he wants to do it. That's the point he's making, see? That I'm a total shit, and he, Lansky, he's got the world by the balls.''

Tom laughed lightly.

"True story, swear to God," Epstein said.

"Did you ever see him again?"

"Who?"

"Lansky."

"Sure," Epstein said. "Plenty of times. But he never said another word to me." He chuckled. "Those other times, I guess he didn't want a bagel.''

Tom smiled. "Hey, Harry, one thing you never told me. How'd you end up in Salt Lake?"

"Lots of detours, my friend," Epstein said. "A couple through the federal penitentiary.''

"Really?"

"Is this the face of a liar?"

"I figured you for Florida. Las Vegas, maybe."

"I can't stand Florida," Epstein said. "Bunch of old farts sitting around showing pictures of their fucking grandchildren." He shivered. "Waiting to die, that's what they're doing.''

"But why Salt Lake?"

Epstein grinned. "They don't have much crime here," he said. "I don't want to go out staring at some fucker with a blade wants my lunch money.''

"You mean that? That's the real reason?"

"Why else would I come here?"

Tom walked to the window. The sky was growing dark, outlining the mountains in black. "Sometimes I think maybe I'll leave Salt Lake," he said. He turned toward Epstein. "You ever think of doing that?"

"Never," Epstein said. "They'll bury me right here. Maybe I'll have a Jewish ceremony with a pink-cheeked rabbi telling the people what a swell guy I was. What's in his mind while he's saying all this bullshit, that he'll keep to himself."

"Sometimes you feel like making a change."

"So make it," Epstein said. "Where you want to go, back to New York?"

"No."

"Hawaii. It's nice there."

Tom shook his head. "Somewhere away from everything. Far away. In the country, maybe. A little house sitting in a pine forest."

"Places like that," Epstein said, "they just exist in people's minds."

"You think so?"

"That's been my experience."

Tom stepped away from the window and walked to the door. "Take it easy, Harry," he said. "I'll drop back in a few days."

"Sure," Epstein said. He did not turn his eyes from the ceiling. "Sure." He lifted his arm. "You run short of tubes, let me know. I got extras cheap."

Tom smiled and walked out of the room. Outside the hospital the air was cool, and he pulled his coat around himself tightly. He could see the mountains far away, beautiful in the dark blue air, the snowcaps raised up like offerings to the slowly drifting clouds.

He got into his car but did not put the key into the ignition. For a moment he thought of Phyllis and wondered what she was doing now, at this moment, in Denver. Then he thought of Gentry, pushed the thought away, and remembered his mother, the way she had knelt beside her bed, going through the catechism: *How many persons are there in the Godhead? Three. How do we know this to be true? It is a mystery.* And not the only one, Tom thought. He placed the key in the ignition, glancing at his face in the mirror the way he had that afternoon so long ago, when the mist had gathered on the glass and he had wiped it away with his hand and had seen them there, clearly, Romero standing rigidly under the marquee, his hand stretched out with a small, yellow envelope, and the other hand moving up to take it, old and slightly trembling. Gentry's.

Tom hit the ignition, his eyes still staring at his own face in the glass, and it seemed to him that something terrible and inexpressible was moving toward him, had always been moving toward him, slowly, but irresistibly, as one is pressed to death by stone.

43

Tom had almost arrived at his apartment when the call came in about a murder on Murphy's Lane. He turned the car around immediately and headed for the address that had been given to him over the police radio. He expected to be one of the first people there, but as he cruised down Murphy's Lane he could see ambulances and squad cars lined up on both sides of the street.

He had to park some distance from the house, inching his way in between a black-and-white and a plain green Chevrolet, which had been assigned to Baxter for as long as he could remember.

After he had parked, Tom got out of the car and walked toward the house, passing knots of people every few yards, mostly neighbors who stood about whispering to each other or simply staring, stricken, at the neat little house near the middle of the block, the one in which, according to the dispatcher, one or more persons now lay dead.

Tom nodded to a uniformed patrolman who stood at the end of the walkway, his body silhouetted by the lighted house. ''What we got, exactly?'' he asked.

The patrolman recognized Tom, started to smile reflexively, then drew his lips together. "Three dead."

"Who?"

"A father and two children."

"Father do it?"

The patrolman looked shocked. "I don't think so. I mean, nobody said anything like that."

"Redmon here yet?"

The patrolman shook his head. "I haven't seen him."

"Okay." Tom turned and began walking toward the house. Halfway up the walk, he saw Philby stagger out the front door and onto the small porch. He slumped against one of the wooden pillars and wiped his face with a handkerchief.

"Multiple," Tom said as he approached the porch.

Philby stuffed the handkerchief in his coat pocket and stared palely at Tom. "This is the worst thing I've ever seen, the absolute worst thing." He clumped down the stairs and stood next to Tom. "What's happening to this town?"

Tom said nothing.

"In there," Philby said, "it's terrible."

"Three people," Tom said.

"Yeah. A father and his two kids, his two sons."

"Carl on his way?" Tom asked.

"Yes, he is." Philby glanced to the right as a patrol car slowly passed the house. "Baxter's here already, and Bemis from the coroner's office." His eyes snapped back to Tom. "He used a magnum on them. Little boys. Four and five years old. You can imagine, Tom."

"Who found the bodies?"

"A neighbor," Philby said. "The woman who lives next door. She'd been helping Ben out because both boys were a little sick."

"Ben?"

"Ben Parker."

"Who's that?"

"The man inside," Philby said sadly. "The father."

"You knew him?"

"We went to the same ward," Philby said. "I live only a few blocks from here."

"What happened in there couldn't be a murder, then a suicide, could it?"

"Not a chance." Philby looked at Tom assuredly. "We know now, Tom. We know what it is."

"What?"

"The motive," Philby said. "For Olsen, and Ben. Even for Fielding."

Tom waited.

"You haven't guessed it yet?" Philby asked. "With Parker, it's all very clear now. What we're dealing with is someone with a terrible grudge against the Church."

Tom said nothing.

"An enemy of the Church," Philby went on, "that's what this is all about. Olsen and Parker were both very prominent in the Church. Fielding wrote articles in favor of Church positions and never hid his connection to the Saints. It's all in his mind, don't you see, Tom? He hates the Saints. He's willing to do anything to destroy us."

"What about physical evidence?"

"It looks like a magnum for Fielding and Parker," Philby said.

"That's all?"

"So far." Philby's face tightened fiercely. "But we'll find the rest. We'll find everything we need." He glanced back toward the house. "I want that place turned upside down, Tom. I want it gone over like nothing's ever been gone over in Salt Lake before."

Tom nodded hesitantly.

"I want you and Carl to nail this maniac real quick, Tom," Philby said in a high, raging voice. "I want him burned. You understand me?"

"We'll do our best," Tom said quietly.

"Do better than that," Philby said. Then he turned and rushed down the walkway to his car, got in it, and slammed the door with such force that the sound reverberated down the quiet street like a pistol shot.

Tom turned and walked into the house. Inside, it was like every other murder scene he had ever visited, except that it was oddly quiet, the men carrying out their various duties with silent determination.

Bemis was standing a few feet away from the front door, scribbling notes in a tattered notebook.

"How you doing?" Tom said as he walked up to him.

"How do you think?" Bemis said without looking up from his pencil.

"Philby said a magnum."

"Forty-four, probably." Bemis looked up at Tom. "Single shot in each case. Just the heads." He glanced down the hallway toward an open doorway. "Nothing left of the heads."

"Anything else?"

"I don't see any sign of sexual molestation," Bemis said. "And no odd cuts or bruises."

"Just clean kills."

Bemis squinted. "You have an ugly way of putting things, Tom."

"Bodies still here?"

"Yeah. In the back bedroom. The kid's room, I guess."

Tom looked toward the doorway. A slant of hard white light sliced through it.

"Go take a look if you got the stomach, Tom," Bemis said. "They're still in there. Stacked up against the wall. Baxter will show them to you."

"Stacked?"

"That's right. Very neatly. And covered with a nice clean sheet."

"They weren't killed that way," Tom said.

"Of course not."

"How?"

"Looks like Ben was killed in the living room here," Bemis said. "You got a blood pattern against the wall about six feet high. The boys were killed in the hallway, blood all over the carpet there. Then they were all taken back into the bedroom, stacked up, and covered with a sheet."

Tom's eyes drifted over toward the back wall of the living room. "I don't see any blood pattern," he said.

"Only traces," Bemis said. "Killer tried to wash it off. Tried to clean up the hallway carpet, too, but I guess he got short of time. He didn't do a very good job."

Looking closely now, Tom could see a circular pink pattern

on the far wall. He turned his eyes back to Bemis. "Anything else?"

"Not yet. If you want to see the bodies, you'd better get on back there. The guys'll be bringing them out soon. I'll do the autopsies tonight. Maybe I'll have something for you in the morning."

"Okay. Let me know as soon as you find anything."

"Are you kidding?" Bemis said. "We're all hell-bent on this one."

Tom nodded, then walked back to the bedroom. He saw a steady stream of bluish smoke coming out of it. Baxter's cigar.

"Hey, Tom," Baxter said as Tom entered the room. He nodded toward the bodies. "Want to see them? Lab guys want them out of here real quick."

The two men from the coroner's office glanced up at Tom.

"Let me have a look," he said to the one nearest him.

The man threw back the sheet, turning his own eyes away as he did so.

Baxter looked at Tom solemnly. "Hard to get used to kids, ain't it?"

Tom could see Tina Rodriguez in his mind, the small white socks stained red.

"Yeah." He turned to the man who knelt beside the bodies. "Okay," he said, "you can take them out."

The two men lifted the first body, the small one, onto the stretcher, and carried it out of the room.

"Things are getting out of hand here in Salt Lake," Baxter said.

"Yeah."

"They're going to have to add a few guys to the squad, shit like this keeps happening."

Tom's eyes drifted back to the clean white sheet. One small foot extended out the bottom of it, a dollop of blood on the tip of the tennis shoe.

"This place is beginning to look like L.A. on a hot Saturday night," Baxter added.

Tom looked at him. "Don't you ever shut up?"

Baxter's mouth closed tightly.

Tom turned quickly and walked out of the room and down

the hallway, jostling the two men from the coroner's office on their way back for the remaining two bodies.

Outside on the porch, he took a deep breath and let it out slowly. The night was very clear, and he could see an enormous array of stars overhead. The sky had been like that the night he met Gentry in the park. "You saw that little girl, Tina," he had said, and Gentry's face seemed to fall away from him, dissolving into the darkness.

"Sorry I'm late," Carl said as he stepped up onto the porch beside Tom. "I was at a ward meeting. I didn't get the call right away."

"Things are getting strange, Carl."

"I heard." Carl looked drained, his arms dropping lifelessly at his sides. "What are we going to do, my friend?"

Tom shoved his hands into his pockets, his fingers digging at the cloth. "I don't know. Philby talk to you?"

"He caught me on the way over," Carl said. "Pulled his car over and started yelling out the window."

"He's pretty strung out on this one."

"He was talking about some crazy hit list, Tom," Carl said ominously, "with prominent Saints on it."

"Yeah."

"Do you think there could be anything to that?"

"I don't know."

Carl shook his head sorrowfully. "A father and his two little boys. Who could hate us that much?"

"I don't know, Carl," Tom repeated.

"There's a Scripture," Carl said. " 'Whom the Lord loveth, he chastiseth.' " He turned away for a moment, his eyes glistening.

Tom said nothing. Gentry's eyes had looked like that, and he had made the same gesture of turning away. "I swear to you, Tom, please," he had said. "I swear to you on my mother's grave, I had no idea."

Carl turned back toward Tom. "You had things like this, didn't you? In New York?"

"Like what?"

"Murders. Like this. Children."

Tom nodded.

"What did you do?" Carl's face shone white in the light from the porch. "To steel yourself, I mean."

Tom lifted his collar against the cold. "Nothing," he said.

Carl stared at Tom piercingly. "I don't know how you live like that. I really don't. I mean with nothing."

Tom began to move away. "Tomorrow morning we'll go over the whole thing," he said softly. "The whole thing from the beginning, and this time no mistakes."

Driving away, Tom could see the light in the back bedroom of the Parker home. Baxter was probably still in there, his blue cigar smoke tumbling over the ruins of a decent family. Tom guided the car slowly down the street, his own face staring back at him as the car passed under the white streetlights, flashing his reflection in the glass. They had stood on the street that night, he and Gentry. And he had told Gentry everything he knew, that he had seen Romero and the yellow envelope and that he knew what the money was for, that Gentry had fingered Carlos Rodriguez as the witness and that Romero had done the rest, and Gentry's old eyes began to glisten in the streetlight and he told him, begged him to understand, that he had no idea that Romero would exact such a terrible price.

And then the old man begged to be forgiven and Tom said no, but never told anyone in the department what he knew, simply left New York forever, as one flees a scene of unbearable misery and corruption and disappointment, and had ended up here, where he had no choice but to remain and dream of some other place, an island in the pines.

PART
FIVE

44

Tom spent most of the night thinking about the cases, and by the next morning he was ready to lay it all out for Redmon. He found him at his desk in the squad room.

"Carl," he said, "I want to talk to you about something."

"Pull up a chair," Carl said. He looked tired, as if he had not had much sleep either.

Tom jerked a chair over to Carl's desk and sat down. "I've been thinking about what Philby said. About his theory. You know, the hit list."

"I think maybe Philby's right about that, Tom," Carl said.

"Maybe," Tom said. "He thinks that the one connection is that all of the victims are pretty prominent Mormons."

"They are." "Except one."

"Well, Fielding wasn't exactly prominent as an official or anything," Carl said, "but he wrote some pretty ringing defenses for us."

"I'm not talking about Fielding."

"You mean Jennifer Warren?"

"No. Rayette Jones."

Carl squinted. "Rayette Jones? What's she got to do with the other murders?"

"She was killed in Room 17, remember?"

"Sure."

"And the guy who checked into that room signed the motel register with the name William B. Thornton."

"Yeah, so what?"

"Well, I was checking through Donald Olsen's correspondence for the last month or so, and he received a letter signed William B. Thornton.''

Carl sat up slightly. ''What kind of letter? Hate letter?''

''That's the odd thing,'' Tom said. ''It wasn't a threatening letter, but there was something in it, an anger.''

''What did it say?''

''It praised Olsen for the way he had defended the excommunication of Barbara Harrison.''

''So you think friends of Harrison may be doing this?'' Carl thought about it for a moment. ''You know you could be right, Tom. She stirred up so much trouble. She could be involved in this.''

Tom shook his head. ''I don't think so.''

''Well, maybe not her,'' Carl said. ''Personally, I mean. But friends of hers. Supporters. They could hate the Church enough to start killing people, Tom. They're fanatics.''

''But why would Rayette Jones be a victim?''

''What do you mean?''

''Well, why would friends of Barbara Harrison kill a black prostitute?''

''I see,'' Carl said. ''That doesn't fit, does it?''

''No, it doesn't.''

''Yeah, Rayette Jones,'' Carl said, thinking. ''What would she have to do with anything?'' He thought for a moment, casting his eyes about. Then he looked up. ''This Thornton thing, Tom, could it just be a coincidence?''

''I don't think so, Carl. There's more. In all these killings, nobody has seen a car. Not at the Paradise Motel, or in the garage where Fielding died. You've talked to the people around the mountains. Did they see any car but Olsen's out there?''

''No,'' Carl said. ''But we don't know about yesterday. About Parker.''

''That's true, but people park their cars on the street all the time in that neighborhood,'' Tom said. ''It'd be hard for anybody to notice a car that *wasn't* there.''

''There's something else.''

''What?''

''Lab called just before you got here. They figure Fielding and the people in the Parker house were killed with the same weapon. A forty-four magnum.''

"That connects Fielding and Parker."

"Yeah."

"And the Mormon angle may connect Olsen," Tom said. "But that still leaves Rayette Jones, and then there's this other thing, this William B. Thornton."

Carl leaned back in his chair. "Jones just doesn't figure in, Tom."

"I know. I know. But still there's something we're missing. Maybe we should check with Vice and see if they've got any new angles. Get them to ask their snitches."

"Already did it," Carl said. "I checked with Tony in Vice. They worked the street on it, but couldn't connect it with anything. Surprising."

"How so?"

"Well, the fact that there's nothing at all. They can usually get some whisper. Street gossip, that sort of thing. But on the Jones killing they get nothing." He shrugged. "Maybe the guys on the street are scared as well."

"Maybe the simple truth is that they don't know a fucking thing," Tom said. "Maybe the street's as empty as we are."

"Could be." Carl looked at Tom seriously. "So where do we go from here?"

"I don't know. Did you talk to the neighbor who found the bodies on Murphy's Lane?"

"Sure," Carl said. "She just found them. The neighborhood canvass shows that they had to have been killed between four and six."

Tom was about to say that that was no help at all when his phone rang.

"Tom, this is Bemis."

"What do you have?"

"Not much, like I said. No prints, anything like that. No sex involved. Just clean murders."

"All right," Tom said dully. He started to put the phone down.

"Don't hang up, though," Bemis said. "We did find something on the sheets."

Tom brought the phone back up to his ear. "What?"

"Stains," Bemis said. "Very light. Besides the blood, I mean."

"What kind of stains?"

"We tested them," Bemis said. "They were basically a saline solution."

"Salt water?"

"Not exactly."

"What, then?"

"Best I can figure," Bemis said, "tears."

"Tears?" Tom asked, almost in a whisper.

"That's right," Bemis said. "Quite a lot, when you get right down to it. What we call profuse."

"How could you explain that?"

"Well, this is the strange part, Tom, but the best guess is that our friend must have been pretty broken up about the whole thing. The way it looks is that while he was covering the bodies, making it all nice and neat, well, he was also . . ."

"Crying," Tom breathed, and it was as if something in him, something very deep, shuddered.

45

All morning he had not drawn the shades. He did not think he could bear the light. He sat in the darkness behind his desk, the little bag at his feet. He had not even been able to take the pistol out of it, and it was as if he could not touch it, could not look at it. Over and over he relived the moment when he had heard that slight sound to his right and then turned and saw them, two little boys he knew well, who during the brief few seconds that remained to them could not imagine what he had done to their father and must have thought of it only as the joke of a moment, a little child's play in the living room between two grown men, one pretending to shoot the other, the other falling back against the wall, playing his part in the game. But the head, their father's head. They must have seen it explode, must have seen the wave of blood sweep out, covering his shirt, gouging up from the blasted head. They must have seen that, he thought, squeezing his eyes tightly shut.

For a long time he sat with his eyes clenched shut. He wanted to embrace total darkness, to be relieved of the mission entirely. It was, he thought finally, too much for him. He had thought himself strong enough to carry it out. But now, with the boys, he no longer knew whether he could finish the task. Then he relived it again, the scene coming at him from out of the darkness. He saw the barrel jerk up and fire, saw the first boy rise into the air, then the second turn and begin to run toward the back room, then the barrel of the pistol jerk up and fire, sending a terrible shudder up his arm.

He turned his head slightly, his eyes still closed. He did not want to open them ever again, and he prayed, whispering fiercely in the darkness, to die.

Then he sat upright, folded his hands in his lap, and waited. He did not know how death would come. Perhaps in a sudden, bathing fury. Perhaps merely in the stopping of his heart or the gentle closing of his throat. He did not know or care. He only understood that he was unworthy, unclean, a stricken warrior unable to complete his task. How could God possibly view him, but as something unspeakably weak and vile, something unworthy of his care, something sunk in failure and hopelessness and irredeemable cowardice?

He squeezed his hands together, waiting. He saw his death come as a fiery and annihilating sword hurling toward his throat. He jerked his head to the left out of reflex, as if warding off a blow. Then he straightened himself, stretched his arms out over his desk, and prayed again: *O Lord, my God, I have offended thee at the peril of my life. Please now, take that which is your due.*

Again he waited. He knew that God could hear him, and he wanted only to be taken quickly. He could see himself bending down over the sheet he had spread across the bodies, huge tears cascading down his cheeks. He had wept like a frenzied child, uncontrollably, and he knew that God had seen this and felt nothing for him, for his pathetic weakness, but an immense and dreadful shame. He had always known that death would be the penalty for his failure as it was the reward for his success. But to die in the glory of achievement was wholly different from this. He wished to die now because he had proved himself incapable of the mission for which he had been selected. He had broken, had allowed his personal feelings to interrupt the journey, had dropped to his knees in that bedroom and bawled out his panic and despair, wiping his eyes with a blood-stained sheet. He could only imagine the furious contempt with which such collapse was greeted in God's eyes.

And so he continued to wait, his arms outstretched, his palms turned upward. He prayed again: *O Lord, my God, I have mightily offended thee. Please, I offer up my body and my soul to your judgment.*

But still there was only the silence of the room and the darkness behind his closed eyes. For a moment he wondered why God was waiting to strike him. Perhaps this waiting, this agony of waiting, was part of the punishment he was being made to suffer.

Finally, after several moments, he opened his eyes slowly. He could see a crease of light slice through the shaded window to his right. He cocked his head slightly. That thin line of light. What could it mean?

46

Tom sat in his car across from the Parker house. It was midafternoon and the streets were deserted, except for an occasional passing car. Glancing down the clean, shady streets, Tom remembered that this was the kind of neighborhood his mother had dreamed of while she gazed out the barred windows of her Bronx apartment. She had been full of dreams, and had sat at the window and watched each one of them pass her by. Her last hope was simply to leave the Bronx forever. She had sat in her small, metal chair beside the window and watched the crowded, noisy, stifling streets and had dreamed of paradise somewhere in Dutchess County, where, she imagined, the world suddenly turned green and peaceful, where the air grew cool and quiet, and the people nodded and smiled and never glanced worriedly over their shoulders, never felt they had to do that because they knew that all their troubles had been beached on some distant shore and could never reach out for them again. But in the end, she had died in that street she had stared down at for most of her life. She had died suddenly, falling to her knees among the scattering crowd, a single ball of cabbage tumbling from her grocery bag and rolling down the sidewalk like a small severed head. And not long after that, Tom remembered, there was Rodriguez and his daughter, Tina, the one dead for his courage and the other for her innocence, and then Gentry with his yellow envelope full of Romero's money, and finally, because of all of this, Tom's decision to leave New York for good and never look back. And his brother had said, "Christ, Tom. The West? You can't run away." And Tom had said only, "Watch me."

Tom got out of the car and walked toward the house. He paused at the door, then knocked. The door was opened almost immediately be a small, compactly built woman with short blond hair.

"Yes?" she said.

Tom showed her his identification. "You're Mrs. Parker?" he asked.

"Yes."

"I know this is a bad time to be . . ." Tom began.

"Don't worry about that," Mrs. Parker said quietly. "I'm alone. Lots of people were here trying to comfort me. I sent them away. But if you're from the police, I want to help you in any way I can."

"I just have a few questions."

Mrs. Parker swung the door open. "Please come in."

Tom stepped into the house.

"They wanted to give me some drugs," Mrs. Parker said, "but I told them that I didn't want any. No sedatives, or anything like that. We have to accept what comes to us, Mr. Jackson."

Tom nodded. "I know you've already talked to—"

"That doesn't matter," Mrs. Parker interrupted. "I'll talk to as many people as I need to." She pointed down the hallway to a door that led to the back yard. "I've been in the house all day. I'd like to sit in the sun for a while."

"Fine."

"It might be a bit chilly, though."

"It's okay," Tom said.

Tom followed Mrs. Parker out into the yard and took a seat in a wicker chair. She sat down only a few feet away.

"Now," Mrs. Parker said, "what can I do for you?"

"I'm not really sure," Tom said.

Mrs. Parker looked at Tom oddly. "Not sure?"

"It's not the details I'm interested in right now," Tom said. "I'm sure you've been over that several times."

"Yes."

"Who did you talk to from the department?" Tom asked casually.

"A Mr. Philby," Mrs. Parker said. "I was staying with my sister after it happened. He came over last night. He was very nice. He seemed almost as upset as I was."

"Well, he's very dedicated to finding the man who—" Tom stopped.

"Murdered my husband and my children," Mrs. Parker said flatly.

"Yes."

"And what do you want to find, Mr. Jackson?"

Tom stalled for a moment. He pulled out his notebook and pencil. Then he looked directly into Mrs. Parker's eyes. "I'm looking for the reason," he said.

"The motive," Mrs. Parker said. "Isn't that what they call it?"

"Yes."

"Well, I can't think of any reason, any motive."

"Well, we're working on a kind of theory, Mrs. Parker," Tom said. "I don't know if Mr. Philby mentioned it to you."

"He didn't mention anything about a theory, or a motive."

Tom nodded. "Well, we're not too sure about anything right now."

"What is this theory?" Mrs. Parker asked bluntly.

"There's a feeling in the department," Tom said. "A feeling

that maybe we're dealing with someone who is specifically killing prominent people within the Church.''

Mrs. Parker's face saddened. "Well, that's our history, isn't it? Persecution."

"So I've been told."

"You're not a Saint?"

"No."

"I see."

"This theory of ours," Tom went on, "do you think there could be anything to it?"

"I wouldn't know, of course," Mrs. Parker said firmly.

"Well, what did Mr. Parker do for the Church, exactly?"

"Devoted his life."

"I mean in his job."

"He was an archivist," Mrs. Parker said. "He did a great deal of research. If a particular problem arose, he could look back at the records and determine what the Church had done in the past, what its position was."

"He was not an administrator?"

Mrs. Parker shook her head.

"Where did you meet him?"

"At Brigham Young."

"You were both students?"

"He was. At that time, I wasn't. I became one later, mostly because of Ben."

"Were you a member of the Church?"

"Not when I met him, no."

"So you came into the Church because of him?"

"He introduced me to the faith," Mrs. Parker said. "In that way, I think, he played a very important part in the salvation of my soul."

Tom nodded.

"He was always correct in everything," Mrs. Parker continued. "He taught me a great deal. Not just in the beginning, but always. Yes, I came to the Church through him."

"When was that?"

"Only a year before we married," Mrs. Parker said. "About ten years ago."

"But you were not a member of the Church before that?"

"No."

"And your family?"

"They are not Saints."

"This may strike you as an odd question, Mrs. Parker," Tom said, "but your family, what did they think about your joining the Mormon Church?"

"Why do you ask?"

"I'm just trying to cover as much as I can," Tom said.

"But what has any of this got to do with my family?"

"Sometimes people get upset if their daughter does something they don't approve of."

"My family loved Ben," Mrs. Parker said defensively.

"I'm sure they did," Tom said, and started to go on to his next question.

"Surely you're not suggesting that they could—"

"We're working on a Mormon connection here," Tom said quickly. "We're interested in anything, any reason why someone would want to hurt members of the Church."

Mrs. Parker closed her eyes slowly. "Of course. I'm sorry. I didn't mean to be uncooperative."

"It's perfectly understandable," Tom said. He glanced down at his notebook. "Does the name William B. Thornton mean anything to you, Mrs. Parker?"

"No."

"You've never heard of such a person?"

"No."

"Could your husband have ever mentioned that name?"

Mrs. Parker shook her head. "Who is he?"

"I don't know." Tom went quickly on the the next question. "Did your husband know Donald Olsen?"

"Of course he did."

"Were they friends?"

"More like colleagues."

"They worked together?"

"Ben was in charge of Church archives," Mrs. Parker said. "He worked with almost everyone."

"Were they involved in anything lately?"

"Not that I know of."

"How about Lester Fielding?"

"The writer? Yes. Ben knew him quite well."

"In what connection?"

"Lester used the archives for his writings," Mrs. Parker said. "My husband helped him in his research."

"Were they working on anything together recently?"

"No."

"It seems like a lot of people had access to the archives," Tom said.

"No, not very many," Mrs. Parker said. "Only people who could be trusted. Some people had access. Some people didn't."

"Only people who could be trusted," Tom repeated.

"Yes."

"What does that mean exactly?"

"People who could be expected to use the papers properly," Mrs. Parker said.

"Properly?"

"In a friendly way." Mrs. Parker looked at Tom knowingly. "You think that's wrong, don't you?"

"I don't know very much about it," Tom said.

"You think it's censorship."

"It's not my business."

"Well, if Ben were here he would explain it to you," Mrs. Parker said. "But since he isn't, I will."

"All right," Tom said.

"These archives, they are not just papers," Mrs. Parker said. "They are the history of this faith, its heart and soul. They are sacred to us, so we guard them very carefully."

Tom nodded.

"You think we have great secrets there, don't you?"

"I wouldn't know," Tom said.

"There are no secrets," Mrs. Parker said determinedly. "I can assure you of that."

"I'm looking into a murder, several murders," Tom said. "I'm not looking into the Church."

"Yes, of course," Mrs. Parker said stiffly.

"Did your husband mention anything unusual happening around his office?"

"What do you mean?"

"Strange people asking strange questions."

"There are always such people," Mrs. Parker said. "There

is such a thing as insanity. There are people who have visions, religious lunatics."

"How did your husband deal with such people?" Tom asked.

"He turned them away. Very politely."

"Did he ever mention any particular person who had made strange requests who wouldn't be waltzed to the door, anything like that?"

"A visible Church attracts people of questionable intent," Mrs. Parker said.

"But did he mention anyone in particular?"

"No one in particular." Mrs. Parker smiled gently. "My husband felt sorry for such people, people who were lost, disturbed, sometimes evil. He had a saying: 'Faith is a rock that attracts the eagle, the serpent, and all creatures in between.' "

"How about odd phone calls or letters?"

"He never mentioned any."

"And none came in here at his home?"

"No," Mrs. Parker said. "He would have told me about anything like that. He was very protective of his family." She looked sadly at the house and then back at Tom. "I'll tell you one thing, Mr. Jackson, if your theory is correct, then that man, whoever it was, chose his victim well. My husband was a perfect Mormon husband and father. A faithful Saint. An example."

Tom folded his notebook. "I won't bother you anymore."

"The Church has suffered a great loss," Mrs. Parker said.

Tom stood up slowly. "I'm sure it has."

Mrs. Parker looked at him. "Do you mind if I let you show yourself out, Mr. Jackson? I'd like to sit here for a while."

"Sure," Tom said quietly. "If you think of anything that might help, I'd appreciate it if—"

"I'll let you know right away," Mrs. Parker said. "I know my duty, and I will do it." Her eyes narrowed slowly. "Your duty is to find the man who killed my family, and I hope you do it, too."

"I'll do my best."

Tom turned and walked through the house and out onto the porch. As he started down the walkway toward his car, he heard a bell ringing. He looked around and saw a newspaper boy wobbliing up the street on his bicycle. He glanced at his watch. It was a little after four o'clock. He raised his hand, hailing the newsboy. The boy turned his bike toward the curb and waited until Tom reached him.

"My name's Jackson," Tom said. "I'm with the Salt Lake police."

The boy watched Tom apprehensively, as if he had done something wrong.

"I guess you heard what happened in the Parker house," Tom said.

The boy nodded. "Sure did. I knew Teddy Parker. We were in the same class at school."

"Do you run this route every day?"

"Yes, sir."

"At about the same time?"

"Sure," the boy said. "I got to. Everybody expects their paper at a certain time, and if it's not waiting for them, they start complaining to the boss downtown."

"So you came by here yesterday at about this time?"

"Yes, sir."

"Did you see anybody around the Parker house?"

The boy's eyes rolled upward as he thought. "No, I don't think so."

"Did you see anybody at all in the neighborhood?"

Something seemed to catch in the boy's mind. "There was a man I passed on the way up from Highland Drive." He shifted about in his seat and pointed behind him. "He was walking up this way."

"Toward the Parker's house?"

"Yeah, up this street."

"And that would have been about now? A little after four?"

"Yes, sir."

"What did he look like?"

"I don't know. Just a man. Tall, I guess."

"Could you see his face?"

"No," the boy said. "He was wearing a hat down over his eyes, sort of. I couldn't really see what he looked like."

"What was he wearing besides the hat?"

"I couldn't really see. He was wearing a raincoat. It covered everything else."

"A raincoat?"

"Yes, sir."

"What color?"

"Dark brown, I think."

"It wasn't raining yesterday."

The boy seemed to catch the meaning of what Tom had said. "No," he said slowly, "it wasn't."

"Did you see him go up to the Parker house?"

"No." I just saw him walking up the street toward it."

"Did you see him again?"

The boy's face brightened. "Well, I saw another man. Could have been him."

"Where?"

"He was standing on the corner when I came back down the street. Didn't have on a raincoat, though, or a hat. Just a suit."

"Where was he standing, exactly?"

The boy turned around again and pointed. "At the bus stop at the corner of this street and Highland."

"At the bus stop?"

"Yes."

"And he was just standing there? He wasn't walking?"

"No. He was standing, that's all."

"Like he was waiting for the bus?"

"Yeah, like that."

"Was anybody else standing there?"

"No. Just him."

"About what time would that have been?" Tom asked.

The boy's eyes shifted as he calculated. "Well, it takes me about a half hour to go up the hill and around and then back down here."

"So you would have gotten back here at about five o'clock."

"Yes, sir."

"When you passed him again, at the bus stop, did you see his face?"

"No," the boy said. He looked disappointed.

Tom glanced down toward the bus stop. "What buses run in this neighborhood?"

"I only see one," the boy said. "There may be more."

"Which one is it that you see?"

"The 26 Holladay. It stops at the corner of Highland Drive."

Tom patted the boy on the shoulder. "You've got a good memory," he said. "What's your name?"

"Mickey Todd."

"Thanks, Mickey," Tom said. "That's all for now."

Tom watched him move up the street, tossing papers left and right. He could feel a steady charge pulsing through his blood.

47

Tom cruised around the central downtown bus station. There were no parking spaces in the lot or near the station, so he pulled into a cab stand, dropped his sun visor down so that his police insignia was clearly visible, and walked into the station. It was very crowded, but he could see the information booth. There was a long line in front of it, and Tom had to wait for some minutes before he finally reached the window.

"What are you having, a convention?" he asked the man behind the glass.

"People are coming from all over for the conference," the man said from inside the booth.

"What's that?"

"Church meeting. Roger Berryman's going to speak." He looked at Tom as if he were some strange creature that had just stumbled in from the Bonneville Flats. "That makes it special."

Tom nodded indifferently. "Look, I'm with the Salt Lake police. I need to see the guy who controls the bus routes."

The man smiled. "That's Benny."

"Where's he?"

"Benny's a computer." The man grinned mischievously.

"Well, who talks to Benny?" Tom asked.

The man pointed to a green metal door. "Over there. Just walk in. Ask for Sam Thompson."

"Thanks." Tom elbowed his way through the crowd and opened the green door. A stocky man with a thin mustache was sitting behind a gray metal desk.

"You Sam Thompson?" Tom asked.

The man looked up from a stack of papers. "The one and only. What can I do for you?"

Tom showed his badge.

"We got a problem?" Thompson asked worriedly.

"I'm checking up on something. You might be able to help me."

"Glad to." Thompson pushed his chair back. "Anything for law enforcement, that's what I say."

"You have a bus that runs up Highland Drive, right?"

Thompson nodded. "Sure do."

"The 26 Holladay?"

"That's right."

"Who would have been driving that bus yesterday at around this time?"

"Just a second." Thompson pulled open a drawer and picked up a roster. "It's all in here. Just a minute." He scanned the paper. "That would be Terry Jenkins."

"How could I reach him?"

"Well, the best thing for you to do is just wait for him," Thompson said. "He's driving the 26 Holladay now, and he'll be pulling into Central here in about . . ." He stopped and looked up at the wall clock. "I'd say about fifteen minutes if he's on time."

"Thanks," Tom said. "Where does the bus pull in?"

"Well, it's sort of hectic right now," Thompson said, "so best thing is for you to wait in the lobby. When Jenkins gets in, I'll bring him out to you."

"Okay, thanks." Tom turned and walked back into the lobby, closing the door behind him.

The terminal seemed even more crowded than a moment before. People were streaming in and out from all sides; whole families stood staring about as if they had no idea where they were. Babies were crying and children were dashing here and there, chasing each other across the terminal. The loudspeakers announcing arrivals and departures could hardly be heard above the steady roar.

Tom slowly made his way through the crowd until he found a vacant space by one of the far walls. He leaned against it casually and looked about. Everyone seemed very cheerful, clutching their children to them or hugging old friends or relatives. Fresh white faces smiling in a fresh white world. The Port Authority Bus Terminal had not been like this, Tom remembered; it was a central Manhattan way station for hypes and drag queens, chicken hawks and whores. Once he had found a dead baby in a garbage can on one of the bus ramps. It had been wrapped in a single sheet of newspaper advertising a fall sale at Bloomingdale's.

From somewhere came a burst of laughter that went through Tom like a tearing wind. He jerked his shoulder from the wall and dropped his hands into his pockets. A couple trotted toward him, then leaned against the wall beside him. The girl was dressed in a pastel-pink dress with a high-button collar.

"And we saw Andy Williams, too," she said.

"No kidding," the boy said.

"It was a super show," the girl said, her voice high, excited. "He's a lot shorter than I thought he was." She seemed disappointed.

"You know Alan Ladd?" the boy asked.

"Who?"

"Alan Ladd, the actor."

"No, I don't think so."

"Old-time actor," the boy explained, "like Humphrey Bogart."

The girl shook her head.

"He was real short, too," the boy said. "When he did a movie, the actors all had to be short to make him look tall."

"Was he a star?"

"Back then he was."

"Oh," the girl said. "Well, anyway, Andy Williams was super." She started to say something else, then bolted forward, her hand waving frantically. "Daddy! Daddy!" She turned to the boy almost as an afterthought. "I have to go. My parents are here."

The boy straightened himself nervously. "Well, look, maybe I'll see you again."

"Sure, okay," the girl said. Then she darted away, a small green valise dangling from her hand.

The boy's shoulders slumped down, and after a moment he drifted away. Tom watched him amble through the crowd. He looked incredibly vulnerable, not much different from a baby wrapped in newspaper. At Port Authority, he would not have lasted through the night.

"Hey, Tom."

Tom turned around quickly and saw Baxter shoving his way through the crowd.

"Christ, we got a regular termite colony here," Baxter said as he finally stepped up to Tom.

"Some sort of Mormon thing," Tom said. "Bringing lots of people into town."

"What are you doing here?" Baxter asked.

"Checking something out."

"Jesus, you should have been around the cophouse about an hour ago," Baxter said wearily.

"Why?"

"The shit hit the fan."

"What do you mean?"

"The word's come down, Tom," Baxter said. "The theory is a Mormon hit list. That's what Philby says all these killings are about. So we're tearing the town apart, picking up everybody who's ever said a nasty thing about the Saints. Man, those fucking guys are going nuts. They're dragging in every teenager who ever sprayed a nasty word on Mormon property."

"That theory," Tom said, "it could be right."

"I guess. Anyway, they got wind some fuckhead was coming into town. Agitator of some kind. I'm supposed to make it clear we got an eye on him."

"Who is it?"

"Can you believe it, Tom? A fucking Indian. Comanche or something. Stirred up a lot of bullshit about Indian lands around Salt Lake." Baxter laughed. "One time he chained himself to the Temple door, said he was going to starve to death right there under the goddamn angel."

"What happened?"

"They unchained him and threw him on a bus," Baxter said. "Shit, Tom, this must have been fifteen years ago. You weren't around then. He's been kicking up trouble ever since, but he's sort of stayed clear of Salt Lake."

"But now he's coming back," Tom said.

"Yeah. Word is he's on the warpath again. Coming into Salt Lake to fuck up the conference. Philby thinks he might even be our friend with the magnum."

"It's worth checking out."

"Yeah," Baxter said unenthusiastically. He took out a cigar and lit it. "What about you, Tom? What are you doing hanging out at the bus station?"

"Just an angle," Tom said.

Baxter smiled. "You working secret these days?"

"It's just a bus driver who had the Highland Drive route. He might have seen something yesterday."

"That was very ugly over there." Baxter blew a huge cloud of white smoke into the air. "Got anything on it yet?"

"Not much."

"Secretive again, Tom," Baxter said. "You trying to be the glory boy on this one?"

Tom glanced toward the crowd. "Be hard for you to find the Indian in this crowd, Ralph."

Baxter waved his hand. "Don't worry about it. I'll meet that bastard at the bus door." He laughed. "Tonto comes out, I'll blow some smoke in his face, grab his fucking arm before he can get to his tomahawk, and that's it. Hiyo, Silver, away."

"When's his bus due in?"

"Five in the p.m."

"You'd better get to the ramp."

Baxter looked at his watch. "Guess so. Well, take it easy, Tom. I hope you get the gold watch on this one." He winked. "I'll give Shitting Bull your best regards."

"Yeah." Tom watched Baxter until he disappeared into the crowd. Then he leaned back against the wall again and waited. He could feel the pictures in his pockets. They seemed to give off a heat of their own, like decaying bodies. He could imagine what must be going on in the squad room. He had seen dragnets before. They pulled in a world of slime, but they almost never snagged the man you wanted. He was always too elusive, a man living in a barren room, quiet, well-mannered, almost in-visible, but with a little spark that sometimes fired in his mind, igniting others until his whole body was aflame.

Tom glanced to the left and saw Thompson inching his way through the crowd. A tall, thin man in a bus driver's uniform walked behind him.

"This is Jenkins," Thompson said once he had made his way over to Tom. "He was driving the 26 Holladay yester-day."

Tom nodded.

"How you doing?" Jenkins said. He put out his hand.

Tom shook it. "I'll try to keep it short."

"Plenty of time," Jenkins said.

"Well, I'll leave you two alone," Thompson said.

"Listen, Sam," Jenkins said quickly. "Keep me in mind for that July vacation schedule, okay?"

"Sure thing," Thompson said. Then he disappeared into the crowd.

Jenkins turned to Tom. "They scheduled me for December last year. I don't want that again."

Tom nodded. "Listen, why don't we step outside and get out of this crowd."

"Sure."

Together, they muscled their way through the crowd and out onto the street.

"I'm investigating the murder of Ben Parker and his two boys on Murphy's Lane," Tom said.

"All over the papers this morning," Jenkins said. "Terrible thing."

"Yes, it is."

"I drive by there. The house, I mean. But I guess you already know that."

"Yeah."

"So, how can I help you?"

Tom pulled out his notebook. "About what time did you drive by the Parker house yesterday?"

"Well, they don't need much bus service out that way. Most of those people have their own cars."

"Would you have passed there at around four?"

"Yeah."

"There's a bus stop at the corner of Murphy's Lane and Highland Drive," Tom said. "Is that the one you stop at?"

"Yes."

"When you stopped there at around four, did anyone get off?"

Jenkin's face suddenly tightened. "Dear God," he said.

"What?"

"Yes. Somebody got off. A strange guy. He was wearing a raincoat and a big, floppy hat."

"And he got off at Murphy's Lane and Highland Drive?" Tom asked quickly.

"He sure did," Jenkins said.

"Did he walk up Murphy's Lane?"

"Yes, he did. I saw him in the rearview mirror."

Tom let the tip of his pencil drop onto the first page of his notebook. "Where did he got on the bus?" he asked.

Jenkins face seemed to blank. "Get on?"

"He had to have gotten on the bus somewhere."

"Sure he did." He thought about it for a moment. "That's funny."

"What?"

"I don't remember him getting on."

"Mr. Jenkins," Tom said, "he didn't just appear on the bus. He had to have gotten on somewhere."

"That's the funny thing, though. He didn't. Or at least I can't remember him getting on. I mean, I would have noticed him getting on the bus. I mean, he was dressed sort of funny. That long raincoat and hat. It wasn't even raining, wasn't even cloudy."

"Maybe you just didn't notice him."

"No," Jenkins said firmly, "I would have noticed anybody getting on my bus that looked that funny. I moved to Salt Lake from L.A. I was a bus driver there, too. In L.A. you learn to keep a close eye on who gets on the bus. You got to if you want to stay alive."

"Maybe he got on with a lot of people," Tom said. "Do you have any particular stops where a lot of people get on?"

"No place in particular."

"Try to think if you might have seen the man in the raincoat," Tom said. "Nothing big, just a glimpse."

Jenkins scratched his chin. "I'll tell you the truth, I don't remember that guy getting on the bus. It's really weird."

"Do you know who was driving the route about an hour later?"

"Leon Tate."

"How could I get in touch with him?"

"He's a buddy of mine. You want his phone number?"

"Yes," Tom said.

Jenkins gave Tom the number, and he wrote it down in his notebook.

"Will Mr. Tate be home now?" Tom asked.

"Well, he's off today," Jenkins said, "but he may be out hunting. He loves to hunt."

"Thanks Mr. Jenkins." Tom walked quickly back into the bus terminal, found a pay phone, and dialed Tate's number.

"Hello." It was a male voice.

"I this Leon Tate?"

"That's me."

"My name is Tom Jackson. I'm with the Salt Lake police."

"Jesus," Tate said. "What's the matter, my ex-wife not get her check on time?"

"I just spoke with a friend of yours," Tom said, "a Mr. Jenkins."

The man laughed. "He turn me in or something?"

"I understand that you drove the 26 Holladay yesterday afternoon."

"That's right."

"And you would have gotten to the corner of Highland Drive and Murphy's Lane at about five in the afternoon."

"That sounds about right."

"You've heard of the murder that occurred on Murphy's Lane yesterday?"

"Sure. It's in all the papers."

"Did anybody get on your bus when you stopped at Highland Drive and Murphy's Lane?"

There was a silence at the other end.

"Please do your best to remember," Tom said.

"Let me see," Tate said. "Well, I think there was one man."

"What did he look like?"

"I don't know. I just remember somebody got on at the corner there."

"Was he wearing a raincoat?"

"Raincoat? It wasn't raining yesterday."

"Did you see his face?"

"Not really," Tate said. "This guy, is he the killer, you think?"

"I don't know."

"Well, I wish I could help you, Tate said. "You know Jenkins, he remembers everything. Paranoid, that's what I'd call it. From all those years driving a bus in L.A. Me? I always lived in Salt Lake. I don't much notice the passengers. I think a man got on at that corner there at Highland Drive and Murphy's Lane. What he looked like? Jees, I really don't know."

"Do you remember where he got off?"

"Got off?" Tate said. "No, I couldn't help you with that either. Like I said, I just drive the bus and keep my eyes on the road."

"Okay," Tom said. "Do me a favor, though. If you think of anything, give me a call. Tom Jackson. Homicide."

"Will do," the man said.

"Thanks." Tom hung up the phone, then walked to the information desk and stood in line until he reached the window. "I need a map of the bus routes in Salt Lake."

"Sure thing," the man said. He reached under the table and pulled out a bus schedule. A map of all the bus routes was printed on the back.

"That do?" he asked.

Tom took the map. "Thanks." He turned and began walking out of the terminal. At the door he glanced back into the room and saw Baxter tugging at a large man with long braided hair. The Indian seemed to resist for a moment, then to recognize his hopelessness and give in.

48

The thin slant of light that pierced the window had now grown to a blazing strip of white, and it was as if he were being summoned toward it.

He stood up and walked slowly to the window, his face suddenly illuminated by the shaft of light. He parted the curtains and looked out. His son was walking about in the yard, and he watched him for a long time, trying to determine the message he knew was beginning to come. What was it? Was he being forgiven? Was he being told that the mission was to continue? He stepped back and pulled the curtains tightly together, darkening the room entirely.

For a moment he thought of remaining in the darkness, of waiting until the message became clear. But he was being tugged gently out of the room, it seemed. He followed his intimations, still not knowing where they might lead, and after a moment he opened the door and walked out onto the grass.

His son was still standing in the yard, his back turned to him, gazing upward toward the trees at the rear of the estate. He felt an overwhelming need to speak to him, and his voice spoke out on its own, without his willing it, and the boy turned.

"Yes, Father?" he said.

He felt his arm move out, motioning for his son to come to him; when the boy came, his hand moved slowly downward until it rested on his shoulder.

"Did you want something?" the boy asked.

"I am your father," he said.

The boy smiled, then looked at him oddly.

"I am your father," he repeated.

The boy said nothing.

He gazed at his son, still waiting to receive the message.

"Is something wrong?" the boy asked.

"No."

"You look worried or something."

He squeezed the boy's shoulder tightly. He could feel a word forming on his lips, a name. "Abraham," he whispered.

"What?" the boy asked.

He glanced down at his son, then back up at the line of trees in the distance. The sun was beginning to set, turning the sky a fiery red.

"Abraham," he repeated.

The boy rolled his shoulder gently. "Who is Abraham?" he asked.

He looked at his son. The message was becoming clear. "From the Bible," he said.

The boy nodded. "Oh, that Abraham."

"God had needed to test him."

The boy stepped gingerly from his hand. "I remember the story," he said.

"Do you remember the test?"

"Yes."

He smiled. "What was the test, son?"

"Well, like you said, God wanted to test Abraham's faith. So he told him to take his son, Isaac, up into the mountains and to build an altar and put his son on it and—"

"And to sacrifice him," he said.

"That's right," the boy said.

"And what happened?"

"Abraham did it. He went and made an altar and he put Isaac on it. But at the last minute God changed his mind, so Abraham didn't have to kill Isaac."

"Yes." He smiled at his son. "Go on with your play."

He watched as the boy skipped away, dancing over the grass. Then he turned back to the house. He knew now that he had been forgiven, that those two little boys had been his test—and that he had met it, he had sacrificed them. He felt himself growing light, as if floating, and it seemed for a moment that he could look down on the whole great globe, this little orb hurling through darkness, this place that would one day be made para-

dise by God's wisdom and His love. He smiled. He had never
felt such overwhelming joy.

49

When Tom returned to the squad room, he found it almost as
crowded as the bus station. Cops were scurrying about, pushing
people forward and backward. Typewriters clattered everywhere. Three people had been shoved into the holding cell near
the back wall; they sat morosely on the wooden bench, staring
toward the far windows.

"What's going on?" Tom asked as he stepped up to Carl's
desk.

"Just a second, Tom." Carl's eyes were fixed on a small,
thin man who sat next to his desk. "Spell the name of that
street," Carl said.

The man flashed a bored look. "S-p-r-a-g-u-e."

Carl typed the word onto a form in his typewriter, then turned
to Tom. "What's up, Tom?" he asked, almost gleefully.

"What's all this in the squad room?" Tom asked.

Carl smiled. "We're through pussyfooting around, that's
what."

"What does that mean?"

"We're dragging the sewer, partner," Carl said. "We're
rousting every suspect we can get our hands on." He shot a sar-
castic look at the man in the chair. "But we're being very nice
about it, aren't we, Louis?"

The man looked back sourly at Carl and said nothing.

Carl turned back to Tom. "We're picking up every creep in
town, Tom, everybody who could be dangerous."

"That's a lot of people."

"Dangerous to the Church, I mean," Carl added.

The little man's eyes rolled. Then he sneered at Carl, his face pure mockery.

"Baxter said something about this," Tom said, "but I thought he was mostly bullshitting."

"He wasn't," Carl said cheerfully. "At least not about this."

"He said Philby ordered the roust."

"That's right."

Tom shook his head. "If you pulled this kind of shit in New York," he said, "you'd be drowning in lawsuits."

"Well, this isn't New York, Tom." He seemed proud of the fact.

"No kidding."

"We've got three prominent people dead, Tom," Carl said. "What do you expect us to do? Just sit on our hands and wait for the next one to drop?"

Tom said nothing.

"You'll never understand us," Carl said. "You'll never do it in a million years. But we have enemies. We've always had enemies. Usually just some nobody like Louis here, a smart guy with a can of spray paint. But this time it's different. We've got somebody out there who's killing us, and we're not going to lay down and take it."

There was a terrible determination in Carl's eyes. It was clear to Tom that any argument he could make would be useless, and that in the end, Carl would come to think of him as just another enemy in a world of enemies.

"You'll have to handle it your own way, Carl," he said finally.

"Well, how about you," Carl said. "Have you had any luck?" There was more than a hint of accusation in his voice, a suggestion that either Tom could care less about catching a Mormon-killer, or his tactics fell miserably short of what was clearly necessary to catch him.

Tom said nothing.

"Well? Have you?"

For a moment Tom thought of telling him about the man at the bus stop, but he was afraid that in the current mood, it might initiate a roundup of everybody in Salt Lake with a raincoat or a floppy hat.

"I didn't find anything important," Tom said. He would work the latest lead alone, work it until it faded into nothing like all the others.

"That says it all, don't you think, Tom?" Carl said.

"Maybe."

Carl quickly turned back to the man in the chair. "Where were you yesterday afternoon, Louis?"

"Movies."

"What movie?"

"You mean the title of the movie or the theater where they were showing it?"

"Both," Carl said irritably, "if your mind can keep up with two things at once."

Tom didn't wait to hear the man's answer. He walked back to his desk, pulled out the bus schedule he had picked up at the terminal, and began tracing the route of the 26 Holladay on the map. He began at the downtown station, slowly moving his red pencil, out along Second South, then onto East Birch, finally turned into Highland Drive.

For a few minutes, Tom merely stared at the map, as if he hoped it might speak to him. Then suddenly it did. He put a small *x* at the location of the garage where Fielding had been shot, then another on Murphy's Lane, and finally one at the location of the Paradise Motel. In every case the red line of the 26 Holladay route intersected with the *x*'s on the murder sites. And finally it passed the Greyhound Bus Terminal, with its direct connection to that area of the Wasatch Mountains where Olsen and Jennifer had been killed.

Tom looked up quickly. "Carl, could you step over here a minute?"

Carl glanced over his shoulder. He was in no mood to be disturbed. "What is it now, Tom?"

"I want to show you something."

Carl turned to the man in the chair. "Don't move, you understand?" he said brusquely.

"Where would I go, fuzzball?" the man said. "To hear the fucking choir?"

Carl flashed a mortal grimace. "Watch your mouth, punk," he said. "You're walking on very thin ice."

The man shrugged indifferently. "Yeah, right."

Carl got to his feet and walked over to Tom's desk. "Make it fast," he said.

Tom pointed to the map. "The red line is the route of a Salt Lake City bus, the 26 Holladay," he said. "The x's are the places where the murders occurred."

Carl looked at the map expressionlessly. "So?"

"Well, it hits them all except out at the Wasatch, but there's a connection at Central."

Carl smiled. "Tom you're hopeless. You just keep grabbing for anything."

"Well, there's something more," Tom said. "I talked to the newspaper boy who delivers on Murphy's Lane. He saw a man walking toward the Parker house not long before the murders. And he saw the same man standing at a bus stop about an hour later."

Carl suddenly looked more interested. "What's this man look like?"

"The kid wasn't too clear on that."

"Did you check with the bus driver?"

"Two of them," Tom said. "The one whose bus the man would have been riding on when he got off on Murphy's Lane, and the one who would have picked him up an hour later."

"What'd they say?"

"The second one couldn't remember anything, but the first one said the guy looked pretty strange."

"In what way?"

"He was wearing a raincoat and a floppy hat. It wasn't raining yesterday, Carl. It wasn't even cloudy."

"So why would he wear a raincoat?"

"Look at it this way. You can't hide a magnum with a silencer in your hand."

Carl was silent for a moment, his eyes moving over the red line, following it out of the city and then back again. Then he looked at Tom. "What do you think?"

"Maybe our man favors public transportation."

"You're connecting all of them, then?" Carl said. "All six murders?"

"All seven murders."

Carl shook his head. "I can see putting Olsen, Fielding, and Parker together. Maybe the girl was a witness out in the mountains. And maybe the kids got in the way, too. But that black whore. What's she got to do with anything?''

"You got the Thornton connection with her, too," Tom said.

"That whore was killed by a drifter. She just doesn't figure with the rest of them." Carl looked at the map again. "And another thing. Using a bus for a getaway? That's crazy, Tom, and these are real professional kills. The guy who's doing them, he's not stupid."

"Not stupid at all," Tom said.

"So why wouldn't he use a car?"

"I don't know."

"Maybe he doesn't have one."

"Maybe," Tom said, "and you wouldn't have a taxi waiting for you while you wasted somebody, would you?"

"No."

"This bus thing, it's worth working," Carl said. "Maybe we should check every driver on that route. More than that. Maybe we we should have a few plainclothes ride the bus for a while."

"I think so, Carl."

"Run with it, Tom." Carl glanced toward the man sitting next to his desk. "You handle it, okay? I got my hands full with creeps like Louis."

"Okay."

Carl walked back to his desk and started in on Louis once again.

Tom leaned back in his chair, folding his hands behind his head. For a moment everything seemed to swirl around, bits of debris in an endless maelstrom: a whore's purple dress, a name scrawled on a motel register, a writer slowly going mad, two bodies sprawled in a deserted woodland, a letter with a phony name, and a white sheet stained with a killer's tears. And it seemed that all of this whirled about in the great pit of the Salt Lake Basin, where things were never lost, but only sank down into the desert sands, never washed away, except through sudden torrents of revenge.

PART
SIX

50

Tom arrived at Mordecai McBride's office early the next morning, and was immediately ushered in.

"I'm surprised to see you again." McBride thrust out his hand.

Tom shook McBride's hand quickly, his eyes studying the office. It was very tastefully designed, with thick, dark carpeting and heavy burgundy curtains to shield the room from the bright Utah sun.

"Please sit down," McBride said. "I have a class at Brigham Young soon, so I'm afraid I don't have a lot of time."

Tom took a seat in front of McBride's desk. "It won't take long."

"I am surprised to see you," McBride repeated.

"Why is that?"

"Well, we didn't exactly part on a pleasant note the last time we met." McBride circled around his desk and took a seat behind it, folding his hands in his lap. "Have there been any developments, Tom?"

"I'm trying to make one."

"Make one?" McBride said. He looked at Tom oddly. "How can you do that?"

"I'm not sure I can," Tom said, "but we're at a dead end in the physical evidence. So I'm working on something else about the cases, and I need a little help."

"I'll do anything I can for you."

"I don't have much to go on," Tom admitted.

"Just an idea, is that it?" McBride said. "Sometimes they're the best things to have."

Tom did not want to get into a philosophical discussion. "I want this to be strictly between you and me, Mr. McBride," he said.

"It will be."

Tom took out his notebook and flipped back the cover, a gesture of professionalism he hoped would have an effect on McBride. "How well did you know Donald Olsen?" he asked.

"Very well."

"And as far as you know, he had no enemies?"

"None at all."

"And Ben Parker?"

"Ben Parker was as good a man as I have ever known," McBride said. "I can't imagine why anyone would want to harm him or his family."

"Did you know Lester Fielding?"

"Very slightly. He interviewed me on one or two occasions."

"He was friendly to the Church, wasn't he?"

"Yes, he was," McBride said. "He was a Saint, and he did his duty as one."

Tom said nothing.

"All three of the men you've mentioned have one thing in common, Tom," McBride said after a moment. "They were Saints. Two of them were high officials in Church administration. One of the two supported Church policies very vigorously."

Tom nodded.

"If your idea is that someone is killing Saints because he is involved in persecuting the Church," McBride said, "then I would say you are absolutely right."

"That's what everyone in the department thinks," Tom said.

"But you don't?"

"I'm not sure. Does the name William B. Thornton mean anything to you?"

"No," McBride said immediately. "Who is he?"

"That's what I'm trying to find out."

McBride shrugged. "I've never heard the name. I'm sorry."

"Someone signed that name to a letter written to Donald Olsen."

"A threatening letter?" McBride asked quickly.

"Not exactly," Tom said. "Part of it praised Olsen on his handling of the Barbara Harrison problem. The excommunication."

McBride's face tightened slightly. "We don't use that word," he said. "A person in the Church is not excommunicated. A person is disfellowshipped."

"Same thing, right?"

"More or less, I suppose," McBride said coolly. "But what would such a letter have to do with anything?"

"I'm not sure," Tom said. "But the man who checked into the room where Rayette Jones was killed signed the register with the same name—William B. Thornton."

McBride looked unperturbed. "Who is Rayette Jones?"

"A black prostitute."

McBride bolted forward in his chair. "A what?"

"A black prostitute," Tom repeated. "She was strangled about a week ago in the Paradise Motel."

"Ah, yes," McBride said, "you mentioned her to me before, I believe."

"Yes."

McBride watched Tom worriedly. "This . . . prostitute . . . she couldn't have been a . . ."

"She was not a Mormon," Tom said.

McBride looked relieved, but then the worry crawled back into his face. "Are you suggesting that Olsen and the others had some connection with this . . . this whore?"

"I don't know. That's one of the things I'm trying to find out."

McBride's hands tightened together. "Look, Tom, I can't speak for Mr. Fielding. As I said, I only knew him slightly. But as far as Donald Olsen and Ben Parker are concerned, such an idea, such a suggestion, is completely ridiculous."

"But the name is there," Tom said firmly. "It's on the motel register, and it's on a letter to Donald Olsen."

"I would say that it's no more than an odd and misleading coincidence," McBride said.

"I have a description of Thornton from the motel manager, and someone fitting that same description was seen near the Parker home just a few minutes before Parker and his two sons were killed."

McBride stared grimly at Tom but said nothing.

"In a way, that connects three cases," Tom said flatly.

McBride's lower lip fluttered. He kept his eyes fixed on Tom's face.

"Three cases," Tom repeated. "Olsen, Parker and—"

"The whore," McBride whispered.

"Yes."

McBride sat back slowly in his chair. "Outrageous," he said quietly. "I can't understand it." He considered the whole terrible set of consequences. "This Thornton," he said finally, "have you checked him out—the name, I mean?"

"Yes," Tom said. "Several days ago, in the phone book. There's no one in Salt Lake by that name."

"So this Thornton, he's from out of town?"

"Probably. If Thornton is a real name."

McBride cast his eyes about for a moment, thinking deeply. Then he leaned forward, lowering his voice. "Tom, I can assure you, absolutely assure you, that neither Olsen nor Parker could possibly have anything to do with a whore, white or Negress."

"Maybe so, Tom said, "but this name, and the descriptions—it's too much to ignore."

"I agree," McBride said, "and I don't think it should be ignored. But there are several ways of looking at it, Tom."

Tom said nothing. He watched McBride's hands fidget.

"The first way is the obvious one," McBride went on. "It makes the suggestion you have already made, that perhaps something was going on between these men and that . . . what's her name?"

"Rayette Jones."

"Yes, something going on between the men and Miss Jones."

"But there's another way of looking at it?" Tom asked.

"Yes, there is," McBride said.

"What is this other way?"

"This could be some sort of conspiracy, Tom. A conspiracy to embarrass the Saints by somehow linking their leaders to a prostitute, especially a Negro one."

"Why especially black?"

"Because of the Church's traditional position concerning Negroes," McBride said. "A position it no longer holds."

"What is that position?"

"Of denying them access to the priesthood. But you must understand, that is no longer the case among the Saints. Still, a connection like that, with a Negro prostitute, it could be seen as an example of extreme hypocrisy and used very well by our enemies."

"Who would want to do that, embarrass the Church?"

McBride hesitated for a moment.

"I need to know," Tom said.

"Well," McBride said, "I don't want you to get the idea that there is rampant paranoia among the Saints."

Tom took out his notebook. "Who?"

"There is a rival organization which has always relished our troubles on this question of the Negroes."

"What is it called?"

"The Reorganized Church of Jesus Christ of Latter-Day Saints," McBride said. "They're based in the Midwest, but they have a contingent here in Salt Lake."

"Do they have a leader here?"

"They have a man who is more or less their spokesman."

"What's his name?"

"Clifford Brannon."

"Do you have an address?"

"Not an address," McBride said, "but he owns a small gift shop not far from the ZCMI. You won't have any trouble finding it."

Tom closed his notebook. "Is there a master list of Mormons?"

"You mean of the Reorganized Church?"

"No. Of yours."

McBride looked puzzled. "Master list?"

"A mailing list, something like that," Tom explained. "You send material all over the country, don't you?"

"All over the world," McBride said proudly.

"Then you must have a mailing list."

"Of course."

"I'd like to see it."

"Why?" McBride asked.

"To find out if there are any William B. Thorntons on it.

McBride looked insulted. "You mean you think this mad-man could be one of us—a Saint?"

"It wouldn't hurt to check."

"Forgive me, Tom," McBride said, "but this sounds like a fishing expedition to me."

"It is."

"Well, the Community of Saints is not a public pond," Mc-Bride said coolly.

"I only need to know one thing," Tom assured him. "Whether or not anybody by that name has been in Salt Lake during the last couple weeks."

"And how would you find that out?"

"It won't be difficult."

"But it might be disturbing to innocent people."

"Sometimes that can't be helped."

McBride's eyes rested steadily on Tom. "That list is a very large one. It's not available to the public."

"Is it available to you?"

"Of course it is."

"Then you check it," Tom said.

McBride considered it a moment, then stood up. "Just a min-ute. I'll be right back." Then he left the room.

Tom waited in McBride's office, browsing over the large bookcase behind McBride's desk. The titles dealt with every conceivable aspect of Mormon history, culture, and theology. A large portrait of Joseph Smith hung on one side of the room; facing it on the opposite wall, a portrait of Brigham Young. The two men seemed to stare at each other across the great gulf of Mormon history, turmoil, and achievement.

After a few minutes Tom heard the door open. McBride stood in the doorway, a single piece of paper in his hand. "Here it is," he said.

Tom stood up, walked over to McBride, and took the paper.

"Only four people by that name," McBride said.

Tom glanced at the list. The names and addresses were printed neatly on the page. None were from Salt Lake.

"I hope I don't have to remind you to be very careful, Tom," McBride said.

Tom nodded.

"These are good people," McBride added. "Not at all the sort you're accustomed to dealing with, I imagine."

Tom thought of all the pimps and whores and junkies he had spent his life meeting in bars and chasing down alleyways, or merely watching from the grim darkness of an unmarked car. "No, I don't suppose they are."

51

Clifford Brannon's gift shop rested in the very shadow of the ZCMI tower, but it was unlike any of the other shops in the area. The back wall was adorned with portraits of Joseph Smith and his wife, Emma, but there were none of Brigham Young. There were none of the replicas of the Temple, the Tabernacle, or the Beehive House that generally filled shelf after shelf of Salt Lake's gift shops. The Salt Lake *Tribune* was on sale, but not the *Deseret News*. There were stacks of the Book of Mormon, but the other titles that caught Tom's eye were unfamiliar.

"May I help you?"

Tom turned from the shelf of books and saw a small, round-faced man in an open-collared shirt and light blue slacks. "I'm looking for Clifford Brannon."

The man smiled. "You found him."

Tom flashed his police identification, and the man's face soured.

"You guys are falling all over each other," he said.

"What are you taling about?"

"I just talked to a cop about an hour ago," Brannon said. "He was asking me all kinds of questions about where I've been and what I've been doing for the last few days."

"Did they tell you what it was about?"

"No," Brannon said. "They were real funny about that.

And when I started getting a little hot about all these questions, they backed off.''

"They were investigating the murders," Tom said.

Brannon shrugged. "That's what I figured. All these big-shot Mormons getting killed, they'd have to get around to talking to me." He looked at Tom carefully. "You a Saint?"

"No."

Brannon smiled. "Least we got that in common."

"That's what I've heard."

"They figured if they sent over a Gentile, he might get more cooperation, huh?"

Tom said nothing.

Brannon smiled. "Well, maybe they were right. What do you want?"

"I'm investigating the murders, too," Tom said.

"And just like I told you, my name came up, right?"

"Yes. Why is that?"

Brannon waved his hand. "Don't kid around. You already know."

"I'd like to hear it from you."

"Okay," Brannon said. "I'm a rival, a member of the Reorganized Church. The Utah Mormons would like to forget that we even exist. But they can't. And in Salt Lake, I'm one of the big reasons they can't." He chuckled lightly. "They'd like to keep us far away, back in the Midwest. They can't stand the idea that we're working right under their own noses, right smack in the middle of their holy city."

"What is the Reorganized Church, Mr. Brannon?"

"What, you want a history lesson?"

"Maybe."

"Okay," Brannon said. "I don't mind taking the time." He winked. "Who knows, you might end up a convert."

"Just tell me about your group," Tom said.

"Sure," Brannon said. "We're the real Saints, the ones who hold to the original doctrines of the Church. We believe in the Book of Mormon, in Joseph Smith as prophet, and in the original revelations. We separated from the Young group in the eighteen-fifties because we didn't believe in all the nonsense he stood for. We didn't believe in polygamy or baptizing dead people or that Heaven would actually exist on this earth rather than someplace else. The Young bunch swallowed all this, and a lot more. Polygamy is just the tip of the iceberg. It's what people know about, but it's not the whole story."

"So your people left Utah?"

"Most of our group never came to Utah in the first place, but some came out here, got a good hard taste of Young's dictatorship, then went back where they belonged."

Tom nodded.

"And it wasn't that easy, either," Brannon went on. "Some of them had a pretty rough time with the Avenging Angels."

"What do you mean?"

"They were chased, threatened. Some might have been killed."

"The Avenging Angles, this was a group?"

"That's right. A kind of Mormon Ku Klux Klan. They believed in blood atonement. What that means is that they believed that there were some sins so terrible that the sinners couldn't be given forgiveness in this world, so, you might say, they sent them off to the next."

"They killed them?"

"Sometimes," Brannon said. "And they weren't just off-the-wall extremists, either. Brigham Young believed in blood atonement. He preached it."

"I see." Tom glanced at the bookshelf to his right.

"Those books," Brannon said. "That's the real history of Mormonism." He laughed. "The Mormons make a big display of how much they care about history. They spend a lot of money on their Genealogical Society, keep all their records in a huge vault in the mountains." He shook his head despairingly. "But they don't really believe in history. They believe in making up their own history, making it what they want it to be, ignoring the facts."

Tom turned back to Brannon. "Do you know of anyone in your group who might take these ideas about the Utah Church a little too seriously?"

"You mean seriously enough to start killing people?"

"Yes."

Brannon smiled. "It's the Utah Church that has a history of that sort of thing, not us." He picked a book from the shelf and showed Tom the title. "You ever heard of the Mountain Meadows Massacre?"

"No."

Brannon nodded. "I didn't think so. It happened in southern Utah in August of eighteen fifty-seven. A bunch of Utah Mormons wiped out a whole wagon train. They killed about one hundred and twenty people. Men, women, and children." He smiled. "And they think *we're* killers?"

"Are there any blacks in your group?" Tom asked.

"Sure," Brannon said cheerfully. "We've always welcomed blacks into the Church. Fully welcomed them. Not through the back door like the Utah bunch."

"Do you know of any particular black member who might want to get even with the Utah Mormons?"

Brannon shook his head. "You're really barking up the wrong tree," he said. "We're not the violent type. We don't preach a lot of paranoid self-defense stuff."

Tom watched Brannon closely but said nothing.

Brannon shrugged. "Oh, listen, we get on the Utah Mormons a little. We do things sometimes that annoy them." He turned to the shelf and picked up a small replica of a house. "Know what this is?" he asked, lifting it toward Tom's eyes.

"No."

"This is a replica of that ridiculous-looking house Brigham Young built for his favorite wife, Amelia Folsom. It's called Amelia's Palace, and you won't find replicas of it sold by any Utah Mormons. We sell it because we like to remind them of their polygamous past. We like to remind them that facts are facts, that they don't go away just because you want them to."

Tom took the house and turned it slowly in his hand.

"Terrible-looking, right? A chunk of bric-a-brac."

Tom nodded.

"Place used to be right across the street from the Lion House, where Young kept all his wives and children. They make a real big deal of the Beehive House, where Young himself lived. Little old Mormon ladies love to hustle the tourists through that, show everybody all the great things Brigham did. But they don't mention the passageway between the Lion and the Beehive. And when you get right down to it, even Young's grave is a problem for Utah Mormons, a real serious problem.

The trouble is, he's got a few wives buried around him. Mormons don't like to call attention to that.''

Tom handed the little house back to Brannon. "Do you know of anybody who might feel strongly enough about the Mormons to start killing them?"

"You mean like the blacks?"

"Anybody."

"The Mormons have lots of enemies," Brannon said. "They've never made non-Mormons, or Gentiles, as they call them, they've never made such people feel at home in Salt Lake." He placed the replica of the house back on the shelf. "Did you know that about forty percent of the people in Salt Lake are not Utah Mormons?"

Tom shook his head.

"Forty percent," Brannon repeated, "and yet the Mormons have almost all the power, all the wealth. This is their town, and everything they do makes that clear to everybody else." His eyes narrowed lethally. "That's not exactly the best way to win friends and influence people, is it?"

Tom said nothing.

"If you're looking for Mormon enemies," Brannon added, "you got a lot of people to choose from."

"Does the name William B. Thornton mean anything to you?" Tom asked.

"No."

"No one in your organization by that name?"

"Absolutely not." Brannon stared at Tom for a moment, then pulled a book from the shelf and handed it to him. "Here, take this," he said. "It's a history of the whole Mormon movement. It was written by a Utah Mormon, but it's pretty good anyway. To my way of thinking, you're going to need to know more about the Mormons if you're going to find out who's killing them."

Tom took the book and put it under his arm. "Thanks," he said. Then he turned toward the door.

"Wait a second." Brannon reached out and grabbed Tom's arm. "That name Thornton, it does ring a bell."

Tom waited.

"I don't know anybody named William B. Thornton," Brannon added, ''but there's a guy I'm familiar with named Thornton Elrod.''

''What about him?''

''You might find it interesting to talk to him.''

''Why?''

''He belongs to a group that has been pretty badly persecuted by the Utah bunch.''

''What group?''

''Polygamists,'' Brannon said. ''Elrod is one of their leaders.''

''Where can I find him?''

''Here in Salt Lake,'' Brannon said. ''Right here in the belly of the beast.''

''Do you have his address?''

''Yeah,'' Brannon said. He took out a pen and paper and wrote the address down. Then he gave the paper to Tom.

''Thanks,'' Tom said. He shoved the paper into his coat pocket.

''Be careful,'' Brannon said darkly. ''Thornton Elrod is not an ordinary man.''

52

Thornton Elrod opened his door before Tom made it up the last step toward the porch. He was very tall and dark, with sleek black hair that hung almost to his shoulders.

''You from the police?'' he asked.

''Yes.''

''The one Brannon sent?''

''That's right.''

Elrod's eyes moved up and down Tom's body, as if evaluating him by means of his own secret system. ''According to Brannon, you're a Gentile,'' he said.

"Yes, I am."

"What you're looking for, it has nothing to do with plural marriage?"

"Nothing at all," Tom said.

Elrod nodded silently, then stepped back and opened the door. "Come on in, then."

Tom followed the man into a large, open room, furnished with only a few tables and chairs. The windows were covered with heavy shades, and the room had an enclosed, musty smell.

"Sit down," Elrod said.

Tom took a seat near one of the windows.

Elrod closed the door, peeped out the shade, then came into the room. "Brannon should have asked me first, before sending you over here," he said.

"I'm sorry to bother you," Tom said.

Elrod did not seem to care one way or the other. He sat down heavily in a huge wing chair. "We have been cursed in this place," he said. "We are wandering in the deserts of Egypt."

"You've heard about the murders, I suppose," Tom said quietly.

"The wrath of God is fierce in its destruction," Elrod said. He looked toward the shaded windows. "The angel of death is passing over the city, striking the evildoers."

"These 'evildoers,' " Tom said. "Did you know any of them?"

"They are the hounds of the devil," Elrod said. "I have done battle with the hounds."

"Olsen, Parker, Fielding, you knew them all?"

Elrod turned back from the window and stared coldly at Tom. "God strikes for me. I do not need to strike myself."

"You don't exactly seem to be mourning their deaths."

"Would you mourn him who persecutes and reviles you, him who drives you from the gates of the city?"

Tom cleared his throat gently. "I guess not."

"They, and all their kind, have made a curse of our names," Elrod went on. "They have set themselves up as principalities and powers. They have done evil to the innocent."

"This evil they have done," Tom said. "What is that, exactly?"

"They have denied the revelation, and persecuted those who have refused to deny it."

"Revelation?"

"The commandment that man is to have wives in abundance." Elrod thrust his head backward. "Bring me water!" he shouted.

Instantly a small, fair-skinned woman darted into the room and handed Elrod a huge mug of icewater.

"Go now," he said to her.

She disappeared into the back of the house.

Elrod took a drink from the mug, then set it down loudly on the table next to him.

"How did you come to know Mr. Brannon?" Tom asked.

"His enemies are my enemies," Elrod said.

"You mean the Utah Mormons?"

"I mean the Utah hypocrites and traitors," Elrod said fiercely.

"But Brannon doesn't support polygamy."

"His is the weaker force. The greater enemy must be slain first."

Tom nodded.

"The topmost tower must first be made to fall." Elrod's eyes narrowed menacingly. "The Saints are demons, wolves in sheep's clothing, liars and deceivers, Pharisees and Sadducees, and the hands of Pilate cannot—"

"Mr. Elrod," Tom interrupted, "I'm with the Homicide Division of the Salt Lake police. I'm investigating a series of murders that I'm sure you already know about. Now, your name has come up in connection with the investigation, and I—"

"My name is a bitter herb upon their tongue," Elrod intoned.

"Yes, I'm sure it is."

"They have tried to destroy me by all manner of cunning."

Tom shifted uneasily in his seat. "I just have a few questions."

"They would bear false witness against me," Elrod said. "They would speak slanders."

"I understand that you're the leader of a small group of—"

"Polygamists," Elrod said. "Yes, I am. Plural marriage

was a revelation handed down to the Prophet Joseph by the Lord God. It cannot be undone by the will of man."

Tom took out his notebook. "Mr. Elrod, have you been in Salt Lake during the last week?"

"Yes."

"Where were you yesterday between three and six o'clock?"

"At work," Elrod said. "Man is commanded to labor."

"Where do you work?"

"I am a barber."

"You have a barbershop?"

"I do not own it."

"But you are a regular employee there?"

"Yes."

"Was anyone else in the shop yesterday between three and six?"

"Many people," Elrod said haughtily. "They will tell you."

"Where is this shop?"

Elrod gave the address. Tom wrote it down, then looked back up at Elrod. "This group of yours, how many people are in it?"

"Jesus said that 'wherever as many as two are gathered in my name, I am with them.' "

"Well," Tom said in exasperation, "not counting Jesus, how many?"

Elrod looked at Tom grimly. "Do not mock me," he said loudly.

"I just need the number," Tom said, "and I need it now."

Elrod folded his arms over his chest and glared at Tom.

"I have some Mormon detectives who might like to talk to you, Elrod," Tom said. "Had you rather I send a few of *them* over here?"

Elrod dropped his hands into his lap and squeezed them together.

"They could be here in about five minutes," Tom added.

One corner of Elrod's mouth jerked down. "I will speak to you," he said.

"Good," Tom said. "How many?"

"Seven males," Elrod said, "and I am certain that they can account for themselves."

"What do you mean?"

"They have killed no one."

Tom placed the point of his pencil on the open notebook. "What are their names?"

Elrod said nothing.

"You can give them to me, or you can give them to someone else," Tom reminded him.

Elrod gave the names and Tom wrote them down quickly. Then he looked up at Elrod. "Can you think of anyone who might want to harm prominent Mormons, or the Church itself?" he asked.

Elrod smiled.

"I mean anyone who might take it to the point of murder?" Tom added.

Elrod's smile disappeared. "God's vengeance is for God, not man."

"All right," Tom said wearily. He stood up, walked to the door, then turned back toward Elrod. "Does the name William B. Thornton mean anything to you?"

Elrod's body stiffened. "Why do you ask that?"

"Does it?" Tom repeated.

"William B. Thornton was my great-great-grandfather."

Tom unconsciously took a step toward Elrod, then stopped. "Your great-great-grandfather?" he said softly.

"Yes," Elrod said. "Do they now wish to further slander his name?"

"Who was he?"

"A holy man," Elrod said proudly. He pointed to a large portrait on the back wall of the room. "That's him. A holy man. Dead now, a hundred years."

Tom's eyes latched onto the portrait. "What do you know about him?"

"A holy man," Elrod said, an edge of terrible anger in his voice. "Unjustly executed for murder."

"Murder?" Tom said. "Who did he murder?"

Elrod stood up quickly. "I will speak no more of the dead."

Tom looked at Elrod and knew he would get nothing more from him. He glanced back at the portrait. It showed a stern, rigid face with dark, fierce eyes that seemed to have their own special gleam. He wore a large, black handlebar mustache and—odd for a portrait—a worn, floppy hat.

53

He placed the bag on his desk, opened it, and pulled out the coat, lifting it high above his head and shaking out the folds. He had washed it carefully after the girl's death, then placed it back in the bag. But now he knew he would have no further use for it. He walked over to the fireplace and threw it in. Then he bent forward, struck a match on the brick hearth, and placed it at the hem of the coat. The flame licked at the cloth tentatively, white smoke rising from the tip of the match.

"Burn, now," he whispered.

He continued to hold the match in place until the coat caught fire. Then he stepped back and watched as the flames consumed it. It took only a few minutes for the coat to disintegrate. He watched with relish as the orange flames moved up the hem, then seemed to explode in every direction, reducing the coat to a lump of charred cloth.

He stepped away from the fireplace and slapped his hands together. Tomorrow it would be over, he thought; only one more day and the mission would be complete. He knew now that it had all been planned from the very beginning, even the deaths of the two boys. They were the sacrifices that had to be made to test his resolution. He imagined them sitting on the lap of God now, their souls clothed in holy light, strange and beautiful smiles spreading over their joyful faces.

He walked over to the curtains and parted them with a quick, forceful movement. The room was suddenly bathed in light, and he could feel its warmth as if it came from within himself—a soft, soothing glow radiating from his soul. He would never close the curtains again. He had only one more thing to do, and that would not be done in secrecy, in disguise. It would be his moment to rise at last, to reveal himself and his mission, and he thought of it as a final and beautiful anointment. He could almost hear God's voice thundering over the Salt Lake Basin at the moment his mission was completed: *Behold this my son, in whom I am well pleased.*

He turned and walked through his office and out onto the front lawn. Far to the north he saw a rim of clouds moving over the mountain range. There had been no rain in Salt Lake for an entire week. That, too, he thought, was part of the plan. He had been given a brilliant week in which to do his work, and now that it was coming to a close, the rain could sweep in again, the perfect symbol for a final cleansing. He smiled. Through the entire week it had been unseasonably warm. Now, he thought, let the cold winds come.

54

Carl's eyes blinked rapidly. "You saw the picture?"

"It was hanging on his wall," Tom said.

Carl glanced about the squad room. The "enemies" of the Church were streaming in and out in a continual flow of confused or belligerent or simply weary faces. "With all these people, we didn't pick him up yet," he said, disappointed. He turned back to Tom. "Let's go get him."

"He says he can prove where he was at any time."

"Anybody can say that, Tom."

"Maybe he's telling the truth."

Carl looked exasperated. "Look, Tom, you've done real good work on this case. Tracking down that Thornton lead. That's first class, really. But this guy Elrod, he's dangerous."

"He has a few too many wives, Carl, but I don't think he's a killer."

"If not him, maybe somebody he knows," Carl said anxiously. "One of his group, somebody like that. These polygamist types—freaks, I'm telling you. The Church has been cracking down on them for years. That's our motive right there. Revenge on the Church."

"Well, there's a problem you keep forgetting, Carl."

"What's that?"

"Rayette Jones."

Carl smiled. "No, Tom. I haven't forgotten that. And now, with this Elrod guy, it all makes sense."

"How."

"It was a smokescreen," Carl said confidently. "They go out and kill a whore first. Plant the name. Clear as day on the register: William B. Thornton. Then they do some more killing. All of it very clean so that it looks like the same guy. The whore is done to throw us off, keep us from seeing that all the killing comes back to them, to revenge against the Church."

Tom said nothing.

"What's the matter, doesn't that make sense?"

"In a way."

"See, that's the whole thing. The whore is just a diversionary tactic, something to keep us from getting on their trail."

"Give me a day to work another angle, Carl."

"Why?"

"Because, for one thing, there are some other William Thorntons."

"What?"

Tom took out the list McBride had given him. "All of these guys are Mormons."

Carl took the list and read the names. "Where'd you get this?"

"Mordecai McBride."

Carl looked stunned. "He thinks one of these guys might have—"

"He doesn't think anything," Tom said. "I asked for the list, so he gave it to me. Simple as that."

Carl waved the list slightly. "What do you want me to do with this?"

"Check it out," Tom said. "Make sure none of those people have been around Salt Lake lately."

"These are all Saints, right?"

"Yes, so any questions might come better from one of their own." He took out the list Elrod had given him. "And after that, you can check these people out."

"Who are they?" Carl asked as he slipped the paper from Tom's fingers.

"Elrod is the leader of a small group here in Salt Lake," Tom said. "The guys on that list are members of it. Elrod says they're all clean, but it wouldn't hurt to check."

Carl nodded. "Okay, Tom. But I still think we should pick Elrod up. I mean, look at the squad room, we've picked all the other trash off the streets."

"Just give me one day."

"What if Elrod skips town," Carl said, "or worse, kills somebody else?"

"If that worries you, send Baxter out to keep an eye on him."

Carl nodded. "That's a good idea. Baxter's not worth anything around here, anyway."

"Good," Tom said. "Do it. Baxter needs the exercise."

Carl smiled. "I had you wrong, Tom. I'm sorry."

"What do you mean?"

"I didn't think you really cared about this case. I mean, who has ever cared about the Saints?"

Tom's eyes wandered over the scene in the squad room, over the officers feverishly questioning blank-faced or angry suspects or striding back and forth from their desks to the file drawers, or simply sitting, staring toward the window as if waiting to see some Avenging Angel sweep down toward the streets, flaming sword raised in assault, and no one to stop him but themselves.

It was midafternoon by the time Tom reached the Salt Lake City Public Library. It was clear to him now that Carl and Philby and the rest of them were right: someone really was exacting a terrible revenge upon the Saints. He had dismissed such a possibility at first as no more than Mormon paranoia, the cautious, watchful defensiveness McBride had mentioned with a kind of stubborn pride. But someone was associating himself with an ancient murderer in a floppy hat. William B. Thornton was the key, and he knew that he had to find out exactly who that old man was.

Tom stepped up to the librarian's desk and showed his identification. The librarian glanced at the badge. He had a short-cropped blond beard and wire glasses. The sign on his desk identified him as Charles McCormick.

"What can I do for you?" he asked.

"I'm looking for books on Mormon history," Tom told him.

McCormick smiled. "Well, you've certainly come to the right place. Did you bring a truck?"

Tom smiled. "I guess you have a lot of books on that."

"Enough," McCormick said. "Is there any particular aspect of Mormon history you're interested in?"

"Not really," Tom said.

"Any particular period?"

"No."

McCormick nodded. "Well, I suppose the best thing is to start with a general survey. We have several of those. Take a seat over there and I'll bring them out."

"Thanks," Tom said. He walked over to the table McCormick had indicated and sat down.

A few minutes later McCormick brought a large stack of books and placed them on the desk in front of Tom. "That should keep you busy for a while," he said.

"Thanks."

"Sure," McCormick said. "If you need anything else, just let me know."

Tom took the first book from the top of the stack. It was a general history of Mormonism, written in a stodgy, lifeless style, but the facts were there, and as Tom read he began to get an idea of what Salt Lake City was all about. It was the haven chosen by a persecuted people, a little village on the banks of a dead sea that a stoical, dedicated, and amazingly industrious people had made into their shining capital. And it seemed to Tom, as he read, that if ever a people had needed a haven, the Mormons had. Theirs was a history of the most relentless persecution. They had been massacred at Haun's Mill in 1838. Joseph Smith had been beaten, tarred, and finally murdered. They had been driven into their fields and there, crouching down among the corn, had watched their homes burned to the

ground. They had been pursued by state militia, driven from
settlement to settlement, state to state, until finally they had
made the great trek across the plains and into the uninhabited
wilds of Utah. "This is the place," Brigham Young had said as
he stared into the Great Basin. And so they had stopped here at
Salt Lake and erected their City of the Saints, a cathedral to
their endurance and a monument to their past.

Tom closed the book and glanced out the window. The sky
was beginning to take on the deep blue of the late afternoon. He
took the next book and scanned through it, his eyes searching
for the odd detail, the curious event, the sudden slant that
would suddenly connect all that had recently taken place in Salt
Lake City with William B. Thornton.

It was evening by the time Tom finished going through the
rest of the books. Most of them only repeated what he had read
in the first, and none mentioned Thornton.

Tom stood up and stretched, then returned the books to Mc-
Cormick's desk.

"Find what you were looking for?" McCormick asked.

"No," said Tom.

"Well, there's plenty more if you want to come back."

"Thanks. Maybe I will." Tom walked to his car and drove
back to his apartment. The sun had already set when he got
there, and for a while he sat in his room, his mind going over all
the details of the past few days, the pathology reports, ballistic
tests, and interrogations. He thought of Mrs. Harrison watching him from her door, of Mrs. Parker's strong, unwavering
voice, of Philby's desperation. All of it seemed hidden behind
the portrait of William Thornton, a man who had killed and
been killed almost a hundred years before. Then he remembered the book Brannon had given him earlier in the afternoon.
He went out to his car and brought it back into the apartment,
turned on the light over his chair, and sat down.

The book's cover was illustrated with a photograph of the
Tabernacle. It was entitled *A History of the Mormon Struggle*.
Looking at it, Tom could feel an aching behind his eyes. He
flipped to the index, his finger running down the long list that
began under a capital *T*.

Suddenly he saw it there among all the other names, flaring
up at him from the page: *Thornton, William B., 74.*

He quickly turned inside the book and found page 74. There was only one short mention of Thornton, in a paragraph concerned with a series of Indian troubles that had plagued the early Mormon settlers in Utah: "As a consequence, certain violent acts were carried out against the local Indian population. The Church was quick to denounce these acts and to punish those who had engaged in them. One such person, William B. Thornton, was executed by firing squad in the late fall of 1858."

Tom closed the book. He knew no more now than he had known before. He turned the book over on his lap and glanced down. There was a picture of the author on the back cover, a man with long, graying hair. The brief biography under the picture said the author, Sanford T. Lambert, was a distinguished historian who served as professor of history at Brigham Young University.

55

Epstein was sitting in a wheelchair when Tom came into his room.

"It ain't motorized," he said, "but it's nice compared to that goddamn bed."

"You look better." Tom held out the boxed chess game. "I didn't forget this time."

"Didn't leave from work, huh?"

"I did," Tom said, "but I went home to get it."

"How is the old neighborhood?" Epstein asked.

"Dusty as always."

Epstein glanced at the game. "Well, let's have a go at it."

Tom pulled a small table over to Epstein's chair, laid out the chessboard, and sat down.

"Snow line's getting lower on the mountains," Epstein said dully as he watched Tom assemble the pieces on the board.

"Winter's coming."

"You like winter in Salt Lake?"

"Better than anything else," Tom said.

"Thought any more about leaving?"

Tom placed the last pawn on the board. "No," he said. "Can't think of much of anywhere else to go." He looked up from the board. "Want to go first?"

Epstein shrugged. "Why not." He moved one of his pawns two spaces forward. "How's work coming?"

"A few things are coming together." Tom brought a pawn forward, facing Epstein's.

"The *Deseret News* is screaming off the presses," Epstein said.

"Yeah."

"*Tribune*'s not exactly mum, either."

"We're doing the best we can," Tom said.

Epstein brought a knight forward. "There was a time when cops just manufactured evidence. Laid a little dope in the back seat of somebody's car. Blammo. Conviction. Possession of a controlled substance. Two to ten."

Tom studied the board. "They still do a little of that," he said, "but not for the same reasons."

"Eliminating somebody else's competition, right?"

"Yeah."

"For a little extra carfare?"

Tom nodded.

Epstein glanced toward the window. "It's the water we all swim in, Tom."

Tom brought a second pawn forward.

"Playing it close to the vest," Epstein said.

"You're more aggressive than I am, Harry."

"That's why I always win."

"That and cheating," Tom said.

Epstein smiled. "I'll play it straight from now on. I don't have to cheat to beat you. You're a pussy at chess. You never take a chance." He brought the other knight forward. "Charge!"

Tom smiled. "You play chess like it's the Battle of the Bulge, Harry." He moved another pawn.

Epstein leaned forward and took the pawn with his knight. "You don't have your mind on the game, Tom."

"Yeah."

"Killings, that's what's on your brain."

Tom continued to watch the board. "I guess so."

"I did some rough things in my time," Epstein said, "but I never pushed anybody's button."

"You're a gentle soul, Harry."

"Didn't have what it takes to do that," Epstein added.

Tom grinned. "Gutless, that's you."

"Knew a lot of button men, though."

Tom kept his eyes on the board. "Yeah, I know."

"Knew a guy named Moe Bloomberg one time. A real mean bastard. Button man, but worse than that. Very nasty. I think he enjoyed it."

Tom hesitatly moved his rook forward.

"Good talker, though," Epstein said. "Bloomberg, I mean." He glanced at the board and instantly moved his queen three squares forward.

"You're really pulling out the heavy artillery," Tom said.

"Blitzkrieg," Epstein said.

Tom stroked his chin, his eyes fixed on the board.

"Moe used to laugh like hell when he'd tell one of his fucking stories," Epstein said. "Cackled. The whole world was hilarious as far as he was concerned."

"Yeah?" Tom said. "Well, in that line, you got to have a sense of humor, right?"

Epstein nodded. "I guess so. Anyway, he had this weird story one night. We were sitting in a bar on Second Avenue. Little hole-in-the-wall place, bugs on the wall, rats in the back, you know the kind of place I mean."

"Yeah."

"Moe loved places like that," Epstein added. "It was his element, you might say."

Tom moved his own queen up two squares.

"Jesus, Tom," Epstein said with a laugh. "You sure you want to take a risk like that?" He moved his knight and took another of Tom's pawns.

Tom shook his head. "You're wiping me out."

Epstein nodded indifferently. "Well, just a couple nights before, Moe had smoked a guy in one of those dumps out on Long Island. Guy's name was Stein. Herbie Stein. Another Jew boy.''

Tom continued to watch the board.

"They'd gone to the races together," Epstein said. "Moe and Herbie, I mean. Spent the whole fucking night on the town with Moe knowing that he was going to waste Herbie in a few hours. That was part of the thrill. Betting horses all night with a guy you knew was going to be dead by morning. Power trip, that's the way Moe felt about it.''

Tom brought out his knight.

Epstein looked at the board for a moment, then moved his queen forward once again. "Anyway, Moe and Herbie, they were fucking pals all evening. Telling jokes. Slapping each other on the back. Hell, Herbie probably thought Moe was his best goddamn friend."

Tom kept his eyes on the board, trying to figure out Epstein's game plan.

"Anyway, Moe told Herbie that maybe they should go out to Long Island, check out the sunrise, you know?''

Tom nodded.

"Sunrise!" Epstein laughed. "Fucking asshole convinces Herbie that he just ain't lived till he's seen the sun rise over Long Island Sound.''

Tom moved his rook up one space, a stall.

Epstein pushed his rook up two squares and took one of Tom's pawns. "Herbie buys the bullshit," he said, "hook, line, and sinker.''

Tom took one of Epstein's pawns with one of his own.

"Well, you got to lose a little to gain a little," Epstein said as Tom swept the pawn from the board. He moved his king to the side. Then he glanced at Tom. "You got to be willing to make a sacrifice in this fucking world, Tom.''

Tom kept his eyes on the board.

Epstein leaned back in his chair. "So, as it turns out, these two nature lovers head out toward Long Island. It's a pretty long drive, and all the way, Moe is bullshitting Herbie about how much they have in common. Two Jew boys in gangland. Moe's going on about the fucking spics and dagos, about how fucking stupid they are and Herbie, he's eating this shit up.''

Tom moved his knight forward and stared hopelessly at the board.

Epstein moved another pawn forward one square. "So, after a while, they end up on some deserted beach waiting for the sun to crack over the horizon."

Tom moved his hand toward the board, then drew it back.

"Move, Tom," Epstein said. "Don't be such a chicken shit."

"Just give me a minute, Harry."

Epstein shrugged. "Take all the time you want. It won't do you no good, though."

"Just relax."

"Sure." Epstein glanced down at his hands, then back up at Tom. "So anyway, these two fucks are on the beach, and Moe's going on about what a great pal Herbie is and then, right in the middle, he says, 'And you know Herbie, that's why it breaks my heart to do this.' "

Tom looked up.

"That's what he said, Tom," Epstein said. "And Herbie, he looks around and his face turns white, but he don't say nothing, just starts to tremble."

Tom watched Epstein's face closely and for the first time saw something that looked like sadness move across it.

"That's when Moe took out the twenty-two," Epstein said. "He pointed it right at Herbie's head, and Moe said this weird look came into Herbie's face, you know, like he couldn't believe it, couldn't believe another Jew would kill him." Epstein looked down at the board briefly, then let his eyes drift up toward Tom. "Then Moe shot Herbie in the face."

Tom felt the fingers of his hands curl up into his palms. "Is that story true, Harry?"

"That story is absolutely true." Epstein turned away quickly, facing the window, watching the snowcapped mountains as they darkened in the distance. "Winter," he said softly. "I don't like winter."

As he watched Epstein, Tom could feel an idea taking shape in his mind. At first it was no more than the vaguest intimation, but then the pieces began to move together toward some central notion, like bodies drifting toward the pier.

56

Tom arrived at Lambert's office in the middle of the morning and found the professor sitting quietly at his desk. His head faced the window, so that Tom could only see his white hair edging over the back of the chair.

Tom knocked lightly at the open office door. "Professor Lambert?"

The chair spum around instantly.

"You're Sanford Lambert?" Tom asked.

"Yes. Who are you?" Lambert asked. He was dressed elegantly in a black suit, a gold watch chain stretching across his midsection.

"My name is Tom Jackson. I'm with the Salt Lake City Police Department."

Lambert's hands moved idly across the top of his desk. "Are you looking for someone?"

"For you," Tom said.

Lambert drew his hands from the desk and let them fall into his lap. "For what reason, may I ask?"

Tom nodded toward the chair in front of Lambert's desk. "May I sit down?"

"Of course."

Tom eased himself into the chair. "I don't suppose you get many cops up here."

"Since this is a great university," Lambert said, "you can make that assumption." He brought one hand up toward his tie and unnecessarily tightened the knot. "What is it that you want with me?"

"You've heard about the murders in Salt Lake."

Lambert smiled thinly. "I have, to be sure."

"Well, I'm with Homicide."

"How interesting," Lambert said dully. "But what has that to do with me?"

"Well, it'll probably sound strange to you," Tom began, "but—"

"It will no doubt sound strange," Lambert interrupted, "but could we get on with it?"

Tom let Lambert's impatience pass. "There is some evidence," he said, "which leads me to believe that these recent murders are connected."

"Indeed," Lambert said lamely.

"You wrote a book on the history of Mormonism," Tom said.

"I've written many books on that subject. Which one?"

"A History of the Mormon Struggle."

"A general survey," Lambert said. "What of it?"

"Well, in that book you mention a man by the name of William B. Thornton."

Lambert watched Tom expressionlessly.

"Do you remember him?"

Lambert closed his eyes slowly. "Of course I remember him. I wrote the book."

"Yes, but there are only a few lines about Thornton."

Lambert rubbed his eyes wearily. "Yes, yes. But as I said, that book is a general survey. It attempts to deal with the whole of Mormon history, at least the early history. You can't go into great detail about isolated incidents, obscure individuals." He drew his hands away from his face and folded them on the desk. "Again, to press the point. What does all this have to do with murder?"

"Well, that name Thornton, it keeps popping up."

"Really? In what way?"

"I'd rather not go into detail about that," Tom said. "But I'd like for you to tell me more about Thornton."

Lambert shrugged gently. "Certainly. What is it that you wish to know?"

"Anything you can tell me," Tom said.

"Beginning with what?"

"Well, just who was he?"

"He was one of the original Utah settlers," Lambert said. "He came here with the party of Brigham Young."

"And he got into a lot of trouble."

"You might call it that."

"Well, he was executed," Tom said.

"Then I suppose you could say that he got into a certain amount of trouble, couldn't you?" Lambert said dryly.

"What did he do, exactly?"

"He committed murder," Lambert said. His eyes shifted away from Tom. "Several times."

Tom took his notebook from his coat and opened it. "Tell me about that, the murders."

"Well, it all began with something Thornton saw," Lambert said stiffly.

"Which was?"

"He was at a trading post in southern Utah one afternoon, and a party of Indians came by. They had two young white girls with them. Very young. Children. They said that they had captured them from white men and that they wanted to sell them back now. That's what they did, the Indians. They offered the girls for sale."

Lambert stopped. He picked up a pen from his desk and twirled it between his fingers. "Unfortunately, either the white men were without funds, or they simply refused to buy the girls. The Indians began to move away. Then the chief turned back and started cursing the white men. He grew more and more angry, and finally he took the smaller child by the heels and began whirling her around, still cursing. The white men watched, but still no one offered to buy the children. That made the Indian uncontrollably angry, and he stepped over to a stone wall and bashed the little girl's head against it. He did this repeatedly, until she was dead." The pencil dropped from Lambert's hand and rolled a few inches across his desk. "That's what Thornton saw. That's what changed him."

"In what way?"

"Turned him into what you would no doubt call a murderer," Lambert said crisply.

"What did he do?"

Lambert took a deep breath and leaned back in his chair. "Are you a Saint, may I ask?"

"No."

"I didn't think so. This whole explanation will take a little longer."

"I have all day."

"All right," Lambert said. "First, the Book of Mormon is the real history of the native American. It teaches that the gospel was preached among the Indians before the first white men came here. As such, it suggests that the Indians are among the chosen people of God. For that reason, Mormons have always tried to deal justly with the Indians, to educate them, to take them fully into the Church, to treat them as Saints on a level of equality. This practice caused a lot of trouble between the Saints and the Gentile settlers. They were forever accusing us of being in league with the Indians, of selling them guns or setting them against the Gentile settlers."

Tom nodded.

"Still," Lambert said, "the Church held to this position of giving the Indians a special place within the faith. They were never excluded—the way, for example, the Negroes were." He smiled. "Are you following me, Mr. Jackson?"

"Yes."

"Well, all of this finally has to do with Thornton," Lambert said. "He was a Saint who had always accepted the truths of the faith, and one of these truths was the Indian's right to be in the Church."

"And then he saw what happened at the trading post," Tom said.

"Yes."

"So he started killing Indians?" Tom asked.

"No," Lambert said. "He was not naturally a murderer. He didn't want to kill anybody. For a long time he argued that the Indians should be denied the faith. He told this to anybody who would listen. No one would. So, in the end, he acted."

"What did he do?"

Lambert seemed to hesitate for a moment, then he continued. "He committed murder, as I've already said."

Tom leaned forward in his chair. "You also said it was more than one."

Lambert nodded. "Yes, more than one. Several."

"And later he was executed for them."

"Yes, shot to death." Lambert picked the pen from the desk and began twirling it again. "He wanted to be killed, to be executed."

"Why?"

Lambert shook his head. "I'm not sure. Perhaps it was simply guilt. Or despair."

"Can you tell me more about the murders?"

Lambert looked up. "No. You should talk to Professor Kraft, down the hall. He introduced me to the story of William Thornton. He can tell you more." He pointed to the left. "He's in his office now, I think."

57

Professor Kraft's door was closed, but Tom heard boxes being moved behind it. He knocked lightly and waited until the door opened.

"Yes?"

Tom showed his identification. "I'm investigating the recent series of murders in Salt Lake."

Kraft watched Tom warily for a moment, then opened the door wider. "I don't know what that could have to do with me, but come in."

Tom stepped into the office. It was cluttered with pasteboard boxes, stacked against one wall as well as in front of Kraft's overly large wooden desk.

Kraft inched his way around the boxes and took a seat behind his desk.

"Have a seat, Mr. Jackson," he said, "if you can find one."

Tom took a small stack of folders from one of the chairs in front of Kraft's desk and sat down.

Kraft folded his arms over his chest and leaned back slightly. "Now, what can I do for you?"

"I was just talking with Professor Lambert," Tom began.

Kraft eyed Tom intently. "About murder?"

"About an old murderer," Tom said. "A man named William B. Thornton."

"Thornton, yes," Kraft said. "How did you hear of him?"

"From Professor Lambert's book," Tom said. "He told me that you know a good deal more about this Thornton than he does."

Kraft smiled. "That's probably true about a great many things."

"Where did you learn about Thornton?"

"I am a historian. Mormon history is my specialty."

"But Thornton's pretty obscure."

"Relevant, however."

"To what?"

"To his time," Kraft said. "To its extremity."

Tom nodded. "His victims, who were they?"

"The first was a young Indian woman," Kraft said. "A beggar of sorts, very poor. She lived in Salt Lake, more or less on the streets, living on handouts of one kind or another."

"How did he kill her?"

"He strangled her," Kraft said, almost casually. "Then he laid her out in a place where he was fairly sure she would be discovered by the Mormon militia."

"What did he do next?" he asked.

Kraft's eyes grew very still and thoughtful. "Perhaps he liked the taste of it, murder. Perhaps it pleased him in some way. Anyway, he killed again."

"Another Indian?" Tom asked.

Kraft shook his head. "No. Did Professor Lambert tell you about the position of the Saints in regard to Indians?"

"Yes."

"And also about what Thornton saw out at the trading post, the way that little girl was killed?"

"Yes."

Kraft nodded. "All right, well, you can understand the rest. There were three Saints who had been conspicuous in advocating the position of the Indian within the Church. One of them was a pamphleteer who had been publishing broadsides on behalf of the Indians for quite some time. Thornton hitched a ride

to Provo. Dirt poor, Thornton. He didn't even own a horse."
Kraft smiled. "Anyway, he hitched a ride in a wagon. When he
got to Provo he found the man—his name was Lancaster, I believe. He found him saddling up his own horse in a stable. He
shot him in the head."

Tom could see Fielding's body stretched out under the covering, his head exploded by the .44. His mind was racing. "Did
he ever kill another woman?"

"No."

"Children?"

Kraft shook his head, watching Tom closely. "Why do you
ask?"

"Who were the other victims?" Tom asked quickly.

"They were both Church officials who had advocated the Indian cause."

"How were they killed?"

"One stabbed in the mountains. The other shot in his
home."

Tom felt his hands grip the arms of his chair. "And then they
caught him."

"Not exactly," Kraft said. "Thornton was too clever for
that. Besides, he wasn't through yet. Or at least, he thought he
wasn't."

"What do you mean?"

"He planned to kill again," Kraft said, and let it drop.

Tom leaned forward. "Who?"

"The Saints in Salt Lake were planning to have an Indian
speak at the general conference," Kraft said. "Thornton intended to kill this person at the exact moment of his speech. He
intended to kill him in full view of the congregation and all the
Church officials. That would make his point. After he had done
that, I don't think it mattered what happened to him."

"What did happen?" Tom asked.

"A witness had seen the last killing. A woman. She had a
good memory, and she drew such a complete portrait of Thornton for the authorities that they were able to spot him on the
street before the conference."

Tom nodded.

"They hadn't put the whole story together yet," Kraft went

on, "but Thornton made his whole plan known during the trial. He was executed a week later."

Tom stood up. "Thanks for your time."

Kraft nodded. "What's all this got to do with what's going on in Salt Lake?"

"I'm not sure," Tom said.

"Well, I hope you catch your man before I leave," Kraft said.

"You're leaving?"

"Oh, yes. That's what all these boxes are. I'm making ready my departure. I'm going to another place. Soon."

"Well, good luck, then," Tom said.

"Thank you." Kraft smiled quietly. "And the very best of luck to you, too, Mr. Jackson. You seem very dedicated. That is a passing virtue."

58

It was almost two in the afternoon by the time Tom got back to Salt Lake. He parked near the corner of South Second and Main. Then he got out and began walking up Main toward the center of the city. He knew not who William B. Thornton had been—a killer who had struck out a hundred years ago, who had killed four people in the name of a deranged religious idea that the Indians must be separated forever from his Church. But this knowledge brought him no closer to the identity of the killer than when he had first walked into Thornton Elrod's darkened room. He knew only that the killer was probably killing out of his hatred for blacks. Thornton had picked an Indian woman and strangled her. The killer had picked a black prostitute, had asked for one specifically, and had then killed her and laid her out for the police to find. Then during the next few days he had killed three men, one who had written in support of blacks in the Church, and two Church officials who had at least gone along with the change in policy. Tom guessed that Jennifer Warren and the Parker children had caught the murderer in the act and been killed only for what they had seen. The first Thornton had been destroyed by a witness. The second had taken no chances.

Tom continued to walk up Main Street, the buildings of the business and financial center of Salt Lake rising above him, casting their dark shadows across the wide boulevard. The city was known for the breadth of its streets, and the openness had appealed to Tom when he had first come here. But now this same expansiveness struck him as almost foolhardy, an invitation to assault a faith that had grown heady with its own power, that believed too deeply in its own resilience and invulnerability. Olsen had walked fearlessly into the woods. Parker had swung open his front door and stared into the face of the man who would kill him. They were like Redmon, ready to storm the door at the Richmont, perfectly at peace with their own courage, unchallenged in their sense of divine protection. In New York, Tom thought, such an attitude would get you only one thing, death.

Tom stopped at the corner of Main and First South. To the left he could see the Salt Palace Convention Center. A crowd milled about the plaza stretched out from the entrance of the building, part of the overflow of people had been sweeping into Salt Lake to attend the general conference ceremonies. He could imagine these people filling the hotels clustered around Temple Square, then streaming out each morning and marching like a strange, civilian army, winding their way up First West to the Pioneer Museum, then down again to the Beehive House, finally ending their day in the darkness arena of the Hansen Planetarium. They were the tourists of their faith and Salt Lake was their Mecca, the place they came to for inspiration and renewal, a city set down within a curve of snow-capped mountains, a fortress against that alien, Gentile world they had no wish to join or understand. And yet, somewhere within the heart of their own citadel, someone was killing them.

Tom stopped for a moment in front of the ZCMI shopping mall, with its shimmering glass architecture, and glanced through the great glass entrance at the shops inside. It seemed a single stone might bring the whole frail structure down upon itself in a huge, shattering collapse.

He turned and walked to the corner of Main and South Temple. Then he crossed the street and stood for a moment under the great brown portico of the Hotel Utah. Knots of people stood waiting for cabs, while others poured in and out of the hotel in a steady bustling movement. To Tom their faces seemed relentlessly cheerful, as if nothing could possibly harm them.

Tom glanced at his watch. In a little while Redmon would give the signal and the police would sweep out again, cleaning the Salt Lake streets of Thornton Elrod and his strange band. They would haul them in, push them into chairs, and grill them relentlessly until they finally came up with nothing, as he knew they would.

Tom pushed through the crowd and walked over to the group of statues at the very center of South Temple Street. He sat down on a granite bench and stared up at the statue of Brigham Young. Young's face was severe and humorless, his figure formally dressed in a long coat, his left palm outstretched and raised slightly: *This is the place.* For a time. Tom stared at the face, then his eyes drifted down the column to the small plaque where the names of the first settlers were recorded. Three were set apart from all the rest—the blacks. He turned away, his mind drifting back to the portrait of William B. Thornton in Elrod's house. Then he stood up, glanced back at the Hotel Utah, and saw Mordecai McBride standing at the curb in the dark shade of the portico. He started to cross the street to speak with him, when McBride suddenly spun around to face someone who had evidently called to him from the hotel entrance. Bending slightly to get a better view, Tom saw the man standing only a few feet from McBride—a tall black man in a light blue suit. McBride moved toward him and gathered him into his arms. A wedge of light fell across the black man's face, and at that moment Tom knew.

59

Thornton Elrod was sitting rigidly next to Carl's desk when Tom rushed into the squad room.

"I waited as long as I could," Carl said. "I really did. Then I had to tell Philby, and he said the bunch had to be picked up right away."

"Is Philby here?"

"In his office."

"Come with me, Carl."

Carl did not move. "What's the matter?"

"I need to talk to Philby, and I want you to be there."

"Okay," Carl said hesitantly. "If you say so."

Tom led him quickly back to Philby's office.

Philby leaped up from his desk as Tom entered the office. "You must be out of your mind, Tom! Holding back on that Elrod thing. Are you crazy?"

"Elrod had nothing to do with the murders," Tom said.

Philby glanced at Carl. "Is he nuts? Is he absolutely nuts?"

Carl shrugged.

Philby glared at Tom. "You blew it, friend," he said, "and you'll be lucky if you don't get busted for it. You'd better get your shoes resoled, Tom, because you're going to end up on the beat again, acting the way you do."

"I'm telling you, Elrod is clear on this."

"How do you know?" Philby cried. "What's the hell's the matter with you?"

"William B. Thornton was Elrod's great-great-grandfather," Tom said sternly. "That's all you got."

306

"In a pig's eye!" Philby shouted. "That guy has more wives than a barnyard rooster."

"That doesn't mean he killed anybody."

"He's got the motive," Philby said, "and you knew it, and you held back on it."

"Polygamy has nothing to do with any of this," Tom said.

Philby looked at Carl unbelievingly. "I think your partner is going to be retiring from the Salt Lake police," he said. He turned to Tom. "Okay, you got the whole story. If Elrod's clean, who do you suggest we hit next?"

"I don't know," Tom said.

Philby smiled. "I didn't think so."

"I don't know who the killer is," Tom said, "but I think I know who the next victim is."

Philby's eyes squeezed together. "Who?"

"I found out who Thorton was," Tom began. "He was a killer. He killed four people over a hundred years ago."

"A ghost?" Philby said. "Tom, you really have slipped into another world."

"Our man is imitating Thornton."

"How do you know that?"

"Thornton got the idea that the Church should change the way it thinks about Indians," Tom said. "He saw an Indian kill a little girl at a trading post in southern Utah. He decided that Indians should not be allowed in the Church."

"So we've got another guy who hates Indians," Philby said, astonished. "That's what you're telling me?"

"No," Tom said. "Thornton killed an Indian woman and laid her out very nicely, just the way Jones was laid out at the Paradise. The guy who killed Jones signed his name William Thornton. See what I mean?"

"So the black prostitute took the place of the Indian woman?" Carl said.

"That's right," Tom said. "Then, over the next few days, Thornton killed three prominent Saints, people who had been very favorable to the Indians, who were trying to get them into the Church."

"Fielding. Olsen. Parker," Carl said slowly.

Tom smiled. "Yeah."

Philby sat down and folded his hands together. "What about the girl? And Parker's children?"

"Witnesses," Tom said. "The first Thornton was turned in by a witness. The one we have, he won't take any chances like that."

Philby nodded thoughtfully. "So where does that lead us, Tom?"

"Well, my guess is that we're dealing with someone who doesn't want blacks in the Church."

"There may be more people like that than you think," Carl said.

"I wouldn't know about that," Tom said. "But if my guess is right, then Olsen and Parker must have had something to do with blacks being admitted into the Church."

"Into the priesthood," Carl said.

"What?"

"The priesthood," Carl said. "Blacks have always been allowed to be members of the Church."

"That's right," Philby said. "But wait a minute. You said Olsen and Parker. What about Fielding?"

"I know he supported the black thing," Tom said. "I read one of his articles."

"So to bring the thing full circle, we just need to know about Parker and Olsen?" Philby asked.

"Yes."

"All right," Philby said. "That won't be hard to find out." He picked up the phone and dialed.

"Hello, Jerry," he said after a moment. "This is Philby. I need to know something. A few years back, during this thing with the blacks and the priesthood, how did Donald Olsen and Ben Parker stand on that?"

Tom watched as Philby quietly nodded his head.

"And what about Ben?" Philby waited, listening. "I see. Thanks, Jerry." He hung up the phone and looked at Tom. "Okay, Tom, it fits. Olsen wrote a lot of press statements on it. All favorable. And according to Jerry, Ben Parker was against the old policy and did everything he could to get it changed."

"That's it, then," Tom said.

Philby smiled. "Not quite. We've just got a motive. We're a long way from nailing anybody."

Carl straightened his shoulders. "So what do we do now? Put an armed guard around every Saint in Utah who's not a racist?"

"No," Tom said. "Just one."

Philby leaned forward in his chair. "That's the victim you mentioned."

"Yes."

"Who is it?"

"Roger Berryman."

"Oh, God," Carl groaned.

"You think he's the man Thornton is after?" Philby asked.

"Yes."

"Why, Tom?"

"Thornton was planning to kill again before he got caught—a prominent Indian. Thornton was planning to kill him at the general conference. Berryman's going to speak at the conference."

Carl shook his head mournfully. "Oh, no."

"So we need to put some protection on Berryman," Philby said.

"Right away," Tom said. "But the problem is, you can't protect him for the rest of his life."

"What do you suggest?"

"The only way Berryman is really going to be protected is if we get Thornton."

"Where is Berryman going to be speaking?" Tom asked.

"The Tabernacle," Carl said. "Tomorrow night."

"I could get in touch with the General Authorities," Philby said. "We might have the conference location changed to the Temple."

"What good would that do?" Tom asked.

"Well, the only people who can get into the Temple are Saints," Philby said. "You can't just walk in there. You have to have what we call a Recommend, a letter from your stake president verifying that you're a Saint."

"Anybody can walk into the Tabernacle," Carl said to Tom.

Tom shook his head. "I don't know what you're talking about."

"Simple, Tom," Philby said. "Thornton couldn't get into the Temple. That way Berryman would be safe. You said yourself that the other Thornton, the first one, wanted to kill the Indian at the general conference."

"If Berryman gave his speech in the Temple," Carl explained, "then Thornton wouldn't be able to get in, so he couldn't kill Berryman."

"But what if our man *is* a Saint?" Tom said.

Carl and Philby glanced at each other quickly.

"Look," Philby said, "do you really think this Thornton, this murderer, could be a Saint?"

"The first one was," Tom said flatly.

"That was a hundred years ago, Tom," Philby said. "This is not frontier Utah anymore."

"Look, Tom," Carl said. "We're not just being naïve in this. To be a Saint is very special. We keep a close watch on ourselves. Somebody like this Thornton, he has to be crazy. If he were a Saint, a practicing Saint, somebody would have noticed, and this Thornton, whoever he is, he wouldn't have continued in the Church."

"So he wouldn't have a Recommend," Philby added.

"All right," Tom said, "maybe he isn't a Saint. But we still have the same problem. We have to catch him, and we won't be able to do that without Berryman."

Carl's mouth dropped open. "You mean you want to use Roger Berryman as a decoy?" He looked at Philby, amazed.

Philby ran his fingers through his hair. "I don't see how we can do that, Tom. This man Berryman, he may be an Apostle of the Church one day. We can't take any chances with his life."

"We're trying to save his life," Tom said. "We don't know if Thornton will give up just because he can't get Berryman during the conference. And we can't keep a houseful of cops around him for the rest of his life."

"My God, Tom," Carl said. "Do you know how it would look if some nut killed Berryman in the Tabernacle? Half the world thinks we're crazy as it is. And if that happened, Berryman murdered—dear God, we'd never get over that!"

"I don't see what choice we have," Tom said.

Carl's mouth closed slowly. He glanced about the room as if for a sudden revelation.

Tom looked at Philby. "We could protect him in the Tabernacle," he said.

"You know how many people the Tabernacle seats, Tom?" Tom shook his head.

"Eight thousand," Philby said. "And it'll be packed for the conference for the simple reason that Berryman is speaking."

"Where will Berryman speak in the Tabernacle?" Tom asked.

"At the front altar, I imagine."

"To get at him from any distance," Tom said, "Thornton would have to use a rifle. We can spot that."

"What about close range?" Philby asked.

"We can blanket the orchestra section with our own men."

"There's no way to be sure we can protect Berryman, Tom," Philby said.

"Right, absolutely no way," Carl added quickly. "I don't see how we can set something like this up."

Philby looked at Tom seriously. "Frankly, Tom, I don't either."

"Well, we're not going to nail Thornton before tomorrow night," Tom said. "And we know that Berryman is in danger. So we don't have a choice, do we? We either protect him or we don't."

Philby thought about it for a moment. "It'll mean carrying guns into the Tabernacle," he said finally. "We can't do that without telling the General Authorities."

"This is a terrible thing," Carl said.

Tom continued to watch Philby. "And you'll need to tell Berryman."

Philby nodded. His face had suddenly turned very sad and remote.

"All we've ever wanted is peace," Carl said softly. "Now this."

Tom turned and walked out of the office. He met Baxter halfway to his desk.

Baxter nodded toward Carl and Philby. "What's got those two looking so down in the mouth?"

Tom glanced back at Philby's office, then at Baxter. "Leave them alone," he said. "They have troubles of their own."

60

It was almost nightfall by the time Philby called Tom and Carl back into his office.

"I've checked with the General Authorities," he said quietly. "I've told them the whole thing. They believe that Berryman should be protected at all cost."

"What does that mean?" Tom asked.

"It means we're going to cover the Tabernacle from top to bottom," Philby said.

"Did you talk to Mr. Berryman?" Carl asked.

"The General Authorities did," Philby said.

"What did he say?"

Philby smiled. "He said his life has always been in God's hands, and he is content to leave it there."

"Meaning what?" Tom asked.

"Meaning that whatever the General Authorities decide, that's what he'll abide by."

"So we can go in," Tom said. "Full scale."

"Yes."

"SWAT too?" Carl asked.

Philby shook his head. "No," he said. "Too trigger-happy, and their cannons are too big. We don't want to blow the Tabernacle away."

"So it's just Homicide?" Tom asked.

"Everybody except SWAT. The uniform guys are going to get a taste of undercover." Philby pulled a rolled paper from the shelf behind his desk and drew it out. "The General Authorities sent this over. It's the layout of the Tabernacle. We're going to have to plot our positions on it before we go in.'' He looked at Tom ominously. ''You're the point man, Tom.''

Tom nodded.

Philby placed his finger near the end of the first pew. ''You'll be sitting just to the left of the lectern.'' He pulled his finger over a few inches. ''It's here. That's where Berryman will speak.''

''With the whole choir behind him,'' Carl said, his eyes fixed on the drawing.

Philby smiled. ''We're going to have two guys in the choir, too.'' He moved his finger to the other side of the Tabernacle. ''You'll be here, Carl. And Baxter will be sitting right in the middle of the first pew.''

Tom let his eyes move over the drawing. ''What about the balcony?''

''It'll be covered.'' Philby glanced back down at the paper. ''But if Thornton is using a close-range weapon, then you three are the only people between him and Berryman.''

Carl shook his head. ''I hate this. I really do. Going into the Tabernacle like this, with guns. It doesn't seem right somehow.''

''Maybe nothing will happen,'' Philby said. ''Tom may be wrong. Let's hope he is. But we can't take a chance.''

Carl looked at Tom. ''Those other Thorntons, the ones on Elder McBride's list. They're all clean. I just thought I'd let you know.''

Tom said nothing.

''All right,'' Philby said, ''that's it. I'll tell Baxter about his position.'' He looked back and forth from Tom to Carl. ''Any questions?''

''Be at the Tabernacle at seven o'clcok tomorrow night,'' Philby said. ''Wear suits. Try not to look like cops, especially you, Tom. And don't be glancing around the whole time. We're doing this to nail somebody, not to scare him off. And I want to make something else clear. If anybody burns their cover in this operation, they're finished in the department. You understand?''

''Yes,'' Carl said.

''Tom?''

''I understand.''

"Good," Philby said. "I want you two to take the rest of the day and tomorrow off. I want you to be alert in every possible way tomorrow night." He looked at Carl. "So leave your wife alone tonight. Let her get a little sleep for a change. And you get some, too."

Carl's face turned bright red.

Philby looked at Tom. "I don't know what your habits are, Tom," he said, "but if drinking's one of them, lay off the booze. You can have a nightcap after this is over." He looked up and down Tom's body and made a face as if he had picked up a bad odor. "That the only suit you got?"

"I have one more, but it's not much different."

"Buy yourself a new one," Philby said. "This is going to be a pretty well-dressed crowd. You've got to fit in, look like you belong. I don't want you wandering down the aisle of the Tabernacle looking like a ragpicker."

"I'll get one this afternoon."

"Fine," Philby said. "Now, both of you, for the last time, any questions?"

No one spoke.

"Okay, then," Philby said. "See you tomorrow night." He looked at them as if they were brothers on the way to battle. "Listen, say a prayer for yourselves." His eyes shifted over to Tom. "You, too, Tom," he said softly. "I mean, what could it hurt?"

Tom spent the early evening hours looking for a suit. He finally found one in a place called The Beehive Clothiers, a dark blue, three-piece type that made him look, he thought, like a stockbroker.

When he walked into The People's Choice an hour later still wearing it, Lucy barely recognized him.

"Jesus," she said. Then she whistled. "What happened to you?"

Tom sat down at the counter. "Hamburger and a Coke, Lucy," he said.

"Really, Tom?" Lucy said, laughing. "Sure you want to eat greasy shit like that in those fancy new duds?"

"I'll use a bib."

"You'll need one," Lucy said. She turned and threw a patty on the grill.

"Where are you going, Tom?" she asked, turning back toward him. "An uptown AA meeting?"

"I'm just a social drinker," Tom said dryly.

Lucy leaned toward the counter. "Ain't seen you lately."

"I've been busy."

"Chasing girls?"

Tom shook his head. "Anything but."

Lucy seemed satisfied. She turned back to the grill. "What have you heard from old Epstein?"

"He's recovering."

"So the bastard lived?"

"Yes," Tom said. "He wants to make it to your wedding."

"Fat chance." Lucy turned back toward Tom. "Heard from what's-her-name—Phyllis?"

"Not a word."

"Poor Tom," Lucy said, smiling. "Woman left him high and dry. Nobody to replace her."

"Luck of the draw," Tom said. "You better flip that patty before you burn it."

Lucy shifted around to the grill. "All dressed up like that. Got a hot date?"

"Just going home," Tom said, and something in the words seemed to hit him very hard.

Tom watched television for four hours straight when he got back from the diner. Then he went to bed, but he couldn't sleep and he knew why. It was his fear, the same one that crept into his belly every time he had to go through a locked door or race down a rainswept alley. It seemed always to be staring down at him from its dark perch somewhere behind the moon. He envied the people who never seemed to feel it. People like Redmon, who had their own special armor. He had never had that, and so he had never lost his fear. Usually he kept it in check, but there were times, when the danger was coming toward him, when he had to swallow it whole, simply drag it down into himself, because if he didn't, he knew that he would simply bolt and run and never stop running. Of all the people he had ever known, only Gentry had been able to sense it. Once, they had

had to walk up a filthy staircase to the top of a tenement. A killer was waiting for them, just behind the metal door, his hands clutching at a .45. Both of them knew it, and both kept moving slowly up the stairs. But suddenly, near the door, Gentry touched Tom's arm and drew him down toward him. "The secret of courage, Tom," he said, "is just to push right through your fear." And that's what he had done, pushed through his fear, and through the metal door, and yet had managed to survive, to hold on to that little string that was his life, all he had, and beyond which, he knew, there was nothing.

61

A light drizzle had already begun to fall when Tom arrived at Temple Square on Sunday afternoon. Storm clouds had turned the air strangely dark, and the klieg lights illuminating the granite walls of the Temple gave them an almost golden cast.

Getting out of his car, Tom spotted Carl slouched against one of the trees that sprung up from the concrete plaza in front of the Temple. He walked over to him.

"You're here early."

"You, too."

"Nobody much here yet."

Carl shook his head. "Most of the time these conferences don't amount to much. They have them twice a year. Not too many people come."

"But since Berryman's speaking," Tom said, "they're going to make an occasion out of it, right?"

"Yes," Carl said, "and there'll be a lot of black Saints here tonight, too. This is a special affair for them." He shook his head. "If something happens to Berryman tonight, Tom, it'll be terrible."

"Well, we won't let that happen, Carl." He patted Carl on

the shoulder. "I'm going to go on over to the Tabernacle and look around."

"Don't burn your cover," Carl warned. "Remember what Philby said."

"I will."

Carl smiled faintly. "By the way, I like your suit."

Tom nodded and walked along the side of the Temple to the Tabernacle, located directly behind it.

Philby was standing at one of the entrances, with Baxter slumped against the wall beside him. He motioned Tom over to him.

"I'm glad you're here early, Tom," he said. "Baxter and me, we're going to go ahead into the building. You just hang around out here for a while and keep your eye on the people coming in."

"Without burning my cover?" Tom asked.

"Just look like you belong. There's a lot of strangers around here tonight. No one will notice you."

"All right," Tom said.

"Let's go, Baxter," Philby said.

Baxter pushed himself away from the wall. He winked at Tom. "This might turn into quite a meeting tonight."

"Maybe," Tom said.

Philby whirled around and glared at Baxter.

"Listen Baxter," he said. "This place is for Saints, and Saints don't smoke. So don't light up a stogie in the Tabernacle, you understand?"

Baxter nodded, winked again at Tom after Philby had turned his back, then shambled on into the building.

Tom walked a short distance back from the entrance to the Tabernacle and stood watching the first few people filter into the building. Carl had been right. There were quite a few blacks, and he noticed that they did not seem to feel at all out of place as they moved through the hallowed buildings of the faith that had excluded them for so long.

Tom glanced to the side and saw Carl making his way toward him.

"I thought I might go on in," he said.

"Philby wants me to stick around out here for a while," Tom said.

"This was a terrible day for me, Tom," Carl said. "I just didn't know what to do with myself. Mostly I just wandered around the house. What did you do?"

"Nothing much. Bought this suit last night. Got up fairly early this morning. Took a nap in the afternoon. That sort of thing."

Carl nodded indifferently.

"Why don't you go on in, Carl?" Tom said. "You'll just get more jumpy standing out here."

"Yeah." Carl edged himself into the growing crowd and flowed with it into the building.

For the next few minutes Tom watched the people making their way from various directions into the Tabernacle. He was surprised how many of the faces he recognized. There was the little man who owned a small grocery store near his apartment, and the man who sometimes worked on his car, and the woman who was the cashier at a movie theater he sometimes frequented. He had always been vaguely curious about what made up their lives, and now he knew at least a part of it. They were among the ranks of that army of Saints whose fortress was Salt Lake. They did their work, made their lives, reared their children, paid their mortgages, and came here to listen to the business of their faith. And then there were the other faces, the ones he would not have known if someone had not started killing people. He saw Jennifer Warren's mother and father drift into the Tabernacle, Mr. Warren holding his wife's arm tightly under his own. A few minutes later Professor Martin passed him, nodded quickly, and shuffled into the building. Mr. Robertson came a few minutes after that, then Professor Lambert, who looked a good deal larger than Tom remembered him, then Kraft, and finally Mordecai McBride, who glanced at him very briefly, then stopped, turned back around, and nodded pointedly.

Finally the crowd dwindled down to stragglers, and Tom walked inside the Tabernacle and down the long aisle to his seat near the stage. The great organ towered above everything at the very front of the building, its huge gold pipes rising high above the stage and finally disappearing into an enormous frame of dark polished wood.

Tom glanced over his shoulder. The seats were almost entirely filled, and the hum of the crowd reverberated through the oval interior of the building. He glanced up at the high, domed ceiling, its weight held securely in place by interlocking wooden arches.

He turned back toward the front as the choir began to take their seats, the men on one side of the stage, the women on the other. After the choir had seated itself, the General Authorities, the highest official body of the Church, filed up onto the stage through a door specially marked for them. They took their seats quickly and stared out toward the crowd.

To the right, Tom saw Baxter sitting casually near the middle of the auditorium, his arm slung over the side of the seat, his legs stretched out in front of him. Philby sat one row back. Across the auditorium on the right side was Redmon.

Suddenly a massive sound filled the room. Tom turned toward the stage and saw the organist's fingers dance along the four-tiered keyboard. Then the choir lifted its music, and the room seemed almost to shudder with the movement of their voices.

Tom waited impatiently for the choir to finish its recital, and when it was over he felt like standing up to stretch. But the program continued without intermission until at last the speaker of the evening, Roger Berryman, was introduced.

As Berryman walked onto the stage from the left, Tom felt his body tense. He glanced about, trying to detect any sudden movement in the crowd. Baxter fidgeted, drawing his legs up and pulling his arm back to his side. Philby leaned forward slightly, his eyes roaming the faces of the choir. Carl did not move.

Berryman was a tall man with graying hair, dressed in a black three-piece suit. He smiled brightly and raised his hands to the crowd.

"My friends and fellows in the faith," he began, "it is indeed an honor for me to address you this evening, here under the dome of this splendid Tabernacle, here in the city that is the symbol throughout the world of a living faith."

Tom could feel tension growing in his hands. He patted his shoulder holster quickly and glanced left and right.

"For some of us," Berryman continued, "it has been a long journey to this moment. I don't need to familiarize most of you with our history. We know it well. It is inseparable from us, and we are inseparable from it.''

He could feel his fear again, building in him with steady force. He sucked in his breath and waited, casting his eyes in every direction.

''And as long as we have our history,'' Berryman went on, ''we have a part of ourselves. For we know, absolutely know, that ours is the Restored Gospel of Jesus Christ.''

Tom turned his eyes toward the stage. Berryman's arms were outstretched, his body fully exposed behind the thin, wooden lectern.

''The Restored Gospel,'' Berryman intoned, ''the completed vision of the Christian faith. And oh, the glory of that completion, that restoration!''

Tom saw something shift suddenly within the ranks of the General Authorities. It was McBride, and his head was twisting right and left as if he were trying to draw something into focus.

Tom tucked his hand inside his coat and felt the firm wooden grip of his pistol. He leaned forward, watching McBride closely, and suddenly their eyes met. McBride's lips were moving slightly, as if he were trying to tell Tom something.

''For once we were lost,'' Berryman said loudly, tilting his face toward the dome of the Tabernacle, ''but now we are found!''

Tom could feel himself edging out of his seat, his eyes fixed fiercely on McBride. And McBride seemed to rise slightly from his chair, drawing up his hand from his lap, his finger outstretched, pointing.

Tom wheeled around in the direction McBride's finger indicated. Someone was moving toward the front of the Tabernacle, but Tom could not make him out. He stood up and moved out into the far left aisle. Then he turned and stared back toward the rear of the building. The man was closer now, and he could make out the face. It was Lambert.

Tom steadied himself in the aisle and watched as Lambert moved toward him with a steady, unhindered gait, as if he had not even seen Tom move to block him.

For a moment, Lambert stopped and faced Tom squarely. Then, with terrific force he bolted forward, his hand flying inside his coat.

Tom felt a cold wave of terror pass through him. For a moment he could not move but only watched as Lambert picked up speed, rushing now, the pistol already in his hand.

And still Tom could not move, except for the trembling in his hands and he could hear a gasp rise from the crowd and then a voice from inside his mind—*You must bite down hard on your fear*—and he felt himself dive toward Lambert, his hand reaching for the pistol, and Lambert's body tumbled under his and he felt his fingers digging into Lambert's wrist, trying to get the pistol and then Lambert shifted and was on top of him, the pistol swinging in the air and he saw Lambert's other hand dive down and then, an instant later, he felt the blade plunge into his side and heard himself moan, his eyes closing, and then the blade again, ripping across his ribs, sawing into his flesh, and he felt his hand weakening, the pistol lowering toward his head, and he opened his eyes and saw them running toward him, Baxter and Redmon and Philby, all running toward him, and the roar of the crowd was like a great engine grinding down upon itself and he felt his blood moving out of him in a great wave and he thought—*Te absolvo, Gentry*—and closed his eyes and felt his breath desert him and then sucked in a final time and thought he caught the smell of pines.

62

Epstein folded the last shirt and dropped it into the open suitcase.

"The wheelchair will be up in a moment, Mr. Epstein," the nurse said.

"Fine," Epstein said quietly. He glanced at the television. Ranks of uniformed patrolmen were marching down South Temple Street, past the Brigham Young Memorial and the ZCMI, then onward toward the stark web of Eagle Gate.

"A beautiful day for the funeral." The nurse watched the screen for a moment, then looked at Epstein. "I understand you knew Mr. Jackson."

Epstein nodded. "Yes."

"Is he the one who came to visit you a few times?"

"That's him." Behind the marching patrolmen, he could see a riderless horse prancing energetically, the reins held tightly by another patrolman. "Giving him a real hero's sendoff."

"He deserves one," the nurse said.

"Ain't it the truth," Epstein said dully. He turned away and closed the suitcase and fastened it.

"To save Mr. Berryman like that," the nurse went on. "And Mr. Jackson wasn't even a Saint."

"Not a Saint at all," Epstein said. He checked the suitcase latches, making sure they were secure.

The nurse shook her head. "Sometimes people just snap."

Epstein looked up. "Who?"

"That college teacher," the nurse said, still staring at the screen. "Just went berserk like that, right out of the blue."

Epstein nodded. "Right out of the blue."

"Paper said he was a real smart man, too. Wrote lots of books."

"Well, that's the way things go sometimes," Epstein said unemphatically. He looked toward the window. "Is it supposed to be clear like this all day?"

"That's what the paper said."

"Good," Epstein said. "Maybe I'll go for a walk."

"Well, you shouldn't exert yourself too much, though," the nurse warned.

"Don't worry, I won't." Epstein looked again at the television. The coffin was moving into view—large and black, carried on a caisson, a wreath or red roses resting on top. "He was a lousy chess player," he said, almost to himself.

"What was that?"

"Nothing," Epstein said, shaking his head.

The door to the room swung open. Epstein turned and saw a wheelchair roll in, pushed by a large orderly.

"You needed this?" the orderly said crisply.

"It's for Mr. Epstein," the nurse said. "He's leaving us to-day."

Epstein looked at the wheelchair—all that metal, the shiny chrome wheels. "They ought to make those things look a little more inviting," he said. "Just sitting down in one makes you feel like a goddamn invalid."

"It's just a short ride," the nurse said. "Got to do it, though. Insurance purposes. We don't want a patient falling down in the hall."

"Okay," Epstein said.

The orderly stepped over and took the suitcase from the bed.

"Be careful with that," Epstein said. He smiled. "It's old, like me. It could fall apart any minute."

The nurse offered her hand. "Easy getting in this thing."

Epstein pulled away from her. "I can handle it." He eased himself into the chair. "Okay, let's go."

The nurse stepped behind the chair and began backing Epstein out of the room.

"Turn off the television," Epstein said.

The orderly hit the switch, and the screen went black, Tom's coffin disappearing into the sudden blackness.

"I guess you'll miss your friend," the nurse said as she began pushing Epstein down the hallway.

Epstein said nothing. For a moment he thought he grasped how it had all gone bad for Tom, then the idea split into a thousand pieces, a glass breaking in his head. "He should have stayed in New York where he belonged."

"Now, you shouldn't say that," the nurse said. "I mean, look how fortunate it was for us that he came here."

Epstein waved his hand, dismissing the idea, but said nothing.

"Are you from New York?" the nurse asked lightly.

"I lived there a while."

"I'd love to visit it. My sister went a few years ago. She said it was very exciting."

"Yeah, it is," Epstein said.

The nurse stopped at the elevator, pushed the Down button, and waited. "Traveling can get pretty tiring, though," she said. "When my sister got back from her vacation, she looked more worn out than when she left."

"That's the way it is," Epstein said.

The doors opened and the nurse wheeled the chair inside. "Why did Mr. Jackson come to Salt Lake?" she asked as the elevator door closed.

Epstein felt the idea coming at him again. He tried to gather it together. "I don't know," he said. "Maybe he was looking for something."

"Just a change of scene, maybe," the nurse said.

"Just something better," Epstein said.

The doors opened and Epstein saw the hospital lobby. People were sitting in rows of chairs, some of them erect and peering about, some of them slumped over, but all of them waiting, some for good news, some for bad. It struck him that it felt good to be alive, and he took in a long breath.

The nurse moved quickly through the lobby and out to the street, where a cab was already waiting.

"You take care of yourself now, Mr. Epstein," the nurse said.

"I will," Epstein said. He got carefully to his feet, his eyes peering upward to where the six spires of the Temple rose toward the sky, sharp and black, like ice picks held to the throat of God.

"Good-bye, now," the nurse said.

Epstein nodded as he eased himself into the cab and closed the door.

The nurse waved as the cab pulled away, and Epstein waved back. "So long, toots," he whispered. Then he leaned forward and told the cabbie where to take him.

The cab pulled away, and Epstein leaned back in the seat. For a moment he thought about Tom, then about a particularly hairy situation he had gotten himself into back in Chicago, then about this blonde he'd known for a while back in Cicero, very curvy with large full lips, a real knockout. He let his head drift back against the seat, closed his eyes, and smiled.

He sat completely immobile, staring out the window. There were voices coming toward him from somewhere, but he could not make them out.

"He gives me the creeps."

"Well, you'd better get used to him, because he's going to be living here for a very long time."

"Maybe it's all an act, you know? A fake. Just a way of avoiding the noose."

"I don't think so. They'll never put him back together."

"You never know. These guys suddenly pop in again. I've seen it before.

"Not him. He's in outer space."

"Something must be out of whack in Provo. I mean, how could this guy teach school wigged out like this?"

"That's the way it is. One day they're just fine. The next day it's completely different."

"It's like you can't trust your own eyes. I mean, here you are talking to me, and tomorrow you might come on the ward with a pistol and blow us all away."

"Most people keep their minds on track, that's all you can say."

"What did Dr. Jaspers say about him?"

"I don't know. The doctors just talk to each other."

"Are they going to try him?"

"How could they? Look at him."

"Yeah."

"He'll just live here from now on."

"Just sit there and stare out the window."

"What do you suppose he sees?"

He saw a wave of blue and thought it must be the sky, or the sea, or perhaps a long, flat lake. Then, suddenly, in the middle of the blueness he saw a light shining gold, a small pulsing light that remained, glinting as if hit by a ray of sun, and the gold swam in and out and in again like a pulse beating in the middle of the blue, a golden pulse, and he moved toward it, peering, and the gold began to move and roll and form itself, until he could see it plainly, a figure towering above a vast, illimitable plain, a figure with a great trumpet stretched out into the field of blue, a figure made of gold and glinting in the bright sun, and he saw the face of gold, the light bringing it to a shining glory, and it was Moroni, the Messenger of God, and he was standing on the highest spire of the great, gray Temple, and he was summoning the faithful to their destiny, and he could hear the sound of the golden horn as it sounded over the white, gleaming city, and he felt a wave of terrible glory pass over him like a shaft of brilliant light, and the peace that came upon him then was like the peace of all completion, of all creation come to rest, and he knew that he was home.